PRAISE FOR CATRIONA MCPHERSON

The Dead Room

"What an absolute treasure—and a joy to read. Completely engrossing—Catriona McPherson is a genius with dialogue and ingenious with suspense, and her deeply emotional and utterly relatable story made me neglect my own responsibilities—I could not wait to get back to the pages. Haunting, cinematic, clever, and wholly original—and beautifully written—you'll be captivated from the first page to the perfect conclusion."

—Hank Phillippi Ryan, *USA Today* bestselling author of *All This Could Be Yours*

"With *The Dead Room*, Catriona McPherson proves once again why she's one of the top crime fiction authors writing today. As usual, she seamlessly blends complex characters with a smoldering tension that amps up with each chapter. A must-read for anyone who loves an atmospheric, slow-burn thriller."

—Kellye Garrett, award-winning author of *Missing White Woman*

"The *Dead Room* is a masterclass in suspense . . . Every page leads the reader on a twisted journey full of dread, with tension taut enough to leave your nerve endings singing. Catriona's best book yet."

—Lisa Hall, author of *Eight Years of Lies* and winner of the CWA Whodunnit Dagger Award 2025

"Catriona McPherson delivers a masterclass in psychological suspense with *The Dead Room*, a haunting tale of a distraught young widow returning to her Scottish hometown. Grief warps the edges of reality—familiar places feel off-kilter, memories flicker, and paranoia takes root. The eeriness of a home seen through a Dutch angle and the precision of Highsmith-like tension are expertly woven together by McPherson's remarkable storytelling prowess. A deliciously complex, unforgettable thriller."

—John Copenhaver, award-winning author of *Hall of Mirrors*

"This book kept me up night after night, disturbing my dreams and rattling my bones. The moment I finished it, I wanted to reread it. That almost never happens, but when it does, it's because the story is as haunting as this, keeping its grip on my imagination long after I've turned the final page. It's so brilliantly woven you won't even see the threads pulling tighter and tighter until it's too late. There's a darkness at the heart of it, which I found truly chilling, and redemption too, although if I tell you much more, I'll be giving it away. What I will say is beg, steal, or sell your soul to get ahold of a copy. Catriona McPherson is one hell of a writer, and this is one extraordinary book."

—Amanda Lees, author of *The Key to the Island House*

Deep Beneath Us

"A tense, beautifully written page-turner with a truly unsettling denouement."

—*Kirkus Reviews*

"Suspenseful . . . plenty of action."

—*Booklist*

"The characters are captivating, the atmosphere is dark and dour, and the wretched weather contributes to the overall tone of the book . . . the untangling is a treat."

—First Clue Reviews

A Gingerbread House

"A disturbing tale of madness and fortitude that grabs your attention from page one."

—*Kirkus Reviews*

"A creepy read . . . that will linger in the reader's memory long after finishing."

—*BOLO Books*

"Nobody does a thriller better . . . a riveting read."

—The Reading Room

Strangers at the Gate

"Another unsettling and cleverly plotted winner from the enormously talented McPherson."

—*Kirkus Reviews*

"I love McPherson's books—the clear and effortless prose, the entirely credible characters, and the wonderfully twisty plots—and *Strangers at the Gate* is one of her best."

—Ann Cleeves

"McPherson delivers a maze of a thriller that will keep you guessing, turning pages, and staying up well past your bedtime."

—Seattle Review of Books

"McPherson spins a tense tale of murder and deception. Fans of Daphne du Maurier's *Rebecca* will find much to like."

—*Publishers Weekly*

"The period authenticity of Victoria Holt, several finely honed settings à la Mary Stewart, and the idiosyncratic familial bloodlines of Shirley Jackson, Daphne du Maurier, and Susan Hill wrapped in an eminently readable and highly engaging style. There is practically nothing predictable about this novel."

—*BOLO Books*

"There were plenty of times that I declared (yes, out loud), 'Oh! I know where this is going!' But I am happy to say I was never right."

—Nerd Daily

"I adored the spooky, small-town, insular setting."

—Tara Laskowski

Go to My Grave

"McPherson provides a virtuoso exploration of guilt, remorse, and revenge in a haunting psychological thriller. The ending will leave you astounded."

—*Kirkus* (starred review)

"Agatha Award–winning McPherson's deliciously Gothic country house mystery with a contemporary twist is devious and suspenseful and keeps readers guessing to the shocking end. Highly recommended."

—*Library Journal* (starred review)

"A Gothic feast of a novel, this is a country house book with a difference: contemporary, punchy and disturbing, but using the tricks and twists of the best of Christie."

—Ann Cleeves

"*Go to My Grave* is both a classic 'country house mystery' and a thriller. Atmospheric, with mind-bending twists, a narrator who may or may not be reliable, and an ending that will take your breath away and leave you astonished."

—Louise Penny

"Terrific! Chilling, entertaining, and profound, *Go to My Grave* is a master class in dazzling structure, layered characters, and even the relentless sociology of the class system. With her signature style and unique voice, Catriona McPherson brilliantly twists and turns the classic manor house mystery into a contemporary psychological page-turner."

—Hank Phillippi Ryan

"*Go to My Grave* is a terrific mystery—sharp, devious, and suspenseful. Catriona McPherson has written another winner."

—Meg Gardiner

"Lovers of classic manor house mysteries are in for a treat."

—*Publishers Weekly*

"Grippingly riveting drama."

—Dru Ann Love

"*Go to My Grave* is a synthesis of the styles, tones, and themes that McPherson previously explored while steadfastly making its claim on the Gothic tradition."

—*BOLO Books*

House. Tree. Person.

"An unnerving and suspenseful novel. *House. Tree. Person.* is McPherson's best yet."

—Karin Slaughter

"McPherson is a master at creating psychological tension . . . a one-sitting read."

—*Kirkus* (starred review)

"Riveting . . . every factor, every character, every movement is pivotal."

—Dru Ann Love

"McPherson knows how to lay on the creep and keep it building for maximum effect, and her talent for domestic suspense is second to none . . . Get a hold of this one ASAP."

—Criminal Element

"McPherson continues to impress . . . *House. Tree. Person.* may just be her best yet . . . one of those books where saying too much will ruin the reader experience, so my lips are sealed. Just know that you need to buy this book!"

—*BOLO Books*

"A complex story whose characters have layer upon layer of hidden motives, which award-winning writer Catriona McPherson deftly peels away. I found the smoky darkness of this slow-paced but relentless Scottish mystery very appealing."

—*Mystery Scene Magazine*

"Beautiful writing, engaging soulful characters, and a wonderful plot. McPherson teases the reader with exquisite delicacy, dotting tiny breadcrumbs of suspense literally from page one."

—Ellen Kirschman, PhD

Quiet Neighbors

"*Quiet Neighbors* drew me in from the very first page, and I stayed up late reading it because I couldn't wait to find out what happened next. That's the definition of a good book."

—Charlaine Harris

"Both cozy and creepy, which accounts for the quirky charm . . . the plot thickens nicely."

—*The New York Times*

"Layer upon layer of deception . . . a fine read."

—*Kirkus* (starred review)

"Luminous."

—Lori Rader-Day

"Outstanding . . . McPherson's literary observations are delightful, her quirky characters are intriguing, and the unfolding mystery highly satisfying."

—*Publishers Weekly* (starred review)

"McPherson is a master storyteller."

—*Mystery Playground*

"Complex and character-driven . . . atmospheric and suspenseful."

—*Library Journal* (starred review)

"Cleverly conceived, skillfully executed . . . bursting at the seams with warmth, wit, moxie, and menace."

—*Mystery Scene Magazine*

"Superb . . . The intensity never let up."

—Fresh Fiction

"Her style and ability to spin a yarn stand out. *Quiet Neighbors* will not disappoint."

—Criminal Element

"Intricately layered and psychologically taut."

—*The Strand Magazine*

"One of those ideal stories that you cannot put down."

—*Suspense Magazine*

The Child Garden

"If you like your thrillers twisty and twisted, you'll love *The Child Garden*."

—Val McDermid

"Just the right mixture of spookiness and mystery."

—James Oswald

"A gripping thriller."

—Ian Rankin

"Both utterly intriguing and eerily disturbing."

—*The Guardian*

"A warmhearted character study . . . that shivers with suspense."

—*The New York Times*

"*The Child Garden* is the best work so far, and coming so soon after her brilliant *Come to Harm*, that's saying a lot."

—*The Globe and Mail*

"A terrific stand-alone that is complex, haunting, and magical."

—*Library Journal* (starred review)

"A stunning combination of creepy thriller and classic mystery."

—*Kirkus* (starred review)

"An enchanting brew of mystery, poetry, legends, and dreams . . . also an elaborate shell game that will keep readers guessing up until the very end."

—Hallie Ephron

"Webs of intrigue so beautiful and intricate she puts spiders to shame . . . This is a book you will absolutely devour."

—William Kent Krueger

"Deeply resonant, utterly original, compelling and satisfying . . . the work of a master—of character, tone, setting, and plot—writing at the thriller-most top of her form."

—John Lescroart

"A riveting, page-turning read; I did not want it to come to an end."

—G. M. Malliet

"The tremulous miracle at the heart of this novel is its heroine, Gloria Harkness."

—Jenny Milchman

"Smart, complex, even a little magical—and absolutely chilling."

—Lori Rader-Day

"Catriona McPherson is a powerful force and major talent in crime fiction. And the last page? I cried."

—Hank Phillippi Ryan

Come to Harm

"Expertly done. Fans of . . . Dandy Gilver . . . should be warned that this is not one of them."

—*The New York Times*

"Shudderingly terrific."

—*The Globe and Mail*

"An immersive experience in completely unfamiliar territory."

—*BOLO Books*

"The latest from this master of psychological thrillers is more cerebral than physical. But every page will draw you in and deepen your dread."

—*Kirkus* (starred review)

The Day She Died

"Cracking read, irresistible narrator."

—Val McDermid

"A tour de force, a creepy psychological thriller that will leave you breathless."

—*Kirkus* (starred review)

"Keep the lights on and batten down the hatches, for McPherson's psychologically terrifying stand-alone demands to be read all night . . . a top-notch tale of modern Gothic suspense."

—*Library Journal*

As She Left It

"A stand-alone that is worlds apart . . . fascinating, mysterious . . . can't put down."

—*Kirkus* (starred review)

"It was stunning. Absolutely memorable world-building and, yes, I was surprised at the end."

—Janet Reid's Sox Knockers

"Stark and bleak, yet funny and deeply moving . . . a total revelation."

—Mystery Loves Company

THE DEAD ROOM

OTHER TITLES BY CATRIONA MCPHERSON

Stand-alone novels

As She Left It

The Day She Died

Come to Harm

The Child Garden

Quiet Neighbors

House. Tree. Person.

Go to My Grave

Strangers at the Gate

A Gingerbread House

Deep Beneath Us

Dandy Gilver series

After the Armistice Ball

The Burry Man's Day

Bury Her Deep

The Winter Ground

The Proper Treatment of Bloodstains

An Unsuitable Day for a Murder

A Bothersome Number of Corpses

A Deadly Measure of Brimstone

The Reek of Red Herrings

The Unpleasantness in the Ballroom

A Most Misleading Habit

A Spot of Toil and Trouble

A Step So Grave

The Turning Tide

The Mirror Dance

The Witching Hour

Helen Crowther series

In Place of Fear

The Edinburgh Murders

Last Ditch Motel series

Scot Free

Scot & Soda

Scot on the Rocks

Scot Mist

Scot in a Trap

Hop Scot

Scotzilla

Scot's Eggs

THE DEAD ROOM

CATRIONA McPHERSON

This is a work of fiction. Names, characters, organizations, places, events, and incidents are either products of the author's imagination or are used fictitiously. Otherwise, any resemblance to actual persons, living or dead, is purely coincidental.

Published by Thomas & Mercer, Seattle

www.apub.com

EU product safety contact:
Amazon Media EU S. à r.l.
38, avenue John F. Kennedy, L-1855 Luxembourg
amazonpublishing-gpsr@amazon.com

ISBN-13: 9781662535598 (paperback)
ISBN-13: 9781662535581 (digital)

Cover design by Damon Freeman
Cover image: © Stephen Mulcahey / ArcAngel Images

Printed in the United States of America

This is for Lucinda Surber and Stan Ulrich
with love and thanks

Where am I now?

I don't understand. I haven't understood any of this.

It's not a hospital although I feel ill enough. It's nowhere I've ever been and nothing I can smell or touch is familiar to me. Smell and touch because it is black as sin in here, so dark I can't see my hand even when I hold it close enough in front of my face to feel my breath on my palm, quick hot bursts of breath as I pant and whimper. Smell and touch because I hear nothing, no matter how long I try to hold those panicking breaths deep inside and strain my ears. At last, I have to exhale and it comes out as a sob. But I have to try to make sense of it. Then I can form a new plan, like the last one. I can escape.

So.

Smell. What do I smell?

Dust and . . . age? Old carpet and old blankets and old . . . What is that staleness? I feel I should know but I can't name it. It doesn't belong here. I don't want to think about it. I won't admit that I know what it is.

So.

Touch. What can I touch?

The blankets are wool. I feel the roughness on the back of my head and they prickle my hands as I push myself up to sitting. I swing my legs and the carpet beneath my feet is cheap and worn. I can feel i—

My feet are bare! I pat myself all over to find out what I'm wearing. None of it is mine. A robe? I feel tape at the neck. A hospital gown. But this can't be a hospital. The bed is made of wood.

Where am I?

How did I get here from—

But thinking about the last place thumps me down into chaos and helpless misery, leaves my thoughts skittering and useless. I thought it was working! I thought I was winning! And all that happened is they moved me to somewhere I don't understand at all.

Who *moved me? Who am I talking about? Who's doing this to me? I don't know and I can't try any more to work it out. I can't do anything to help myself and I can't make any of it stop. I can't.*

I curl back up on the bed, scratching up the blanket to cover myself, wailing.

Prologue

March

We lived here in Hawaii, where the ocean is warm and the air smells of flowers, for eight years, Kai and me. We were happy. Even last year. Even this. But what am I going to do all alone, seven thousand miles from home, for the rest of my life? What's keeping me here now?

Kai died.

It's an excellent sentence, resonant and rhythmic, a vocal exercise of a sentence. Compare "My husband has passed." That's a prissy, bridling quitter of a sentence, isn't it?

They're both true. But the sound matters. Thing is, I read out loud for a living. Audiobook narration. And Kai wouldn't mind me noticing the best way to announce his death, because he was an audiobook narrator too. He had heard of me before we even met. He crossed the main exhibition floor at the annual convention in New York City and stopped in front of my booth. "Are you Lindsay Lord?" he said, as if I wasn't wearing a lanyard. "And are you free for dinner, if we can find somewhere where the air isn't too dry and the music isn't too loud?" It wouldn't have sounded romantic to anyone else, but the offer of a first date with someone protecting *their* voice, getting that I'd protect mine, charmed me.

I *was* free for dinner and to marry him and leave Scotland and move to Hawaii and spend all day every day together, mostly right here in our dead room. I suppose that's why I'm in here now: not because the soundproofing soaks up all my rage and grief without the neighbours hearing but because this is where I feel closest to Kai. Of course, we shared our bedroom and the kitchen and the deep shady porch, and Kai died in a hospital bed in the living room, but here is where he designed and built sound decks for us, stacking the equipment, wrapping wires into thick ropes with insulating tape like a horse bandage, choosing just the right plug board, with nothing left over, getting a sprawl of mics, keyboards, monitors and control boxes Tetris-ed in.

I look at myself in the mirror, since that's my only option now. We always had a mirror each, to check posture and make sure we had that slight smile that comes through in the voice, but I usually had mine angled so I could see him instead as he concentrated so hard on whatever he was preparing. Kai's bent head was what made me smile.

Get him onto discussing the tools of our trade and he made me laugh out loud. "PreSonus Studio One, for sure," he used to say, "*but* Aston condenser mics." That punch on the *but* cracked me up and he had no idea why it was funny.

Start a conversation about the human voice, though, and I stopped laughing as my heart filled. Different kinds of books need different kinds of voices, obviously. Technical manuals, straight and simple; business guides, punchy and bright; memoirs, not quite sad but on the way there; self-help, the less said the better about my one brush with that genre. Kai used to say romance novels were tough. Unless your life was a love story. "Like yours, babe—you're welcome. Producers can *hear* our marriage. I should get a cut, really."

I slip Kai's phone out of my pocket and plug it in to charge, flooded with the memory of the day he took his fingerprint off the lockscreen so I could use it once he'd gone. He would kill me: a phone in the studio? But it's not connected to anything now that I've closed his account and there's no way it's ever going to make a sound, even if I was working at the moment, which I'm not. When it's at 1 percent, I swipe it on, gazing at the picture of the two of us sitting on the porch of this house, grinning like the idiots we were back when we thought we were bulletproof.

"I can't stand being here without you, sweetheart," I say into the warm silence. "But how can I break all this down? I'll never be able to rebuild it on my own. But I can't leave it behind me if I go either."

And anyway, go where? Home? Or, as I like to call it with a hollow laugh and a good attempt at being over it all, "home." There is a difference. My audible scare quotes are second to none.

Whatever I decide, I need to clean up my files. So I switch on all the output gear and move one headphone into place. I have no recollection of what I was doing just before Kai's last step down to the end and I'm shocked to realise that it's been months. I delete out-of-date samples and bids for work long since contracted to someone else.

There's only one recent file I don't recognise. I click it on.

Kai's voice.

At first I don't pay attention to what he's saying, too drunk on the sounds. He was a born audio artist, with a deep, sonorous tone, a talent for silent breath and that unplaceable accent; the faint Hawaii lilt intriguing everyone who heard it. Publishers loved it. He sounded so close to American, yet there was nothing to put him in a region and turn off anyone from the others. Plus there was that slight mystery in his plosives that made you keep listening.

I slide the second counter back to the start and prepare myself to hear whatever he's going to tell me.

If you're there, Lindsay, he says, *that means I managed to shift this file to somewhere you're going to find it. I didn't want to leave it too long. I wanted to sound like me and I can feel my range narrowing every day. Anyway. So I died, huh? What a downer. You okay, babe? I want you to be okay. I want you to be happy. I want you to meet a nice guy—not too nice, but solid, you know? He'll cope with living in my shadow if he gets you thrown in. And then you and him can get started on those babies we were going to have if it had turned out that way. Deal? We got a deal? Try not to mind them being basic issue and not the angels we would have made. Love them anyway. And even if he doesn't show up, just go ahead and have the babies.*

Seriously, Lin. I'm not going to tell you not to mourn. I would be ready to burn the earth to embers if it was me losing you. So, mourn. Grieve. Don't forget me. But be happy. You're living for two now, hon. You're living for me as well as yourself. No slacking.

I wait and wait. There are eleven unused minutes on the track and I have sat in silence through nine of them before I believe that's it.

Because he didn't even say he loved me. *Downer? Basic issue? No slacking?* If he wasn't dead already, I would kill him.

"You fucker!" I say, cursing his skill at dead room design because I want my anger to ring out, not be folded into a perfect audio-cuddle. "You fucker!" I say again, jumping up and opening the door to the corridor outside. That's better. "You spent ten years turning me from a standard, sarcastic Brit-bitch to someone who thrives on all-American emotion and then you leave me with this-this—"

It's at this precise moment that my phone goes. It's my brother. Not my sister-in-law on my brother's phone, not one of the boys calling to thank their auntie for birthday money, all in one breath with their mum standing over them, but my brother calling me.

"John?" I ask. "Is everything okay?"

"Everything here's okay," he says. "How are you?"

I don't answer. There's no answer.

"Listen, Lindsay," he goes on when he realises it's still his turn, "why don't you come home? Why don't you just . . . come home?"

"Where do I start?"

"Yeah, but . . . I'm here. Shelley's here. Zak and Nicky are a laugh. And it's different now that . . ."

It must be, I suppose. He lives in the house where we both grew up. He owns the business that used to be our mum and dad's. He'd hardly be there if it made him feel what I'm scared I'll feel, if I go back.

"Really?" I say. "Promise?" I sound like a child.

"Truly," he tells me. "Hope to die."

And so I do.

Part One

June

Chapter 1

I'm lost. I can't be more than ten miles from the house where I was born, but the roads have changed since I learned to drive here, and I've been travelling for twenty-six hours now, and somehow I've missed the turn. I'm crying so hard I can't see the road properly and I don't even know if I care.

When I finally pull in to the side of the road and park, I'm on a market square. There's a church, a bank, flowerbeds . . .

And a gold pillar box.

"What's a pillar box?" Kai asked me once.

"Mailbox," I told him. "But like the blue ones on the street, not the things on sticks at the end of the drive."

I really am ten miles from home then. This is Dunblane, where Andy Murray survived a school shooting and trained for all those medals. They painted this pillar box gold for him, because he belongs.

The air is cold around my ears when I step out and the solid flank of the pillar box is just as cold against my palms. I let my head drop forward and stand hugging Sir Andy's tribute like a drunk with a lamppost, sobbing, making raw, painful noises that will wreck my voice for days, as if something at the core of me has broken. Because something at the core of me has.

Even when I see the old woman, walking stick held in one hand and letter ready to post in the other, I can't catch a hold of myself and get normal. She comes towards me slow and steady, her back still straight although she must be eighty if a day, smartly belted into a mackintosh and wearing the kind of shoes you have to get your foot width measured for.

"Who have you lost?" she asks, in a clear voice, when she's close enough for me to look into her grey eyes.

"How-How-How did you know?" I gulp it out on a tide of snot.

"A long life with its fair share," she tells me. "There, there."

I take a sniff and swallow, then screw my eyes up tight to try to choke off the tears. When I open them, she's holding out a packet of tissues. "There, there," she says again.

I don't think anyone has ever actually said those words out loud to me in my life and before today I would have guessed they'd infuriate me as much as all the other platitudes, but there's something about her calm voice or her kind face, or maybe it's the absence of any eagerness in her expression. She lacks avidity. She doesn't want to know all about it. She's not compiling an anecdote for later about the messy woman she met at the postbox. She's being calmly kind. Kindly calm. Like no one has been to me since—

"My husband," I tell her.

"Oh, I'm sorry," she says. "That's awful. You poor thing."

They're the same words people have written in texts and on cards, the same stock phrases people murmured at me in the receiving line. But they mean something coming from her, and they comfort me.

"We're— We've always been— We were very happy." I still have to take a good run at putting him in the past.

"And so young," she says. "I got fifty years of that happiness. It's cruel that you didn't. It's an outrage."

"I'm sorry too," I say. "For you. It can't be easy no matter when."

It's the first time in the whole three months since Kai died that I've managed to summon a shred of sympathy for another person. She brushes it aside. "I got what lucky people get. You're either left or you leave. Quite different from your calamity, my dear."

Calamity. A perfect word. It slams and it leaves you rattling.

I find myself nodding. "And I'm jet-lagged too. I came home from Hawaii."

"Were you on holiday?" she says. "Was it an accident?"

"No, we lived there. He was from there. I'm from here."

"Welcome home," she says, smiling. "It's a great pull, isn't it? Even when away is Hawaii, it seems."

We've reached the natural end of what must be an insignificant encounter for her but feels like balm to me. As if to confirm it, the red post van draws up beside us and the postie gets out to empty the box. I try to keep smiling back at her but my face must fall because, instead of moving off, she puts her hand out and says, "Peggy March. Why don't you come and have a cup of tea?"

I take her hand, as thin and soft as a bird's wing, and shake it gently. "Lindsay Hale," I say. "Thank you."

She sets off at a decent clip, after a nod for the postie, and she doesn't feel the need to talk. So I get a chance to pull myself together as we go up the high street, past shops and businesses, to where stone walls and neat hedges suddenly begin. I can see chimneys and gables and the tops of copper beech and oak trees.

"Here we are," she says when we've been walking for another few minutes. "Saint Helen's."

"What a nice house," I say. It's not effusive enough by half, because "Saint Helen's" is a beautiful house and enormous too.

"I love it," Mrs. March says. "I always have. It's Edwardian, not Georgian, not even Victorian, so house snobs are horrified, but I've always been very happy here. Come away round the back and I'll put the kettle on."

Round the back, beyond a boot room, there's a kitchen with red tiles on the floor and the kind of comfortable mishmash of odd chairs and cupboards that takes decades to gather.

"English breakfast?" she says. "Milk? I'm going to insist on sugar whether you want it or not. And a biscuit. See what there is in that black tin there. See it? The jubilee biscuit tin."

I'm looking for a spanking new tin from Queen Elizabeth's diamond jubilee, so it takes a while to spot the battered black-and-gold drum with Victoria's little pudding face in a medallion on the front. I prise it open and find KitKats and Penguins inside. I take one of each and, once the kettle's boiled and she's dunched the bags against the sides of our mugs, she leads me through a warren of passageways and across a hall until we get to a room that's all windows at one end, overlooking a garden. The furniture is more of the same, shabbier than shabby chic but grander too. I settle into an armchair with a faded linen slipcover and put my mug down on one of those brass tables like a tray with a clothes airer holding it up.

"So," she says when she has unwrapped the Penguin and dunked the end of it in her mug. "Are you sure about leaving the place you were happy together, dear? Haven't you heard the adage about big decisions? A year, they say. And it's surely been nothing like a year."

"Twelve weeks," I tell her.

"Unspeakable," she says. "I'm furious for you." She sucks the warm chocolate off the end of the Penguin then takes the bare biscuit out of her mouth and adds, "But you have decades of life ahead of you." She must think that's comforting, but to me it sounds bleak. So I say nothing. I just peel open my KitKat and dunk it, since she is.

"And no one will try to tidy you away as if you're too old to count," she adds after a while. I shrug. I've lost all squeamishness about old people referring to their imminent death. After Kai, at forty, they sound smug.

"When Richard died," she goes on, "people kept informing me that I would be moving somewhere small and dull. I got sick of having to say I would stay here in my house until they nailed the lid down on me. 'But the garden!' they'd say. 'I shall get a gardener,' I told them. 'But the stairs!' 'Ah, but the wonder of a house that is miles too big is that I can live in the *down*stairs, should I ever need to.' Which I don't."

"Good for you," I say. "When I find a house I like, I think I'll do the same."

"And where are you going to look?"

I laugh. "Here. My best friend still lives here. My family owns the junkyard in Menstrie."

"Lord's Yard's is still on the go?" she says with a smile. She sets her empty mug aside and, no matter what she says, I think she's very vital for a woman her age. She's downed the hot tea while I'm still blowing on mine. "My days of treasure hunting are long gone, but Richard used to love a poke around Lord's Yard."

"It's home," I say.

"Home," she agrees, looking around at her walls and her floor and her furniture. "Never let anyone tell you it's only bricks and mortar. Home matters."

"The house in Hilo—" But my voice breaks. "I better go," I say instead, then I thank her for the tea and all the sugar, and explain that John and Shelley are expecting me.

"Very well then," she says, but she doesn't stand up and neither do I. She rummages for the remote down the side of her chair and clicks on a smallish and oldish telly sitting on a side table. I have no idea what show it is that starts up, but it's unmistakably British daytime telly: gentle and jaunty and familiar . . .

I open my eyes onto dark blue. The sun has gone and the moon is out, shining right in the wall of windows, casting a grid onto the floor. There's a cushion behind my head and a blanket of crocheted spirals drawn right up to my neck. I push it off me and stand.

"Mrs. . . ." What the hell was her name?

The door is opening onto a lighted passageway. "Welcome back to the land of the living," she says, standing in silhouette.

"What time is it?"

"Almost eleven. I was just about to wake you before I went up." She lights a lamp, not the overhead but it's enough to make me squint anyway.

I start to bluster about how sorry I am and try to tell her all over again about the jet lag, but she shushes me.

"I'm flattered. I'm glad I could give you what you needed. Sanctuary." She reaches out a hand and rubs the doorframe as if she's petting a dog. "While you were asleep, I wondered what else might help. How about a book?" I notice then that she's got one in her hand.

"A self-help book?" I ask. "I've had a bad experience—"

"Heaven forbid!" she breaks in to say. "This is a novel."

"I used to love novels," I say, "ever since I could read. Stories saved— What I mean is, storybooks were such a refuge from . . . boredom when I was a kid."

She holds the book out as if it's a dog treat.

"Then I didn't need saving," I add. It's so hard to explain when you're trying not to say anything. "I had Kai." I blink three times, willing my eyes not to fill.

She's practically pushing the book into my hand.

"Anyway," I tell her, "the problem now is that I'm an audiobook narrator by trade." She cocks her head, asking for more. "I start counting characters and planning what I'd do to differentiate them all. If it hasn't been narrated, I can't resist trying to get in touch. If it has, I can't help listening and usually deciding I'd do better. So it's not very restful, usually."

"Ah, but this is a Christie," she says, showing me the front cover. It's one of those gruesome seventies paperbacks and this is a particularly horrible example: half a blue-fleshed head with knitting needles stuck in it. "If it's been made into a talking book, it'll be Jenny Agutter or Alan Rickman. Unimpeachable."

I think her arm must be getting tired, holding a book out like that. It would be rude not to take it. "Thank you," I say.

"It's all about a young woman coming home," she tells me. "It's years since I read it, mind, but it's a lovely story as far as I recall. Perfect for you while you're house hunting."

"Thank you," I say again.

Then she shows me out, through the front door this time. I think it's to display more of her beloved house. We go through a square hall with arches and half pillars, past a monster of a hatstand, and emerge into a marble-tiled vestibule open to the front garden.

“We’re sure to run into one another,” she says on the doorstep. “If it’s here you’re settling.”

“I’ll look forward to it,” I say, sincerely. If she was younger, I’d ask for her contacts and text her in the morning.

I stop, halfway down the drive, overcome with the urge to go back and ask Peggy March if I could stay the night in her house. *Succour* is such a terrible word for a beautiful thing. I even turn and look back at the open door to the vestibule, at the glass door into the hallway. Then the light snaps off and I remember that she was on her way to bed, so I content myself with scribbling my phone number and email on a business card and easing the letterbox open as quietly as I can to let it drop inside.

Chapter 2

I find my way back to Menstrie on muscle memory this time, and old habit makes me switch off the engine and coast in silently so as not to wake them, even though it's hard to say whether they're up or not. On the one hand, the big gates are still open and there are three strange cars parked in a row, besides John's van and Shelley's little runabout. On the other hand, the house is in total darkness.

Or so I think until I see a chink of light coming from a gap in the dining room curtains and feel a wash of memory. That was always where Mum and Dad sat, fists on the table, to chew us out if we got home too late on a school night. I creep towards the window half expecting ghosts but, when I peek in, of course it's not the pair of them, worried sick and fuming, both in their dressing gowns. My brother's sitting facing my way at the far side of a small, square table, lit by a low-wattage bulb in the hanging lamp. There are three more people gathered around and I don't recognise any of them. Not the beefy man in a checked shirt with his scalp shining through his hair; not the slick-looking guy with his suit-jacket hung on the back of the chair and a cigar in his mouth, the smoke hiding so much of his face he must surely be puffing at it like a steam train. Obviously not the thin, grey-haired one opposite my brother. From the back, he could be anyone. I glance at John again and just for a second there *is* a ghost as my dad's face meets my gaze.

I tiptoe away from the window and climb the steps to the kitchen door. It's locked but I reach up and feel my fingers close around the spare key right there where it always was, like nothing's changed. But it must have. John said. Everything's different now.

And anyway, it's not as if I've never been back here, since I left. I've visited. I brought Kai to meet them. I'm fine.

Before I can fit the key into the keyhole, the door swings open and Shelley is standing there in the darkness.

"Lindsay? You're not supposed to be here till tomorrow."

I can't see her face and I can't read her voice, even though I've known her for twenty years and I can read any voice. Even the voices of strangers, even in a foreign language, even underwater or through a wall when the words are muffled to nothing and only the tune is left.

"Is my bed not ready?" I say. "It doesn't matter. I can sleep on the—"

"I got the time difference wrong," Shelley says. "I added instead of taking away."

That doesn't make any sense but it doesn't matter. What matters is the way Shelley's standing square in the doorway like a nightclub bouncer.

"Are you okay?" I ask her.

She reels away from me, clicking the light as she goes, and then stands at the sink with her head bent.

She doesn't seem the least bit okay. She makes a sound I think at first is retching then realise is sobbing. I've never seen Shelley cry. She got tears in her eyes when she was first breastfeeding, but that doesn't count. The thing about grief, though, is it makes you so selfish. I don't care what's wrong with her.

"I'm sorry," she says. And even though I don't ask what for because I don't care about that either, she goes on. "I'm sorry I'm crying. I'm sorry Kai died. I'm sorry we didn't make it to the funeral. I'm sorry we haven't got space for you to stay here long-term."

She's lying. And she's not very good at it. One reason would be better than four, for a start.

"Are you hungry?" she says. I shake my head. I haven't been hungry for months. But she sees through this. "Have you eaten?" she tries next. "Sausage sandwich?"

Right enough, as well as the olive-green laminate units and the rattling fridge, not to mention the lumps on the carved back of this orange pine chair that are digging into my spine, there's a smell of white sausage fat congealed in the grill pan, same as ever. *Nothing's* changed. How can John live here? How could he ask me back?

"I made them for John's poker night," she says. "Plenty left over."

"Yeah, I saw—" I begin, but she cuts me off.

"He needs to know you're here." She goes off into the passageway. Were there cards on that table? There must have been. And actually why else would four men be sitting like that at nearly midnight? Even though who the hell has poker night on a Monday? I hear Shelley bang on the dining room door. "John? It's Lindsay."

There's a stretch of total silence then a click and low voices. Shelley's is so neutral it sounds robotic. John's is . . . John's voice is . . . My heart is guttering in my throat. John's voice is another ghost, like his face was.

"Your old room's all set," Shelley says as she comes back. "Zak's in with Nicky tonight already so I could give it a good clean round."

John is behind her. He lifts his chin once and says, "Lindsay. You change your flight?"

I almost laugh. This is the bosom of my family that I've come home to?

"Give Lindsay a cup of your wonder stuff," John says to Shelley. "I'll see you in the morning, eh Sis?" And he's gone again.

"It's only herbal tea," Shelley says. "But it'll help you sleep. What time does your body think it is?"

I haven't got a clue. My body thinks it's *Kai died*. But I accept a cup anyway, take one sip and try not to grimace. Typical that Shelley's carried on with terrible food but given up on a decent cuppa. I take it upstairs to my old room and stand at my bedroom window, staring out into the past.

I can't see much detail, just hummocks in the dark. If I didn't know it was a scrapyard, I could believe I was looking at shrubs and gazebos out there. What I *can* trace, though, is the boundary against the fields beyond and it's familiar enough to make me feel dizzy. The fence, high and sturdy, is still like a garden-centre showroom—odd sections all different styles, one after the other, with no thought to appearance.

I let my eyes travel down to the far end, to the Barrens. That was John's secret hidey-hole, named after something he read in a book, back when he was too old for toys and started reading instead, same as me.

Before that, we shared everything. We were pirates with a ship made out of a feed trough. We were spacemen with the guts of sit-under hairdryers and a dentist's chair. We were Ghostbusters, with weedkiller-backpacks that probably still had the dregs of absolute poison in the bottom. I squint out into the dark, wondering if any of it is still there—feed trough, dentist's chair, backpack sprayers. But it's hard on the eyes, or maybe it's the jet lag. Certainly, my vision is doing something it's never done before. Has it? The scene outside the window seems to flatten and flutter as I gaze at it, as if all those wood and wire-mesh panels are so much tissue paper, the black silhouettes of the trees beyond no more than painted card. I turn away, blinking.

I brush my teeth and wash my face, knowing I'm never going to get to sleep after that nap, but I climb into bed anyway, angle the lamp towards me, and start reading. It only takes a page or two to know I was right about this book: I can't see past my job to relax into it. There's a young New Zealand woman and I can do that; there's a posh English man, young though, so I could do that too; the doctor . . . he could be Scottish to distinguish him, if that's not too much of a cliché; an elderly lady . . .

But Peggy was right about the book too: It's a sweet tale of a young couple buying their dream home. And I can't bear it. I set it face down on my bedside table so I can't see that unsettling cover and pick up Shelley's special tea.

My second sip tells me I should have drunk it hot, because it's even worse lukewarm, but I gulp it down anyway and switch the lamp off, expecting to lie staring up into the darkness until the morning.

Shows what I know. Almost immediately, I feel exhaustion licking around the edges of me and my thoughts start to roll towards dreaming.

Where I find nightmares waiting for me. Kai is sitting at a small table with three doctors I've never seen before, although one of them is John. Shelley is walking round behind their chairs delivering those flavoured build-up shakes I used to pour down the toilet and swear blind to the nurse he had drunk. The lightbulb over the—it's not cards and I can't see what it is—gets dimmer and dimmer and Kai is gone and now it's just blackness in front of my eyes, a sweaty twist of blankets all around my body and scuffles and mutters inside my skull. It feeds on itself until the mutters grow into shrieks that are loud enough to wake me. I lie still in the tangle of sheets, waiting for my ears to stop echoing and my breath to find a rhythm, for my heart to settle back down into my chest. Did *I* make those noises? I can't have, because Shelley isn't bursting into my room and the boys aren't crying. But was it real? Vixens can sound like terrified children in the still of the night, I know.

I keep listening as my pulse stops pounding and my sweat begins to cool and dry. There's one weighty thump, somewhere outside, as if a pile of something soft and heavy has collapsed, and then silence. Fox, I decide. It knocked something over but nothing breakable, by the sound of it. Maybe it was hunting birds in the dawn. Certainly, I see grey light stealing in around the curtain hems and I can hear at least one bird singing as my limbs get heavy and I sink back down.

Or maybe all of that was a dream, because the next time I wake, it's still pitch black, and Kai's so real that I reach out to feel the warmth of him and knock my hand against the wall beside this single bed. I lift up on one elbow and grope for the glass of water I didn't bring upstairs with me, drain the teacup instead to slick my throat, and crash back, making Kai huff and thrash. He was always such a light sleeper, and so sour about me moving or reading or God knows snoring, despite his white noise machine and sleep band and black-out mask and now, back in Hawaii, the noise machine beeps and hisses, half compression-sore mattress and half lorry reversing to come and take him away. Because he's cold beside me, the worst dream of all. He's lost in masks and tubes and wound tight in sweaty blankets, and it's not Hawaii.

Rattray Walker are delighted to present this rarely available late-Georgian villa of excellent proportions and stately bearing, quietly situated in an enviable residential location in the Kingdom of Fife. While some modernisation is now advised, pride of ownership shows in a myriad of preserved original features and extensive, carefully tended grounds, including a former tennis court with pavilion and a small area of woodland. The Hollies has been in the same family for sixty years, and its appearance on the open market is therefore a once-in-a-lifetime opportunity for the discerning buyer to realise its potential as a showpiece for both family life and elegant entertaining. The subjects include an impressive drawing room with open fire in an original hearth, a dining room of equal proportions, leading to . . .

Chapter 3

"Did I wake you?" Shelley says, as I arrive in the kitchen and sink down at the table, using my arms to lower myself into my seat. "I wasn't sure whether to leave you or not. I did look in once or twice to check you were okay. Coffee?"

"Anything," I say. "Coffee, tea, a muddy puddle . . . I'm parched."

"Well," Shelley says.

"Well, what?" I know it's not even nine o'clock yet and it was gone midnight when I went up. Shelley puts a mug of Nescafé in front of me, granules clinging to the teaspoon. I reach for the sugar bag.

"You slept round the clock, Lindsay," she says. "It's Wednesday."

I blink at her and take a slug of the horrible coffee. "I think I was tired," I say. "My eyes were playing tricks. Still are." Because Shelley, who should be as large as life sitting opposite me, looks as flat as a paper doll, her clothes held on with tabs over her shoulders. It makes me feel sicker than it should somehow.

"Have you been sleeping?" she asks me. "Before this, I mean."

I laugh. I've been sleeping like I've been eating.

"Well, there you go then," she says, back to brisk normal. Then even brisker, "So what's on the cards today?"

Got it, I want to say but don't. No snivelling. She's already standing up and turning away from me to face the sink, where she has dumped out about a wheelbarrow load of muddy spinach to start picking over.

"Chloe, I suppose." She's my oldest friend, one fifth of the reason I'm back here, as well as John, Shelley and the boys.

"Ask her for dinner."

"What are you making?" I can't imagine my brother eating any dish that green.

"This isn't for us," she says. "This is for the free fridge."

I don't know what that is and I don't ask. Another thing about grief is how dull it turns you. I don't mean to other people, although that's probably true too. But I feel dull to myself. Uninterested and unenthusiastic, I let news and gossip, sights and sounds wash over me without bothering to have a single thought about any of them. I know why. It's because there's no point finding out what a free fridge is, or when John started playing poker, even what the hell was in that herbal tea that knocked me out and filled my sleep with nightmares. I can't tell Kai any of it, so who cares.

"I need to find a place to live," I say.

"Don't talk daft," Shelley tells me, wiping her hands on the front of her jeans and turning away from the sink again. "This is your home for as long as you need. Anyway, when does your stuff arrive?"

It's true that my container won't be quick getting here from the dot in the Pacific that used to feel like my whole world, but I don't need to wait for it.

Upstairs, I sit on the bed for a while, summoning the energy to put my shoes on. It's in the same place as mine always was, this new bed, and the rest of the furniture was too solid and well fitted to change, but the carpet and walls are grey now and my pony stickers have gone from the drawer fronts, replaced by monsters and villains. I suppose some of them must be heroes, but they look like pure evil to me. I go to stare out the window instead.

In daylight, the view is so much the same that I can almost believe, if I push the blue and grey curtains out of sight, that I'm twelve again, with my mum downstairs in the kitchen.

Except I wouldn't be up here looking at it. I'd be out there in it, with John, on an adventure. Even once we'd grown out of pirates and spacemen, there were still plenty of adventures. Breaking and entering was the one that lasted longest: My brother and I knew more secret ways into the back of Lord's Yard than my dad ever dreamed of. Other kids sneak out of their houses to go and get up to mischief. We sneaked in.

There was a tree hard against the fence at one corner. After John had hammered nails into its trunk as footholds, we'd wriggle out along an overhanging branch on our bellies and drop down the other side. He did it in a single smooth movement, lengthways to crosswise to letting go to landing. I never got that bold, no matter how many times he told me it was easier without all the hesitation. "You're losing momentum," he'd say. "You're making it harder." I knew he was right but still I sat upright on the branch, took a moment to consider the drop, then carefully edged my body over to one side, hands sweaty and scraped, and I always dangled for a good long time before I let go, ignoring him laughing at me.

I preferred the other way anyway. A bit farther on from the tree, there was a section of corrugated iron that looked as secure as any of the rest of my dad's mishmash fencing—more so perhaps—except John and I knew it was only leaning on the post it should have been screwed to. Better still, underneath it was a sheet of laminate from an old wardrobe, slick as a skating rink, that the iron slid over more or less at a touch.

"Bo-ring," John would say. "Yawn."

So when I found a third entrance, I kept it from him. I scan the boundary now, searching for the right place, for the bright mustard paint of a shipping container and the snarl of barbed wire rolled up on top of a row of filing cabinets. I can't see either of them, never mind the dark stretch in between, and that makes sense.

Because a junkyard is an ecosystem all of its own, not that different from a compost heap, just a bit slower. Stuff comes in—microwaves and medicine spoons, toasters and bud vases, walking sticks and fireplace inserts. It gets picked over and shuffled. Then, if no one buys it, it gradually sinks under newer stuff. Weathered barrels collapsing, sun-faded plastic shattering, it succumbs to the elements until it's right at the back or right at the bottom. Eventually, like all of us, it returns to the earth.

It's a gentler way to go than how Kai was ripped from me.

I blink and turn to let the grey chevron strips of my nephew's bedroom curtains resettle me in the present. I don't want to pretend I'm back in the before, with my life to live over again. I wouldn't go in a different direction and I couldn't change how it all turned out. I would still say yes when he proposed. I would pick eight years with Kai over fifty with anyone else. So wishing my way back to my childhood would mean having to live through this again. And that would break me.

Maybe I broke anyway, I think, as once again the view thins and flattens, sliding around until I'm dizzy. I squeeze my eyes shut. Jet lag. Keep moving. Like Shelley said: *What's on the cards today?*

I can go out into the bowels of the yard and look around, like a customer. I'm grown up. It's different now. I need a table, a couple of chairs, and somewhere to sleep, if I'm going to move out of here. A couch would be nice too, and, as my dad's advertisements used to say until someone from the Pentecostal place in Alloa complained about them: *Lord's will provide.*

I sit back down to do up my trainers, the villains and monsters watching me. My pony stickers were just shiny, but these guys have holograms built in, moving eyes and shimmering ghosts of their other selves. I decide to call the worst one Glioblastoma. That's what he looks like to me. "What will we call that little slimy one?" I ask Kai. "Radiation? Chemo suite? Cranial saw?" Ugly words for ugly things.

Outside, I avoid the Portakabin where my dad would be sitting then, where John sits now, taking calls and watching the cameras, all crowded round with crystal decanters and carriage clocks, resting his arms on the glass counter of a jeweller's display case full of worn rings and strings of pearls, barricaded in with sets of golf clubs. John lives here, works there, and he's fine. I'll be fine too.

Next to the cabin is the big shed with the best security that was always kept for appliances, the real money spinners. Decent sets of furniture were in the least rickety of the other sheds, along with the hotel refurbishment overstock. Odd chairs and occasional tables were stacked in the polytunnel, where damage wouldn't matter so much; curtains and carpets went in a kind of carport that kept the rain off but let a breeze through. China and glass was out in the elements on old shop fitments, gradually filling with rain and leaves, fading if no one bought them, eventually breaking as they were shoved back to put new things in front.

I skirt the appliance shed, since surely anywhere I rent will have a cooker and washer already, and I don't bother with the suites and good couches covered in plastic wrap. I ignore the battalions of toilets, sinks, and baths, all with their taps, plugs, and handles neatly taped inside them, and I carry on past the gates and sections of fencing leaning hard enough against the books trailer to make it look as if it might tip over. Eventually I get to where I need to be. I snap a picture of a new, line-end mattress sealed in its cover, switching off the flash to make sure the item number, scrawled in marker pen on the plastic, is visible. I text it to John in the Portakabin.

I pick out an armchair that looks clean and feels comfy, and is small enough to fit in my hire car if I put the seats down. Then I carry on, deeper into the archaeology of the odds shed. There was a vinyl table with chrome edges the last time I was here. That's gone, although I find a school laboratory desk still with its graffiti fresh and proud: *Hibernian FC, Keep Beliebin', Chloe is a slag*. Different Chloe, but I take a picture anyway.

Out of the corner of my eye, I catch sight of what looks like the corner of a pinball machine outside the shed's back door. It must be wrecked to be this far back in the yard, with the half bikes and the bashed lampshades, but I clamber over to check it out anyway. It was always like this: down the rabbit hole, glimpse by glimpse, until you end up . . .

All the way back among the living room units, once someone's ultra-modern pride and joy, now with their shelves collapsing behind the smoked-glass doors and the veneer lifting on their ash or teak or beech finish. Back here with the deep, flimsy cabinets for old-style tellies and the moulded MDF headboards that turn into a table on each side like the curled horns on rams' skulls.

And I am fine. I'm not scared, not shaking, not crying, not praying for help. It's nothing more than kind of depressing. And I'm so steeped in sadness anyway that the sight of something depressing can't touch me.

The smell touches me all right. It's faint but it's there, and I'm glad I don't have to deal with it. Of course, Lord's Yard always smells a bit, always did: of dust and must and mould; of mushrooms growing in soaked wood and leaves rotting in the shallow pools that form in tilted sinks and on buckled tabletops; of slow decay and what we used to call disco decay—the way cheap carpet, discarded dirty, ferments when it sits in the rain. There's not another smell like it. But all those smells are vegetative and harmless. They come and they go. This smell is animal in origin, an unmistakable trace of dead rodent or bird blooming somewhere. Once a bat got stuck in the outflow pipe of a water butt it had fallen into. It might be that again.

I retreat until it's gone and, on the way, something catches my eye. Against all the odds, I find myself smiling. In a faded milk crate, so brittle from the sun and rain that it's starting to crumble, there's what must be a reproduction Victorian jubilee biscuit tin. I edge over that way and pluck it out of the jumble of pillowcases and dust busters where it's ended up.

That kind old lady who found me crying by the pillar box had completely slipped my mind, but I think I'll drive over there and see if she's in, show her my find, disapprove of the fakeness along with her. It's a pretty good attempt, mind you; much better than all those distressed Guinness signs that were once so treasured and are now stacked dozens deep in Lord's Yard, never to be chosen, never to be bought for so much as a penny.

"What you after, Linds?" John's voice makes me jump. He must have come round the outside edge somehow. There must be a straight path to here these days, where before we always had to thread a way through the aisles in the sheds and climb over the collapsing piles between them.

"Nothing," I tell him. "Just wombling." That was what we always called wandering the yard, seeing what we tripped over. John's face is blank, as if he's forgotten, or at least as if he doesn't want to share a happy memory with me.

"Sorry," I say. "I didn't mean to gloss over things."

He shrugs at me as if he doesn't understand this either.

"What are *you* doing away back here?" I ask. "Playing hunt the smell? Because something certainly whiffs a bit."

He pinches up his eyes and shakes his head at me. No way he's forgotten *that*. When we were wee, my dad would often have to track down a dead mouse or even a rabbit and "hunt the smell" was what he called it. Is this how John has managed to live here? Has he buried everything so deep that he can't even remember what I'm referring to?

"I was checking you're okay," he says. So he *does* know I might not be. "What makes you think you need a mattress?"

It takes me a moment to change tracks. "Right," I say, thinking, okay, surface it is. "You got my texts? I'll pay for it, obviously, but if I give the other bits back when my stuff arrives—"

"But you're staying here," he says. "You're staying here with us."

"I'm not moving *today*," I agree, "but I need to get back to work. So I need somewhere *to* work. So I need somewhere to live."

"Do you though?" he says, sharp looking suddenly. "Are you short of money? I thought—"

As if he's nothing but my father's son. Or maybe it comes with the job. Maybe you can't be in the house-clearance business without seeing death in pound signs.

"Not for income so much as for . . ."

"Would the boxroom be big enough?" John says. "We can easy clear it."

"I wasn't hinting."

"Yeah but," he says, sounding awkward. "Oh you know, Linds. I'm not sure you should be on your own, not this soon."

I give him a quick hug with one arm, the only kind of hug he'll put up with. I'll check it out later to be polite but I'm pretty sure John's work set-up, Shelley's big screen, and the boys' games have the bandwidth tapped out already without me siphoning. Still, I appreciate the offer.

"So long as you're okay," he says, turning to leave. "We worry about you."

"John, I can't interpret any of this," I tell him. "You assure me it's fine here now, encourage me to come back. Then you act like you don't know why it wouldn't be. And you didn't exactly fall on my neck when I got here, by the way. Then you check whether I'm coping, like you know damn well I might not. You're making me dizzy."

His face is a mask. "We're worried about you because you're *grieving*," he says.

"Right," I say. "Got it. We know, but we can't know, so we don't know, though we do."

"Talking utter bollocks doesn't exactly help us *not* worry."

I stare at him. There's no way on earth he can have forgotten the Lord family motto. He invented it. I open my mouth but, before I can chip away at even a tiny corner of this, the fight goes out of me.

"Don't you need to go and open up?" I say.

"Not today. We've had a big clearance over . . . well, down Stirling way, and we need to sort it out. So we're closed to walk-ins." He hesitates. "Just . . . Mind how you go, away back here, eh?"

Which makes no sense whatsoever. Because either he's really talking to me after all, in which case, as we both know, there's nothing to be scared of now. Or he's making out that we didn't play all over this bit when we were kids. We were never told to stay away from tyres or broken glass, not to climb on the *Les Mis* mountains of semidigested broken things. We were only warned away from what was clean and new, in case we scuffed or dented something that could make our mum and dad some actual money. It was always okay to be this far back.

Then I catch myself. How did John know where I was? Is there security away back here these days? High-tech surveillance of the broken television cabinets and the rusted space heaters? I dismiss the idea, tuck the biscuit tin under my arm and start edging through the beds shed towards my hire car and my new friend. Just the once, I have to stop and close my eyes when that visual glitch turns the world flat and false on me, but still. I've got a feeling inside about seeing Mrs. . . . I wish I could remember her name . . . that feels almost like optimism. I've given John lip. I've taken a funny picture to send to Chloe. Maybe it was the round-the-clock sleep, or maybe I was right to come home.

Shelley's out on the step when I finally make it back to the house. "You okay?" she says.

"Jesus, not you too."

"You seem . . ." Shelley says.

"I'm fine," I tell her, deciding not to mention how my eyesight's gone wonky four times now.

"You should get yourself a doctor sometime soon," Shelley says. "Our practice in Alva is pretty good."

"I don't need a doctor," I say. "I thought it was America that medicalised grief and us that just got on with it?"

"I don't mean happy pills," Shelley says, frowning. "Lindsay, I'm worried about you."

"Both of you, eh?" I say. "Did John just text you or something?"

"No," she says, but she turns bright red and she knows I saw it happen.

"I'm fine," I say again and leave her.

The opportunity has arisen to own a truly exceptional equestrian property tucked away in a surprisingly tranquil corner of Clackmannanshire, with excellent access to the smart shopping and café culture of surrounding towns. The main house offers excellent family accommodation and would be admirably suited to multigeneration living, having as it does both a stairlift and shower hoist, as well as front and rear ramps, included in the asking price. The impressive range of outbuildings offers business potential, subject to all necessary permissions, and also includes a gate cottage which could serve as a temporary base, should the new owners wish to begin a comprehensive programme of refurbishment, after which this hidden gem could form an enviable rural retreat. Torrie Mains Farmhouse awaits an owner with imagination and flair to bring it back to its former glory. Rattray Walker expect lively interest in this stunning property and interested parties are advised to arrange viewing without delay.

Chapter 4

The Hillfoots Road is quiet on this school-day mid-morning, and I let my gaze take in the sheep in the fields, lambs getting more sturdy and less playful, settling into their life of eating. Then I turn my eyes away from the low land and look up.

Other people say the Ochils loom over the Hillfoot villages strung out along their base but, on my one trip to Lincolnshire, the flatness unnerved me, and I was instantly happy in Kai's family home, under the black gaze of the big volcano. Hills are comfort if you grew up with them.

Comfort. It's a horrible word for a beautiful thing, the opposite of *effluvia*. *Comfortable* is even worse, full of lumps. That's why people say *comfy* instead.

I ache for Kai. John and Shelley would be embarrassed if I went banging on about the sounds of words and their meaning.

I suddenly feel sure that Mrs. . . . won't mind it one bit and I find myself looking forward even more to seeing her again. I wonder if she's ever been to Hawaii. I assume not, since she didn't say so. Maybe I'll tell her about the smell of flowers on the breeze. I could try, because she won't mind if it makes me break down sobbing. She's seen too much in her long life to be bothered by a few tears. And she'll show me that women like us can be okay on our own.

Not, I tell myself as I slalom down the side of the hill into Bridge of Allan, that I'll *be* on my own. I was born here. I grew up here, went to school here, came back home here from uni most weekends once the term's money had run out. I know people all over the place.

It's a complete whim when I stop in the middle of BofA, mostly because I've seen an empty parking space right outside a property centre with a name I know from online listings, but when I open the door I reckon I've proved my own point. In the front office, there's a man in a farmer's tie and a windowpane-checked shirt leaning over the receptionist's shoulders looking at something on her computer and I recognise him.

"Hiya," I say.

Both the receptionist and the leaning man look at me with polite smiles.

"Sorry," I say. "Lindsay Hale." It's clear to them both that I'm talking to him, so she goes back to her screen. His smile is starting to look fixed and his eyes are blank. "Lindsay Lord?" I try next. His smile is completely gone now. He even takes a step backwards, as if—ludicrous as this would be—I'm trying that old haven't-seen-you-for-years chat-up line, on a Wednesday morning in an estate agent's instead of half eleven in a nightclub.

"Sorry," I say again. "I could have sworn we knew each other. Maybe at school?" Damn it, that's the follow-up line.

"He's got one of those faces," the receptionist murmurs with her eyebrows raised.

I can feel *my* face warming, because she's right. He looks like a Perthshire farmer from central casting: ruddy cheeks; crisp, fair hair thinning in its sensible cut; the start of a beer gut under that shirt that he probably bought in a men's outfitters that sells a lot of Barbour jackets too. I glance down, and he's wearing brogues the colour of conkers.

"And what can me and my face do for you?" says Farmer George. "I'm Robert Walker, by the way." He comes forward with a hearty handshake, and I try to ignore how I'm even more sure we know each other.

"It's probably just that your photo's on your website," I say to him. "I've been keeping up with the listings." I know my voice dries out before the end of this.

"Are you okay?" the receptionist says.

I tell her I'm fine, and I tell myself it's nice to be home where everything's so familiar, but at the edge of my vision I can see the display window starting to flatten and wave around as if a breeze is blowing it.

"Let me make you a nice hot drink," the receptionist says. "I'll bring it in, Bob."

So Farmer George has got no choice but to usher me into his office for an impromptu meeting. Over a cup of bad coffee, I tell him I'm back from Hawaii, need a house, want a nice house, can pay for a lovely house, and am willing to rent till the right one comes up.

"Trouble with the rental market these days," he says, at last, "is Airbnb. If you wanted a *weekend*, you'd be laughing. Six months on a lease, though?" He shakes his head and sucks his breath in over his teeth.

"What's the longest you can rent an Airbnb for?" I ask him, not quite joking.

"Where are you right now?" he asks. "Believe me, you don't want to stay anywhere that hasn't got bookings in place for the summer by this time in June."

"I'm bunking with my family," I say. "And they've been lovely. They've both said I can stay as long as I like, but I'm not daft."

He's nodding so hard he looks as if he can hear rock music. "Let them be there for you," he says. "We all need our families at a time like this."

Time like what? I think. Then I realise he's probably assuming I'm newly divorced. It's more likely at my age, and why else would someone leave Hawaii?

"You're right there," I tell him. "I'm a widow."

His face falls like a dropped pudding. Those cheery, ruddy farmer faces aren't made for dismay. He opens his mouth to say something, but nothing emerges.

"Don't feel bad about guessing I wasn't okay," I tell him. "I don't mind. I wish we still did armbands, to tell the truth."

"There you are then," says Farmer George. "I reckon if your brother and sister-in-law are happy helping you, you should be letting them."

I stare at him. "Did I actually mention my brother?" I try to focus on his face, scared that if I look around, the room will be curling up at the edges.

"Lord, you said," he comes back with. "Lord's Yard? Your brother owns it, and his wife lives there too." He's staring me down, really trying to make me think that was a normal thing to say. I hold his gaze for a minute, but then I lower my eyes. It's me that's not normal. Where do I get off looking sideways at this guy? I thank him and leave as quickly as I can get out of there without actually trotting.

Jet lag, I tell myself. It doesn't feel like jet lag. Grief, I tell myself. It doesn't feel like grief either. So, I reason, this is what grief and jet lag feel like together. Who knew?

I drive on past birch trees with their young leaves fluttering green and silver like sequins as the breeze moves them, past the monument on its hill, past the park with the stately villas looking over it, and scoot over the motorway to the Dunblane road. This town's changed since I used to know it, now that I'm paying attention. There's a pet grocer and a Turkish barber, but there are cobbles still and kids in bright-blue blazers with bright-blue futures.

I turn into the road of hedges and high trees and roll along it, slowing down when I'm close to Saint . . . whatever it was. I'm not sure whether I can just drive through the gates onto the gravel or if I should park on the road and walk in. If it was me, I'd rather have the sound of a car than a knock out of nowhere, but Mrs. . . . comes from a time when people at your door was normal.

It looks different today, I think as I pace towards it. The front door is shut over the vestibule, so maybe she's out. And she must be out for the whole day, or away on a trip, because it was open when she'd only popped to the postbox.

The closer I get, the more sure I am that she's off on her holidays or something. The house looks cold and dead, somehow. Or maybe it's just that I can't see anything inside the front windows, not even an edge of curtain or frond of fern. It looks neglected. I ring the bell and knock the knocker, but I'm unsurprised when she doesn't answer.

As I step away, I can't help glancing in the nearest bay window. My feet still. The room is completely empty. There are no curtains to see an edge *of*, and no carpet, no sofas or chairs, nothing on the mantelpiece and only paler squares on the wallpaper to show where pictures used to be.

Maybe, I think, she's having it decorated. I cross the step and look in the window on the other side but it's the same story: bare boards and a gaping fireplace with not so much as a wire screen across it. Poor old lady. She must have sold some of her furniture. No wonder she had me sit in a back room.

I trot round the side, then stop dead, staring in through the French window at where we sat. It's stripped and dusty beyond the naked panes: no armchairs, no telly on a trolley, no brass table with wooden legs, nothing. I stumble to the kitchen window instead, desperate to see the jumble of gathered treasures. There's nothing but empty shelves and scuffed floorboards.

I let my head fall against the glass. I can feel all the same old helplessness, like when Kai was sinking for the last time, after his final rally, a time when the world seemed to be upending itself to tip him out of it as quick as he could go. I am so angry at myself for looking forward to coming here. And I'm angry at her for playacting a future when she was on her last legs. All those lies about staying forever! She knew what I've been through. How dare she use me for a fantasy? The rage courses through me on channels slick and deep from wear, unreasoning rage, honed sharp. Such a habit now. So efficient at consuming me:

Why did she lie to me? I bellow at her.

Why couldn't she just have left me at the pillar box? I demand to know.

Well, look where all her big plans got her! I sneer.

And then the anger is gone as quick as it came, leaving me sick with shame. "I'm sorry, Peggy," I whisper. "I didn't mean it."

And anyway, I tell myself, I missed thirty hours. I couldn't find my way to Menstrie from the airport. I keep seeing things not the way they really are. So how sure am I that I *was* actually here two afternoons ago? That the house was occupied and I got invited for tea? By a total stranger who let me fall asleep for hours? It doesn't seem that likely.

I turn away and trail back down the drive, where I find an old man, in his eighties at least but dressed even older than that in his smart clothes, waiting by my car.

"You're quick off your blocks!" he says. "It's not even on the market yet."

"I'm not," I assure him. "I'm a friend." I'm pretty sure this is true.

"Some friend, that thinks she's still here!" he says.

So there *was* a "she"! That's something. "She didn't tell me," I say.

"How could she? She didn't know herself."

"It must have been very sudden," I say.

"She's not dead," he snaps. "As you would know, if you actually had any connection to Mrs. March." Mrs. March. That's it! Peggy March. I didn't imagine her. And she's still alive. Then he sags a little, sadness taking over him. "She just got sick of looking after this big old place all on her own. Moved to a nursing home. Not that a complete stranger needs to know that."

"Are you—?" Sure, I was going to say, but he cuts me off.

"You're asking *me* who *I* am."

"No, it's just—"

"Tell the truth," he thunders at me. "You've never met Peggy March in your life, have you?"

"I-I-I don't know," I say, hounded into honesty. "I know her name."

"Oh, I'm sure you've found out her name. But listen to me, young lady, I'm a resident and a Neighbourhood Watch member. So don't bother telling the rest of your gang that there's rich pickings. The house is cleared and I'm always on duty."

He's as good as his word. He stands watching me until I've started the car and driven round the corner to park again. I don't know whether it's leftover anger, another fresh bout of grief, the scolding I just got, or the fear of not knowing what's real but when I call Chloe, it's with shaking hands.

When I struggle awake, I'm on the move, in a car. Have I been rescued? Am I safe now? Of course the problem is that I haven't actually woken, because I wasn't asleep. What's happened is I've come round from unconsciousness and that's why it takes a moment or two for my thoughts to arrange themselves.

Safe?

Rescued?

I am not going to let myself hope again. I know this is the same as last time and I need to be alert and see what I can learn before we get wherever we're going and I'm put wherever I'm to be put.

First, I need to make sure I don't faint, or even suffocate, from trying to breathe through whatever is over my head, sucking against my nose and my mouth every time I inhale, clouding the hood or whatever it is with my own steamy heat every time I exhal—

Against my mouth? My mouth! If this thick woollen whatever-it-is is sucking against my mouth—and it certainly is! I can taste it, rough and wet on my lips—then I'm not gagged. If I can stay awake perhaps I could scream when I get the chance.

But first, I must settle myself and gather my strength. I stretch my neck as long as it will go and tuck my chin down towards my chest. It works. I'm no longer breathing in stale wool and breathing out my own suffocating heat and wetness. With my chin tucked tight I am sucking in cool air from outside the hood and I am blowing my breath out over my chest, even lifting the wool a little so I can see, very dimly, something beyond this stifling dampness.

In and out. In and out.

When I'm sure I won't swoon, I start to feel around, because this time my hands aren't tied either. They're either starting to believe I'm no threat or they're simply lazy. In any case, I can tell by groping around that I'm in the boot of a car, the lid about ten inches from my face and the locking mechanism digging into my knees. I shift but then the wheel arch presses hard against my ankle. There is no way to lie that doesn't hurt somewhere.

When I've shuffled myself to a diagonal and got as comfortable as I can, I start to pay attention to how we're moving. I would have said from the speed and smoothness and from the fact that we haven't turned any corners, that we're on a motorway, or at least an A road. I wish I knew how long I've been unconscious. Because without knowing roughly when we started, there's no way to tell how far we've come.

We could be anywhere, bowling along.

K-chnk!

I catch my breath. What was that? We just drove over something in the road.

K-chnk!

Another one. And that's not all. The sound of the wheels has changed.

K-chnk!

We're on a bridge, rattling over the metal joins between the sections of tarmac.

K-chnk!

And suddenly I think I know where I am.

K-chnk!

There are twelve in total and that seems about right. Half a mile. And now we're slowing and the road smooths out and there are no more jolts. If I've worked it out, then we'll be in a town now. If we stop at a traffic light I could fill my lungs and scream at the top of my voice. You never know. Someone might hear me.

But I've been so taken up counting the sections of bridge that I forgot to keep my chin tucked and I've been breathing in that muffled, damp wool, until my head is reeling and my thoughts start to spin away from me.

And I'm gon—

Chapter 5

Lord's Yard is the last thing before the speed limit sign at the east end of Menstrie. The second-last thing is Victoria Terrace, where the Croziers lived, so we've been friends since we were three. Kind of. Depending how you're counting.

Back at the start, we played together whenever we could persuade one of our mums to take us along the side of the busy road, chubby hand held tight, chubby leg stung by nettles and scratched by brambles, but protected from the whizzing cars by that maternal bulk. Then we met up in the reading corner on the first day of nursery school, charmed and thrilled to find out that we would see each other every day now, no pestering required. We saw each other every day for the next thirteen years. We saw each other through puberty, first loves, first heartbreaks, and her wedding. She got me through my mum's early, savage cancer and my tests for genetic markers, my dad's heart attack and all the left-over trauma I felt when John went to have his arteries checked out. She celebrated with me when it turned out we both got my mum's healthy heart and my dad's lack of cancer genes. She never bugged me about celebrating in quiet settings, so I didn't have to scream over the hubbub and end up wrecking my voice for work.

Then, somehow, we lost each other. I suppose it must have been my fault because I met Kai and moved, but I kept emailing, sending birthday cards and Christmas cards, inviting her over. It was Chloe who vanished. John kept me up to date, telling me she'd left her restaurant job and started a cleaning business, she'd got divorced and was working her way round the county, rugby teams first. I wrote to her then but got no reply and didn't push it.

So, it's an understatement to say I was surprised to hear from her after Kai's diagnosis. "John told me," she said, on a phone call that showed she had no idea what time it was in Hawaii. "Is the invitation still open?"

It was, and it stayed open for the nineteen months Kai was dying. She said, the day after his funeral when we went for one last walk up the canyon, that what I had lived through day by day, too close to focus on it, was five snapshots for her: both of us looking healthy but stunned right after the diagnosis; Kai stumbling over his words but still cheerful, after surgery, and me spending down my capital of hope; Kai bloated on steroids in his electric wheelchair and me thinner than I'd ever been, with my hair dry and breaking; Kai lying wordless in the hospital bed we drew up to the window so he could watch the birds while I watched him, marking every breath; finally, on the last trip, a box with the lid shut and me . . .

"What?" I said. "Me what?" We had stopped at the lookout on a ridgeline path, jungle laid out before us and ocean winking in the distance. I screeched the question from my ravaged throat, work the last thing on my mind now, my voice a broken croak. "Me what, Chloe?"

"You wrapped up in blankets and fed off a teaspoon," she said, handing me a tissue. She had bought the good ones, with the lotion, but still I could only dab at the raw skin under my nose where I'd blown it with the cheap ones before she arrived. "You coddled and cared for. I'm scared when I look at you."

"Are you applying for the job?" I said, snorting instead of blowing my nose again, then turning away to spit. "Coddler, carer, blanket wrapper?"

"Of course," she told me. "Who else?"

So it's Chloe I phone, sitting parked on the road outside Saint Helen's once Neighbourhood Watch Man has seen me off. She doesn't answer, because it's a workday and she runs the cleaning business she owns like she ran the restaurant she managed. She used to stalk around on those high heels she swore were comfy, head going side to side like a raptor, looking for empty glasses, dropped crumbs, customers trying to catch an eye. These days she's in trainers, and she's looking for stray hairs on porcelain, watermarks on chrome, balls of dust. But she's the same old Chloe. It's like those missing seven years of our friendship never happened.

"It's Lindsay," I say to her voicemail. "Look, I've had a bit of a shock. That's too extreme. I've had a bit of a disappointment. And I'm having these—" Except, thinking I knew Farmer George in the property centre was nothing really. And I'm mad to question whether Peggy was real. It was only yesterday that I— Although I missed a day, didn't I? And the visual stuff? I've already decided that's grief and jet lag. "I've had a disappointment," I say again. "Any chance you're up for a drink tonight? I need you."

I really do hope she's free, I think, about a minute after I get back to Lord's Yard, because John and Shelley are at me again, tag-teaming, worse than this morning, and not even seeing my nephews again can make it bearable. I need a break.

The five of us have sat down for early tea because the boys have got football. I don't know how they can run about for ninety minutes after one of Shelley's dinners, but they're shovelling down rice and some kind of ham-and-pineapple concoction she tells me is curry. I've taken a spoonful of rice and a spoonful of salad. I don't want to let on that Hawaiian food has ruined me but the sweet-and-sour sauce coating the lumps of meat makes me think of orange toffee.

John starts. "You can't be on your own yet, Lindsay."

"You're the boss," I tell him.

The boys snigger.

"He's right for once," Shelley says. "You're not okay."

"Of course I'm not okay!"

"Yeah, but we don't mean that," says Shelley. "We both noticed—"

"It's probably jet lag," John says, making my heart thump in my chest. Noticed what? All of a sudden, a sob escapes me, like a bubble that's got no choice but to rise and burst. Tears roll down my face and tremble on the edge of my jaw.

"Mu-um!" Zak says, like a flare of danger. Poor kid.

"Mu-um!" says Nicky, mocking him.

"Behave!" John snaps.

"John, for God's sake don't take it out on them," I say, wiping my face and sniffing. "I'm sorry, you two."

"Tell Auntie Lindsay you're fine sharing a room while she's here," Shelley says.

Zak and Nicky look warily at me, at their mum, then their dad, nod once and go back to eating. I think they were primed, and they just failed. Certainly, John's looking daggers at the tops of their heads and Shelley's smirking, like she always does when the boys are typical. I can't imagine what it must be like to love someone so much you love them even more when they're annoying.

"Just don't make any rash decisions," John says.

"Like what?"

"You're so subtle," Shelley says, and he glares at her, but he looks uncomfortable too.

Then we hear a car, and we all turn our eyes to the door, grateful for the distraction.

"Here comes the casting vote," I say, hoping I'm right. "Here comes the real boss."

Right enough Chloe appears after tapping on the window with her nails. She dumps her bag down, gives me a bone-cracking hug and a smacker of a kiss on the top of my head, then and goes to the kitchen tap to get a drink of water, her uniform hugging her figure in a way that makes Zak glue his eyes to her back. She always wears the same uniform as her cleaners: a navy blue tunic—big white logo on the back, a smaller version of it on the breast pocket—and a pair of navy yoga pants. For all the bending and kneeling, she said when I saw her in them for the first time. Her white socks and trainers are scuff-free and blinding, and her hair is pulled up in a high knot, showing a face free of make-up. She wears no jewellery at all and, although she says she can't ask her staff to take their wedding rings off, she usually gets them stud- and chain-free in a couple of weeks.

"I needed that," she says when she's gulped down half a glassful. She knew where to reach for the glasses, and I wonder if Shelley minds my friend acting as if this house is still the place she used to come to play after school, where she would ask my mum what we were having before she decided whether to accept an invitation to stay and eat.

She's eying up the ham-and-pineapple gloop as if she could be persuaded now. That's one of the things I love about Chloe. She's very successful. She might even be rich these days. But she has no airs about her. Tap water and tinned ham get the same response as Veuve Clicquot and Wagyu beef.

"Welcome home, Lindsay," she says. "And don't argue, because I have made an executive decision for you, like we agreed."

"Eh?" I say. "When did we agree that?"

Kai said, one time about a year ago, that I let Chloe boss me around too much and asked me how come she was the leader in all our exploits with me just following along uncomplaining. I said nothing, only smiled. "What?" he asked me. We were having this conversation in the house that he'd grown up in, on the island where he was native, before I went to work in the bespoke dead room that he preferred to either a sound pod or a rented studio. I was his perfect wife because I was Chloe's perfect friend. Equally happy to be both. Still, I'd like to know what she's on about.

John and Shelley are nodding in approval, even though they can't have any more of a clue than me.

"You need a place to stay," she goes on, steamrollering me as usual.

"She's staying here," says John.

Chloe waves a hand at him. "And you're in no position to be making tough choices, so I'm going to make them for you."

"Now hang on—" John says.

"I'm going to find you a house," Chloe says.

"I can find myself a—"

"She's not moving," John says.

"But it's more fun if I do it," Chloe goes on, ignoring both of us. "Like a property show. I'll scope them out, and you swan around and say there's not enough hanging space."

"She just got here," says John.

"And yet I'm leaving," I say, standing up. "But only to go for a drink. Chloe?"

"Phil Inn?" Chloe says. "Like we're sixteen again? Only I'm driving, so I'll have to drink less than I did then."

We're halfway there when her phone goes, and she frowns at whatever voice is coming through her Bluetooth.

"Wait," she says. Then she turns to me. "I need to deal with this."

I shrug my permission but, to my surprise, she pulls over, switches the engine off and gets out of the car, moving away too far for me to hear her half of the conversation. She's pacing up and down, gesturing as if the person on the other end can see her, and I can tell from the way she pumps her arm as she dinks the end-call button that she wishes she was slamming down an old landline.

She stalks back over towards me, stalling a step when she sees me sitting with the passenger door open.

"Friends die in hot cars," I say, which is no lie because the evening sun is firing right in through the windscreen.

"Did you hear any of that?" she replies, without smiling.

"Nope. What's up?"

She doesn't answer. She's sitting back in the driver's seat, knuckles white on the wheel, eyes darting back and forth.

"Hear any of what?" I say.

"Work shit." She spits the words. Then she sorts her face out and turns to me with a smile. "You run a business, Lindsay. You know how it is. Oh!" she clutches my arm. "What have I said? Why are you crying?"

I shake my head. She wouldn't understand, best friend or no best friend, that Kai was the arse kicker and BSP-merchant and innovator and I'm as terrified to start my own business, actually on my own, as I've ever been in my life.

"Is it Kai?" Chloe says, and I nod because it is and I don't want to tell her the details and have her despise me.

She lets me talk about him for one drink, passing me hankies and nodding, not trying to cheer me up or make me see some other side to it all. Then she bangs her hands flat on the table, sends me to the loo to fix my make-up and goes to get another round in. There's a bag of crisps waiting for me too. She noticed that I didn't eat much dinner, I reckon.

We spend the rest of the time in the pub with her delivering the highlights of domestic grossness from clients' houses and me half laughing and half retching at them.

"How could you not flush a full toilet even if your cleaner *isn't* coming?" I say. "How would someone stand up and walk away from that?"

"It might be a fetish. No, listen, listen! Because what I don't know about fetishes now, Lindsay, is not much. I rub leather conditioner into harnesses and roll them up neatly on the bedside table. These people have no shame."

I settle into the comfort of her. *Ease. Soothing. Alleviation.* So many words *sound* better—those three are each a joy to say aloud—but *comfort* is the only real option.

"So what was the shock stroke disappointment?" she asks when we're on our way back to the car after that second glass of wine, still barely mediocre even with ice cubes. We've just decided enough with nostalgia; next time we'll get a taxi somewhere.

But I decide not to tell her about Mrs. March. She's been such a pal not just tonight making up those tall tales (surely), but over the last two grim years. Some of the people we thought were our friends drained away like bathwater. Some others stuck around, true. But only Chloe repaired a pretty dead-in-the-water friendship just so she could be there to help me. Who needs an elderly acquaintance when you've got a friend like that?

That's what I tell myself. The truth is I still can't decide if I really went for tea in that house. The memory feels locked on the far side of something I can't name, unless sleeping so long always feels like that. Or, like I keep telling myself, it's grief and jet lag.

So I lie.

"It doesn't even matter now," I say, "but a house I was looking at to rent didn't work out. There was nowhere to fake a dead room."

Chloe's steps slow at my side and, before I know what's happened, I'm two paces ahead of her.

"What's wrong?" I say, stopping and turning back.

"Fake a dead room?" she says. "What does that mean?"

"You know what it means, Chlo!" I tell her. "I'd need a windowless room with no pipes or electrical noise that I could line with quilts, till I get my permanent house and install a proper one."

"A proper . . . dead room," says Chloe.

"Right. Like the last one. Didn't you ever see it?"

She's walking again. "I didn't know what it was called," she says. "Can't you call it a recording studio?"

"Bit pretentious," I say. "It's just an expression, Chlo. Why's it freaking you?"

"No idea," she says. "Maybe I need to calm it with the true-crime podcasts. So listen, shut up about the disgusting habits of the rich and spoiled for a minute and tell me what else you need in your forever home. As well as the *dead room*."

I still don't know what's bothering her. Even when Kai was dying in a room across the corridor, it never occurred to me to call my dead room anything else.

But her mood must have affected me because, when I go to bed, after we've hugged goodbye outside the big gates and I've let myself in and double-checked the lock behind me, made a cup of sleepy tea and gone upstairs, I find myself having a brand-new nightmare. Kai is in our dead room in Hilo and I'm trying to open the door, but it's jammed. I shout but I know he won't hear me through the soundproofing, so I go round the back of the house, that's now made of grey stone and sits on a gravel drive in a green garden. There's a window I can look through and I catch sight of the foot of Kai's hospital bed and two peaks of blanket that must be his feet. I bang on the glass, but it makes no sound, except to startle a fox behind me in the bushes and make it scream. I don't turn. I can't see this fox. Awake, I wouldn't know what it was or have any clue where the noise was coming from, but in the dream I'm sure it's a fox. And suddenly, I'm running around a cobbled yard, with half-open stable doors on all sides, looking for something to help me smash the window and save it, because it's trapped inside with Kai now.

I wake filled with dread and have to concentrate hard on my breathing so I don't whimper. I should be used to nightmares by this time and all of them about Kai have been me trying to reach him and failing. Whether I'm locked out or struck dumb or lost or wading through glue, every dream has been about barriers and impediments and impossibilities, my mind trying to teach itself that I've lost him. There's no reason this one should be any worse than the others.

I sink back down on my pillow and turn to pick up my phone. What I see makes my lips curl in a seed of a smile. My phone isn't on my bedside table. I've made an inch of progress and, although no one else would break into a cheer, I'm proud of myself. For the first time in two years, I've left my phone in my bag downstairs and not gone to bed primed for disaster.

I bash a dent into Zak's horrible foam pillow and turn onto my side hoping to go to sleep again.

I could read but—

I sit bolt upright and let out a laugh before catching my teeth in my top lip and freezing, hoping I didn't wake anyone.

I *could* read, I realise, clicking the light on. I could read *Sleeping Murder*, which is right there on my bedside table, because the real Peggy March really gave it to me on my real visit to her house. It's horrible if she was pretending to be settled there, when in fact she was a day away from having to leave, but she was real and I liked her. Maybe I could find out where she moved and give her book back, once I've finished it.

I settle back with it, even though my head is swimming and the print dances in front of my eyes. And besides, what with the big spooky house and the woman all alone in the world, it isn't exactly comforting. People get that wrong about Agatha Christie all the time. Even Peggy had forgotten what was actually on the page, after too many hours in front of the telly on Sunday nights. No book then, I decide, letting it fall. I start to drift. No foxes, I tell myself. No voices, no screams, no thumps, no flat paper world, no poker games. I must be nearly gone though, because what's scary about a poker game, right? Or a fox, actually.

Seldom do Rattray Walker have the honour of presenting a house the equal of Cairnside to the waiting market. Enviably situated equidistant between Stirling and Edinburgh, this imposing Victorian former manse sits in its own expansive grounds with views over rolling farmland to the south and easy access to Scotland's motorways. The subjects for sale include lavish accommodation in the main house, whose spacious public rooms boast working shutters, deep cornicing, elaborate ceiling roses, original fireplaces and countless further period features. Upstairs there is the potential for five en-suite bedrooms. In addition, outbuildings and garaging might be suitable for conversion and the large grounds of just over two acres are admirably suited to division into separate plots for further development. Cairnside is structurally sound and has been in use as a residence until comparatively recently but would benefit from considerable upgrading and renovation to form a luxurious family home.

Chapter 6

I'm still shaky the next morning, eyes playing tricks again, and I can't face looking at listings, but I need to start working no matter what John says. Not that I can shrug off what John says across the board. Which is another thing I need to deal with.

There's nothing except the dead room stopping me working, because with good enough Wi-Fi anyone can work anywhere. Kai and I couldn't have lived in Hawaii if that wasn't true. We certainly wouldn't both have been at that APAC convention in New York, both of us thousands of miles from home, meeting each other, changing our lives forever. So—again in theory—I haven't made any difference to my career, running home like this. My accent is what it was when I lived in America, only less exotic. My contacts haven't got harder to access, as long as I remember when they're sleeping. But the longer I leave it, the more work I'm missing out on and the more subscribers my YouTube channel is losing from lack of new content.

I've forgotten the password for my SoundCloud, but my website is in good shape, with show reels and raw reels right there on the home page. The raw reels were one of Kai's great enthusiasms. He even offered to raw read any extract a prospective client sent through, in real time. Like he was holding up a copy of that day's newspaper or something. I never dreamed anyone would take him up on it. Shows what I know. "They humanise us, Lindsay," he'd say. "Plus producers see how clean our first reads are and they know we won't waste studio time. It's all about the Benjamins. You know that."

I would sound like a Galápagos turtle if I tried to raw read right now. I would sound worse than I did when I tried for that self-help book. I have got to stop crying and get some honey. And a dead room, I think, coming full circle. I need to speak to John. Two birds, one stone.

He's sitting there in the Portakabin, like my dad always did. But my dad wasn't using a laptop. John's going to wreck his neck or at least his wrists if he doesn't ditch the jewellery display case and get a proper table to put his knees under. A better chair than the old leather recliner he's slouching in wouldn't hurt either.

"What's up?" he says. His hands are very busy suddenly, as if he's clicking away from a web page he doesn't want me to see. I make a point of not looking.

"You've made some changes, right?" I begin. I wave around the cabin. There's a Keurig instead of Dad's grimy old kettle and a stack of disposable coffee cups instead of the chipped mugs with their whole history ground in around the handles. The small electronics on the wall shelves are MP3s and Xboxes instead of CD players and video cameras. "Up front here and back in the Barrens."

"What do you know about the Barrens?" His voice is loud and hard, and his chest rises and falls far too fast.

"Oh, John," I say, dropping into the duct-taped office chair he keeps for elderly customers. They use up a lot of time, poring over coins and medals, but they spend decent money so he takes care of them. "When are you going to stop pretending you're all right?"

"When are you going to turn back into my sister instead of a therapy-mad bloody daytime-telly social worker?"

"For God's sake," I say, "if you and me can't talk about this to each other, what's the point of me being back here?"

"There's nothing to talk about," he says. "You should deal with your own shit, Lindsay, and not . . ."

"Project it?" I say. "Okay. I'll deal with my own 'shit.' Meanwhile, I was wondering if you've got anything like an unused trailer or something."

He's staring at me and his breath is picking up again.

"It doesn't need to be kitted out. In fact, it would be better if it was empty."

I can see a vein in his neck. I feel cruel but I need him to stop shutting me out. "You know what would be perfect?" I say. He narrows his eyes. "Remember the caravan?"

The blood drains out of his face so suddenly that I can see the dark shadow of his stubble against his white skin. I reach out and his hand is damp against my fingertips. I don't think he even notices I'm touching him.

"What caravan?" he says. "I've got no idea what you're talking about."

"Oh, John," I say again.

Then I'm back in the past. It was our best-ever find. My dad had salvaged a two-berther, or agreed to take it as part of a house clearance maybe. He probably meant to use it for something specific, like he used a horsebox for books and a tent for toys. But there must have been a busy flu season. Or maybe it was the Christmas that Cellardine's Works folded and he got all the contents: strippable machinery, goods to resell, endless metal shelving, catering equipment and canteen fittings from the proper old-style works cafeteria, not to mention the office furniture that some feckless manager had just refurbed in a doomed attempt to show off to potential new customers. Dad replaced his and Mum's cars with new ones, cash down, off of Cellardine's.

But anyway, then or some other time, he managed to overlook a caravan. John and I found it hidden behind a stack of insulation panels. It was like hacking through vines and uncovering a castle. It was a fort, pyramid, spaceship, galleon, submarine, Tardis and sometimes just a caravan, one that we hitched to a pony and took around the quiet lanes of a magical summer, home from boarding school and free as a pair of birds. It was everything to John and me. Until it wasn't.

When he speaks again, I realise I've been quiet long enough to let him rebuild all his walls. "Why do you *want* a caravan anyway?" he asks me. "Where are you going?"

"I don't," I assure him. "Nowhere. I want somewhere to set up a temporary . . . audio pod."

"Dead room," he says. "Chloe told me."

I nod, but what I'm thinking is when exactly did Chloe tell my brother she hated the name of my workspace? And why? Does she text him like she texts me? I still can't get my head round the fact that I left and these people carried on without me.

"Dead room, right," I say. "So that I can start working again. I'm too scared to look at my contact page and see what I'm missing, but there's no point if I've got nowhere to do it."

"So leave it."

"I need to get back in the game, John," I tell him. "Keep my name current. I can't slip."

"In the dog-eat-dog world of audio narration," he says, deadpan.

"As opposed to the hard-bitten mean streets of house clearances and scrap dealing," I say.

"Speaking of which," says John, because a car has pulled up in the parking spaces outside the gates and someone is approaching, setting off a beeper on John's computer. The Portakabin door swings open and it's the kind of couple you never used to see in Menstrie when I lived here before. Two men, gym honed and dressed to the nines in tailored shorts and leather sandals, both with severely sculpted beards and one-shouldered backpacks. One of them is wearing blue aviator shades, which tells you that blue aviator shades are in fashion again, rather than that he might not be.

"We're looking for vintage sinks to make a water feature," one of them tells John.

"No problem, gents," John says, getting to his feet. "Sounds nice. If you promise to tag Lord's when you post the finished project, I'll knock a few quid off for you."

I see both men let their shoulders drop when they realise that this rough-sounding scrappie isn't the bigot he might have been. I smile at John's back and think, if he needs to keep it all tamped down, why don't I let him? He's grown up into an okay kind of man despite everything.

He turns and walks backwards to talk to me. "Why don't you do something more like settling in, Lindsay? Not moving again or starting work when you're still not able for it. Do something nice for yourself, eh?"

More evidence that he's basically all right. Kind in his own way, coping the best he can. And he's got a point. There *is* something else for me to do, something that definitely counts as settling in. Making friends is something nice for myself, in anyone's book. Not letting another person slip out of my life is something nice for myself.

Peggy March is in a nursing home. How hard can it be?

Just my luck to be trying this where four counties meet, though, instead of bang in the middle of Yorkshire or something. I sit on Zak's bed, with the monsters watching, copying and pasting until I've got a page of numbers to try. There are more residential care homes than I can believe in Perthshire. Quite a few actually in Dunblane. Stirlingshire is just as bad. Clackmannanshire isn't but it's too close to home for me to tackle before I've honed my spiel. West Fife is much more manageable, with no more than a dozen that look like the kind of place Mrs. March's kid might have moved her into. Did she say if it was a son or a daughter? Probably a daughter, I decide, from the way the old lady was so instantly at home with me.

I lift my phone.

"Can I speak to Peggy March?" I ask when someone answers at the first one.

"No Peggy March here." And they hang up.

I stare at my phone for a moment then redial.

"Hello again," I say. "Did you mean to cut me off like that?"

"What? Wait, are you *not* cold-calling?"

"What?"

"Oh man, hen," the voice says. "You wouldn't believe the cold calls we get. Our residents—no offence to them—are not great at protecting personal data. It's half the effing job some shifts."

"But Peggy March isn't actually one of your residents?"

"Yeah, no, but they do that too. Make up random names to ask about."

Okay, I tell Blastoma and Chemo and the rest of the monsters once I've hung up again, What I need here is the personal touch, my honest face. Which is why, half an hour later, I'm at the farthest away bit of coastal Fife with a residential home on my list, prepared to work my way back or until I find her, whichever comes first.

"Hi," I say to the uniformed girl who lets me in on the buzzer and then slips behind the reception desk to deal with me. "I wonder if you can help. My name's Lindsay Hale—I *was* Lindsay Lord, from Lord's Yard up in Menstrie?" I wait for recognition even though the whole point of coming to Fife was to put a bit of distance behind me. Besides, this kid isn't the junkyard type and looks back at me blankly. "Anyway, I've been living overseas for a while—look." I get out my Hawaii driving licence and put it on the desk between us. "But I've moved home. And I'm trying to get in touch with an old friend. Her name's Peggy March and I know she's moved into a home recently, but I don't know which one."

That's my devious plan: the unvarnished truth. Well, close to the unvarnished truth except for that little bit of fancy footwork where I said "old friend" hoping this girl will think "close friend" and not "new friend in her eighties." Even "new friend" is pushing it: One cup of tea plus a business card left behind isn't what anyone would call a friendship.

"Can't you ask her family?" the girl says. "She could be anywhere really. What made you think she was here with us?"

"It's near where she lived before," I say, lying now.

"But her family might have chosen a place near them. Where do *they* live? Has she got kids?"

"Just the one," I say. "But I don't really want to ask *her*. She doesn't . . . Truth is, she doesn't . . ." I don't want to keep lying but, if I say Mrs. March's daughter doesn't know me, I'm going to look dodgy.

"You think she might not approve of you visiting?" the girl says, pulling her brows down.

"No idea," I say. "Does she have to approve?"

"Absolutely not, no way!" I realise that the frown wasn't for me; it was for this imaginary daughter who's trying to stop her mum seeing old friends. "Even if she's responsible for her mother's legal and medical, she can't stop the old lady's social life." She twists her mouth to the side and shakes her head, joined with me in distaste for this woman who's controlling her own mother for no good reason. "But like I said, Mrs. March isn't here."

I thank her—from my heart because she's left me much more sure of my ground as I move on to care home number two.

It works there, and in the following four, but then at a place in Kincardine, halfway home again, something goes wrong in a way I can't immediately understand. I walk in—there's no buzzer here—and a man looks at me through the vertical blinds covering an office window then comes out to the foyer to see what I'm after. My heart sinks when I realise that he's another one my messed-up mind is telling me I know from somewhere. At least I don't embarrass myself by trying to claim an acquaintanceship.

"What can I do for you?" he says. I falter as he's reaching out to shake my hand. I'm surprised, for one thing, because I would have thought that if anyone was still practising distancing it would be the staff in places like this. But that's not all. His hand looks not quite real as it comes towards me, rippling at the edges. I take it but step back again after we finish shaking. This is a serious day-long smoker, and the stench of tar and tobacco coming off him is strong enough to be off-putting.

"My name's Lindsay Lord," I say, looking away from his fingers and back at his face. I've ditched the married name bit; it was distracting.

"From Lord's Yard up in Menstrie?" This guy definitely knows it. "I'm just back home from living overseas," I go on. "I can show you my American driver's licence to prove it, if you need to see ID. Thing is, I'm trying to get in touch with an old friend, called Peggy March. She used to live in a house called Saint Helen's—I don't know the name of the road, sorry—in Dunblane, but she's just moved into a care home somewhere near here, only I don't know which one. So I'm going round asking."

I sense someone else in the office and, as I look up, the vertical blinds twist shut, so all I can see is my own reflection.

"There's no Peggy March here," says Nicotine Ned. "And I don't think it's a good idea to go on the hunt for old ladies, you know. How many other places have you asked?"

"Seven," I say, including the one on the phone because he's put my back up. Everywhere else, a nice lady or girl has politely told me that I've struck out, without any of this sinister hinting that I'm doing something wrong.

"You've been round seven homes asking for Peggy March?" he says. He's not the healthiest-looking man I've ever seen, having that yellow-grey complexion with eye bags that look like oyster shells, but unless I'm imagining it, his face is darkening as I speak to him.

"No one else seemed to mind," I tell him. "What do *you* think the problem is?"

He looks behind himself at the half-open office door. If I had to guess, he wants whoever is in there to come out and deal with me but he doesn't want to ask. It's probably his wife.

"We take safeguarding very seriously," he says, spitting the words. Literally spitting. I take another step backwards. "So I don't want to have to let anyone know that your organisation is using predatory tactics to—"

"Whoa! Whoa! Whoa!" I say. "My organisation? Predatory? What the hell are you on about?"

"Lord's Yard," he says. "You're sniffing round for a house clearance." I open my mouth to tell him that the house is clear, but he sails on. "We work pretty hard to stop funeral directors, furniture dealers, e-scooter reps or anyone else from bugging our friends. Take a hike."

I find myself smiling. I've had the sharp end of it but it's still good to know how well-protected these people are.

"I *will* go," I say. " I mean, you're wrong about me, but I can't prove it, so . . . I'll try something else."

"You do that," he says, turning away. He's back in the office before I'm out of the front door, and whoever it is who's lurking in there says something I don't quite catch. It sounds like "Now shave," but even if that *is* his wife, it surely can't be.

Nestled in the charming hamlet of Pool O' Muckhart, this quaint and comfortable former shooting lodge brings together old-world charm and the possibility of elegant modern living for the visionary buyer. Habitable but in need of major refurbishment, Grayson House has retained all the character and traditional features one expects after settled ownership of several decades, but is now ripe for refreshment to bring it to contemporary standards and meet the needs of today's country dweller. Lot 1 comprises the house, half an acre of garden and unimproved outbuildings. Rattray Walker are also representing the seller in regard to two further lots of land with residential possibilities subject to planning. This is a true gem which must be viewed to be appreciated.

Chapter 7

Now shave?

It eats at me all the way back to my car. He didn't need to shave. His chin was fine. *New shade?* But I know sound and that first vowel wasn't a thin high sound. It was rounded and mobile, a diphthong. And the final sound wasn't a definite stop. It went on and faded.

I get in and put my seat belt on, then a horrible thought strikes me. What if I misheard, like I've been mis-seeing? What if the voice in the office said "All okay?" or "Who was that?" even?

What if trying to find Peggy at another home after this one brings another familiar face that shouldn't be, more solid objects shimmering like underwater and, worst of all, sounds that don't ring true in my ear?

Give it up, I tell myself. I've got Chloe. And that receptionist at the estate agent's looked like the book club type too. And, once I'm not trying to stay out of Shelley's way to make it less annoying that I'm in her house, I'll have Shelley. We could all get together once a week for dinner, like a family should. I could watch the boys splashing around on the football field the odd Saturday if I really wanted to bed myself in.

She's out on the front step as I pull into the yard, holding an enormous gold tray that bounces the sun back in my face, half blinding me. God I hope she is. I hope I'm not imagining either the tray or the caveman club in her other hand. Is that a shield? It's too big and too round, surely. But at least I know, as I walk towards her, that it's really there.

"Bird scarer?" I say, guessing.

She's hanging over the side railing now, trying to attach the disc to a set of hooks there.

"Gong," she says. "Your brother never takes his phone with him when he's away back there in the wilds and I'm sick of shouting for him." She lets the big brass tray go and it swings on the hooks, clanging against the brick base of the porch. Once it's still, Shelley squares up the club as if she's taking a swing in a game of rounders and hits it smack in the middle. The sound is deep and resonant and reverberates in waves, sending two wood pigeons up out of the sycamore tree, fussing and flapping.

"Wow," I say. "That would make me take my phone."

John steps out of the Portakabin. "We could have sold that," he says.

"Jesus Christ, John," I say, "you sound like Dad."

"Worse things I could be," he says, which is the kind of jet black joke that makes me feel as close to him as when we were children. No one else would get it except me. I grin so wide my cheeks hurt, but he only stares at me. "What you been up to, Linds?"

And just like that the gap between us is a mile wide again. "Why?"

"*Why?*" says Shelley. "For God's sake, Lindsay, how many times do we need to tell you we're worried about you?"

The honest answer would be "a few less than you have" so I say nothing.

"Only, tell us now if you're already feeling as wobbly as you look," Shelley says, "because Chloe's on her way round and you'll need all your strength to stand up to her."

"I don't want to stand up to her," I say. "It's only a bit of fun." John looks unconvinced. "It's no different from you finding me a car," I tell him. "If you can keep me from having to deal with car salesmen and Chloe can keep me away from estate agents—lucky me. I met a real weirdo of a one down in BofA yesterday."

"What tinpot car dealer have you found in BofA, for God's sake?" says John.

"Not a dealer," I say. "A property centre and not tinpot either. He looks like a farmer and he knows you and Shelley. I even thought I recognised *him*. He didn't recognise me, mind. Maybe he was all over me at a barn dance once and he was too blootered to remember. Anyway."

John stares at me, saying nothing. And I can't think of anything to say to him either.

"Go and have a lie-down till lunch," Shelley says. "You look like you need it."

I wish I could argue. Instead I go inside and upstairs to sit on Zak's bed with the monsters.

I've got myself together by the time I hear John come in, and I go downstairs to the smell of Shelley's homemade soup warming up in the big pot that's been a mainstay of this kitchen since my mum's day. They're standing together at the cooker, John's arm round Shelley's waist, her head on his shoulder.

"—brilliant as well as beautiful," I catch him saying.

That's why I should stick with the plan to find Peggy. She's alone, like me. That receptionist was definitely married and Chloe's never single for long, or not unless she changed more than it seems in the years I didn't see her. I'm actually surprised she's single now. I push the door wider open and try to tread heavily so they hear me.

"So, Lindsay," Shelley says, still stirring the soup, which is starting to splat and fart. "We're agreed. You're staying."

"Are we?"

"Let's agree now," says John. "You need to take your time and make sure you choose wisely. You've had enough upset. And you're not . . ."

"I'm not what?"

"Come on," he says. "You know you're not."

"That smells . . ." I try to say *good*, to change the subject, but what it smells like is mutton fat. My mum's day indeed. She always made potato soup with a flank of mutton too. I can still remember watching her lift the disc of fat off the top on the second day, knocking bits of carrot and turnip out of its underside before she threw it away.

Shelley ladles out three bowlfuls and sets mine down in front of me.

The disc of fat from this pot of soup is sitting on a square of kitchen roll and, as I watch, Shelley wads it up into a ball, then rolls it in a load of seeds she's got spread on a plate. She plops the whole thing in a plastic bag and heads out to the scullery.

"What the hell?" I ask John. "Tell me that's not for dinner."

"She's freezing it for the birds in the winter," he says.

Shelley comes back in, massaging the fat into her hands. I suppose it must be good for the skin but, when she plonks a loaf of bread down on the table, I can't take my eyes off the greasy fingerprints on the wrapper.

"Anyway," she says, "Even if you were tip-top, this is your home. You've got as much right to live here as us. More maybe." As if she didn't just serve me first.

"Excuse me," I blurt and I slip out of the kitchen before the tears can fall.

As the door is closing, I hear John growl, "What the fuck did you say that for?" But even this sign that it's not all as rosy as they make out doesn't help me.

I'm still hiding in the downstairs loo trying to get a hold of myself when I hear a car arriving and Chloe's voice calling my name. I should answer but for some reason I sit where I am, making a fan out of the end of the toilet paper, as I hear her come in and the three of them talking. When curiosity gets the better of me, I stand and open the door a crack. I used to be able to do it silently but I've lost the knack and there's a sudden silence before the back door opens and closes. I open the toilet door all the way and go back to the kitchen. Shelley and Chloe are huddled together on the far side of the drive, close to the Portakabin steps, deep in discussion.

"What's that all about?" I say.

John gives a theatrical sigh and rolls his eyes. "Some daft crap," he says. "Shelley'll set her straight."

"Set *Chloe* straight?" I say. I lean over the sink and bang on the window, startling both of them. "I don't need a keeper, John. I don't need a minder. Chloe's my oldest friend."

"Just hear me out," Chloe says, barging back in with Shelley on her heels. She always did that: started in the middle of the conversation she'd been imagining before I got there. She was the first person I knew to kick off with "So" like everyone does now. She sat down next to me on the school bus and said, "So about the party." Once, she got off a plane in Honolulu and said, "On the other hand, Lindsay, if I stay with him you could have a break."

"I'm listening," I tell her.

"The thing is, of course you should check the market and all that. Make no big decisions, blah blah blah—only there's this one house . . ."

"Is there?" says John in a voice that could flash-freeze the sun. What is his problem?

"Chlo," I say. "I've got no idea what you're on about. Any of you."

"I want to take you round it," Chloe says.

"That was the idea," I remind her.

"And I want you to stay here where you belong," says John. "Until it's the right time to move."

They stare at each other. Mad as it sounds, I look to Shelley to give the casting vote. "So much drama," she says. "It's. A. House. You're talking about moving house."

"Oh Shelley, the Queen of Crime wrote a whole novel about folk moving into a house," I say.

"You need to be here with your family," says John. "We know what you need."

"You're getting a bit *Handmaid's Tale* there, John," Chloe says. "Speaking of books."

I really need this to stop, even though I have no idea what it is, why they're fighting. I need them to cut it out before the kitchen starts to flatten or I hear a phantom voice or—God forbid—one of them shows me that they can see any of that happening to me.

"What like of a house?" I ask Chloe.

She squeaks and leaps into my arms, whirling me round. "Couple of days to set it all up, Lindsay. That's all."

Of course that's not all. She grills me in excruciating detail about what I need, what I want and what I hate, leaning over to dip a piece of bread into my soup while she texts herself the answers with her free hand. John goes back to work, without another word, and Shelley retreats to the living room to iron in front of the telly, turned up loud to tune us out.

"Right," Chloe says at last. "So that's what *you* want: character, detached, at least two bedrooms, your own bathroom—ten years in America, that is—a manageable garden, bit of privacy, big kitchen and a wood burner? Same as everyone else. Plus a dead room. Same as no one else ever."

"It's an industry term, Chloe," I tell her for the hundredth time.

"Which just leaves the numbers," she says, ignoring me. She's looking down so as not to appear overly interested. She's always loved money and she's good with it. She told me once, if she can't retire at fifty she'll have failed.

"Seven hundred," I tell her.

"Seven hundred grand?" She lifts her head from her phone screen. "Seven hundred thousand pounds?"

"All in. That's got to cover the conversion of the boxroom or whatever."

"I had no idea audio work was such a goldmine," Chloe says. "That's live sex-chat money."

"It's mostly insurance," I tell her, feeling mean but needing to shut this down before she steps in it by literally congratulating me. Even Shelley has come to the living room door with a half-ironed school shirt in her hands.

"Oh," Chloe says. "Right. Of course. Sorry. Look . . ." I wait. "Are you actually up for this?"

"Yeah, you didn't give Lindsay much chance to say no there," Shelley chips in.

I stand up and go round the table, leaning over to hook my chin over Chloe's shoulder and wrap her in my arms. She smells of ten different kinds of household cleaner and a trace of nice soap from this morning's shower. Shelley goes back to her ironing board, but she's fiddling with her phone, the forgotten shirt crumpled under her arm,

"Because I know I can be a lot," Chloe says, mumbling into the forearm that's crossing her body just under her chin. I can feel her warm breath on my skin.

"Who told you that?" I ask her, kissing the top of her head. *I've* told her that more times than I can remember. The last occasion was when I came home to find her laying shirt-and-tie combos on top of Kai's blankets, trying to help him decide what he should be cremated in. If he hadn't been laughing, I would have punched her.

She licks my arm and blows a wet raspberry, sending me springing back. "I'll be in touch," she says. She shouts through to the living room, "Thanks for the weird soup, Shel!" And she's gone.

I make my escape too, and try to avoid both of them—all of them once the boys are home—for the rest of the day.

There's nothing wrong with my ears, I tell myself near bedtime. I am an experienced and talented audio artist and this is the perfect moment to take a step back towards my business again. I wait for the thought to overwhelm me, for the very idea to give me the cold chills. When that doesn't happen, I check my inbox for requests and find someone self-publishing a "vintage" recipe book I suspect is probably her granny's. She's offering a share of royalties rather than an upfront, so I send her my standard regretful pass. A company I've worked with before in London wants to re-record a new edition of a textbook and I reply asking for dates. I check the Jenny Colgan school stories like I started doing this time last year. She's had three different narrators for four books. That's like a shark smelling blood in the water, and I know I should throw my hat in the ring for any forthcoming book five but I'm not keen if it's as sad as the last one. There's a line between emotional delivery and snot bubbles. Plus I would need to explain what happened last time, since the producer is someone I know and she'd remember me enquiring then not following it up. I was nursing Kai and then grieving for him, but I can't tell people that. Anything that hints at unreliability is a strict no-no in this game.

Anyway, it's not time for jobs yet. I click onto the sound-pod website I've bookmarked, declining the cookies because I don't want to find out how much they cost in case it's outrageous. Or in case they're dead cheap and I end up buying one. Kai didn't rate them, so I'd feel like I was letting him go all over again. I click away from the site before the products load, the way I always have whenever I don't want to admit what I'm doing.

New job, new home, I say to myself in the mirror while I'm brushing my teeth. The sleepy tea is only herbs and water, so I won't have to get up and rinse with mouthwash.

New job, new home, I repeat, settling into bed to read. There should be another thing, of course, because change, like witches and monkeys, comes in threes. *New friends* takes me back to Peggy and the nursing home and *Now shave* and not knowing what's wrong with me. There is another potential third new thing rumbling around somewhere inside. But how can I even be thinking about that already? *Sleeping Murder* doesn't help. When it's not the heroine all alone in that unsettling house, hearing things and imagining things and concluding that she's going nuts, it's the pair of them, so young and so in love. So maybe it's the book's fault, not mine, when I dream that I'm with someone—like *with* someone—who definitely isn't Kai.

Bright side, it gives me a break from the true nightmares, but I wake up weeping with shame. "I'm sorry," I tell him. I leap out of bed and open the curtains, clutching the windowsill to steady myself. Now I *want* the world to flatten and flutter. I want to hear things wrong, forget and remember where I shouldn't and should—I'd take any proof that

I'm not myself and it wasn't really me who dreamed about a stranger in bed with me instead of Kai back again.

But all I see is two pinpricks of light away down at the end close to Shelley's veg patch—John out on a tour of the yard. Maybe this is his therapy. Maybe this is how he keeps the demons at bay. One of the lights is a torch beam bobbling around and there's a steadier but much dimmer glow a little higher up, coming from a phone. Maybe he listens to soothing music to help him breathe his way through it.

"Oh, John," I whisper to him, putting my hand flat on the glass.

We're both surviving in our own broken way.

I know where I am! I'm sure I know where this is!

If I'm right, then there should be chinks of daylight showing. So, since it's dark, I can be sure the sun isn't up. That means it's only been an hour or two that I was unconscious. I don't know why, but that matters a great deal. I am proud.

Now to strategise!

When I start to move, though, it comes home hard that my spirit might be willing, my resolve fierce and brave, but my body is weaker than it's ever been.

I stand, so slowly, so many different timid movements. First I roll onto one hip, feeling the hard floor bruise me as I go. Then I bend my legs under me, scraping one of my ankles. Scrabbling for purchase with my fingernails, I haul myself up onto all fours and stop there, swaying, with my head hanging down and my mouth hanging open like a dog. Like a tired-out donkey. I shuffle and creep my way forward until I feel a wall in front of me and then slap first one hand and then the other against the paint. I am sweating, foul-smelling to myself, but it helps my clammy palms stick to the wall and gives me the courage to get one foot underneath me and push as hard as I can, dragging the other leg and pawing my way up until I can whip that second foot forward too. I bang my toes against the skirting board and go over hard on my ankle but I don't fall. I lean against the wall with my arms wide, my cheek pressing in painfully as I slump, my mouth open, letting trails of drool fall. I feel the liquid on my bare shoulder.

It's hard not to let go and crumple up again. All I want to do is curl into a tiny ball and weep like a child. Instead I make my way around the room, as careful and as slow as I've ever moved in my life. There is tape everywhere, around the door, around the window, covering the light switch. I can smell it and I can feel the edges of the strips under my fingernails. I pick at it for a moment or two, but I can tell it's something stronger than I've ever encountered before, thick and unyielding.

I move on to a section of flat wall and roll around until my back is against the paint. Then cautiously I let myself slide down until my knees are bent like hairpins, screaming and aching. I stretch my legs out in front of me and wait until my breathing settles.

Here I am then. And perhaps I should be glad. It's warm and dry here. It's better than the other place. The place I wish was a dream but fear, with banging heart and ragged breath, is a memory.

Chapter 8

John's still in the kitchen with Shelley when I get up the next morning, although the boys have gone to school already.

"Listen, Lindsay," he says. "I'm serious now. You can't let Chloe boss you about. You shouldn't make any big decisions for at least a year, you know."

"Viewing a house isn't a big decision," I say. "Letting my friend do a nice thing for me isn't a big decision."

"Friend," says John. "Right, well I'm saying nothing." He stands, puts his mug in the sink and bangs out of the door.

"Why's he got it in for Chloe?" I say. It doesn't seem likely that they'd have enough dealings to make it a possibility but the atmosphere between them is unmistakable.

"He hasn't!" Shelley says. "Anything but."

"Christ, you don't mean—" I blurt out before I manage to stop myself.

Shelley laughs. She's wearing wellies and a raincoat, spreading newspaper on the table ready to tip out a barrowload of wet beans to top and tail before she packs them. "Now, *that* I would pay to watch," she says. "Nah, it's just Chloe thinks she knows best about everything. You ever notice that? Her business, our business, no doubt your business. And John reckons she's always got another angle beyond the one she tells you. Same as him. He's jealous, I think."

"So . . . they've locked horns professionally?" I say. House clearing and house cleaning in the same small town are not a million miles away from the same thing, I suppose.

"No way!" Shelley says. "No, I mean about you. John wants you here. Chloe's desperate to show you houses and move you out."

"What about you?" I ask her.

"Well," Shelley says, "this place *has* been feeling tight recently, if I'm honest. And there's only one of you. At the moment. What I think is maybe getting your family home back is just what you need right now."

All I can do is stare at her. Is she saying what I think she's saying? How can I tell her I don't want a seventies chalet bungalow in my brother's scrapyard, that I don't want the place she's been living for twenty years?

"I thought you were settled here," I said. "Does John—"

"Don't tell John I said *any* of that!" She's mugging alarm and panic. At least, I hope she's mugging. "Rain's off," she says, and I watch her trudge up through the yard towards her garden.

I sit with my eyes closed for a good five minutes, sipping coffee. Is that what's going on here? Shelley wants to move and thought I'd slot back in and ask to stay forever? John thinks I'd make a good night watchman? Peggy said it all—the way women on their own get shunted about and expected to go wherever and do whatever they're told. She said it with false bravado, pretending to a stranger she was staying put in her house, but she said it. More than ever, I want to find her, and I think I know how. Unless it's a wild idea for here. I borrow a coat from the pegs beside the door and head up the yard.

"Shel?"

She's doing something in her vegetable garden that looks like washing the bean plants. I can smell soap.

"Best way to get rid of aphids," she says. "Greenfly," she adds. My face must have told her I had no idea what aphids were. "That downpour's given me a head start and I don't want to waste it. What can I do for you? Have you thought about what I said? About living here if we move out?"

I can't begin to find a polite way to say what I'm thinking.

Shelley pushes her lips out and nods. "Fair enough. Just don't tell John."

He might work it out when I buy a different house, I think, but I say nothing. Or rather, I change the subject. "You know how I made a fool of myself saying I would get a Lyft from the airport that time?"

"You didn't make— It was funny. But yes, I remember."

"What about private detectives? Are they like Lyft and Uber, or are they like nail bars and kombucha? Are they here yet?"

"Private *detectives*?" Shelley's tone gives me my answer. "As a business? Instead of the audio work?"

"As a customer. Me employing a private detective to do a bit of work for me. To find someone I've lost touch with." I don't really know why I'm being . . . not quite dishonest . . . about Peggy March. Maybe I feel stupid to be so fixated on someone I only met once. Maybe I don't want them to tell me it's because of Kai—like I don't know that. Or tell me they're "worried." They'd get more worried when I started screaming until my eyes bled.

"Why not do what everyone else does and use Facebook?" Shelley has stopped washing the beans and stands with the spray bottle dangling from one hand while soapsuds drip off the plants and pop on the earth below them.

"I don't think she's on Faceb—" I say. "You know what? I didn't actually check. She's local so it seems like it would be easier to track her down by asking around."

"Or getting Inspector Whatshisname up from Midsummer to investigate for you," Shelley's winding me up but still I get the sense that I've rattled her.

"Barnaby, but he's a policeman," I tell her. "It's not a police matter. She's not missing. She's just gone."

"Well, to answer your question, no. It's not a normal thing in Clackmannanshire to hire a private detective to find an old friend. Or to hire a nanny for your dog or a therapist to listen to your troubles. Get a grip, Lindsay."

"What's not a police matter?" John has appeared from nowhere, or rather from behind the hedge—new since my last proper visit—that separates Shelley's garden from the Barrens. It must have cost them a fortune to put in hedge plants this size.

"Lindsay thinks she can get a private investigator," Shelley says. "Maybe in Alloa? Or were you thinking you'd have to go all the way to Stirling? Why not get a lawyer too, and sue somebody?"

"What's not a police matter?" John says again.

"I'm trying to track someone down," I tell him. "A local woman who's gone missing."

"You said she wasn't missing," John says. "What's her name?"

"What difference does *that* make?" I don't know why I'm being so awkward, except I've had enough of Shelley making fun of me and it's easier to be rude to your brother than your sister-in-law.

He stares back at me for a while before answering. "I might know where she moved to," he says. "If I took any of her stuff off her hands before she went."

As he speaks, I remember the black biscuit tin I meant to show Peggy. It must have rolled under the passenger seat of my car while I was driving. Then it went out of my mind in the shock of finding her gone.

"Don't worry about it," I say. "Like Shelley's just pointed out, I haven't even checked Facebook yet. But message received: No private investigators."

"And don't go running to police if you don't have to," John says.

"Well, don't you be so weird for no reason then," I shoot back. "Deal?"

Shelley laughs. "She's got you there, pal." She pumps up the air in her spray bottle again and goes back to firing jets of soapy water at the invisible pests on her precious beans.

"When was I weird?" says John. He's not kidding. He turns to disappear back through the hedge but stops before he's quite out of sight and adds, "Don't bring the polis sniffing round, Lindsay. I mean it."

I find my own route back through the yard. At the Portakabin, I see John sitting in his recliner, talking nineteen to the dozen on the phone and banging his hand on the top of the display case. I walk on by.

It's not as if I ever thought my dad's business was squeaky clean. I knew there was often something stored at a friend's house that he didn't want to have lying around the yard, just in case. He never said in case of what. But that was no more serious than a work crew taking the leftover materials at the end of a job or, at worst, an abandoned car getting stripped out before the tow company arrived. Dad was never wary of the police. Not like John's just been. The one time we had a break-in, in the appliance shed, Dad was on the phone before the alarm had finished ringing. Maybe. I think to myself, the less I know about how the yard's being run these days, the better.

Which is so ironic, it's almost funny in a hollow, unbearable kind of way. It's like, back then, the daylight business was an acceptable shade of very pale grey and we lived in an adventure playground, John and me. Now, if I've understood John's warning, the daylight business is a good bit murkier. On the other hand, that murk is all I'll find, no matter how hard I dig. There are no depths here now. Which is great, obviously, but there are no heights these days either.

In fact, as I look around, it's hard to believe this is the same place that made such a wonderland for John and me. Maybe it's just being taller, so I can see over everything and none of it looks like an enchanted grotto anymore. I wonder if even my third and most secret entrance would still feel like magic, the way it used to because it was all mine and because it was so unlikely.

The thing is, my secret Welsh dresser looked as sturdy a piece of furniture as my dad ever lugged from a house clearance and then despaired of selling. Its front was carved with urns of flowers and foliage and its drawer handles, cupboard handles, and fat wooden feet were solid balls of walnut. Flanked on one side by that barricade of full filing cabinets, impenetrable and off-putting with the rolls of barbed wire along the top, and on the other with the long side of the twenty-foot shipping container, it seemed the most impossible corner of Lord's Yard to dream of getting into. But I knew better. As solid as the front, back, sides and even the decorative touches of this dresser might be, as square and true as the hinges and catches might have been made back in the factory where it was carved and glued and polished, the base was loose. Maybe it was interchangeable with a zinc one, if this cupboard ever stored meat, or a mesh one to keep grains aired but, in any case, there was a groove along the back and, when you gave it a good tug, the whole base slid out like the lid of a domino box.

Then, if you were small like me, you could wriggle into a secret cave. I would crouch for a minute in the thrilling dark before I pushed open one of the doors and emerged in the yard proper. I can still remember the excitement mixed with soothing comfort of pausing there, no one in the world knowing where I was. I made sure never to appear suddenly enough to make John wonder how.

He might never have wondered anyway. Because the reason it stayed all mine *wasn't* him teasing me about how I climbed the tree. I was lying when I told myself that. The truth of it is, I hadn't found the dresser by the time John started to pull away from me, to boys his own age, to football games in the park, or in the school playground once they'd vaulted over the gates. To bus shelters, litres of cider, cigarettes hidden in your palm. I couldn't forgive him. I was still in the land of adventure, where our Menstrie childhood was no different from the boarding schools and hiking holidays in the books we read, and he was ruining it for me, fleeing into the base and tawdry life that was waiting for both of us once the bright covers of our paperbacks closed for good.

That world is certainly all that's here now. There's no magic to be found wandering around the dripping lean-tos leaking onto the headboards they're supposed to be protecting; the soggy, disintegrating heaps of cushions and sleeping bags that even mice surely can't nest in as they rot; the half pallets of odd roof tiles and shrink-wrapped sheets of plasterboard, every nick in the plastic backed by a bloom of damp and decay.

I know it's always been this way. Stuff either sells or rots. The sights and sounds, even the smells, are exactly what they were when this was Treasure Island, the chocolate factory, and Oz rolled into one. This sad, closed-up, shut-down feeling deep in my bones is a normal response to the flotsam and jetsam of other people's lives. The wonderland is gone.

But at least the nightmare is not what it was. Maybe John's had the right idea all along: Stay here and face it down. Maybe if I hadn't run away so far, I wouldn't be right back—

I gasp so loud that even the clustered junk and packed-in layers of endless stuff can't absorb the sound. I've been judging *John* for denying his memories and, all the while, I've been saying this visual stuff is new and scary and God knows where it came from.

The truth is both bigger and smaller than anything my wild imagination could have conjured for me. Because it's happened before. I did it when I was a kid and it was absolutely deliberate. I turned my world inside out so I could live in it, didn't I? I made my storybooks real—wondrous worlds where I had adventures that always ended well for everyone. And this world? This world of Lord's Yard and Dad and the caravan? I turned it into flat paper nothings that I could close and lay aside as I walked away.

It's happening to me again because I'm back where it happened last time, and now I've brought grief and exhaustion with me. That's all. Nothing more.

And I bet it wouldn't be if I hadn't bid for that job. If I hadn't tried to read that self-help book, it might all have stayed buried where it belongs even after I got back here, no need to remember that I turned the real world into stories and stories into my whole world. No need to think about how I did it. No need to ask *why* I did it.

I don't exactly know how *John* did it. And I won't ask him again, in case I stop it from working. I'll never mention the caravan to him and make him go pale that way. We're lucky, John and me. We made it! We never even stopped loving Lord's Yard and our adventures here.

Still, I think, looking around at the sets of five sundae glasses, the chipped platters and lidless tureens here on the old shop fitments, right now maybe isn't a good time for me to be reminded day after day that everything comes to an end and what's left behind doesn't matter.

My phone buzzes, bringing me back to reality. It's Chloe video calling me.

"Right," she says when I answer. "We're on."

"Weren't we already on?" I say. "But I'm glad you phoned because I'm having a bit of a breakthrough here—they're never what you think they're going to be, are they?—and I want to ask you something." There's no one else in the world I *could* ask, but Chloe is unshockable.

"If it's about why John and Shelley are so worried about you . . ." Chloe says. She's got me on her laptop and she's texting someone else on her mobile at the same time.

"Are they though?" I say. "I'm not so sure."

"Meaning?"

"Never mind," I say.

"Yeah, there's a delicate balance between caring for a bereaved person and treating them like a child," she says, still texting. "Not everyone has my instincts." She is so deadpan, I can't always tell if she's joking.

"Well, speaking of children, funnily enough," I say. "That's sort of what I wanted to ask you. I'm in a kind of a turn-round-and-face-the-future mood and . . . what would you say is a decent interval?"

"Between kids? Three years?"

"Between relationships," I say. "Between mourning and dating."

She looks up. I have made Chloe Crozier look up from a phone. "You?" she says. She looks intensely interested but not appalled.

"I've been having steamy dreams," I tell her. I always could tell her anything.

"Who about?" she says.

"Faceless mystery man," I say.

"And it's been . . . three months?" Chloe says.

"Almost."

"Technically," she adds.

"Exactly!" I say, letting out a huge rush of relief. *Technically* shows that she understands. I did so much of my grieving, and quite a lot of celibacy too, before Kai actually died. And I'm thirty-six and the truth is I *do* want kids.

"Can you do sex on a one-night stand, though?" she asks. "I can so I wouldn't judge you, but . . . you've always been such a sap."

"I love you too," I tell her. "So is that how things are with you at the moment? You haven't mentioned anyone and you're usually pretty on it when you're single."

"On it?"

"Like a heat-seeking missile, yes."

"Or—just a thought—maybe I haven't been rubbing your nose in my burgeoning love life because you're my friend whose husband just died."

"You don't need to tiptoe around me," I say. "If you're just about to get engaged, I'm up for being your best maid and, if you're still shagging your way through the county, I could use the entertainment."

"Right," she says. She's staring at me and I can see the mechanism working.

"Don't set me up!" She's chewing her lip and her gaze has drifted off over my shoulder. "Chloe! Seriously. Do not set me up."

"I'm thinking about the house," she says. "And something's just occurred to me. I might need to shoot off."

"What kind of something? I don't believe you."

"Got it," she says. "Later, Linds." And she's gone.

◆ ◆ ◆

And what would *you* think? I ask Kai when I'm getting ready for bed that night. He made me promise to be happy, but he must have meant there to be a bit of a gap before it started. If it was me, if I was gazing down from my candyfloss cloud and it was three months after my funeral, what would I think of Kai looking around at his options?

Maybe time works different in heaven, though. Maybe it's been an eternity for him and he'd be fine with it. Or maybe it's been a blink and he'll think I didn't really love him. Or maybe time is the same up there as it is down here and he's been watching me through every sleepless night and bleak impossible morning.

If only any of those was true. But I don't believe he's watching. I don't believe he's *gone*, like everyone says, gone to another place where eventually I'll be joining him. He hasn't left me, or moved on, or passed over. I was there when it happened and what happened was that he stopped.

I finish up and go down to tell them the bathroom's free. All four of them are packed onto the couch together watching something violent. At least, John and the boys are watching it. Shelley's scrolling on her phone, but she tucks it away as I come into the room.

"We've had a talk," Shelley says.

"Who?" I ask her.

"Shoosh, Mum!" Zak says and grabs the remote to turn the volume up even though it's only gunfire and explosions.

"The patriarch and me," Shelley says. John doesn't react until she reaches out and pokes him.

"Right, sorry," he says. "Shelley's convinced me that you need your own place again. And you're not going far—for some daft reason, even though you could go anywhere—so I should stop bugging you."

"And Zak and Nicky get their rooms back," I say, but their eyes are glued to the screen and they don't hear me. "Anyone want anything out the kettle?" I ask, but John lifts his beer bottle, and I can see that the boys have got cans of something horrible so I leave them to it. They're so snug, the four of them. I'm really glad Chloe didn't say it was wild to contemplate moving on already. I want what they've got. I do.

What I get, though, is another night of horrors. Some of it is the kind of thing that's a horror in the dream but you don't know why. Why would watching someone lather his face up, standing at a bathroom sink, fill you with dread? Who knows but I run from the sight and search through empty rooms until I find Peggy, or my best attempt at dreaming about a stranger I only met once anyway. John's there somewhere, watching a screen. Shelley's there, skulking in the background, scraping mud off her hands with a . . . it looks like a cutthroat razor. I don't know where the boys are and, in the dream, I'm trying to find them. Or maybe I'm trying to find Kai. He's lost, like he always is, but this time he's a child. I can hear him crying, wailing like a toddler, except when I wake it's me. There are tears on my cheeks and my bedroom door has just clicked open.

"I'm okay," I croak. "Just a bad dream. Sorry."

I can't tell if it's John or Shelley out there on the dark landing and the longer they stand there the more sure I am that it's neither, it's no one. I'm still dreaming.

When I get myself truly awake, I text Chloe. Might need 2 back off on evrythg. Head fried.

The dots tell me she's still up and I wait for her answer, but I'm planning to ignore whatever she orders me to do. I need to sleep without horrors and, if that means I don't move, or find Peggy, or work, or . . . anything else I've been contemplating, then so be it.

But she surprises me. Course it is, wee sausage. Let's do smthg totally diff this wknd. Member nice g.c. with walled bit???

I do remember but I can't believe Chloe's suggesting it. Garden centre? R we 80??? I text back.

Smell flwrs toes in gr grass creamcakes, she texts me.

I text her back a thumbs-up and a wow face, then give myself five minutes of the latest listings and drift off to dreamless sleep.

The whimsical misnomer "Burnside Cottage" belies a stunning property of great distinction, with magnificent views over historied Stirling and a rarely equalled measure of potential awaiting the discerning purchaser. Traditionally built of red sandstone in the Scots baronial style, with countless enviable architectural features such as crow-stepped gables and decorative turrets, Burnside Cottage has been in the same notable family for four generations and it is Rattray Walker's honour to usher it into new ownership for the next stage in its life as one of the town's most recognisable and cherished homes. In recent years, the major proportion of Burnside has been unused, the current residence being confined to a fully accessible portion of the ground floor, and a full structural survey is highly recommended before the next chapter in Burnside's history begins.

Chapter 9

So I'm in the walled garden attached to the garden centre as soon as it opens at nine o'clock on Saturday morning, wandering around with my sandals in one hand, enjoying the damp of the grass under my bare feet, when I sense someone staring at me. She waves and smiles when I look up, heads over when I give her a little twitch of the hand and hitch of the lips in return.

"Lindsay?" she says, stopping in front of me. "Lindsay Lord?"

My stomach lurches. I have no idea who this is and clearly I should. I would have said she was a bit older than me. She might be someone's big sister, I suppose. She's dressed in serious busy-weekend gear, with a phone and keys in one hand and a water bottle dangling from one finger of the other.

"You don't remember, do you?" she says. "Aileen." She waits with her eyebrows raised. "Aileen Murdoch?" The eyebrows go up a bit further. "Aw, come on! The choir trip to Saint Andrews? When we were all sick on the bus? I was in your class for French, geography . . ."

"I'm really sorry," I say. "Aileen?" I still can't bring her to mind at all. "I've been— Recently, I've been finding— Maybe I need—"

But she's not listening. "Pfft. I've lost a lot of weight. And my mum doesn't cut my hair anymore." Then she leans forward and hugs me. "I heard. How are you doing?"

For once I don't have to find an answer to that unanswerable question because a man has come in through the turnstile, spotted us, and lifted his arms as if he's been searching for hours. He stalks across the grass, making a beeline for Aileen.

"Hi," he says, kissing her on one cheek and nodding at me. "I wondered where you'd got to. Are the kids in the café? Did you need anything lugged into the car?"

"David, this is Lindsay. Lindsay, David. No, I only bought plants. Thanks, though."

"Right," he says and turns my way. "Pleased to meet you." He shakes my hand and gives a tight, closed-lips smile that doesn't quite make it to his eyes. He's so much her other half they could have come in a set, Posh McBarbie and Celtic Ken. They've got the same confident air, the same neat weekend clobber. He's even got the iron-grey hair Aileen would have if she didn't dye it.

"Okay then," she says. She squeezes my arm, turns on her heel and leaves. Her husband doesn't go with her. He stands next to me watching her go.

"Uh," I say, confused. "Can I help you with something?"

"What?" he says, turning to face me again.

"Shouldn't you . . . ?" I gesture at Aileen's back as she disappears through the turnstile.

"Oh!" His face softens. This smile shows straight teeth and goes all the way to his brown eyes, breaking out in two fans of fine lines that reach halfway down his cheeks. "We're divorced. This is us handing over the kids on neutral territory."

"Ah," I said. "Right."

"So you're not a *close* friend then," he goes on. "If you didn't hear the saga."

I feel it in my stomach again. Recognising when I shouldn't, failing when I should, and now memory loss. Even if I've explained away the visual stuff, I can't ignore the rest of it anymore. Everyone thinks it's headaches that tip you off, but this is how it started with Kai too. Only, I can't blurt out to this complete stranger that I think I've got a brain tumour. So I make something up. "I'm an old school friend and I've been overseas for a while," I say, which is technically true.

"Are you okay?" he says, dipping his head to catch my eye.

"Um, well, I was abroad because I was married but . . ." I take the kind of big breath required to let me tell someone, but I can't do it. "It's a long story," I say instead. Then I wonder if that's a strange thing to say. Next I wonder if I'm editing because he's quite attractive. I can feel my neck starting to go red in patches. I tell myself he is a million miles from being my type. He's wearing a signet ring, for God's sake.

He dips his head again, even lower, looks up at me from under his brows and says, "Tell me the sordid details over a coffee?"

The red patches have joined up and I can feel my ears getting hot. I'm making heavy weather of not much, but my mouth is too dry to speak.

"Lindsay!" Chloe is marching across the grass. "Put that poor man down."

My whole head is purple now. I can feel a line of sweat along my hairline.

"For God's sake, Chloe. This is the husband of an old friend I just ran into."

"Ex-husband," says David.

"What old friend?" asks Chloe. "*I'm* your old friend." I've always loved how possessive she is. There's nothing like feeling wanted.

"Aileen Murdoch?" I say. "From school?" I still can't remember the name or the face and I hope Chloe can't either; then there's nothing to explain away.

"Oh yeah," Chloe says though. "Big Aileen."

"She shrank," I say. I try again. "You must have passed her in the café and didn't recognise her either."

"And so you're the husband?" Chloe says, giving David a look up and down as if he's a room in a client's house that a cleaner on probation has submitted for her approval. "Well, well, well."

"See?" he says to me. "*She* knows the sorry tale. Chloe, is it?"

"I would have asked for details anyway," she tells him, "before I let my best friend get mixed up with you."

"Chloe!" I say. "Behave yourself!" But then I add, "What details?" David snorts and I feel my flush start to take over again. "What I mean is, no one's getting mixed up with anyone. We were just passing the time of day."

"Very convincing," Chloe says. "You always could lie to me so skilfully. And don't tell me you wouldn't ask a divorce case why his marriage broke up before you'd let him date me."

"Have you been sniffing the Pledge?" I hiss at her. "Get a bloody grip."

"I find it refreshing," David says. "It was the usual thing, by the way. Another woman."

"Oh," I say. "Well, that's . . ."

"Very funny," says Chloe. "You're hysterical."

"It *was* another woman!" David says, putting a hand on his chest in mock affront. Then he turns to me. "Not me, though. Her." His smile has faded a bit.

"Oh," I say again. "Poor you. I mean, did you know she was bi already or was it like a—"

"Ton of bricks, yes."

"Although even at school . . ." says Chloe.

"So is that better or worse?" I ask him, ignoring her.

"Oh, better," he says. "Miles better. I mean, with the best will in the world, you know?"

"Yes, yes, we know, great, excellent," Chloe says. "So swap numbers."

He takes his phone out and waits for me to recite my number but, instead of giving me his, he produces a business card—plain white, engraved in plain black—kisses me on one cheek, and leaves.

"You're a maniac," I tell Chloe as we both watch him walk away.

"Absolutely no arse at all," Chloe says. "Does that bother you?"

But I'm looking at his card: David Minto LLM, CC, and a bunch of contact details. "What does 'LLM' stand for?" I ask her. "And 'CC'?"

"Not a clue," she says. "You need to fix your make-up. And you need to buy better make-up that doesn't melt when you blush. And you really need to grow up and stop blushing."

When I'm on my way to the toilet mirror, I catch sight of him driving a large, clean car with one teenage boy in the passenger seat and another one, identical but a bit smaller, in the back. He toots the horn and gives me a wave. I see both boys' faces shut down as if someone's flipped a switch, instantly hostile. He's not perfect, then.

But no one in my age range is going to be perfect, I tell myself, looking in the mirror over the row of sinks. They'll either be late starters who've got something wrong with them, or they'll come with exes and kids who've been through stuff. Like David Minto and his extra letters. And anyway, all I want to do is go on a date to see what it feels like.

I can't deny how my spirits have lifted, though. I can explain not knowing Aileen, what with all the weight loss, and I *didn't* think I recognised David. And right now the sinks and taps and plants on the windowsill are all in glorious, plump 3-D.

A cubicle door opens behind me and someone joins me at the sinks. She's late middle age with a waxed jacket and a silk scarf round her neck. I don't fake recognise her either.

"Excuse me," I say. "Can I ask you something? Do you know what 'LLM' stands for? On a business card? Or 'CC'? It's nothing to do with plants or gardens."

"I think 'LLM' is a master's degree," the woman says. "Certainly 'CC' is Crown counsel, so that would make sense." Then she takes pity on me. "Advocate," she says. "Barrister? Lawyer, you know. White wig, black robe."

I go back out to tell Chloe but she's already googled it. "*Rumpole of the Bailey*," she tells me. "You lucky pig. The last time I swiped right, he was a driver for the Blood Transfusion Service. It creeped me out too much to let him touch me."

◆ ◆ ◆

She phones after dinner, another video call, not just to boast about how right she was, although she starts there. "See? See? You stopped thinking about it and did something else and bang! A lawyer drops right into your lap."

"Yeah, you covered that over tea and cakes," I say.

"Right, stop distracting me," she says. "I've got news. We can get in to view the house tomorrow. It's definitely for sale, so how early can you be ready?"

"Wait, what?" I say. "Wasn't it definitely for sale before?"

John and Shelley are doing the dishes, but the clinking and sloshing have stopped. They're listening.

"*Still* for sale, I mean," Chloe says. "Nobody's nipped in. But I've got to warn you: It's a bit of a fixer."

"I've seen *Escape to the Country*," I tell her. "I watched the episode where it was a tin shack with a warning sign on the door and they couldn't even go inside. I watched the episode where it was a field with an architect's impression on a tablet."

"It's not a shack or a field."

"Right then," I say.

"You sound weird," Chloe says. "What's up? Is it the guy? Because it's too soon? Because I don't think it *is* too soon and neither do you really."

"It's not that exactly," I say, with a glance at John and Shelley, who're in stasis now and not trying to hide it.

"Well, what is it?"

I leave the kitchen and go upstairs to sit on my bed. I'm still scared that talking about it will make it more real, but I can't resist now she's actually asked me straight out. "I'm having odd symptoms," I tell her. "I keep not recognising people. Well, one person. Aileen. And then I keep thinking I know people I don't. And a couple of times I've had this weird glitch that I used to get when I was a kid, but that's probably just because I'm back, right? And I don't want to think about it too much because I really hate it now. I can't believe I used to use it for comfort."

"Lindsay, tell me you don't mean self-harm," Chloe says.

"No!"

"Okay, and for the love of God *don't* tell me if you mean self . . . woo-hoo." She makes a whistling sound and waggles her eyebrows.

"Shut up!" I say, laughing. "It's not that. It's a whole pile of weird symptoms, and it's scary."

"Lindsay, you total slavering maniac—no offence," she says. "It's grief. How can you not know that? Grief can feel like arthritis. Grief can feel like an ulcer."

"But the thing is that brain tumours can feel like anything. And so, for all I know, they can make you think you've met an estate agent and a nursing home manager that you don't know from Adam."

"Yes, I heard about them from John and Shelley. Not from you, which hurt, but I'm over it."

"Way to miss the point, Chlo. The point *is* . . . Kai had cognition and memory glitches long before anything else." Chloe says nothing. "Well, cheers for that," I say, trying to laugh. "You've set my mind right to rest there. Thank you."

"Can't you . . . listen to a podcast or something? Try to relax?"

"You know I can't relax listening to other people's audio work."

"Or, I don't know, read a book! I know John and Shelley aren't exactly literati but there must be an old Jilly Cooper or a Clive Cussler knocking about the yard."

"I've got a book right here on my bedside table," I tell her. "Agatha Christie."

"Perf—"

"But the cover's creeping me out too much to pick it up."

Chloe lets out a huge puff of breath and she's right. Even I think I'm whining now. So, after I put down the phone, I go down to ask if it's okay to tie up the bathroom while I take a long, hot soak. John and Shelley are still in the kitchen.

"—north wind and the sun," I hear John say as I push the door open.

"Aw," I say. "That's sweet."

Their two faces turned towards me wear such identical frowns that for the first time I realise they've been married long enough to start looking like each other.

"What?" John says.

"*The North Wind and the Sun*," I say. "Have you made me a surprise dead room?"

"*What?*" says Shelley.

"Quilts, is it? Bathmats? Egg boxes?"

They share a worried look and I snap my head to face the other way before their edges start to curl. "Sorry," I say. "I misheard you. It's a test text. For a sound test? It's got all the English sounds—I thought you were talking about my business."

"Lindsay, what the actual are you on about?" says John. "Are you okay?"

"Added two and two and got five hundred and eighty," I say, trying to laugh. "What *did* you say?"

"While you were coming downstairs?" says Shelley. "We were arguing about who's going to pick the boys up from—"

"But what were you *saying*?" I ask, and even to myself I don't sound normal.

"I said, 'They're old enough to walk home,' I think," John offers.

No way. That's nothing like what I heard. Why won't he tell me? I turn away to the kettle, check it's got water in and click it on. Maybe it was married-couple talk. Or maybe my ears *are* going the same way as my eyes and my memory.

Now shave.

It's only when John says "Eh?" that I realise I've said that last bit out loud.

I have a bath, get into bed, and pick up *Sleeping Murder*. Whatever's making the woman in the story think she's going nuts, it'll turn out to be true and then it'll get solved. I could do with a bit of that.

But I've only turned one page and taken two sips of tea when I feel myself drifting down and down to where Kai is waiting. The nightmares have let go for once and it's one of the wonderful dreams that I yearn for every day but am lucky to stumble into once a fortnight now. He's in an empty house, wearing board shorts and flip-flops, his chest brown and bare, still muscled and with the tiniest embryo of a potbelly, exactly how he was right before the diagnosis. "Is that a coyote?" he's saying. "What *is* that?" He's using his sleeve to rub a steamed-up bathroom mirror that turns into a caravan window, because this house has caravan windows and he's got sleeves even though he's topless. I can't see what he's looking at but Peggy says, "I know what it is." She's trying to give me something. It's so small that it's completely hidden by her hand. "Look," she whispers, "it says it right there. It's a fox."

The phone wakes me.

"What is it *now*?" I say into it.

"Very rude," Chloe says. "But I'll press on anyway. It's a brilliant idea."

"Sorry," I tell her. "I was dreaming about Kai and it was nice to see him again, even in a creepy, empty house that turned into a caravan."

"Shit," she says. "Sorry. But listen, if he was in a creepy, empty house . . . maybe you'll dream about him every night after you move in."

"*Is* it a creepy, empty house?"

"It's not a caravan," she says. "I promise you that."

"Big whoop," I say.

"Well, medium whoop anyway. What size of whoop is right for appreciating what I'm doing for you? You know, when you were in a really tough spot, and I bent over backwards to help you out."

"Are you going for a Heart of Gold award?"

"Not that you have to," Chloe says.

"Because you're getting weird."

"I wouldn't want you to feel obliged."

"Good night, Chlo."

"As long as you're not feeling beholden or anything."

"Sleep tight."

"Don't you want to hear my brilliant idea?" She waits. "Why not put a brown paper cover on your creepy book like we did at school, if it's bothering you so much?"

"That idea," I tell her, "is actually not stupid."

She pauses. "But still no thanks, eh?" And hangs up.

When the phone rings again a minute later, I say, "All right, all right! You are the best thing in my life and I would be lost without you. I love you and I will never be able to repay you for all the gifts you bring me."

David Minto, on the other end of the phone, says, "Well, this is going better than I expected, I must say."

Chapter 10

"Oh my God. Kill me now," I say. "I thought you were my friend Chloe."

"From this morning? Pretty *close* friends then."

I start to laugh and then remember why his wife left him and turn it into a cough. "Nice to hear from you," I say. "How's your evening going?"

"Well, my boys are watching the stupidest film that's ever employed five hundred animators in the service of galactic destruction and I've burnt the dinner. How about you?"

"I'm sitting in a bedroom decorated with those same destroyers—I'm staying at my brother's house and it's his son's taste in stickers—but my dinner was pizza."

"Mine too. I put the box in the oven to keep warm and set it on fire." He heaves an enormous sigh and I think I hear the sound of ice cubes in a glass. "They still ate it. I could serve them toothpaste and toenails on a pizza base and they'd wolf it down."

I find myself laughing again. Then I find myself leaning back against the pillows with my legs tucked up, which I haven't done during a phone call since the last time I slept in this room. I get up and go to look out the window instead. John is on the wander through the back sections of the yard, headed goodness knows where. *His* phone rings too, lighting up his pocket, and I watch him fish it out and listen to whoever's on the other end. Then the way he swings round to look straight up towards this room makes me think whoever called him is talking about me. I lift a hand to wave, but he ignores me.

"So anyway," David Minto is saying when I start paying attention again, "I was wondering: Do you like the theatre?"

"Going to see plays, you mean? I suppose so. Not musicals, and I wish so many of the other ones weren't so depressing."

"You don't like musicals? How about opera?"

"Makes me giggle," I say. "Especially the death scenes."

"So I'm guessing you don't think much of ballet."

I spin round so John can't see the smile that breaks out on my face. "Wrong," I say. "I love ballet! I cried buckets when I got too big to keep doing it but I still love watching it."

"That is amazing," says David Minto. "Because I told you I was divorced and I told you why. What I didn't say was that it was pretty acrimonious. *I* was pretty acrimonious. It's no joke when two lawyers divorce each other. And one of the things I screwed out of Aileen was our season tickets for Scottish Ballet, who are currently doing *A Streetcar Named Desire*. I've got two seats for Thursday night."

I turn to face out of the window again. I might need the moral support of family to navigate this, even if it's only my brother gawping at me. But John has disappeared. "Do you mean you've got two tickets you can't use and you're kindly offering them to me?" I ask. "Or . . . ?"

"Or," says David Minto. "Definitely or."

"Well, then I'd love to. Although it would be quite funny to hear what Chloe made of modern ballet too. But I'd love to. Thank you."

"It's in Glasgow," he says. "So we could have something to eat as well and make a night of it. Are you . . . Look, I know you're younger than me but are you so young you'd prefer a late supper afterwards or an early dinner precurtain?"

"Oh, before!" I say. "I'm not that young. If I tried for late supper after, I'd be face down in the soup."

"Thank God for that," he says. "I'll book somewhere nice and text you details about picking you up. Okay? Lord's Yard on the main road through Menstrie?"

As I hang up, I think to myself that I'm pretty sure I didn't tell him where I lived, so the acrimony has died down enough for him to have asked his ex-wife to tell him what she knows about me. I go to brush my teeth, then get into bed and have a serious, silent discussion with Kai to find out how he feels about this development. As far as I can tell, he's fine with it. Leastways, I go off to sleep quicker than I have since I got here and don't wake up until eight dreamless hours later.

I skip out of the door the next morning and down the steps to where Chloe's waiting for me in the car. John seems to have opened the gate for her. He's hanging in the driver's window chatting.

"Lindsay," he says, coming round and opening the passenger door for me, like a doorman.

"I know, I know," I tell him. "Don't let her talk me into anything." He doesn't know Shelley blabbed about talking me into taking on this place.

"I changed my mind, remember?" he says. "What I was actually going to tell you was: Go for it. Knock yourself out."

"Yeah, why was that?" I ask. His face shuts down so entirely, I'm immediately convinced I should know why and I've forgotten.

So when Chloe leans past me and says, "Yes, John, why *was* that?" I'm flooded with love for her. I kiss her on the cheek while I'm fastening my seat belt. "So where is it anyway, this not-a-caravan?"

"Wait and see," Chloe says, twisting round to see where she's going as she reverses—always dicey in the front apron of Lord's Yard. There could be anything, anywhere. But she gets the car turned without any scrapes and puckers up to John as we go by. He's still glowering. For so many reasons, I'll be happy to get away.

"You know something," I say as we emerge onto the road. "You were so shy around John when we were kids, it's weird to see how chummy you are with him now. With both of them, really."

"Chummy," says Chloe. "Is that what you'd call it?"

"Yeah, you're right," I say, giving it a bit of thought. "It's not even chummy. It's beyond that. Intimate."

"Puke. No offence."

"Shut up. I mean intimate like family. Or like workmates. Past politeness."

Chloe says nothing for a minute. "Yeah, you turn your back for ten years and anything can happen" is what comes out in the end. I decide to change the subject.

"So, can we stop and get coffee for the road?" I ask.

"Not worth it."

"Must be close."

"Oh my, Lindsay," she says, all singsong sarcasm. "You nearly tricked me into revealing the location."

At the Wallace roundabout, she stays in the left lane and slows down for the first exit that would take us to Cambusbarron. I feel a slump. I'm sure there are nice bits, but you've got to look for them. Then I realise Chloe has swept on right past the second exit too and is indicating for the third.

"Ha ha! Fooled you," she says, taking the road to Dunblane. "Oh piss off, lane Nazi," she mouths at a van driver behind her.

"I'm glad it's Dunblane," I say. "I—"

"Don't prejudge," she says. "You might still hate it."

So I don't react when we skirt the motorway and come into town on the dual carriageway, or when we peel off to the left at Saint Mary's Episcopal, not even as Chloe slows down and starts to peer in through the gateposts, even though there's a feeling of inevitability beginning to creep over me. A fixer, she said. Complicated sale, she implied. She definitely told me it was big.

"Here we are," she announces, at the open gates to Saint Helen's. "We'll park on the road and walk in."

I manage to get out of the car but I walk nowhere. I grind to a halt and stare from the gate.

"Linds?" Chloe's frowning at me.

I'm ready for the scene in front of me to thin and flatten, wheel and tilt, shatter into shards even. This can't be happening. But the shadows stay dark and the peaks and points on the roof stay light where the sun hits them. And actually . . . when I get a hold of myself . . . I suppose it *is* an empty house. And a small world.

But there's still one very good reason why this can't be real.

"What are you playing at?" I say and, although my face feels numb, my voice comes out in a hiss as if I'm clenching my jaw.

Chloe gapes at me and takes a step back.

"Wh-What do you mean?" She looks at the house and back at me. "What have you— What did— Who's been—?"

"I know this is a bit of fun for you," I say, cutting her off, "but it's serious for me. I need to buy a house, to live in, to recover in. What's the point of showing me something I couldn't afford in a million year— Wait. Is it subdivided? Is it half the house? Or one floor? Sorry!"

"Th-*That's* what you're so upset about?" says Chloe. Her throat sounds dry, and although she went pale when I laid into her, her face is flushing now. Her cheeks have gone a bright, familiar red that makes me want to hug her.

"Sorry," I say again. "Bit of an overreaction." I give her a smile she doesn't return. "Are you seriously telling me I can afford this house?"

"I don't want to tell you the price before you've seen round it" is all I get back from her.

"Why?"

"Because that's how they do it on those stupid shows. I thought you liked all that."

"Well, for one thing, this isn't one of those stupid shows," I tell her. "This is my stupid life. What are you up to, Chloe? And why isn't there a sale board?"

"Nothing!" She blinks. "I don't know. Bylaws, maybe?" She pauses. "Seven dead."

Which of course she can't have said, can she? *Now shave. The North Wind and the Sun.*

"What?" I ask her.

"Seven hundred thousand on the nose," she says.

I let out a laugh that's half a gasp too. "That's not a way you say—I thought you were telling me I could afford it because the last seven owners all died! Or . . . seven people died in there and that's why it's a bargain!"

"Jesus Christ, Lindsay." She's not laughing.

"Or that seven must die to break the curse that means no one wants to live here!"

"Stop it!" she yelps at me. "What is *wrong* with you?"

"*Me?* When did *you* get so jumpy?" She's still not laughing. "Okay, so what *is* wrong with it?"

"You tell me once we get inside," Chloe says. "I thought it was okay."

I really want to tell her I'd rather look at a house I can afford than daydream my way around this one, but she's been the boss of our friendship since the day we met and it's too late to change now. And, if I'm being completely honest, I'm a bit nosy too.

We walk up the drive, and Chloe unlocks the door with an iron key. She opens one half and loosens the bolts to open the other. "First reaction?"

"My honest first reaction would be 'Where's the catch?'"

"Oh come *on*, Lindsay! First reaction?"

"Okay, how's this? 'Gosh, Chloe, it almost feels too good to be true that this lovely house could be in my budget.' That do you?"

I expect her to snap but she surprises me with a grin that makes her eyes dance. "Perfect," she says. "Let's go in."

Saint Helen's is less of a warren coming at it from the front door, or maybe it's because I was half asleep, wholly jet-lagged, the last time. There's a drawing room, panelled and pillared, on one side of the hall and a dining room on the other. Someone has gone to town with the paintbrush, filling in the panels in crimson and picking out the thistles on the ceiling medallions in green and purple: representational but misguided. I don't say that to Chloe, though. To her, I say, "Wow!"

Through a butler's pantry from the back of the dining room we get to the kitchen, sad and empty with all the furniture gone but big enough to dance in.

"There's a utility that would be a big kitchen in most houses," Chloe says, ushering me through. "This door in the curved wall here is like a cloakroom, and check out the stairs."

I dutifully check them out. The paint is a bright egg-yolk yellow on the panels, and the plaster is the same white as all the other rooms, but the woodwork—the doors and skirtings, the deep pediments and ornate banisters—have never been painted in their long life. They're the same warm honey-coloured wood they were when the carpenter first polished them. I remember Mrs. March saying "not Georgian, not even Victorian."

"Edwardian, isn't it?" I say to Chloe. "The stairs are amazing."

"Finally!" she says. "A bit of enthusiasm. But don't go up just yet, there's more to show you."

Then we are in the garden room where I slept so soundly, the floorboards showing wear and tear where Peggy's chair was positioned. I rub the marks with my toe, imagining her feet resting there over the decades.

"That just needs a buff," says Chloe. "Overall, I'd say the place has been carefully looked after."

"I agree," I say. "You can tell it hasn't churned through lots of hands. Whoever lived here stayed a long time and loved it."

"You're right," Chloe says. "The last owner stayed for donkeys and only left when she got too frail to manage the place. The downside of that is no Jacuzzi baths and no kitchen island. The upside is all the original features survived unscathed."

I don't know why I'm so loath to tell her that I know this house. Maybe I don't want to dilute how proud she is of showing it to me. Or I don't want to set her off again when she's been so touchy. I manage to work out a halfway point. "I've been here before, you know," I tell her. "Just once. I came to tea here. I got to choose a chocolate biscuit out of a tin."

"Are you sure? There's a lot of big old houses in Dunblane."

"Positive," I say. "It was a Mrs. March."

She doesn't look annoyed exactly and Chloe's never been one to call a coincidence spooky, but she's definitely bothered. The things that bother her seem so random sometimes.

"Well, speaking of the good old days," she says, still pretty sour, "all the chimneys are still working. And these French doors lead to the back garden. Suntrap patio, mature trees, shed and greenhouse. Upstairs first though."

I follow her up and through four bedrooms—spacious, empty, dowdy and grand—and peek round the door of the only bathroom, then up again on a smaller staircase to two attic rooms and a boxroom in between them. There's a French window up here that gives roof access. We open it and edge out onto something that's not quite a balcony but definitely a bit more than a parapet, looking down at the garden. The lawn is cut in stripes and all the bushes around the edge are clipped into tight little mounds.

"The way I see it," Chloe says, turning away and pulling me back inside; she's never had a head for heights, "is you sacrifice the little room and the big cupboard—remind me to show you the big cupboard off the second bedroom—so you get an en-suite for every bedroom on the first floor, and you've still got five in total. It's hardly squalor, is it?"

"Oh, just casually put in new bathrooms all over the shop using the fifty pence that would be left in my budget?"

Chloe comes and stands in front of me with her hands on her hips. "I thought you were pretending you didn't know the price." She spins on her heel. "Let's try that again." And she repeats her lines word for word. Then I say, "What a great idea. Depending on my budget, that is. I wonder how much this house would cost me?"

"Could you sound any less sincere?" says Chloe, but she's smiling.

"Anyway, I couldn't sacrifice all the small bedrooms for showers," I remind her. "I would need a dead room."

"Oh of course," Chloe says. "A house isn't a home without a *dead* room." And just for a moment, as I look at her, I remember the day she told me her parents were getting a divorce. Except, no. It's not that day I'm suddenly reliving. It's the day she stopped pretending the divorce was a bore and no biggie. It was the day she sat in a toilet cubicle at school, hunched on the shut lid, blowing her nose with toilet paper, and whispered, "I'm scared, Lindsay. Why does everything have to change?"

I don't understand what's wrong with her today, but I still care. "Let's call it the audio pod," I tell her. "You don't need to hear that phrase ever again."

"Sap," Chloe says. The moment is over and I can tell she means to make out like it never happened. "One dead room coming up. Follow me."

She leads me down the attic stairs, across the landing, down the big stairs, across the hall, into the kitchen and out the far end to the back lobby, then she opens a door to reveal steps leading up and ushers me ahead of her. At the top is a room about ten feet square with one small window and a low, plank-lined ceiling.

"Maid's room," she says. "What do you think?" I walk in. Chloe hovers by the door.

"Ideal," I say. "Do these shutters still work? Yeah, ideal. I reckon I could convert a room this size for about seven hundred quid not including the equipment."

"Seven again, eh?" Chloe says with a ghost of her troubled look drifting over her face. I would make a joke about deadening sound, if it was anyone else, or even the usual Chloe.

"And I've already got the equipment," I say instead. "If it survived packing, transport and storage."

"It's surely insured with the mover," says Chloe, unmistakably latching onto a preferred topic. "I'd help you deal with them if they get arsey. I've dealt with plenty of those guys when I'm doing buy-sell cleaning."

I turn away so she can't see me smiling. Chloe truly believes that cleaning a house while it changes hands makes her a property expert, like she believes cleaning a house after a death makes her practically a coroner. God help us all if she ever breaks into the crime scene cleaning game, like she's been trying to.

"There's not many plugs," I say, as this strikes me. I can only see a single outlet tacked onto the skirting board under the window and my computer and sound gear need at least four. I crouch down for a closer look, thinking maybe if the wire's painted onto the top of the woodwork it wouldn't take much to put in a board.

"Poor housemaids," Chloe says. "Nowhere to plug in their straighteners if their phone was charging." She waits. "Come on. Not even a chuckle? That was funny!"

But all my attention is caught by something I've just seen under the windowsill. There is something scraped into the thick, many-layered white paint there. It's a message. Or words, anyway. It's crudely done and hard to read but I'm sure the first word is *Help*.

I turn to tell Chloe, but she's gone.

"Lindsay?" she calls from halfway down the stairs. "Are you coming? I want to show you the garden."

I bob up from my crouch and follow her. Some kid locked in the maid's room as a punishment? Or two kids, playing at kidnap. Maybe this little attic was given over as a playroom once maids were a thing of the past. Or it might have *been* a maid, away back in the day, overworked until she thought she was going to drop. I will myself to stop thinking about it, even though there's a niggle somewhere that I can't quite put my finger on and, if I get distracted now, it'll escape me permanently.

Anyway, I tell myself, picking my way down the narrow stairs, in a house this age, a melodramatic maid or kids playing pretend aren't the worst that must have happened. In a hundred plus years, at least one person must have died here. "Richard" probably died in the biggest bedroom, the one I'd take for myself if this was real.

Chloe has found a prime spot, in the full sun against a backdrop of something I'd say was a passion flower if this was Hawaii. She's all in on the idea that we're doing a property show. "So, Lindsay," she begins, in a presenter voice. "What did you think?"

"Beyond my wildest dreams," I say. "I'm guessing you've gone way over my budget, just to mess with me."

"Would I!" Chloe shoots back. "Oh ye of little faith. Would you care to take a stab?"

"All this house in this location? Nine hundred and fifty thousand pounds," I say. "More likely well over a million. But I love it, so my question for you is, Will you lend me a tenner?"

Chloe's laugh is clear and high. She's delighted with me for playing along properly now.

"I'll lend you a fan," she says, "to revive yourself after hearing the news that this lovely house has just hit the market at a fixed price of seven hundred thousand pounds. That's bang on your budget, Lindsay!"

"Well, that's certainly a lovely surprise," I say, unable to keep the sarcasm out of my voice any longer. "I'm going to buy it." Then I shove her, not *that* hard but hard enough to let her know I mean it. "Right, you've had your fun," I say. "I'm guessing you couldn't resist giving me a look round. But can we go and see the real one now? And can you tell me how much this one actually costs?"

"Eh?" says Chloe. "I just told you. Seven."

I am staring at her with my mouth open. "Seriously?"

"It's kind of sweet that you love it so much you can't believe you can afford it," she says. She goes back to her presenter voice. "Guessing too high is a sure sign of true love. Some people would be put off by the lack of upgrades and the old-fashioned style. It's wonderful that you seem to have taken to it." She laughs again and I know she carries on talking but I can barely hear her. If I maxed out my budget and bought this place, I could have Mrs. March round for tea anytime she wanted to come, after I find her. She could stay the night. I still don't believe her health has changed so much so quickly that a visit would be beyond her. I could make it a happy move all round. As well as these giddy plans, though, I've got to admit there's still a trace of something else.

"Do you want to go for another look round, now you know it's in your price range?" Chloe says.

I'm on the move before she's finished speaking. But it's not only to pirouette in the grand spaces or dance up and down the soaring stairwell. It's also because I want to see that scratched paint again. I'm pretty sure my eyes passed over something else without me taking it in.

I pad through the empty rooms, listening to my footsteps, much louder now without Chloe's chatter. Drawing room, dining room, garden room, cloakroom, up the stairs. One, two, three, four bedrooms, the dressing room that Chloe called a cupboard, the bathroom, up again. One attic room and then the other, the boxroom between them, all the way to the ground floor again and through the butler's pantry to the kitchen, the utility room, the back lobby. Finally up the crooked little stairway to the maid's room, my dead room. I look out of the window again and run my fingers over the message scratched into the paint under the sill. I crouch and close one eye.

Help. They are going to kill m—

I scrabble backwards, heart hammering. *Seven dead.* I can almost hear the words, although I know they're inside my head. *Seven dead in the dead room.* Stop it, Lindsay! *Help. They are going to kill m—*

And I can't pretend this is a symptom of grief or illness. This isn't stress. I wish it was, but this is a physical fact. I can feel it on my fingertips, under my nails.

Melodramatic maid, I remind myself. Kids playing. I stand up. Chloe is looking at me from down in the garden. She must have been watching the window, waiting for me to appear. I brush my fingertips on my jeans and wave to her. I tell myself again that, in a house a hundred years old, of course there's history. Lives have been lived here. Games have been played. More than one person has probably died here. Seven might be a conservative estimate. I should concentrate instead on the fact that more than one person has probably been *born* here. Or reborn, like me.

Occupying arguably the finest position in the whole of Perthshire, adjacent to the world-famous Gleneagles Golf Club and with distant views over the fairways, this eagerly awaited offering brings a never-to-be-repeated chance to make a home or luxurious retreat in one of Scotland's most enviable settings. Currently the house comprises four public rooms and five bedrooms with the usual offices, oil heating and single-glazing, but it lends itself to a level of transformation limited only by the vision of the owner. Viewing is strictly by appointment and the full particulars are available upon registering interest with Rattray Walker. A suitably early closing date for final offers is expected to be set soon, and serious buyers are advised to move quickly.

Chapter 11

"It really is a beautiful house," Shelley says, looking over my shoulder.

I've been unable to think about anything else except Saint Helen's ever since Sunday, poring over the photos I took on my third walk-round. Right now, though, I'm dressed for my date at the ballet, in a blue silk dress and strappy sandals, with my hair up and dangly earrings. It feels weird, midafternoon, but we've got to get to Glasgow and have our dinner before the curtain.

"And we're behind you all the way, Lindsay," says John. He is over in the house on a tea break instead of boiling the kettle in the Portakabin. I think he wants to inspect the man who's coming to collect me. It's part caveman but part sweet too, so I haven't said anything. He leans back in his chair, stretching.

I glance round at Shelley, who lets go of the back of my chair and turns away.

"I'm going to ask again," I say. "Why *have* you two changed your tune?"

"Do you really want to talk about it right now?" says John.

"Jesus," says Shelley. She's working at the sink now, rinsing little lettuces under the tap.

"Seriously," I go on. "You were dead set against me moving and now you're all for it. What changed?"

"Nothing," John spits out between clenched teeth.

Shelley snorts and finally turns to look at me again. She's wiping her hands on a towel and she screws it up into a knot and lobs it into the open door of the washing machine before she speaks. "We're worr—"

A small moan escapes me.

"So we thought," Shelley says instead, "that we should keep you here and look after you, but then we realised that maybe space and quiet would help. That maybe being here was part of the . . . And the boys are a lot."

"Help with what?" I say. "I'm fine." Shelley gives me a long, considering look. "Grieving is work and I'm doing it. I loved Kai and grief is the bill to be paid. I'm paying it." She opens her mouth to argue and I decide to save her the trouble. "I'm aware of the irony," I say. "Talking about grief and love and Kai while I'm all dolled up for a date, but see? I'm going on a date. I'm fine."

"It's more than grief though, isn't it?" Shelley says. John shifts in his seat.

"Because I misheard something, while I was clattering downstairs and opening a door? Big deal." This is pure bravado because the *North Wind* thing is still raw enough to make me feel sick when I think about it.

"It's more than that one time and more than that one thing too, though," says John. "It's the memory stuff." I freeze. "The forgetting folk. The imagining things. The not recognising—"

"But I didn't tell you any of tha—" I blurt out.

"You didn't have to *tell* us," Shelley says. "We've seen it. And we're worried about you."

"Oh, you're *worried* about me?" I say, and even to myself I sound untethered. "Why didn't you *tell* me?" But the sarcasm is laid on top of a jolt of shock and fear. They've *seen* it?

"Enough," says John, but he's smiling at his wife. I don't understand why. Maybe that's the whole point of what Shelley's getting at. Maybe I should. What exactly *have* they seen? I thought I was hiding everything.

"I agree," I say. "Enough. If grief and stress are sending me doolally, talking about it's not going to help. Free fridge?" I add, nodding at the boxes. I want to prove I can remember things just fine, but I know my voice is still strained.

Shelley nods. "If you did buy that house," she says, "and you weren't going to use the greenhouse, John could dismantle— Yes, I know, John, but for me though!"

John has just flinched because he, like my dad before him, has a blanket veto on greenhouses. They're too fiddly and too unlikely to survive intact. I'm so grateful to be back on solid ground with them, understanding the argument, that I blurt out: "Or you could have the use of it where it is."

"Yep," says John. "Much better idea to leave it where it is." A look passes between them and, just like that, I'm lost again.

"Okay," I say. "Okay, maybe I do need to talk about it. I admit it. I thought I recognised a couple of people, and I didn't recognise someone. And I've been having really weird dreams and sometimes, even when I'm awake, it's like I'm not quite . . ." Then I hear a car come in and park in the **No Customers** spaces reserved for family. I don't know if it's a relief but it's certainly a reprieve.

"Don't go to the door," says John, actually putting a hand on my arm. "I want to see if he comes and knocks or sits and toots."

After a silent moment, we all hear a rap at the kitchen door, and the three of us let a laugh go. I leap up to answer and there is David Minto, with his grey hair newly washed and brushed straight back, his face looking raw from a second shave. He's wearing a dark-blue silk shirt that matches my dress or as near as damn it.

"Gosh," he says. "You look incredible."

I was braced for him to cast an eye at the yard or the house, the bikes and boards abandoned on the step, Shelley's weird new gong and her **Leave Us Alone** doormat, but he's only got eyes for me.

"Ready?" he says, but he's got one more hoop to jump through.

I pick up my bag with my cardigan through the straps. "David," I say, stepping to the side, "this is my brother John and his wife Shelley. This is David Minto."

John wipes his hand on his overalls to get rid of some crisps dust before shaking. Shelley holds hers up to show the soil from the lettuces. David steps back. But he's laughing, not judging.

"Have her home before midnight and no funny business," John says.

"Oh my sides," I tell him, pressing a hand to my ribs. "You're hysterical."

Then we make our escape.

"Sorry about that," I say when we're in the car and he's reversing, neatly and without any fuss, back out through the gates.

"I don't blame him," says David. "I wish I'd had a big sister shaking a stick to ward off trouble when I was a newly divorced babe in the wood."

"I'm thirty-six," I say, laughing. I wanted to get that in quick to see if I can find out how old *he* is. Not that it matters, for one date. It's not as if—

But then his words hit me: when *I* was newly divorced. Is it possible that I didn't tell him why I'm not still with Kai?

"You okay?" he asks, and I think I must have been quiet for a while.

"I need to clear something up."

Then it's his turn to be quiet for a while. I don't know how long him and Aileen have been divorced but he's obviously not recovered enough for another knock, no matter how small.

"My husband—his name was Kai—isn't my ex-husband. He's my late husband."

"Oh God," he says. Then, "I'm sorry." Then, "How long—?"

I know he's asking when Kai died but I can't face what he's going to think of me if I answer so I cut in as if it was a different question. "Ten years," I say. "Eight married, but we knew within weeks, and the rest of the first two years was just planning and working out the logistics. Ten years."

"I can't imagine," he says. "Well, I *can* imagine. I *did* imagine Aileen wrapping her car round a tree or getting knifed by a mugger, but I'm assuming you loved your husband so I can't *really* imagine."

I'm too stunned by this answer to say anything for a while. When I look over at the driver's seat, his brows are drawn up and his mouth's turned down. He sees me looking. "I can't believe I just said that," he murmurs. "Do you want me to turn the car round?"

"What?" I yelp. "No! Are you kidding? You just said something I haven't heard ten thousand times already. That's a miracle." I'm still watching him and the side of his mouth nearest to me quirks up a little. "And you know what else?" I've found the guts to continue. "I did love him, but it's still complicated. Because the thing no one got was that I knew it was coming for two long years and did so much advance grieving and sorting that, when it finally happened, after I'd slept for a week, I was so relieved for him—but a tiny bit for me too—that, after I did the wiped out bit, I've kind of fast-tracked through some of the stages to get to tonight. That bothers some people, let me tell you."

"What people?" David says. "Unless they were his other wives, they had the right to tell you exactly bugger all."

Now I'm smiling too. "He died a bit over three months ago," I say. "Do *you* want to turn the car round?"

"Are *you* kidding? I've got a table at La Bruyère d'Étaine. And an Uber booked to get us to the Tramway after." He takes his eyes off the road to see if I'm laughing, then he gets serious. "Bad joke," he says. "I mean, are you kidding? I've just said no one knows better than you what stage you're at. Certainly not me."

I sit back in my seat. "What's La Bruyère d'Étaine?"

La Bruyère d'Étaine, it turns out when we get there, is a posh, celebrity-chef kind of place where you're more likely to find beetroot in the ice cream than the soup, and no way is the carpaccio anything to do with beef. Its other feature, at least tonight, is that they play reservation roulette, and ours has rolled right off the table. David does his best, trying to walk the line between kicking enough arse to get us our dinner while not being rude to staff, which everyone knows is death to a first date, until I put my hand on his arm and say, "Let's go somewhere else, eh? I'm starving."

But it's central Glasgow on a sunny Thursday night at the end of the month. Which is how we end up in a plastic booth at the Blue Lagoon, looking at each other over the ketchup bottle, waiting for the waitress to come and ask us if we want haddock and chips or haddock and chips.

"Stop beating yourself up," I say. "I saw some of the food in that other place and I'd have ended up getting a bag of chips to eat in the taxi anyway."

"We're pushing the boat out," David tells the waitress, as she arrives and takes an order pad out of her apron pocket. "So haddock *and* chips *and* mushy peas *and* bread and butter *and* tea, please."

"Same," I agree.

"Two fish teas," she says. Then she gives me a look. "Do you want a tea towel to tuck into your neck, hen? You don't want grease falling on a silk dress."

"Bet they wouldn't have brought me a tea towel for the grease at Snail Mousse Acres," I say when she's gone. At last he relaxes and starts smiling.

"So how's it all going?" he asks me. "Your friend—Chloe, you said?—seemed very businesslike for a Saturday get-together."

"You've no idea," I tell him. "She's helping me house-hunt, see."

He waits for me to go on. Meanwhile the waitress brings a fat teapot and warns us that the handle's hot.

"She showed me this one place," I tell him. "And I liked it a lot. But it's my whole budget. And I don't have any idea how much it costs to do the purchase of a house in this country, so maybe I overestimated what my budget *is*. But now I've seen it, it's soured me for anything else."

"You sure?" He checks the teapot handle, winces and wraps it with a paper napkin to lift it and pour. "My God," he says, looking at the opaque, teak-coloured stream of liquid. "This'll put hair on our chests."

"Sure . . . ?"

"Sure you like it. You look troubled."

I flash again on the words scratched into the paintwork under the windowsill, then will myself back to the explanation I've concocted for myself. Homesick maid, kids playing. "It's not that," I say. "The house is perfect. I knew the old lady who lived there last. Well, I met her. I went there for tea."

"Shit!" he hisses, as the cup overflows. "I was looking into your eyes."

That's not true. He was staring at the teapot, but he doesn't want me to know he's clumsy.

"She loved the place and it shows," I say, watching him pour the saucerful of tea back into the pot, burning his fingers again.

"Does it bother you that she died there?"

"She didn't!" I say. "And it wouldn't anyway. I don't think. I was planning to find out which nursing home her family moved her into so I could invite her back to visit." I hesitate, trying to read his face. Maybe he's only trying not to suck his fingertips and swear. "Unless . . . Does that seem like a crass idea? Hurtful? My judgement might be off at the moment. My family think I'm . . ."

"Not at all," he says. "It's very kind." But *something's* bothering him, I can tell. "Won't the family tell you where she is? Now you're moving in."

"I won't be moving in," I tell him. "The asking price doesn't leave me so much as a tenner to pay a lawyer's bill. And I shouldn't anyway, because it's so cheap there must be something wrong with it. Or maybe I should ignore my brother and sister-in-law and my best friend and not make any decisions at all. Like everyone tells you. Although my brother's not exactly been consistent."

"*Not* buying your dream house is a decision too," he says.

"But buying a house is stressful and I haven't been coping well with what's on my plate already."

He's looking at me so calmly, and so kindly, that I actually consider telling him all about my "not coping." On a first date. Thankfully, right then the waitress bangs down an oval plate of food, still sizzling, in front of me.

"Err you go. Gerrit ett," she says. I love this place, I decide.

"I love this place," says David Minto. "They'd never have said *Gerrit ett* at La Bruyère d'Étaine."

"It would have been *bon appétit* if we were lucky," I say. "But it might have been"—I put my head on one side and breathe the word out slowly—"*Enjoy.*"

David shudders. "Enjoy *what*?"

"Exactly."

"The only thing worse than"—he puts his head on one side too—"*Enjoy!* is *Believe!*"

"Believe *what*?" we both say in chorus.

"Not that I'm a stickler," I add. "I just love language."

"Exactly," says David. "Now, gerrit ett."

We would come here for every anniversary, if this was a fairy tale instead of real life, I'm thinking, at the exact moment David Minto says something that certainly sounds like a fairy tale to me. "I could take a look at the home report for you. That would answer one of your questions."

"Are you . . . ?" I don't want to say qualified.

"Qualified? Oh, I think I'll manage. What's the address?"

I tell him and watch him tapping away at his phone. "That's something else they wouldn't let you do in the tea towel desert," I say. But he's not really listening. So I make a chip sandwich with my share of the buttered bread and let him get on with it.

"Nice," he says after a while. "Good solid house at first glance."

"Can I have a look?" I ask, sitting forward. "I can't get enough of it."

But he lifts his phone to face his chest. "We're not *both* sitting looking at a phone!" he says. "That's dating death."

I sit back so sharply my chair legs scrape. I hope he doesn't notice my face as the restaurant starts to tilt and slide, like a disc with a picture on it. If John and Shelley could tell something's been happening to me, David Minto might twig too.

"It doesn't strike me as a particular bargain," he says after a while, looking up at me. "Never been done up, not as many bathrooms as people look for these days. Old-fashioned layout. If it gets flipped by someone with an eye for design, it'll be worth a packet next time but, if you like it as is, I'd say go for it."

The thought of Saint Helen's being "flipped" by someone who would blow out the kitchen wall and put in those basins in the bathroom that always make me think of sick bowls on a table is enough to clear up this latest episode of the symptom that scares me most. The one I couldn't tell Chloe about. The one even John and Shelley didn't actually mention. The one I *know* is just a leftover from childhood and shouldn't bother me at all.

"Penny for them?" he says.

"Oh. Yeah. I was just— How much does it cost to do the . . . it's called *closing* in America, what do we call it here again?"

"Conveyancing," he says. Then he grins at me. "Depends. Do you happen to know any good lawyers who're trying to impress you?"

My mouth drops open. "Don't toy with me. I love that house."

"I'm not," he says. "I wouldn't. I love . . . the idea of being able to help. I like you, Lindsay Lord, and you deserve a break after everything."

I take a breath to tell him it's Lindsay Hale, but I manage to stop myself. All things considered, it probably better not be.

"Good call on the chip butty, by the way," he says, taking the other two slices of bread and laying them on his side plate. So, no matter how much he was focused on the home report, he was still watching me.

◆ ◆ ◆

"Good night?" Shelley says as I let myself in. She's in the living room, clearly waiting up for me.

"Wonderful night," I say. "The ballet was brilliant." Shelley snorts. "Is John crashed already?"

"I'm here," says John, appearing in the dining room doorway. "What about the rest of it, that wasn't ballet?"

"Nice dinner," I say. Shelley groans and lets her head fall back. "And David's . . . Well, what did you think of him?"

"Clean, good teeth, seemed normal," says Shelley.

"Bit of a posho," says John.

I see Shelley's jaw stiffen. But I've got more on my mind than whatever's wrong with this pair now. "I like him," I say. "What the hell am I going to do? I *like* him. He was supposed to be a toe-in-the-water, first-attempt guy, not an actual prospect. It's too soon. It's a waste of him, meeting him already."

"Oh no!" Shelley says. "You had a happy marriage to a nice man and then you met *another* nice man but the timing isn't perfect. Poor thing."

I want to argue but then I think a bit harder and realise that she's got a point.

"I'm away back to work," says John.

"Night-night," I say, and go to bed grinning, with my transformed *Sleeping Murder*, now covered in some brown paper I unearthed from my mum's old bureau on the landing. It came back to me as if it was yesterday that I last folded and cut and taped and ended up with a neat smooth block to write my name on. Peggy would be proud of how well I'm treating her book. Will be proud, when I find her and show her. I can hear snores from one of the boys and I put my head round the door of their room. Zak, the snorer, is splayed out like a starfish on the bottom bunk with his quilt twisted round his middle. Nicholas is curled up on his side on the top bunk with his quilt held tight round his face like a shawl. I close the door softly.

I'm thirty-six and I need to be honest with myself. If I want to have the full shebang, including the kids—and I'm halfway to admitting that I do—then skipping a year of mourning and a year of dating duds is ideal, possibly essential. As my spirits lift, I tell myself that probably the atmosphere between John and Shelley is nothing to do with me. There must be something up with the business, for John to go back to his office at this time of night.

But I'm too full of leftover cheer from the date to let thoughts like that stay in my head. I slip my dress off, smiling at the thought of the waitress with the tea towel and the tip David left her.

Generous guy all round, David Minto, offering to be my lawyer and not even mentioning money.

Which, I think as I'm brushing my teeth, is too good to be true. I try to unthink that, but there's no stopping my brain now it's started. What if I buy the house and David Minto isn't a lawyer after all and so it's not a legal sale and I lose it again? What if that woman in the garden centre toilets on Saturday simply didn't want to admit she had no clue what those letters stood for?

Once I've cleaned off all my make-up and rubbed in my night cream, I wipe my hands, grab my phone, then google "David Minto, LLM CC," hating myself for being so paranoid, so cynical, so different from the girl who met Kai and moved to Hawaii with two suitcases and not a care in the world.

John and Shelley's woeful Wi-Fi gives me plenty of time to reconsider, but I steel myself. It's only when I see 89,300 results with all the search terms, there at the top of the still-loading page, that I click Cancel and stand up to draw the curtains.

Which is when I see that the office is in darkness and John and his phone are out in the yard again.

There's no way that's business and my heart hurts for him. I can't keep kidding myself, looking down at those lights, that he's over it all. I wish he would talk to me, just once, before I move out. I wish I could be sure he'll be all right if I move on again. Because why did he ask me to come back? I don't blame him, but why hasn't he let me help?

I watch his phone light for a minute or two, then jam my feet into sandals and put a jumper on over my nightie. I trot down the stairs and out into the yard, mapping in my head where the light was, slipping past the sheds and in between towers of nameless black objects, scuttling along dark corridors of stacked wood and metal, no idea what any of this is in the pitch dark, or where I am actually, which way the house is, which way the Barrens lie.

"John?" I shout. "Are you still out here?"

I hear the sudden scrape of startled feet on rough, gravelled ground but he doesn't answer me.

"John?"

He's moving—I can hear him—but still he says nothing and, as I stand holding my breath and straining my ears to work out which way he's going, a crawling cold slinks up the back of my neck and sets my heart hammering. That's not John. It can't be.

I blunder away but now the footsteps are following and everywhere I turn there's something sharp that scrapes at my skin, something hooked that catches my hair. I can't see anything. I don't know where I'm going and when I walk into a wall, smacking it with both my palms, I can't stop moving in time to keep my head from hitting it too.

I curl my fingers and the squeal of my nails against the painted plastic is so familiar and so horrific that I'm five again, tear stained and pee soaked, with my sweaty hair plastered to my head, huddled in the dark and shrieking.

"Lindsay?" John's voice, less than a foot away.

"You kept it?" I say. "You *kept* it? I can't believe you kept it!"

John clicks his torch app on. "It's not the same one," he says.

Through my tears and terror I can see the truth of it. This caravan is white and square with a beige stripe. *The* caravan was so small it was almost round and it was a duck-egg blue colour.

"Of course I didn't keep it," John says. He comes up beside me and together we sit, shoulder to shoulder on the metal step that leads to its door. We're together again. It's taken all this time, but at last, once again, it's John and me.

"How can you live here?" I whisper.

“I made my peace with it,” John says. “You did it your way, Lindsay, and I did it mine.”

I nod, hoping he can feel the movement, although it’s too dark for him to see it now his phone’s off again.

“And I was older than you,” he said. “No two kids in the same family ever have the same childhood.”

“We shared some of it,” I say. Now *he* nods. I feel it.

“We know,” he says.

“But we can’t,” I add.

“So we don’t.”

“Though we do.”

“I thought you’d forgotten,” I say.

“I have,” says John. “You should forget too.”

Awake!

My head knocking against something hard at my side forces me up out of the dark inside to this dark all around me.

Then it happens again. Because I'm moving. I'm in a car, or maybe a van, stretched out flat and I can hear the road rumbling along underneath me. I can't see, no matter how I strain my eyes in the blackness and the sound of my breath is loud in my ears.

Am I saved? Have I been rescued? Is someone beside me?

I try to speak but I can't open my mouth. All that happens is my cheeks feel tight and my eyelids drag downwards. What's happening? I try to lift a hand to feel my face but they're . . . stuck.

What's happening? I feel my breath pick up pace and suddenly I'm struggling, as if there's something over my face. I twist my head and feel snagging and a rough touch on my nose and forehead and oh no, no, no. There's a cover over my head, filling with damp air as I breathe, panicked and fast, and I can't open my mouth because it's taped and I can't move my hands because they're tied and I'm going to suffocate in the hot, wet, cloying closeness of this hood on my head and I didn't think it could get any worse but what if they're taking me somewhere that is *worse?*

I need to calm myself down.

I refuse to die whimpering into a gag and struggling alone in the dark.

I shift my head so it won't hit that hard thing again. Then I roll to my side to get my weight off my wrists and I stretch my fingers and clasp my hands together. I scrape my head backwards and make a tiny gap in front of my face. The damp wool is an inch or two from my nose now.

There. See? Better. Now I must slow my breathing and my heart until I am quiet, then I can begin to work out anything I can glean about what's happening.

But the van is slowing and stopping and two doors slam, one side and then the other, making me rock onto my back again, crushing my wrists and my knuckles. I moan in my throat at the pain. A door near my feet opens and someone grabs them and drags me. My arms buckle at the elbow and I thrash and kick as hard as I can, scared my bones will snap.

"Shit!" A harsh, hissing voice and I'm shoved over onto my side. My arms jerk free of the singing pain and someone is clambering in beside me to shuffle me towards the open door.

Rough and quick, I'm bundled down the length of the van and then my body swings out into the open air, just hands at my ankles and hands under my armpits holding me up. I feel air on my bare skin where whatever I'm wearing has ridden up. I hear gravel under shifting feet and a voice says, "Wait."

That's—

Then a sharp sting in my leg and a feeling of cold spreading inside my calf.

But that voice was—

I'm soft now. And warm too. I'm losing . . .

That voice was—

I'm leaving . . .

Peace.

Part Two

July

Chapter 12

"Uff," Shelley says as we turn into the drive. "You need to water the garden."

It was a dry spring and we're having a dry summer and, now that I look closely, the front garden—*my* front garden as of noon today—is indeed a bit wilted here and there. The trees are okay but the grass is yellowing and the bushes—I need to learn their names—are drooping.

"At least the weeds are dying," I say, pointing at the gravel drive.

"They'll set seed as a last gasp," Shelley says. "And they're harder to pull out of baked ground."

If it was anyone else, I'd say she was jealous of my beautiful house. And Saint Helen's *is* still very beautiful, even rising up out of this neglect. But Shelley isn't subtle enough to be so indirect. If she was jealous, she'd call me a lucky pig and nip my arm.

"I'm going to miss you," I tell her. "All three of you. You and the boys."

We both burst out laughing because I *will* miss John, but we've regressed over the weeks of trying to live together. After we had that heart-to-heart about the caravan and after he stopped being so worried about me, he started laying into me like the old days. And when I stopped being so worried about myself, I gave it back as good as I got. I realised, you see, that he wanted me back here because he needs me, like I need him. We survived the same childhood, John and me. He was braver, growing up, staying put, letting all the memories fade. I ran away from them, into my books, into my marriage, across all those time zones. Now I'm back, he doesn't need to be so brave all on his own. Now he's near me, I can face it without it destroying me.

I still get the odd wave of—I've decided to call it *psychic vertigo*—when I can't remember telling my family what they seem to know, or I can't put my finger on what they tell me I'm experiencing.

Twice the world went flat and fluttery again. Once was looking out the window at the yard in the dark, and once was talking to Chloe about David, wondering why she wasn't hassling to hang out with him. But I had already solved that little puzzle: It's because I'm back where everything happened to me. The plot thins.

I haven't thought I knew any strangers for a while. And it was only ever Aileen I couldn't remember. What else? I haven't misheard anything. The only thing that's not improving is the dreams: night after night of furious, chaotic nightmares—strangers who know me, friends who look past me, empty houses, endless foxes, and splinters and iron filings under my nails till my fingers bleed. The dreams are all so similar that I wake in the small hours thinking I should surely be able to crack their code, but by the morning they're no more than a shudder when I look in the mirror to brush my teeth—*Now shave*—or a sudden breathlessness if I'm outside and a breeze sends the clouds scudding fast enough across the sky that the light keeps changing—*The North Wind and the Sun*. That and the endless news every morning that no matter how hard I've been searching for Kai all night, I'm never going to find him. One bright spot is waking up knowing I can look for Peggy. Her bit of my dreams is the only thing that's no mystery. It's so clear it makes me cringe. That thing she keeps trying to give me is a business card—a business card, for God's sake!—like I was generous and kind enough to drop through her letterbox. "I'm sorry," I tell her. "I should have done more. I'll find you. I promis—"

"Speak of the devil," Shelley says, looking in her rearview mirror.

"What?"

"That's John. I hope your new neighbours know the Clampetts are moving in."

Of course John offered to move all my borrowed belongings. And of course, when it was too late to make other arrangements, he realised that the big van was booked, so here he comes in the pickup truck with bedposts and chair legs sticking up and a bandana tied to the bit of the couch that's hanging over the back bumper. I wave at him and start windmilling my arms to tell him where to turn and where to reverse to, to get in the front door with the least lugging. He shakes his head as he passes me and, with one arm hanging out of the side window, he reverses up to the steps in one go, leaving just enough room to get past the pillars and drop the tailgate.

I rummage in my bag for the big key I picked up at the estate agent in Bridge of Allan as the clock struck twelve—Farmer George himself, as it goes. He didn't remember me today, which is just as well after I had bugged him for places to rent and then never followed up.

I expected David to be there in BofA, if I'm honest. But I suppose, given that he handled the whole thing for me and has never once mentioned money, I can't complain about the service. I can't complain about any of the services: not David either comping the lot or paring his rates to the bone and all set to wait a while before he bills me; not Chloe finding the house in the first place but not snapping it up for herself; certainly not John and Shelley taking the time to help me move in.

"Have I told you how grateful I am?" I say to John's bent head as he's untying the binder twine holding the tailgate shut. Clampetts is not an overstatement.

"Say it with pies," says John. "I'll have a hot steak slice and a cream horn for after."

"I don't know the bakers yet," I tell him. "But you're on."

Then I can't concentrate on him anymore because I have opened the front door and am stepping inside my new home. The rest of the keys are laid out on a shallow table in the vestibule, just like Farmer George said they would be. I open the inner doors and throw them wide.

Inside, it's cold and damp despite the two months of dry summer and it smells as if there have been mice making the most of getting the place to themselves. But the light is pouring down from the top of the stairwell and the wood still looks burnished to glowing under the lightest film of dust that blows away at a breath. And it's so, so, so solid. Nothing fluttering here.

"Where do you want the couch?" says John. He's got a hold of one end and he's dragging it out of the pickup, the legs screeching on the metal.

"Leave it a minute," I say. "Come in and look round."

"I've seen it," he tells me, then he bites his lip.

"When?" I ask him. "Did you clear it? Why didn't you tell me?"

"Numpty," John says. "I picked up a piano years back from the old dear that used to live here then. I went for a nose about."

"You're such an arsehole," Shelley tells him, in that affectionate way of hers. "Why couldn't you keep your gob shut for once and look round Lindsay's new place instead of having to come out on top every time?"

"Sorry, Lindsay," John says, making my mouth fall open. "I didn't see everywhere. Give me the tour before we start unpacking, eh?"

"Hallebloodylujah," says Shelley, and does that thing with her hands as if she's writing a headline. "Man in Forties Shows Signs of Growing Up."

"Family Stunned," I add, matching the gesture.

"Two Women Pushing Forty in Hospital After Lifting Couch on Their Own," says John. I let him have the win. Apart from anything else, that was funny.

Then I show them round, not even trying to stop myself getting insufferable about the space and the number of rooms, the size of the windows, the original keys for the locks of all the doors, the four-oven Aga I'll never be able to afford to run on the oil it takes, the nifty cupboards in the butler's pantry that I haven't got enough china to fill, the lovely bathroom with the dark wood surround to the bath.

"That was in a book," Shelley says. "A mahogany bit round the bath. Some woman had a flashback."

"I'm reading that book!" I say. "Or trying to, till I packed it by mistake." I'll make sure and tell Chloe there's a downside to a plain brown wrapper after all.

"You do know the only way that wood's still in good nick after a hundred years, don't you?" says John. We wait. "No shower. Is there a shower room somewhere else?"

"Not yet," I say, "and I haven't got a penny left to put one in. I'm going to have dull, flat hair for a while, unless I join a gym and shower there. And I can't afford the membership fees."

"Rather you than me," John says. "Is there decent Wi-Fi?"

"No, and I'm going to have to put the start-up fees on my credit card and work like a dog till I've paid it off."

"Work where?" says Shelley.

"Ah," I say. "The final stop on the tour. Come into my dead room, said the . . . I don't know who would say that."

"Zombie to the blonde," John offers.

Shelley shakes her head at him and rolls her eyes at me. "Don't scrape up Lindsay's new floors, dragging your knuckles on them."

"I'm okay for looking at a cubbyhole, actually," he says as we're recrossing the main hallway. "I'll crack on here." I think he has exhausted both his interest in houses and his capacity to fake it, but he's done pretty well, and neither of us is so desperate to lug furniture that we're going to stop him.

"Won't it creep you out working hidden away here in a big empty house?" Shelley says as she goes ahead of me up the crooked staircase. The door at the bottom was locked and so is the one at the top but the key is there and turns easily. "Especially if you're going to block up the window, right?"

"Of course not," I say, but even as the words are leaving my mouth, it hits me.

I have made a huge, stupid mistake and I genuinely had no idea.

I've heard of this mistake in people's thinking. It's famous. It's probably even got a name. It most usually happens around funerals, or at least that's where I've come across it. People lose a loved one and they've got a ton of paperwork and organising to do. They need to make decisions and plan the send-off, tell friends and other family where it is and when, what they've decided about flowers or donations. They know they need to get all this done before life goes . . . and this is the mistake coming now . . . back to normal.

But, of course, life isn't going to *go* back to normal. Life is going on, it's true, but changed forever. That's why so many people crash right after the reception, surrounded by cards and leftovers. That's when the real work of grieving, the real hard hurting, begins.

Only not for me. Because when I was planning Kai's cremation and memorial, I was also denying that I had to—and then accepting that I had to—sell up, pack, come home, find a house, and move in. Then, I only right now realise I've been mistakenly believing, life would go back to normal at last.

Somewhere inside my heart, unknown to my brain, too deep for common sense to reach it, I didn't really believe I was going to live in this big empty house all on my own. I thought once I'd got it ready, Kai would come and join me, where he belongs.

This is the first time I've faced the truth that, just like Peggy March, I'm going to be alone here, and for the same reason: Richard and Kai are both gone.

"Linds?" says Shelley. I must have been quiet a long time.

"I won't have time to fret," I tell her. I tell myself really, but she can hear me too. "I need to buy some acousticware, get it fitted, and get cracking."

"Is there really such a rush?"

"I need to start making a living. The only thing I'm worried about is staying on top of the garden."

"Subtle." She gives me a nudge. We're both looking out over the back lawn to the greenhouse. "Yes, Lindsay, I well might run the lawnmower round and clip the odd shrub, while I'm here making use of your lovely old greenhouse. Out of gratitude, you know."

"Cool," I say. "Can you do me a key to the plants too, if I draw a plan? Like, what's that one there that can't be a passion flower?"

"Clematis," says Shelley. "Nelly Moser." Something in her voice makes me turn and, when I do, I'm sure she's close to tears.

"Shel?"

"I want nothing but happiness for you, Lindsay," she says. "Ignore me."

We head back downstairs to discover that John has manhandled the couch, the table and chairs, the bed, and the chest of drawers out of the pickup without us and only needs a hand up the stairs with the big stuff headed to my bedroom. In another ten minutes, we've done that too and he's standing whistling through his teeth, desperate to get going.

"What about your pie?" I say.

"Drop it round," he tells me. "Throw in a bag of crisps to thank me for getting you a cheap car. You ready, Shel?"

"Give my love to the boys," I say. "Tell them they're welcome anytime. Tell Zak there's a wee something in his room for him to say thanks for letting me use it."

"Nicky won't like that," Shelley tells me.

"And a wee something for Nicholas to say thanks for putting up with Zak," I add.

"You've spoiled them," says John.

"And tell them they'll be spoiled some more, every time they come and see me."

I'm sounding pathetic even to myself now, an old lady filling her biscuit tin to make the kids visit. In fact, once John and Shelley have gone, that black biscuit tin from Victoria's jubilee is the first thing I unpack. I'm still chuffed I remembered to fish it out from under the seat before I took the hire car back.

It got dented at some point, though, and the lid is stuck on. When I find where I've put my phone down, I'll google how to unstick it without damaging the enamel. Meantime, I set it back on the high shelf where its twin used to live when Peggy March was here. I smile at it, looking forward to showing it to her, once I find her, if she's able to visit, if she wants to, if her health didn't take a nosedive. Which it might have, I suppose.

I lock the front door. Whoever cleared this house made a proper job of it. They've even taken the basket that should be hanging inside the letterbox, the one that was full of junk mail when I pushed my business card through. I find myself hoping I don't remember my half-heartedness every time I go in and out. Then I tell myself that no one goes in and out the front of their houses. I close the inner glass door of the vestibule and head back to the kitchen.

Making sure I've got the right key for the back door, I step into the garden. This is mine. I own these ornate washing line posts and the old rope sagging between them; I own that tree, whatever it is, and "Nelly Moser" the clematis too. I own the shed full of pots and mysterious tools—one like a huge flat sieve, one like a giant's back scratcher with a handle six feet long—and the greenhouse that Shelley covets so much, although to my eyes it's just ten feet of dry dirt with cobwebbed glass around it and warped wooden shelves, furry from soaking.

At the far end, past the beds full of enormous plants that should be vegetables but surely can't be, unless vegetables turn into these monsters if no one picks them, there's an area I never got round to exploring with Chloe, or the day I came back with David, while he double-checked what the home report had told him, before he let me proceed.

There are trees here even a fool would recognise, because the apples and plums are fully formed on them, though green and tiny. The branches twist and buckle, reaching almost all the way to the ground, so the shaded grass underneath isn't as dry and dead as the rest but instead still lush and silky feeling when I slip off my shoes and wander around in my bare feet.

I find the most comfortable-looking tree trunk and settle down against it, wriggling my shoulders. The bark is rough enough to make me tingle. "We're going to be good friends, you and me," I say.

"Who's that?" comes a querulous voice. "Who's there?"

For one moment, my heart leaps and all my childhood tales of magic gardens and enchantments come streaming back. Then I turn and see the top of a bald dome showing over the boundary wall. I'm pretty sure it's Colonel Nosyparker, but he can't do anything to me now.

"Your new neighbour," I say, taking a run at the wall and managing to toe myself up high enough to hook my arms and look over. It is indeed him, still dressed in shirt and tie, although without his jacket today. "Lindsay Hale. We met last month. But you were thinking about security and I didn't get your name."

"Mr. Boyle," he says. "Bunny Boyle."

Not laughing takes every bit of my self-control, and I don't quite make it. But he appreciates the effort and only shakes his head and sucks his teeth. "For the first fifty years of my life, it was just a jolly, unremarkable moniker," he says. "And then came that dratted film. Aye, well."

"Do you remember what I was asking you when I came poking round, Mr. Boyle?" I say. "When you quite rightly sent me packing."

To my surprise, his bottom lip quivers and I think his eyes start to water. Or maybe it's just that he's looking up into the sun at me hanging over the top of the wall.

"Not at all," he says. His voice has gone a bit husky too and he clears his throat before he goes on. "I wouldn't have been right, my dear, even had I known. I was officious and misguided and, if I'm honest, I was hurt that I was in the dark. I mean, what harm would it have done for you to know where poor Peggy had been taken off to? What harm would it have done for *me* to know? We could both have gone to see her and brightened her day. I owe you an apology . . . Linda, was it?"

"Lindsay," I say. "But please don't worry. I'll find out where she is and then I could take you too or you could take me." I know men that age don't like it when women drive them.

"I haven't had a car for six years," he says. "Not since I turned ninety. And I'm very much afraid to tell you, Lindsay, that you're too late. Not by much, but too late all the same. Peggy's boy stopped round only the other day and broke the sad news that . . . well. My old nanny used to say 'gone on ahead.' It struck me as a mealy-mouthed way of alluding to a plain fact, back then when I was a child, with all of life before me, but it sounds about right now when I won't be long at her back."

I should say something comforting, as if he hasn't just let me know he's ninety-six, but I am numb at this news, and silent too.

"And she left instructions that more or less prevent any of her friends from marking her passing too. Most unlike her. Not that we ever discussed it. We should have, given our ages."

"Oh, Bunny," I manage to say. I can't keep clinging onto the wall with my bare toes braced and my shoulders straining. I slither down and hit the grass with a soft thump.

"Sorry, Lindsay," he says, out of sight now.

"Me too."

I trail back inside, expecting the house to feel colder and sadder now. I pause in the lobby, looking through the open door to the kitchen and the yards of empty red-tiled floor ready to ring out at the clack of my sandals crossing it. I look up the little staircase towards the dead room, where I really will be spending most of my time very soon, every day until I retire. Something in me shrinks at the thought. I find myself rubbing my fingertips together, without knowing why, and then I slip my shoes off again and tiptoe as lightly as I can towards the front of the house, where my boxes offer occupation and distraction. "I'll love the place for you, Peggy," I say out loud. I wish it didn't echo so much, but I mean it.

The boxes don't work. I spend the rest of the day spreading my few temporary possessions around, first trying to space them out and then, when that leaves the whole house looking bleak, bunching them together in key spots, telling myself I'll ignore the empty places until my container gets here. I go to the shops and lug home two bulging carrier bags of the kind of healthy food you home in on when there's a new start on the go.

Later, I look it over and then acquaint myself with the handful of Dunblane carry-outs who deliver. I eat three quarters of a pizza and go to bed, almost missing the company of the holographic monsters, definitely missing *Sleeping Murder*, which I haven't found yet.

It's still light when I turn in, the midnight sun only a month and a bit gone and the sky rosy until well after ten, so it doesn't matter that John plonked the big old bed he's lending me smack in the middle of the floor, *far* too far from the wall for me to plug in the lamp he included in my haul. But, when I start awake in the pitch black with my heart hammering, I've forgotten all that. I grope around, helpless and confused, checking and rechecking both sides of the bed, until I finally remember that the nearest light is yards away.

What woke me? I wonder, swinging my legs out from under the covers. I am padding confidently towards the door when I hear the click of a latch closing and am suddenly sure that what disturbed me was the sound of it opening.

Draughts.

Surely.

But I want the light on. Only, I've completely lost my bearings. With both arms stretched straight out and waving wildly, I blunder around, waiting to hit the wall or the window, to scrape my shin on the edge of the bed or stub my toe on the fireplace surround. It seems to go on for an endless stretch of panicky, impossible time and I force myself to stop moving when I feel a whimper start to gather in my chest. I must be going round in circles. I take a deep breath and start to walk in baby steps, placing my heel against my toes to make sure that I keep a straight line. Right enough, this time it takes only eight paces until my outstretched fingers brush against the silky stripes of the wallpaper and I can feel my way round to the door to hit the light switch. As I'm letting my head fall forward to rest on the wood, I hear that same sound again. A door clicks softly open, and then even more softly closed.

Draughts. Old house. The ghost of Peggy March. Imagination. Draughts. The ghost of Nelly Moser. Old doors. Draughts. With old latches. Seven dea—

No.

There's no one here.

Chapter 13

When I open my eyes the next morning, I expect everything to be back to normal. Of course I do—the sun is streaming in the hastily drawn curtains and I can hear birds chirping through the old single glazing. No one would expect midnight wobbles to withstand all that. But instead of feeling sheepish, I find my mouth dry and my heart high in my chest before I've moved a muscle.

"I've got to stop looking at listings," I say out loud to the high ceiling above me. "This isn't a scary place. This is my house." But then I turn my head and see, on my bedside table, that wrapped book I thought I'd lost that I definitely didn't put there last night. My pulse picks up even more.

I must have, that's all. I was too tired to notice what I was unpacking. I know for a fact I was tired enough to sleepwalk round my bedroom and imagine the noise of a door opening.

But *do* you remember sleepwalking?

And do you suddenly start sleepwalking in your mid-thirties?

Grief can give you arthritis and ulcers, I remember Chloe telling me. Of course it can make you sleepwalk.

"I love my new house," I say out loud. "I'm safe here."

Immediately, a door bangs somewhere downstairs and I sit up as if someone has kicked my pedal. I feel my back twang and try to relax it: I've got a lot of lifting to do. But I'm sure that, over the sound of a bin lorry in the street and those birds who must be nesting in the creeper right outside the bedroom window by the racket they're making, there's another sound. Shuffling feet, I would have said.

"Oh Peggy," I say. I'm performing this—this light-hearted exasperation—although God knows who for. It can't be me, because I don't believe in ghosts, and Peggy March wouldn't mind me living in her house, and she didn't shuffle. I remember trotting along beside her that day we met at the postbox, her metalled heels clip-clopping.

I decide the noise is a draught excluder shushing over a bare floor, or maybe dry leaves blowing around in the back garden, and I spring out of bed, making as much noise as I can with my bare feet, march out to the top of the stairs, and head down them.

"Ocht, I didn't mean to wake you!" Bunny Boyle is standing in the front hall, wearing rubber gloves and with a black bin bag in his hand. He blinks up at me, half blinded by the light pouring in the glass cupola.

"I heard the door," I say, although that was last night and surely he hasn't been in here since then.

"Bin day," he tells me, brandishing the bag. "I didn't think you'd have it all worked out yet, so I thought I'd help you. I mean, I say 'bin day,' but it's all so complicated now. Landfill this week. Green wheelies that. I can write it down for you."

"So . . . you've got a key?" I say, coming down the rest of the stairs. It sounds worse than I meant it to, so I add, "That's handy. Thank you."

"Only to the very back door into the wee lobby there," he says. "Which room have you picked for yourself, if you heard me easing *that* one open?"

"Thing is though," I say, "I think the bins have been past."

He lays a finger along the side of his nose and taps it. "I tip like a lord at Christmastime," he tells me. "They'll stop for me on their way back down." He rustles the bag again and shuffles off towards the back door.

I know how offensive it is to lump old people in together as if they're not as varied and unique to themselves as everyone else, but I decide right here and now that I'll make up for missing Peggy by being Bunny's dream neighbour, and if that means he lets himself in and out of my house, so be it. I've just filled the kettle when he's back.

"What did I tell you?" he says, stripping off his gloves and tucking them into his belt. He goes to the sink and starts to wash his hands. "They stopped and picked up your bin without blinking. Fifty quid a year well spent."

"I'm so sorry about Peggy," I tell him. "She didn't last long in the home."

"It's the way of it," Bunny says, pushing his lips out and pursing them. "That's why I'm determined to stay put. Use it or lose it."

Exactly what Peggy said to me.

"You must miss her."

"It was a terrible shock," he says, nodding as he sits. "I had no idea she was leaving. We didn't get to say goodbye. In a funny sort of way, I hope her health *did* collapse completely overnight. She'd have been awfully upset otherwise. And she'd never have left without taking her leave of me, if she could."

"I still want to find out where she was," I say. "I'd like to make a donation of some kind. In her name. Only I don't know where to start."

"The son would know," Bunny says. "I take it you haven't met him in the course of buying the house?"

"My solicitor handled everything," I say, squirming a bit, since the truth is my boyfriend handled everything. "I actually thought it was a daughter." Although maybe I only decided it was a daughter when I was pretending to be a family friend, for the nursing homes. "Is he a . . . is he likely to be helpful?"

"I don't know him well," Bunny says. "A terrible stealer of pea pods when he was a little boy, but he must be well past forty now. Once I get these rusty old cogs turning, I'm sure to come up with a name for you." He sighs. "Robert? William? John, even? It's one of those Tom, Dick and Harry names. But it's not *Mr.* March, that I *can* tell you. The chap's a doctor. Nothing as handy as a GP in the local clinic, though. Some big hospital in Glasgow, and I couldn't tell you which bit of the body he paws around in. Sorry." He stares down into the dregs of his coffee. He's got the same asbestos throat as Peggy. "It hurt my feelings dreadfully not to be told where she went after all the time I knew her," he says.

"How long were you neighbours?"

"Three years." It surprises me until he adds, "And forty-seven more years being dear friends."

Then he claps both his big papery hands onto his knees and hauls himself to his feet with a grunt. "Welcome to Dunblane, Lindsay," he says.

"Thank you," I say, absolutely sincerely. "Having you next door makes me feel even happier to be here."

He leaves by the back door and I wave him off. See? I tell myself. All's well. You had a bad dream. You forgot you unpacked a book. You've got a lovely helpful neighbour. There's no such thing as gho—

And that's when I hear smart, tip-tappy footsteps behind me and feel a cold hand on the back of my neck. I jump what feels like a foot in the air, rewrenching my back, and coming down in a crouch with hands up, crooked into claws, ready to fight.

"Jesus Christ!" Chloe says, stepping back. "Didn't you hear me? Have you got earbuds in?"

"What are you doing here?" I say. "How did you get in? How long have you—?"

"What am I *doing* here?" she says. "I'm your oldest friend. I'm amazed I managed to give you a bit of space yesterday, Lindsay. It was torture."

"But how did you get in?"

"You shouldn't leave your door open overnight, though. Even in Dunblane. I locked it after myself, by the way."

"I didn't leave my door open," I tell her.

Chloe has started making more coffee, sniffing inside the kettle and running a finger along the rim of two cups. She doesn't mean to be offensive—it's second nature now, from checking the work of her staff before she signs off on her customers' houses.

"First night in a new place," she says. "Don't beat yourself up."

I don't want to tell her why I'm so sure I didn't leave any of the doors open last night. I don't want to admit that I checked and rechecked multiple times before I went up. I certainly don't want to tell her that I thought someone was here in the night. "Have you been upstairs?" I say.

"Today?"

"Did you put a book by my bed?"

"What? When? Lindsay, you've got a real thing about that book by your bed, you know. Read something else!"

"It wasn't just the book. I had a weird . . . I don't even know what to call it. But it's probably the house, right? It's an old house. It's bound to have quirks. Right?"

"Even a new house this size would have quirks if you got it for sev—"

"Don't!" I say. She starts and lets some coffee granules scatter off the spoon, so she has to shake out the front of her shirt. She's not wearing her uniform today. "Sorry," I tell her. "Just, you know how you hate the phrase *dead room*?"

"I don't. What do you mean?"

"Oh come off it, Chlo! Anyway, I don't care for *seven dead*."

"Seven dead what?"

"Jesus, I'm losing my mind. You probably weren't even going to say it."

"*Seven dead?* Of course I wasn't going to say it. I don't even know what you're talking about."

"I'm not the only one with memory glitches, then?"

She looks at me for a long moment then sniffs and finally turns to tip the spoonful of granules into a cup. "How about some coffee and some good news?" she says. "I got onto the movers. Your stuff's coming today."

"What?" I say. "How? You got . . . ?"

Chloe laughs, delighted at the effect she's having. "Didn't you hear John yesterday morning, swearing down the phone? That was me on the other end. Asking him for a direct line to the Scottish branch of the firm that moved you. He deals with them all the time—course he does—and no way was he going to call in favours. He made me promise not to mention his name."

"But . . . today? How did you get my delivery bumped up . . . what is it? Nearly three weeks?"

"I can be very persuasive," Chloe says, waggling her eyebrows. "I refused to take no for an answer. And who really needs two kidneys?"

Right on cue, a rumble comes from outside the front of the house. Chloe beams. The lorry's here. I'm just about to see all my belongings again, Kai's and mine.

Saint Helen's swallows them up like it did my stopgaps, with barely a gulp. Our big squashy couch, our solid blanket box, our bed that it took four people to manhandle into the house when we bought it—they look lost and spindly. I can feel my chin start to wobble as I wave goodbye to the movers. I've been telling myself that once the house is clothed in cushioned and woven things, soft things, it'll feel like somewhere to curl up. What have I done?

"Come on, Pudding," Chloe says, catching me at it. She hasn't called me Pudding since I let my haircut from hell grow in, in the nineties.

"I don't know why I thought this was the place for me," I say. I keep a hold of my voice, just. But the effort turns it croaky.

"What? What's wrong with it?" she says. "Empty? Yes. But I say 'lean in.' You need some wide open spaces to make up for your creepy 'dead room.' So leave the floors bare and put nests of fairy lights in the corners as uplighters. Paint the walls white and buy really big pictures. You could fan your curtain hems out over the floor like trains."

"Trains?"

"On cloaks. On wedding dresses."

"You're not describing a home, Chlo," I say. "That's a photo shoot. I want to be cosy and safe."

"Safe?" she says. "Of course you're safe, you doughnut." But she's not really listening, I don't think. She's walking away from me, into the dining room, still so empty that her footsteps ring out, and then on into the butler's pantry. I listen for where she's going next. I need to learn the house's sounds if I'm ever going to sleep through the night without thinking someone's broken in. I think she's in the kitchen, so I go round the other way to meet her.

"Love you too," she's saying into her phone when I get there.

I open my mouth to wind her up, but she hasn't heard me and I decide to be kind. I tiptoe back a few paces then reapproach, letting my bare feet slap on the tiles. She still startles a bit as she slides her phone into her pocket, but I pretend not to notice. Instead, I wrench at the tape on the nearest box to start unpacking. On top of the pile of tea towels Kai and I collected over the years is one of the knitted dishcloths we got at a farmer's market in Santa Barbara, one of the few items we could afford. Kai used to tell the dishes they were honoured to be scoured with such an artisanal piece of craftsmanship. I smile and go to hang it over the taps, plucking out the top tea towel—Christmas at Radio City—to put over the Aga rail on the way.

Then I look out of the window, and here comes David, sneaking round the house with one of the ugliest, fleshiest, most garish and misshapen bromeliads I have ever seen, complete with a red bow. I knock on the glass, and he jumps, then holds the plant up, grimacing. I go to let him in.

"Well, hello, m'lud," says Chloe, getting a lot of syllables out of it. "It's been a while."

"Waste of time," David says. "I've heard enough about you to know you're not really flirting." He kisses me on the cheek and says, "Are you good with houseplants?"

"I'm a ninja with houseplants."

"Oh God, that's a shame. You might be stuck with this for years then."

"They grow outside in Hilo," I say. "It'll make me feel right at home."

"How was your first night?" he asks me. Chloe is drifting away to give us privacy but I reach out and haul her back.

"Shit, thanks," I say. "I had nightmares with all the usual stuff—searching for someone I can't find, straining to hear things no one's saying, struggling to get splinters out of my hands. Only this time there were people in the house too. So I'm going to change all the locks. Unless you tell me that's mad. It would be a bit of a shame to ditch the originals."

Chloe and David commune silently, then Chloe speaks. "It's a *bit* paranoid, to be fair, Lindsay. And a *huge* shame to junk all the old locks. That's my tuppenceworth."

"Add bolts," David says. "Same job and a hell of a lot cheaper. You could get antique ones from architectural salvage."

"Or maybe I'll feel better once I've filled the place," I say. "Sorry, Chlo. I'm just not a minimalist."

"And can you think of anywhere you could source any household junk at a reasonable price?" Chloe says.

I laugh. "It's actually kind of weird it wasn't John who cleared it," I say. "What I'd really like is to find out who it *was* and buy it all back again. Put everything back where it belongs. You can't fake a lived-in house."

As a start, I take the poor dented biscuit tin and bang it hard on the edge of the nearest worktop to knock it straight again. The lid springs open, which seems like a good omen, and a shower of wrapped biscuits cascades to the floor. Penguins and KitKats.

"Lindsay?" says Chloe. "Are you okay? You've gone white."

I am so far from okay I can't even begin to describe it. There *was* someone in my house last night. They put a book by my bed. And my brother's been lying to me. I know those are three very different things and one of them is ridiculous but I've had enough.

"I-I-I need to speak to John about something," I say. "I won't be long."

Chapter 14

He's in the cabin, looking at his screens. I can tell from the reflection in his reading glasses that, once again, he clicks to a different window when he sees me.

"Why didn't you tell me you cleared Saint Helen's?" I say, putting my knuckles on the glass of his stupid nondesk and leaning over him. "In fact, why did you tell me you hadn't?"

"Eh?"

"Stop it!" I say. I bang the flats of both hands down hard. Nothing breaks, more's the pity. "How can you lie to me? You know better than anyone how hard it is for us to— What are you *playing* at?"

"Lindsay, I have no idea what you're on about," he says. "What's up with you? I swear on Zak and Nicky's lives I didn't clear that house."

"Huh," I say. That's that then.

I fall back into the old-rich-people chair. "God, I'm sorry," I say. "Listen, what chocolate biscuits would you say a random granny would keep in her tin?"

"Is this a joke?" John should know me well enough to know I don't tell jokes, but he sticks with it. "I don't know—what chocolate biscuits *would* a random granny keep in her tin?" When I don't answer he adds, "Penguins, Clubs, Twixes, KitKats."

I slump in the chair until it creaks.

"Jesus," I say. "I'm such a wreck. Sorry. God, John, I'm sorry."

"What happened?" he says.

I think hard about how to answer. "Nothing," I say in the end. "Stress, grief, nightmares. Possibly sleepwalking." Will I say more? Should I actually try to tell him about the intruder last night, about the book? Instead, I say, "I really do admire you, you know. You're as solid as a rock and all it takes is moonlit walks round the Barrens."

He frowns and says nothing.

"Good self-care," I say.

"Self-care!" he says, scoffing at me. "That's all bath salts and whingeing, isn't it? Not for me."

"So you really are that over the caravan?" I ask him. "And goan just answer me straight, this one time."

He gives me a sober look, considering. "We both are," he says at last, and I breathe out in a rush. "We got over it with the tree," he goes on. "We got over it with the sliding section of metal. You know we did."

"Christ, John!" I blurt. "Please! I call it 'the caravan' same as you do. But you know what I mean. I'm talking about what happened to us when we were wee. All of it. Dad."

"Dad?" he says. *"Dad?"*

I am frozen. About a hundred different things have just become clear. Or one big thing, maybe, a hundred times bigger than me. Our family motto isn't just a slogan for John. It has worked. It's worked so well, the last bit of it is no longer true. He knows, but he can't so he doesn't. The end.

"Lindsay?" he says.

"What?" I say, aiming for clueless. I have no idea if I hit it. I have no idea if he'll buy it.

"You just said 'Dad,'" he tells me, giving me a screwball look.

"Piss off," I say. "Stop messing with my head."

"I'm serious, Linds," he says. "You just made out like if we weren't going to call our childhood *the caravan* then we had better call it *Dad*."

"Wow," I say, shaking my head and keeping my eyes wide. "Hell of a tongue slip. I meant *Mum*. Obviously."

"Paging Dr. Freud," says John, laughing.

"Why did I leave my good medical insurance behind?" I say, laughing along with him. "What's the waiting list like for a head doctor on the NHS?"

He cracks up again, then sobers. "You don't need a doctor," he says. "You got over it. *We* got over it. And under it and past it. You and me."

With him smiling at me, the memory is so close that I can feel the rough bark of that overhanging tree branch as I dangle, John jeering at me from below. I can hear the squeal of that leaning panel scraping across the laminate underneath it. For a moment I feel guilty for not telling him about my dresser. But he didn't need it. He was fine by then. Tall and strong and happy to hang out in the park till whenever.

"Sorry," I say. "Sorry if I've destabilised—" He groans. "Just . . . all round sorry, okay?"

"Fine by me."

"And look, let me make it up to you for going off like that by being your best customer of the month? Maybe the year. Any massive old wardrobes you can't shift? What about a piano? Have you still got that fairground horse in the back shed where the keyboards go? I need . . ."

I know I sound manic. I *feel* manic as I set off into the belly of the junkyard. He's got the right idea. He's got it layers deep. We got over it and under and past it, I tell myself. John and me.

We did, so long as we call it *the caravan* and pretend it was a one-time thing. I'm not arguing that we got over the time when I was four and John was seven and we made a den in a pristine, mint-condition caravan that my mum and dad had let slip their minds. We holed up in there day after day, night after night: spacemen, cowboys, knights that we were.

Once, Mum found us coming out of it. She chased us—we thought she was playing. She dragged us all the way back there, holding one little arm in each of her big hands, and she locked us in. "This is where you've been hiding?" she shouted through the door. "This is where you've been when Da— When we've been looking for you? You want *this* instead of two bedrooms full of expensive toys? Parents who love you?" She thumped hard on the flimsy door with the side of her fist, making us both jump. "You've got it."

We were there for twenty-six hours. John missed Cubs and it was the next day—light again—that Mum came and let us out. She hugged me so hard, I could feel her bones and mine clashing together, as if she'd got thin like I had, from not eating all those long hours. "You shouldn't have run away," she said. "Your dad has been going out of his mind with worry."

"But, Mummy—"

"Your dad and I told the police you never knock about the yard, so they knew you weren't hiding."

"But Dad knows we play—"

"And if you run away again, they'll take you away to a children's home, you know."

"But we didn't ru—"

"That's what the police told us."

"But you knew where—"

"If anyone ever finds you outside these fences where you don't belong, you'll get taken off us and live in a children's home."

"But—"

"Go and get in the bath and wash yourselves. I need to tell all the kind people who've been looking for you round the clock that you've stopped being spoiled little brats and come home."

A police lady came and asked us if we'd been in a car, if we'd been with a stranger, if anyone had told us to keep a secret. I was sitting on Mum's knee, with her arms tight round my middle, and John was sitting next to Dad, on the couch, with Dad's big hand on John's little shoulder and I could see the white in his fingernails and John was shaking.

"Sorry," I said. "I wanted to do an adventure. I'm sorry."

"Adventure is for your storybooks, Lindsay," said the police lady. "You read about adventures safe here at home from now on, eh?"

"Sorry," said John. "We won't run away ever again. We want to stay at home."

The three of them, and the man who was police too but didn't wear a uniform, went outside onto the step and talked for a long time.

"We can't ever run away again," I said to John.

"They'll put us in a children's home if we run away again," John said to me.

Then we tried on her police-lady hat that she had left on the coffee table, but she only smiled when she came back in and caught us.

And that was all that happened. Because if nothing happened before that day, to make us hide in the first place, and nothing happened *after*, then we're over it. Our family motto has worked beautifully. We know, but we can't, so we don't, though we do. And we call the bit we *do* know *the caravan*. Which we're over, John and me.

And now it's thirty-two years later and I'm just a woman with an empty house, the lucky sister of a generous junkman, wombling again.

I slip past the gates and barrels and baths, searching out bulk like a raptor hunting prey. There's a chaise longue that's been on top of a pile of school blackboards for at least nine years. It probably needs resprung, definitely reupholstered, but it's huge and I want it.

And the fairground horse *is* still there, slightly wormy and chipped, with its saddle crumbling and only the faintest gleam of gold where its painted harness used to be.

"You and me both," I say to it. "We were made for each other."

I pat its neck, marvelling at how it hasn't moved except to be borne back on the tide, like everything always is.

Except—

I'm standing deep in a nest of household textiles—towels and tablecloths and bedsheets and pillowcases—and they shouldn't be anywhere near here. It's like John's stopped trying to organise the stock the way my dad did, with my mum helping. No!

Not going to think about anything Dad did, with Mum helping.

I'm shopping for household items. I'm grown up. John lives here. It's different now. I'm fine.

This looks like one complete lot of assorted linens, I think, forcing my mind back to the present. As if it's from one clearance, stuffed in beside half a dozen rolled rugs that are balanced along the tops of two dressing tables and four bedside tables, the matching wardrobes at the back. I ease open a mirrored door and see clothes still hanging in there, a pile of shoe boxes on the floor.

Well, maybe it's more fun for customers that way. But it's harder to forget that this was someone's life that's been scraped together and junked. If I was in charge, I'd sort things out the way my parents did, group like with like. Because who's ever going to buy a whole bedroom set these days?

Me, maybe? It would fill a lot of house.

Or maybe I should be thinking about more practical items. There's a letterbox basket, just along a bit, and I definitely need one of them. I open the flip top and take out handfuls of junk mail—Land's End catalogues, seed-and-bulb catalogues, Innovations catalogues, flyers galore, a couple of envelopes that look like real mail, but they're so clever at faking it these days. I stuff it all into a drying pile of old magazines inside a cracked plastic washing-up basin, and tuck the basket under my arm.

What next? There's a hall stand near where the letter basket was and of course there is, if this is a house hastily cleared and dumped in a pile. Which is still bothering me more than it should. I know it's because of Kai, really, but Peggy has completely taken over. It's the way she was scraped out of her house so efficiently, even if it was me who got the benefit. And then to have all her precious things—

But these aren't Peggy's things, I remind myself. John didn't clear Peggy's house. He just swore on his children's lives he didn't. That only makes it worse somehow: that she's not the only old lady this has happened to.

Helplessly, there in the mess and loss, I feel all the grief of the last year surge up to submerge the outside of my body, bubble up to drown the inside like it used to all the time at the start. It's as if I'm back at Andy Murray's golden pillar box again, and so I let myself cry.

It's when I finally sniff hard to help the tears stop that I smell it. There's something rotten back here. I breathe in again—a proper big whiff this time—and it's even stronger.

It's not the first time. Once when we were kids a rat died in a drawer and wasn't found for a week. It was summertime and the customer who came to tell us was waxy looking, the colour of cake mix before you bake it. John and I took off on our bikes as my dad headed back into the sheds with a bin bag.

This, I think, sniffing again and feeling my early-morning coffee shift in my stomach, is bigger than a rat. I hope it's not a stray cat or a lost dog. I keep following my nose but the stench is growing with every step, and I don't think I can stand it. I turn away and, blundering for an escape route, I find myself on John's new path he's made right up one side of the yard. I trot along it all the way to the front, only letting my breath go when I'm back at the big sheds again.

"Bad news," I say, letting myself into the cabin. "Something's died back past where that merry-go-round horse is. And it's not a mouse, I can tell you that much."

"It's probably slurry," says John. "On the fields." He glances at the letter basket still in my hand and lifts his eyebrows. "Help yourself, Lindsay. As ever."

I shake my head. "Nothing else smells like death, John. Cow shit smells *absolutely* nothing like it. Go and see for yourself, if you don't believe me. And I'll leave a fiver for this, of course. Only you need to refund me if it doesn't fit."

John frowns deeper than either a dead cat or a lippy sister should make him do and hauls himself out of his chair.

"Sorry about earlier," I say, taking a guess at what's wrong.

He doesn't answer, just takes a mask from an open packet on the counter and hooks it over his ears.

"They're handy, those last masks we never used, aren't they?" I say. I'm surprised, if I'm honest. I never thought of John as the squeamish type and I certainly didn't think of him as the mask type. He was first back in the pub after they lifted the lockdown.

"Take the bypass," I say, following him out. "You'll smell it up at the end."

"Bypass," he repeats, giving me a hard look from over the nose piece that he's pinched in hard.

"Your shortcut," I say. Then, to lighten the mood, I add, "Have you got a wee man cave back there or something?"

"I'm not that sort of man," he says, turning away. "Catch me being hounded out of my own house to live in a hut in the garden. Catch me marrying a woman who would try that on me." As if he doesn't spend three quarters of his life in a Portakabin. Mind you, I realise, he did have that poker game right in the dining room, cigar smoke and all. I feel uneasy remembering it, probably because of the state I was in that first night. I'm glad when Shelley comes out onto the step.

"I thought that was your car," she says. "Everything okay?"

"Rough night," I tell her. "Weird morning." Then I scrub my face hard, like you're not supposed to.

"Are you looking for John?" she says. She takes hold of the club hanging by a piece of string next to her makeshift gong and bangs it three times.

I hear pounding footsteps and John comes clattering round the appliance shed. "What?" he says. He looks wildly about the yard.

"Lindsay's here," Shelley tells him.

John pulls his mask down, spits on the ground and puts his hand on the side of the cabin to steady himself. "Jesus Christ, Shel. I nearly jumped out of—" He clears his throat. "Aye, I know Lindsay's here."

"Where were you?" says Shelley.

"I was right back in the Barrens," says John. "Christ almighty. So there's nothing actually wrong?"

"Is that where it was coming from?" I ask him. I was nowhere near that far back when the smell got too much for me. "What the hell is it? It can't be a rodent, as bad as all that."

"What's this?" says Shelley.

"Something's died," I say.

Shelley screws her face up and turns to John. "It might be the comfrey tea I made for my garden," she says.

"It's a fox," John says. "I'll bury it."

"You'll puke up your guts," says Shelley.

"Can't you just phone the council?" I ask.

"Don't you dare," says John, far too fierce. Then he rubs under his nose with the side of his finger and attempts a laugh. "Too many of my pals are on the council pick-up," he says. "I'd never live it down, calling them out."

"*I* could try," I say.

"You'd puke up your toenails," says John, which is true. "Leave it to me, Lindsay. You've done enough."

"Me?" I say, looking between the two of them. "What have I done except smell it?"

Shelley is shaking her head at him.

John stares at me for a moment or two before he speaks. "You came home," he says at last. "You're taking things off our hands, letting us clear out. The boys like having you near."

Shelley snorts. "You're bloody hopeless," she says. "Lindsay, he wants to stage some of our nice stuff in that big front room of yours and sell it online. Only he hasn't got the bottle up to ask you yet. Only he forgot he hasn't and just blabbed anyway."

John gives me a sheepish look and shrugs.

"Of course," I say. "What a good idea. It's the future, isn't it? Selling online. And speaking of my house, I better get back there. I've abandoned Chloe and David. Good luck with the fox." Shelley snorts again.

As I'm driving away, I can see them huddled together talking furiously at each other, neither one listening. It looks like an argument, but that doesn't make any sense. Whoever said no one knows what goes on inside a marriage might have based their conclusions on John and Shelley. I can't imagine what they've found to argue about in the two seconds since I left them.

Chapter 15

Back at Saint Helen's, I go in by the front door and the letterbox basket is a perfect fit. It hooks right onto a pair of old, overpainted nails sticking out there. I'm all set for my very own Land's End catalogue, as soon as they track me down, and my first *AudioFile* magazine, as soon as I restart my subscription.

I wouldn't have said I've got enough stuff to take them this long, but David and Chloe are still unpacking the kitchen, and I'd only get in the way. Anyway, thinking about *AudioFile* has fired me up and I want to see to my work equipment. I go up to my dead room and empty everything out of the packing cases. I'll only have to box it up again to install the sound insulation, and I haven't even ordered that yet, but these are old friends. Almost without thinking, I start to set them where they'll need to go.

When I'm finished, the workstation looks nothing like what Kai would have done, so neat and trim. Mine is a robotic sea creature, loops and clumps of wire trailing over the floor and switches underfoot as well, crammed onto the desk. The shock mount and boom arm are solid though, and the lights are green, the cursors blinking. It's ready for me to start. The last thing I do is set Kai's Earphones Award where I can see it every day.

Playing back first, to remind myself how good the sound was in Hilo, my own voice makes me realise how much I softened my accent without knowing. Maybe I better dial up the Clack now I'm home. They always say a Scottish accent is one of the most trusted, don't they? Then there's that last file from Kai. Maybe I'm remembering it worse than it was.

If you're there, Lindsay, that means I managed to shift this file to somewhere you're going to find it. I didn't want to leave it too long. I wanted to sound like me and I can feel my range narrowing every day. Anyway. So I died, huh? What a downer. You okay, babe? I want you to be okay. I want you to be happy. I want you to meet a nice guy—not too nice, but solid, you know? He'll cope with living in my shadow if he gets you thrown in. And then you and him can get started on those babies we were going to have if it had turned out that way. Deal? We got a deal? Try not to mind them being basic issue and not the angels we would have made. Love them anyway. And even if he doesn't show up, just go ahead and have the babies.

Seriously, Lin. I'm not going to tell you not to mourn. I would be ready to burn the earth to embers if it was me losing you. So, mourn. Grieve. Don't forget me. But be happy. You're living for two now, sweetheart. You're living for me as well as yourself. No slacking.

When it's finished, I'm as angry as I was last time. I put on my headphones and prepare myself.

"My nice guy is here," I say into the mic at the perfect distance. "And I *will* be happy." Only that little speech doesn't cover anything like all the danger sounds. "Fudge, chairs, groping," I say. Those were always my bêtes noires.

What I really need is the text with *all* the sounds. I know it off by heart, of course. All audio artists do. "The North Wind and the Sun," I say into the mic, ignoring my pulse beginning to lift and lighten. There is no way on what Kai always used to call "God's green-and-blue bowling ball" that I misheard John and Shelley that time and only imagined that's what they were saying. "The North Wind and the Sun had a quarrel about which of them was the stronger," I say, slow and steady as a lullaby. "While they were disputing, a traveller passed along the road wrapped in a cloak." And on and on until, "The North Wind was obliged to confess that the Sun was the stronger of the two. The end."

What did John claim they were saying?

"They're old enough to walk home," I say into the mic.

"Now shave," I add. "Naaooow shaaaaave."

I flick the counter back to hear how it sounds, and I don't even notice the echoes and buzzing telling me I'm going to have to spend a fortune in here. All I'm listening for is what a degraded version of those two phrases might sound like. The first gets me no further forward. It's either what I thought it was or it's *morth* (not a word) *wind and* (maybe *on*) *the Sun*. The second little snippet though, is a different story. My crappy far-from-dead room recording, played back, gives me a version of "now shave" that makes perfect sense. In one way. Although it raises even more questions in another.

"Nice save," I say to myself. *"Nice save?"*

They're *still* at it when I go down. Slow as they must have been going, though, they've got a good system running and they work in companionable silence. I watch as Chloe unravels the packing paper and hands it to David to fold and stuff back in an empty box, before he hands her another wrapped dish from a full one. I should wash them, I suppose, but for one thing I haven't got a dishwasher in this house and anyway, I like the idea that those tea stains on the cups I use all the time are made of the tea I bought in the ABC store and the water that came from our well. I like the idea that the dust on the big dishes I hardly ever use blew into the Hawaii house on the trade winds. It might even have bits of Kai in it. That's what they say about dust, don't they? Dead skin cells, mostly.

"What's wrong?" Chloe says.

"It sounds like a 1980s answering machine up there," I tell her. "Impossible. I just hope I can get the panels quickly. I can install it all myself—trained by the master, you know—but God knows how long the delivery time will be."

"I told you Lindsay thinks Britain is a third-world country," Chloe says to David. Then she blushes. She clears her throat and says to me, "Can you take over here? I need to run."

"You shouldn't have been unpacking stuff when you're all dressed up anyway," I say.

"I'm not all dressed up," she says, colouring even more. Maybe she's got a date with "love you too."

And then she's gone, with no more than a quick peck on my cheek, before I can ask her what's the matter.

"That was weird," says David. "I mean, unless she's always like that."

"No, that was weird," I say. "Like everything else. I kind of hoped you two would get on when I finally unleashed you on her." He gives me a look I can't begin to decipher and, far too late, I realise I've made it sound as if I think he's a long-term fixture.

"Lindsay." He looks as uncomfortable as I feel.

"I know!" I say. "Sorry. I'm kicking myself."

"What? Can I say something?"

"You don't have to," I tell him. "That was a slip."

"I wanted to wait until you were moved and everything before I brought this up." It's something else then. "The thing is," he goes on, "I was wondering if we could slow down on the 'going out' thing."

It is the most awkward, mealy-mouthed sentence I've ever heard him say. The suave top lawyer is gone. And, even as break-up lines go, it's one of the worst I've been treated to. This soon after listening to Kai's half-hearted goodbye again, it enrages me.

"Nah," I say. "I'm not interested in 'slowing down.' Let's just call it quits." God, I'm proud of myself.

"What?" It comes out in a yelp.

"I don't like games, David. Never have. If you don't want to go out with me anymore, then just tell me. I'm a big girl. I'll live."

He has put his hands over his face and now he pulls them down, stretching his lower eyelids until he looks like a basset hound, leaving white finger marks on his cheeks. When his hands drop free, I can see that he's smiling. "Oh my God!" he says. "I don't mean stop seeing you. I mean literally stop 'going out' so much. Drinks, films, dinner, bloody *brunch*! I'm falling behind at work and between us painting the town and the boys there half the time, I'm knackered."

"Oh," I manage to get in.

"I *meant* now you're moved into your own place and we're approaching Aileen's probation-period milestone, I thought you could come round to mine, eat pasta and watch the telly. Or I could come round to yours and do the same."

"Oh," I say again. "Right. So, pretty much the exact opposite of stepping back and slowing down, then? Much more like stepping forward and speeding up." He beams at me. Then my brain catches up with the rest of what he said. "What do you mean about Aileen?"

"Ach, she's hard-nosed about the boys not meeting anyone until they've proved they're suitable," he says. "As if she didn't take them straight to a flat she was already sharing with a woman they'd never met."

"And even *I* have to do probation?" I say. "I was at school with her."

"That's a good point," he says, looking startled. I think he had forgotten. "And you haven't changed much." I frown. "You still call what we're doing 'going out.'" He crosses his arms and taps his foot. "Ma pal's not going out with your pal now, so I'm not going out with you." It's a perfect imitation of a mouthy schoolgirl and it makes me laugh.

"What would *you* call it then?" I say. "What we're doing?" I'm joking, mostly. I want to unsettle him, for payback. To my surprise, he takes it seriously.

"We, Lindsay Lord Hale," he says, "are trying again. You up for that? Hey!" He leaps forward because, me thinking about everything standing in the way of "trying again" has made a sob wrench itself out of my chest and now suddenly tears are pouring down my face. Snot forms bubbles at both my nostrils and I'm wailing. "I am so sorry," he says. "I'm rushing you. I can wait. Please don't cry."

"It's not that," I say. "It's something else."

"Tell me."

No way, I think, then I find myself telling him everything. I tell him I'm scared of the house and I've made a mistake. I tell him I heard noises last night that sounded like an intruder and that my book moved. I tell him I think the person who used to live here before doesn't want me to live here and is trying to drive me off.

"But you don't really believe that, do you?" he asks me.

"No!" I wail. "I think I'm going mad. I keep thinking I don't really own this house, even though I bought it. And I thought John was lying to me about clearing it, because of a bloody biscuit tin with bog-standard biscuits in it, as if they were some kind of Sherlock Holmes cigar ash or something. It's not *just* this house though. I was freaked out at the yard because a fox died in the back bit where no one goes. And I think I recognise people I've never met—that poor estate agent in Bridge of Allan. He thought I was trying to pick him up! And then I *don't* recognise people I should! I can't remember Aileen for the life of me, but Chloe knew her and Chloe and I were joined at the hip all through school, so that makes no sense at all. And it's *sounds* too now. Words. That's my job. That's my whole— That's what I do and if I can't do that, I'm . . . And I'm having nightmares. I've started having this one about there being splinters under my fingernails and when I try to pick them out I just drive them in deeper."

"Yes, you mentioned the splinters," he says. "Nasty. But it sounds like normal stress at a stressful time." He tucks my head in under his chin and rubs my back.

"I know," I say. "I mean, it must be, right? But that's what I mean. It doesn't *feel* like that. It feels as if there's something big and horrible just out of view and I keep seeing scraps that I can't make sense of. Like everything's connected and I don't know how. That's what I'm telling you: I think I'm going mad. And that's not even the truth of it. I *hope* I'm going mad."

He waits.

"Because the other possibility is that there's nothing wrong with my mind but there's something wrong with my brain. Like Kai. That the sounds are auditory glitches like he had, and the visual stuff too—even though I kind of know what that is and it's just childhood shit, but then there's the memory loss and face blindness. Because it's unrelated, him and me. People get brain tumours all the time and Kai's cancer makes it not one iota less likely that I'll get the same thing. It's magical thinking to say his cancer inoculated me. But I've got no balance issues or nausea or—"

David takes my arms in a firm grip and moves me back. "You don't have a brain tumour," he says.

"Are you a doctor?"

"You've got stress and exhaustion—"

"But, even when I had the stress and exhaustion of tracking Kai's symptoms, I never psyched myself into having them too."

"—stress and exhaustion, I was going to say, and a family and friends that, frankly, tell you what to do far too much and then have the nerve to call it supporting you."

I blink at him. He's right. But how did he know? What have I said that's clued him in so completely?

He lets go and turns away to pour me a glass of water and, as I stare at him, his back flattens to tissue paper. I squeeze my eyes hard shut and when I look again it's a tiny bit better. Painted card, but with a jolt like an extra step in the dark, I think I recognise him. Then I laugh. Of course I recognise him. It's David! I *know* David. My head has scrambled itself because I've been letting all my fears out at last and sharing them.

Once I've drunk a good bit of the water, he pulls me back in close. "What you need," he says, rubbing my back again with one hand but also now smoothing my hair with the other, "is a short course of treatment that consists of eating pasta on a couch and watching trashy telly, beside someone who cares about you very deeply." He squeezes me. "And a project or two. Get your dead room sorted out and get back to work. In the meantime, find where your old man was and make your donation."

"Old lady," I say, mumbling into his chest. "There's an old man next door, but it was an old lady who lived here and died. Peggy March."

"Find your old lady's nursing home and give them a massage chair or a croquet set or whatever you were thinking. And I bet you'll stop hearing noises in the night."

Chapter 16

He didn't so much as hint at it, but that night I don't slip my nightie over my head as soon as I shed my clothes. Instead, I rub lotion onto my knees and elbows and inspect the rest of me. I need a waxing and either a pedicure or a long soak in a bath and a good go with a pumice stone. Right now, he would have to be pretty drunk. Although, of course, I haven't seen any of him except the bottoms of his legs when he's had long shorts on, his forearms when he's rolled his sleeves up, and a vee at his neck where his shirt lies open. His grey hair might be premature, I suppose. He might be lean and smooth. Or maybe he's fifty and things are beginning to droop. I kind of hope so; that would be so much less intimidating. I was twenty-six the last time someone new saw what I'm looking at under the bathroom light right now.

In bed, I pick up my plain brown book but I don't so much as open it. Even without the jacket, I can't face a story about a woman younger than me, married to the love of her life, with a wise old lady waiting in the wings to help her out of all her troubles. I put it back on the bedside table and pick up my phone to look at listings instead. I've got my house and I'm never moving again but I need the escapism. Who doesn't love casting a critical eye over a house they can't afford and deciding the kitchen isn't up to snuff?

But it's palled, since the last time. Nowhere is as amazing as where I am and too many of the big old houses have got stairlifts and walk-in baths, showing how their owners fought back against the inevitable.

I add "recently sold" to my search filter and try again, but still there's none of the charm I'm used to finding. I close the app and settle down to sleep.

"Nice save," I whisper to myself, proud that I stopped scrolling as soon as I realised I wasn't enjoying it. *Nice save.*

Weird that Saint Helen's wasn't there in the recently sold, I think, turning onto my side, and Chloe seemed to suggest that the sale was unusual, back when she was organising a viewing. And it really did feel like a massive bargain. But David vetted everything . . . David . . . If he *is* fifty, he might not want to contemplate more children. And he could be. The way he spoke to me, comforting and assured, it was like our family doctor calming me down before jags. I hunch over onto my side. It wasn't just David though. There was Farmer George the estate agent too. Estate agents aren't dodgy. I've seen them on the property shows, respectability shining out of their eyes and trustworthiness oozing out of every pore.

Only he *was* dodgy, wasn't he? He was sketchy as hell from the first moment I clapped eyes on him. The first moment, according to *him*, that is. *I'm* still sure I'd seen him before. Although I was in such a cloud of misery then that everything's hazy.

And, again, the proof of it all being above board is the fact that I'm here. Of course I bought the house. Yes, Peggy moved out suddenly, but the house was for sale and I bought it and here I am. Safe at home. I just need to stop my brain from spiralling.

I'd give anything for a cup of Shelley's sleepy tea right now. When I get a doctor, I'll ask for a prescription. We used to joke about Kai's big tub of drugs. If I had kept some, would I take something now, just to stop all this swirling in my head and go to sleep?

But I do sleep—I must—because I spring awake again in the small hours at the sound of a banging door. This time, the footsteps I hear aren't ghostly and drifting. They aren't Bunny's shuffles or Chloe's tip-tap heels either. These feet wallop along so hard that the house shakes. I jump out of bed, heart hammering, looking round for a weapon in case he comes up the stairs. Of course he'll come upstairs. He's not a burglar—they're stealthy. This, right here, tonight, in my house, is a—

I won't finish that thought. Instead, I tug at the lamp, to arm myself, but the stupid British three-pin plug stops me dead and means I only wrench my wrists and stretch the cord. An American lamp would be in my hands like a baseball bat by now. What else is there? I pick up my water glass and my book—paperback or not—and crouch behind the door, like a cat ready to spring. After counting ten shaky breaths, I slowly realise that the steps are disappearing towards the back of the house on the ground floor. I chuck the book, set the glass down and lunge for my phone.

"I'm looking at him right now," I say to the police dispatcher, minutes later, as she tries to convince me I was dreaming, or it was a fox in the bins, maybe kids in the street. "He's running through my garden." She interrupts. "Yeah, but he *was* inside. I heard him come in. That's what woke me. And he's no kid. He looks like a . . ."

He looks like an ogre is what he looks like, pounding down the length of the garden towards the back hedge with his shirt tail flapping and his big boots leaving deep dents in my grass, even as dry as it's been. Ogre? No, of course not. That's only because I've been asleep and probably dreaming. He's just a big, solid man. That's bad enough, but I'm talking to the cops. I'm safe.

I go downstairs, still on the phone, ready to say that my front lock is burst and my kitchen door is hanging open. But the front doors are locked tight, the glass one and the wood one too. I scurry through the kitchen to the back lobby. This door is locked from the inside.

"Lindsay?" the dispatcher says. "Are you still there?"

"He shut the doors after himself," I say. "Or wait—no, he went out a different way. Hang on."

"Intruders don't generally—" she says before I click her off speaker. She's right, but I don't want to hear it. The garden-room doors are shut too but he slipped up here. The key that should be in the lock is lying on the floor, as if he pushed it through from the outside. In fact, I know he did, because he made another mistake. As he bent down, he put one of his big ogre hands against the glass to steady himself and he has left a perfect print, showing clearly with the moonlight behind it.

"There's a handprint," I say. "There's a clear print of his palm and all five fingers."

"Inside?" says the dispatcher, doubtfully.

"Well, no, because he was outside and he pushed the key under the door after he locked up."

There's a long pause. "Are you alone in the house?" she asks me, as if the next question might be whether she can talk to my minder.

"Yes," I say. "And this isn't the first time this has happened. I only just moved in and I don't know who all's got keys, see? But someone was inside the first night too."

"You just moved in?"

"My husband died recently and I've moved here all on my own."

My ploy fails. "Stressful time," she says.

I could scream. Apart from anything else, reminding myself that I really am alone has started me shaking. It shows in my voice as I try to persuade her.

"I didn't imagine it," I say. "A man in a checked shirt and big boots got into my house, ran through it and left the back way. The last one that was in here left something by my bed. You might be able to get fingerprints off it."

"What did he leave?"

"A book." It sounds stupid. There's no way I'm going to tell her it was the book I was reading.

"Did you get a picture of him? Either the one tonight or before?"

I know she thinks I'm high on something or a fantasist, so I tell her I'll get a picture of the handprint and any footprints too and that I'll be in tomorrow morning to make an official report of the incident, bringing the . . . bedside item with me. I wish I sounded less feeble. I wish she sounded less bored. I ring off.

The flash dazzles when I try to take a photo of the glass but it's too dark to get anything at all without it. Lights on or off, inside or out, it's all hopeless. And the grass has sprung back already. I can't pick out his route through the garden no matter how I squint and stoop. I trail to the far end and check the hedge and the wall there. There are some broken branches, the sharp, soapy smell of bruised privet leaves rising above the rich stink of the blossom. I had forgotten that summer smells like floral cheese in Scotland when the privet hedges are blooming.

There are a couple of scrapes on the top of the wall. But even I have to admit that they could have been caused by anything, anytime. I turn and pad back over the grass in my bare feet, feeling the dry blades squeak and snap under my weight. I lock up tight and take the key out. Then I sit in the echoing garden room just about exactly where I fell asleep that first day with Peggy March. Who will I call? John? Chloe? David? Who *do* you call when the police don't believe you?

I tell myself I'll make them sorry in the morning, then I go to the kitchen, get a sandwich bag and head back to my bedroom. My book is lying open, face down on the floor where I threw it. I put the bag over my hand as if I'm picking up dog shit and flip the pages to close it.

Then I stop. I'm looking at the first page of the first chapter and something's wrong. The first sentence is about two people called George and Kathy Lutz and a place called Ocean Avenue. It *should* be about Gwenda Reed arriving at Plymouth docks. I turn back until I'm at the title page. The book slips out of my hand and smacks to the floor again.

I was reading *Sleeping Murder*. That book lying on the bare boards of my bedroom is *The Amityville Horror*.

I have never owned this book. Kai didn't own this book. We were too young for the splash when it came out, far too young to watch the film when it hit the big screen. So I know for sure, I didn't pack this book. I didn't unpack it. And I've only put a brown paper cover on one book since I left school. There is no way this is some innocent mix-up. No, I think to myself, so strangely calm that I'm almost floating, this is . . .

But I can't finish the thought, because the only thing this could be is something I will not let into my mind. At first, Kai's hallucinations were . . . not funny, exactly . . . but interesting, like clues to be solved, like dreams to be unpicked over breakfast the next morning. And I know what he would have said about this one. "It was there in your brain, babe. You set up your dead room today and remember we once listened to a sample of it? Worst. Narrator. Evuh! So you're having a back-to-work anxiety hallucination. That's my girl."

I leave it where it lies. Then I go back round the house again and double-check every window latch, every lock. I lock all the doors and take all the keys with me. When I go back to bed, I fall asleep with a heap of keys on my bedside table and my phone clutched in my hand.

I dream of faceless strangers, and warrens of abandoned furniture that I'm racing through, filled with rage and terror. I dream of the splinters again and whispers too this time and Kai, of course, always Kai, out of sight and fading. I dream of Dr. Cho, in Hilo, asking if I'm sleeping and telling me I need to take care of myself if I want to take care of David. "Kai," I tell her. But she's gone. She's a tarot reader now. "Morth binned on the sun," she tells me. "Those aren't tarot cards," I say. "They're not big enough." There's another doctor here now and I don't know who they are. "It's only a story," I say. "No," says the new doctor, "it's true." Then Kai is right there, like I've found him. "I don't think you got it yet, babe," he says. "Sorry." And I start awake, shaking.

It was years ago. It was before the pandemic. It was just a regular casting for a popular self-help book coming to audio for the first time.

"Huh," Kai said, looking at my marked-up excerpt. "PTSD?"

"And its more complex cousin, C-PTSD," I said.

"Nice," he said, but I knew what he meant: Those crisp sounds all in a row like little soldiers would be a joy to speak, an anchor in every sentence, bright and clean, like a garnish on a meal, or a touch of snare on top of a melody.

I was so cocky, years into my happy marriage, thousands of miles away, wrapped in my stories, everything else safely locked in a caravan back in the old country.

I didn't have a clue.

It was a wonderful book, kind and wise and startling to someone like me who knew none of it. She wrote about kidnaps and car crashes, about combat veterans and battered wives, about first responders and refugees. And children, of course. Because a book about trauma and terror and darkness that didn't cover adult survivors . . . would be like trying to do *Jaws* without the shark.

I recorded my excerpt, spitting out those bright sounds, slowing on the medical stuff, lightening on the case studies. Then I just kept reading. I read until my file was full and I read on. I read until my voice was a croak and then a whisper and then I was mouthing the words and the only sound was the click of my throat when I swallowed.

Afterwards, when I was lying on my bed, staring at the ceiling, watching the fan revolve, Kai went looking for me in the dead room and found my abandoned station. He must have listened to a minute or two. Of course he did. I would have. We had no secrets.

He came and sat on the edge of the bed, putting his warm hand on my clammy skin where my sweat had cooled in the blades of the fan.

"I don't think you got it yet, babe," he said with a rueful twist of a smile. He didn't enjoy having to be that honest with me. "Sorry."

No secrets.

Kai filed it under: My wife doesn't have the right voice for self-help.

And I did too.

This can't shan't mustn't cannot be happening. This cannot be happening to me. Did I pass out? Where am I? Am I alone? I hope I'm alone and then I wonder for a second why that's what I'm hoping.

Only for a second, though, until I remember the alternative. Until I remember who would be here, if anyone was. Not that I know a name or a face or even a voice. All I know is that I'm in danger if they return. Much better to be on my own.

I knew it right away—dramatic and unlikely as that might seem. I knew I wasn't being foolish, knew I wasn't misguided or mistaken. I knew.

I knew once before, you see, one night when a man got onto a train and chose to sit near me in an empty carriage. I knew he wasn't preoccupied with his own thoughts. I knew that no matter how fixedly he looked in the other direction, all his attention was trained on me.

After that night I swore I would never be polite again. I was done with what good girls and nice ladies get.

And yet here I am, here I am, here I am again and worse than last time, even though tonight I kept my old promise to myself. Tonight I refused to worry about feeling foolish. I refused to care about overreacting. I didn't—for one second—consider waiting and seeing what happened next, when already in the first split second I knew.

Tonight, I screamed as loud as I could until I thought my lungs would burst, kicking and jabbing and ready to bite if I could. I scrabbled desperately for something heavy, or sharp, and I would have lashed out like a . . .

I should think a falcon because they are the fastest, but what I imagine is striking like a rattlesnake, earthbound and vicious, out of nowhere.

Lashing out as I did caught them off guard; that was clear. And it bought me a second or two. But it didn't work.

The next best time is now. I wonder if I made that up, or did I hear it somewhere? It doesn't matter and I mustn't let my thoughts drift. I must concentrate my wits, summon all my strength, and then, when I get the chance, I shall strike.

Only . . .

It is so cold. And it is so dark. And I have no idea where I am or even what kind of place this is or why this is happening to me. Or whether, in fact, this is really happening to me.

This cannot, it suddenly seems quite obvious, be happening to me. If I sleep, then when I wake, it will all be gone like a dream.

Chapter 17

My palm is sweating when I wake up, my fingers cramped from clutching the hard corners of my phone case. I feel pretty foolish when I look over and see the keys, like a little iron bonfire on my bedside table. I feel even more ridiculous when I get out of bed and pick up the book from the floor, flipping it open to chapter eleven of *Sleeping Murder*, with Miss Marple out for a walk on the prom at Dillmouth. I climb back under the covers and lie listening to the rain that started overnight. It's lashing against my bedroom window like someone hurling gravel. He would have left prints on the grass if it had rained even an hour or two earlier. If he was real. He *was* real. He left a handprint on the—

I leap out of bed and go downstairs at a gallop, holding my bottom lip in my teeth as I wheel round the finial post and into the garden room.

"No!" I say, loud enough to make it ring out in this still almost empty room. I go closer to check but I know already. The rain has washed that handprint off the outside of the glass, leaving no trace.

If he was real. If I wasn't dreaming.

"I *wasn't* dreaming," I say out loud to myself. But I'm not sure I believe me. Because I was dreaming the switcheroo of books. And wasn't I half convinced I knew who it was, that "ogre" who ran through my house exactly the way someone would in a dream? The way no housebreaker or mad axeman ever would in real life. And isn't it much more likely that I would half recognise a man inside my dream than in the real world, in the dead of night? I crouch down at the French windows and try to wiggle my fingers in under the stiff bristles of the draught excluder. It could be done. I can feel raindrops on my fingertips, so he could have pushed the key back inside, couldn't he? But it's much more likely that a draught in one of the chimneys of this house, whose habits I've yet to learn, shook the frame, waking me and dislodging the key. Maybe the wind, maybe the north wind, was already picking up, just about to bring the rain, instead of the sun. And I dreamed the rest.

I didn't realise I had brought my phone with me, and I jump when it buzzes in my hand.

David Minto, the screen tells me. I try to sound cheerful when I answer it and say hello.

"How about starting Operation Old Farts tonight?" he says. "Why not come round to mine and let me make you a delicious Italian meal? At the twist of a Ragú jar lid, that is. It's a decent night on the telly."

Suddenly nothing sounds better than getting away from this house.

"I've got to warn you, it's a bit of a bitter divorce cliché," he says. "But as long as you don't judge me . . ."

My heart sinks a bit, although I say nothing. I wanted to be in a *home*, messy, full of football boots and Xboxes. Photos on the fridge. I accept anyway and tell him I'll bring wine.

When the phone rings again a minute later, I assume it's David telling me red or white, but it's Dunblane Police Station, doing a follow-up, and I get to live through total humiliation for a long five minutes, confirming that nothing was taken from or left in my house and no one was there and all the doors and windows were locked at all times and, yes, I probably do need to speak to my doctor, thank you.

I spend the rest of the day flattening boxes, wondering why I didn't make any attempt to clear out before I packed up. Of course, I had just been forced to let go of my most precious gift, so the thought of discarding school report cards or old playbills was horrendous. But as I flip through them now, I think I'm more than ready to let them go. I don't want to find places for them in my new home, folding them into my new start. It still is a new start, if a bit dented by the mess inside my brain. Still something to hold on to.

◆ ◆ ◆

David is wearing an apron when he answers the door at six o'clock, but not in a jokey way to have an effect on me, just as if he's got good shirts and doesn't want to splash them with sauce while he's piercing the film. His house is not what I expected, not at all what I thought he was warning me about. It's the Doune equivalent of Saint Helen's, in fact. A big square of stone with a carved peak on the porch and mullioned windows.

"What kind of bitter divorce cliché is this then?" I say, waving around as he takes my jacket and slings it over a hall stand with antler pegs and a chinoiserie umbrella stand underneath.

"Well," he says, "Aileen didn't particularly want to keep the family home—because Mrs. Aileen didn't want to move in and who can blame her—so I just about bankrupted myself hanging on to it."

"I thought you meant black leather couches and a monster TV," I say.

He laughs uncomfortably and points the way into a room across the hall, where I find three leather couches, in charcoal grey, and the biggest telly I have ever seen in my life, hanging on the short wall.

"I've been in cinemas with smaller screens than that," I say. "Have you got a waterbed?"

"And a mini dressing gown in red satin, to match the sheets," he says. "Drink?" He gives my bottle of wine an approving look and carries on into a kitchen stuffed with stainless steel and more knives than a professional chef would need, even if he filleted his own fish straight from the market and butchered sides of beef.

"So how have you been?" he asks me.

"Terrible then fine," I tell him. "Mad, weird, waking nightmares then six hours of *sleeping* nightmares and an okay day." He gives me a concerned look and I do consider telling him, but who wants to hear that their girlfriend called the cops and gave them a load of nonsense. "I've been wandering down memory lane all day, unpacking papers," I say instead, sitting on a high stool and watching him debag and rinse a salad. "I still can't remember Aileen, you know. I don't suppose you've got photos of her from years back, have you? It's bothering me."

"You're kidding," he says. He puts the salad in a wooden bowl and opens the fridge. "I cut the family photos into origami, trying to get her out of them but keep the boys and the dog." He's looking at the sell-by dates on a selection of bottles of salad dressing.

"Kirigami," I say. "Origami is folds." I hold my breath. This could be the moment I find out that, like most men, he doesn't like being told things.

"Honey mustard okay?" he says. Then he looks up. "How the hell do you know that? Are you crafty? Will you start giving me candles and scarves if I don't nip it in the bud now?"

"I narrated a history of paper," I said. "It was surprisingly interesting. But I wouldn't have thought it sold many copies, so I won't be narrating the sequel."

"What would the sequel be?" he says. He takes two trays of food out of the fridge and slips them free of their cardboard wrappers. "The *future* of paper? The history of plastic?"

"You've got a very logical mind," I tell him.

"Goes with the job," he says. Then, for some reason, he watches me very closely to see what I make of this. Maybe he thinks he's boasting. Or maybe he thinks I'll think he's boasting, ramming it home that he's a posh lawyer and I'm just someone who reads things out for people. I hope not, because I'm proud of my job and the business we built up, Kai and me.

"Speaking of jobs," I say, "you know the compliment I get most often from people who email me?" I accept a glass of the wine he seems to think has been breathing for long enough now. I know letting wine breathe is an old wives' tale, but I don't tell him this. "They say they listen to the books I read to help them go to sleep."

"Rude!"

"Not at all," I say, even though I'm glad he thinks so; I'm glad he doesn't realise I was doing a bit of boasting right back at him. "It's rude to the author if the content doesn't keep them awake, but it's high praise for me if my voice sends them off. I think so, anyway."

He has closed the fridge door again and he leans forward until his head is resting against it and starts snoring.

I take a big drink of wine, feeling my heart open and rise up like a burp bubble. It's been a long time since I talked nonsense with someone puttering around in a kitchen on an ordinary weekday evening. They're dead right that it's the small things you miss. This is such a tiny thing I wouldn't even have been able to name it, but I flood with happiness, welcoming it back again.

"So I spoke to Aileen again," David says, sliding onto the stool opposite me with a full glass. The trays of food are still sitting on the worktop. "About you coming round when the boys are here. Bloody ridiculous, as you pointed out. I pointed it out too and she said all she knew about you was that you were a dab hand at painting trainers and onions, hated PE, and once melted a sink drain in the science block."

"Wow, she really does remember me, doesn't she?" I say. "I wasn't a vandal, by the way. It was the chemistry teacher's fault. We were pouring away some noxious stuff and he told us to pour the acid before the alkaline."

"So you did an experiment? Out of intellectual curiosity?"

"No! He said pour the acid first. Don't pour the alkaline first. The alkaline must follow the acid. If the acid doesn't precede the blah blah blah . . . pour the alkaline and the acid in the right order."

"Well then he was a complete pillock," says David. "I can't remember which way to pour them out now either."

"Exactly!" I take a drink. "So . . . was Aileen *in* my chemistry class? I was looking through school stuff earlier and, like I said, I still can't remember her. I feel terrible. When you're going to bat for me. And like I also said, I don't like brain stuff I can't explain."

"Only natural," he says, rubbing his knuckles over mine. This is even better than the winding up. If he can sort of half allude to Kai without making a big deal of it, he'll be a very unusual sort of man.

"Haven't you got official school photos?" he says next.

"No idea what happened to them. They're probably in Shelley's loft. Anyway, don't bug Aileen *too* much. She's only being protective."

"You might well think so," David says. "I probably shouldn't comment."

This very mild bitch about his ex-wife is the only bum note in the entire evening. Not to mention the night. I go to sleep with his arms around me, after both of us agreeing that we'll literally just sleep together this time. And sleep I do: no dreams, no drama. When I wake up, the sun is lasering through a gap in the curtains. He has moved away from me at some point and banked me up with a pillow instead of his shoulder, but I never even stirred. I prop myself up on one elbow and look over at him lying flat on his back on the other side of the bed, with his arms over his head as if he's trying to look slim in a picture. The covers are around his waist and there's a four-inch band of skin between the top of the sheet and the bottom of his T-shirt. There's a promising looking tent-effect at his hips too and I feel an answering twinkle inside myself. Not that I'm not grateful to take things slowly, but it doesn't hurt. I look beyond him at the rest of the bedroom. The big windows are aggressively clean and the pale carpet too. There's no clutter and no lapses of taste. He must have shed his share of the married furniture and started afresh with a designer to help him. And he must have a cleaner too, I reckon, if it's not too sexist to think so.

"Do I pass?" he asks suddenly.

I jump and then laugh, relieved that I'm inspecting the room and not his body, although he sounds completely alert. He was probably awake when I *was* inspecting him, just keeping his eyes shut to trick me.

"Do you always wake up like that?" I say. "Bang! Hit the On button."

He turns away and swings his legs out without answering me, picks a dressing gown up from the floor and swirls it on as he walks towards the door. "I'll spare you the en suite," he says. "I'm a noted farter first thing. But *you've* got five clear minutes while I'm downstairs getting coffee." He turns back. "Or tea?"

"Black coffee," I say. "And thank you."

My whole mood has swung back round again. Was I always such a weathervane? Is this part of grieving? Can I still blame things on grieving when I'm in another man's bed? Whatever. This morning I feel ready for life. I'll register with a practice and speak to my new doctor. And I'll inhabit my house better, spread myself through it and make it a haven.

Or I could think about something else entirely. Something bigger than yourself, as they say. I could concentrate on finding the last home of Peggy March. When I do, I'm going to make much more of a contribution than just donating a box set or a board game. I'm going to visit someone there, the way I would have visited Peggy if I could. I might even try to organise a whole raft of visitors for all the nursing homes. I'm still smarting about the reception I got that first day when I tried to find her. No way it should be so unusual for friends to drop in that it puts all the staff on high alert.

"What do you know about the Freedom of Information Act?" I ask David when he comes back with a pot of coffee and two cups on a tray. "Or wait! Death certificates! They're public record, aren't they? Do they include last addresses?"

"Is this your old lady again?" David says. "I don't think FOI is for personal details. And death certificates take a while to work through and get into the searchable record. I think it would probably be best to ask at the council offices. They regulate the nursing homes, don't they?"

"Huh," I say. "Perfect for this neck of the woods." He frowns at me. "Right here, where the four counties meet. It's a nightmare." He gives me a blank look as if it's never occurred to him. But then it wasn't part of his childhood, listening to his dad ranting about hazardous-waste restrictions and bulk-collection rates from four different local authorities. "What did your dad do?" I ask him.

"Same as me," he says. Then adds, "Law. He was a proper country solicitor. Wills, conveyancing, disputes over trees on the boundary. In fact, now you mention it, forget the four councils. Despite my treachery in going to the big bad city, I might be able to lean on some of his old pals and get your info."

"You mean through her son? Through her will?"

"That's a bit roundabout," he says. "I meant, get someone to call Register House and sweet-talk them into accessing the pending records and find her last address."

"Couldn't a Flash Harry like you do that yourself?" I say. "Wouldn't they jump higher if *you* asked them?"

He laughs. "You've got a lot to learn about Edinburgh politics," he says. "If I asked, it would be an imposition, but if some sweet old buffer phones up from Yetts o' Muckhart, they'll delight in helping him. I know just who I'm going to ask to do it too. His name is Stourton Stout. He's a legend."

"Stout?" I say. "That was Chloe's married name. I wonder if he's an ex-in-law."

"What did Chloe's husband do?"

"Um, he drove a van for a tyre-supply company," I say and burst out into disloyal giggling. "Probably not, eh?"

David waggles his eyebrows and says, "I wouldn't have thought so."

Chapter 18

Stourton Stout, the legend, comes up trumps. It's barely lunchtime on Monday when David texts me apologising for not calling over the weekend but telling me that Margaret March, formerly of Saint Helen's in Dunblane, moved to the HDU unit at Forth Valley from the Elms, in Kincardine.

"That's quite a smile," Chloe says. "What's put that on your face?"

She sounds the tiniest bit put out and I suppose she's got a point. After all, she got three complete sets of different grades of acoustic panel and filler, delivered overnight, with free returns on the two unwanted packages, then she organised the fitting and whisked away every scrap of cardboard, plastic, tape, Bubble Wrap and paper, except the VAT receipt, which she offered to file for me. And she did it all over a busy weekend when I didn't actually see her, hence this weekday lunch date.

I'm sitting in her office perched on an upturned mop bucket, with two meal deals on the desk between us. I called her on the off chance she was free to be taken out and spoiled and decided to go ahead even though she said she only had half an hour and didn't want to leave HQ because of a big delivery of her own. HQ, at the other end of Menstrie from Lord's Yard, is more or less an oversized lock-up garage with this tiny office carved out at the back beside an even smaller staff toilet. There's room for the two vans she uses for major commercial cleaning jobs and a run of shelves where tools and products, uniforms, and car clingers are stored in meticulous order, with tick sheets to approve the removal of even a single pair of rubber gloves. I've seen dentists' surgeries grubbier than Chloe's nerve centre. It's as clean as David's bedroom.

I unwrap my sandwich and flatten out the cardboard to make a plate, Chloe's sharp eye watching for bits of cress dropping out.

"David's helping me find my old lady," I say.

Chloe snorts and then coughs. "Sorry, that sounded filthy." I feel myself flush. True to form, Chloe takes that as permission to plough on. "How far *have* things advanced? I liked him from what I could tell the other morning. He seems . . . normal."

"I thought you were going to say nice!"

"Normal's much harder to find than nice," she says. "I bet you're being 'nice' to him at the moment too. Anyone can do *nice*. Did I tell you about Cling Film Clifford?"

I take a bite of sandwich and waggle my eyebrows. Chloe's bad boyfriends are always an entertainment.

"He saved food," she says. "He'd save half a pat of butter from a roll in a café. He saved teabags—used teabags, this is—from motorway services. He took home a sprig of parsley and a wedge of lemon from the side of a plate of scampi once."

"Where the hell did you find scampi?" I say. "Was he a time traveller?"

"Okay, calamari," says Chloe. "Not the point. The last straw was when he poured half a wee tub of long-life milk into a Ziploc bag and told me it freezes."

"What was the upside?"

"Absolutely fantastic in bed," Chloe says. "Attention to detail, if you catch my drift."

"And was he really called Clifford?"

She pauses. I'm not sure if she's reluctant to tell me, or if she's building up my expectations. At last she says, "Lance."

"Lancelot?"

"Short for Lawrence. Except it's not, is it? So he had to deliberately choose it."

"Better than Larry," I point out, on my way out the door.

R U sure about Elms? I text back to David when I'm sitting in my car again. Cos I'm 90% certain I *asked* them when I first started. If it's the big one with the steep bank down to the river just as you head into the town.

It's the longest text I've ever sent.

He texts back a shrug made of dashes and brackets. He can't be very busy this afternoon. Anyway, it's silly to imagine he'd know anything about the Elms one way or the other. I roll my eyes at myself in the rearview mirror and head down to Kincardine to ask—again, I'm convinced—if Peggy March ever lived there.

David texts me again while I'm driving, and I read it off the display. Yours tomorrow? it says. Otherwise I'll have to go shopping. It should be offensive but he makes such a bad job of hiding his enthusiasm under unconvincing casualness that I find it charming instead. So I'm smiling when I slow down to turn into the nursing home drive. And it *is* the same place where I met the *now shave* man who smelled like an ashtray. I'm peering out at the slalom of shallow ramps and the net-muffled windows of the very nursing home where I got sent packing with a flea in my ear. But this time I'm armed with information, not questions, and I come bearing gifts. Or promises of gifts anyway. I march up the steps that are still there beside the lifts and ramps and walk inside.

It's that same man I thought I recognised last time, sitting at the desk, still stinking of smoke, but dressed up like a country laird today instead of someone who's come to fix the photocopier.

"Afternoon," he says, blandly polite. He doesn't remember me and he doesn't know I overheard *Nice save.*

"Afternoon to you too," I say. His shirt and sideburns are making me talk like someone from *Monarch of the Glen.* "I'm here about Peggy March."

"Ah," he says. "Well then, I've got some bad tidings for you. Mrs. March died, I'm afraid. It was sudden and painless but she's gone. I'm sorry to have to break such sad news."

I nod along with him while he's speaking, managing not to let my lip curl. It would be odd anyway that he doesn't seem to care who I am this time, when he was so fierce before—although, I suppose, being generous, dead residents are hard to disturb—but *Nice save* changes everything and I can't think of this guy as a straight dealer anymore. "I heard that she had died," I say, "and, the thing is, I want to make some sort of gesture in her memory. I'd like to donate. To your home." It's not the residents' fault he's such a weirdo.

"To the Elms?" he says. "Donate what?"

"A bench?" I say. "A piano, if you need one." That's less generous than it sounds. Lord's Yard is always full of old pianos. John would be delighted if I took one off his hands.

"Can you play?" the man asks. Then he tuts. "But where are my manners? Would you like to sit down and have a cup of tea?"

I glance at the frosted glass of the window that separates the front desk from the back office, at the vertical blinds three quarters closed.

"In the lounge," he adds, pointing the other way.

I go through, expecting to see old people in high-set chairs and maybe a television on too loud, but the lounge is deserted and the chairs look like the ordinary comfortable kind that go with couches and end up in John's front shed. I glance around and see that there is already a piano, and an indoor quoits set, as well as the telly and a couple of desktop computers. I look out at the garden and see that the Elms is well served for benches too. There's no one sitting on any of them.

"Here we are." He's back, with an oval plastic tray set for one in a practised fashion: spoon, tiny milk jug, two straws of sugar, a saucer with a bulge that accommodates a single biscuit. "So you were saying: donation?"

"What sort of thing do you need?" I ask. "Streaming service subscription? Mobile nail technician?"

"We're still on videos," he tells me. "A lot of the residents bring their favourites with them. And it's more likely to be a chiropodist they need, to be honest with you."

"I also wondered about time," I tell him. "Visits. Or outings, even. A wee walk to a coffee shop. I was wondering if that wouldn't be the best donation of all." I look around at the empty sitting room. "Unless they're all out right now, I mean. Unless family and friends take them out as much as they want to go."

He points upwards, jabbing with both fingers, and for one wild moment I think he's telling me that everyone who lived here has died. "Nap time, Lindsay," he says. "It's much better for them to lie down and lift their feet than sleep in the chairs. We encourage a proper nap in the afternoons and a wee wash and brush up afterwards. Makes dinner special."

"And the idea of donating time?" I ask him.

"Sounds great," he says. "I don't suppose you've got a dog, have you? A visit from a friendly dog always goes down well."

I tell him I don't have a dog but, even as I'm speaking, I ask myself why not. I work at home. I've no plans to travel much, for a while anyway. I could have a dog. A big chilled-out one like a retriever or one of those enormous ones that looked after the kids in *Peter Pan*. It would bark at night if people broke in. Or rather it *wouldn't* bark at night and I'd know for sure I was dreaming. Not that I don't know already. Because I do.

We chat back and forth for the length of time it takes me to drink the tea and finish the biscuit, then I stand up to leave. I sing out a casual goodbye in the direction he's gone when he takes the tray away and make my escape.

I'm glad to be back outside, with the wind in the trees and the sound of birdsong and traffic. It was so silent in there. You would think that a houseful of elderly people, at nap time, would produce at least one buzz for an attendant, or a loud snore. And where *were* the attendants, by the way? Do they have to take a nap too? *Nice save.* Letting my imagination run riot, for a minute, I think that, if they make life easy by keeping the old people in their rooms all the time, there would still be noise. But if they sedated—

I'm relieved when another car pulls up beside mine, stopping me from going there in my mind. I turn with a smile on my face to nod a greeting at a relative or a carer on a back shift. Then my mouth drops open. Aileen Murdoch is sitting in the other car staring back at me.

I step out and go to speak to her, taking my chance to prove I'm a suitable adult to be around her boys.

"Lindsay?" she says. She's more astonished than I can quite account for. It's as if we've met in Zanzibar instead of in an unexpected setting five miles from where we both live.

"Aileen," I say. "Have you got a relative . . . ?" But I blink and stop talking. Surely David would have known that. He would have mentioned it to me, if an ex-parent-in-law lived where Peggy March ended up. But then it was only two short texts. I'm being daft.

"Aunt," Aileen says. "She's not been here long but she seems to like it." Obviously she hasn't mentioned this family detail to her ex-husband and it's hardly the sort of titbit that two boys would itch to pass on either. "I thought . . . aren't your parents . . . ?" she goes on. Like I couldn't have an aunt too.

"Long story," I say. Then, since the boys have crossed my mind, I add, "David mentioned that you're being cautious about me meeting the kids. I understand." I hold up both hands when it seems she might be about to protest. "But I was just wondering what I could do to set your mind at ease."

"About you hanging out around two boys of . . . their age?" she says. It was a strange hesitation. It was as if she didn't want me to know even *that* detail about them. I want to tell her I saw them in the car on the first day David and I met. "Go for it, if that's what floats your boat," she tells me, and I can't help the expression that crosses my face. I know she must mean to ridicule me, out of some misplaced jealousy, but she's pretty much done it by alluding to her boys as targets for unhealthy interest. It strikes me as a very weird thing to say.

"I wouldn't go that far," I answer carefully. "Just that they're part of the package and it'll get awkward otherwise."

She doesn't flush. She's got the wrong colouring for it, apart from anything else. But she looks distinctly uncomfortable, as if she's only just realised what she said to me.

"Whatever," she says. It sounds peculiar coming out of her mouth. She can't possibly talk like that at work. Maybe she talks like her sons when she's talking about them. I smile at the thought.

"Thanks," I say. "I'm glad I've managed to reassure you."

"What you do is all one to me," she says. "But I'll certainly be having a word with *David*." She's either in a really foul mood or she's a really unpleasant person. I hope for David's, the boys', and her wife's sake that it's a bad day. Or maybe it's me.

"Look," I say. "I'm sorry I didn't— I'm sorry I can't dredge up school memories, Aileen. The last few months have taken a toll."

"What's been happening in the last few months?" she says.

I wave the question off, but it bothers me. Didn't David tell her about Kai when he was presenting me as a suitable person to be around her sons? Or is that *me* being weird, thinking widowhood confers respectability?

As I set off, I try to think about how popular that retriever or mountain dog would make me with my boyfriend's sons. I don't quite manage it though, and I find myself wishing I could tell all this to someone, then wondering why I'm not driving back to Chloe to tell her. As I'm slowing to turn into Saint Helen's, however, I see the perfect person. Bunny has just left his own drive on foot and is heading my way.

"Are you taking the air?" I ask him. "Or could I persuade you to a cup of tea?"

"Always," he says, climbing into the passenger seat and pointing up my drive with one long, arthritic finger, his nail as thick and curved as a talon. "Is something troubling you?"

"I mean, I don't need a reason to have tea with a neighbour, but yes as it happens."

"The therapist is in," says Bunny, making me laugh.

"Let's get inside and I'll tell you everything," I say.

"I'm having boyfriend trouble," I begin, as I'm filling the kettle. He toddles over to the mantelpiece and reaches down the biscuit tin. "Can I tell you and you just nod and maybe tut?"

"I shall do my best," he says. "I don't pretend to understand your ways, you young creatures, but I shall do my best in this very different world where I find myself. No judgement from this corner, Lindsay."

"Okay, here goes," I say, putting teabags in a pair of mugs. "I stayed overnight at my new boyfriend's place last night."

"*Last* night?" says Bunny. "You slept elsewhere? Gosh! I see. Well, I hope you— Sorry."

This is not a great start if I'm hoping not to shock him, but I plough on. "Well, the point is, it was when his kids weren't there. He said his wife—we were at school together, although I don't remember her—but anyway he said she was cutting up rough about me hanging around them so soon. Fair enough. I'm not moaning about that."

"His wife?" says Bunny. "I know I assured you—"

"Bugger!" I say. "Ex-wife."

"Phew," he says. "It's such a different world, but I have my limits. I must say, I applaud you for getting off your blocks so smartly, Lindsay. Do you use an app?"

"Um," I say. "I don't, actually. But right, okay, yeah—back to the ex-wife. I just ran into her, by pure chance, and she didn't *seem* bothered about me meeting her kids. At all. But she did seem hacked off with her ex-husband. So either she *is* bothered but she was too embarrassed to tell me to my face. Or—and this is what's worrying me—*he* lied."

"Hm," says Bunny. "Where did you run into her? Might she have been on the back foot, as it were?"

"That's a good point, but I don't think so. It was at the nursing home. Oh! I found out what nursing home Peggy went to."

"For your plan to donate in her memory," says Bunny, nodding.

"Yes, my boyfriend found out which one it was and I went round there and it turns out his ex-wife has got an old lady in there too.

Which, I thought it was weird he never said, but it's only an auntie so he wouldn't necessarily know."

"And how did he manage to do what outwitted you?" says Bunny.

"Through work, but the thing I'm needing help with is— That's two potential strikes, right? If Aileen was straight with me when I just met her there, then David's been lying to me. And he's been running Aileen down, bad-mouthing the mother of his children."

"Absolutely," says Bunny. "He's keeping you at arm's length—one. And he's blaming his ex-wife for it—two. Explains why she didn't know what you were talking about and why she seemed miffed with him when she found out."

"I knew it was too good to be true," I say. Which is a lie. I didn't know that at all. I leapt into it, trusting that I deserved something this good after all the bad stuff.

"Or," says Bunny, holding up that long, bony finger again, "this ex-wife is thoroughly nasty to him but doesn't have the guts to be equally nasty to strangers. Or perhaps she's bitter about him, even about men in general, but she's fonder of and fairer to women. What?" he adds when I can't help reacting.

"She left him for a woman," I say, wondering if this is where I lose him.

"Heavens," he says. Then he surprises me. "Poor chap. Poor wife, trying to deny her nature. Are they terribly religious or something?"

"I don't think so."

"What does she do for a living?"

"She's a lawyer."

"One does slightly wonder then why she wasn't open all along. Different in my day, of course. People led heartbreaking lives through no fault of their own. I am a big fan of a great deal about the modern world. Never feel you have to water any of it down for me. You're a long time dead, Lindsay, as you know. Why not, is all I'll ever say to *you*."

"Why not what?" I ask him.

"Why not whatever takes your fancy," he says. "And now I've made you blush. Have I been 'inappropriate'?"

"You've been perfect," I tell him. "Thank you."

Chapter 19

So of course I accept when David phones me up and asks me round again that night, to meet the boys. "Did Aileen speak to you?" I ask him.

"She did."

"Did she bollock you?"

"What for?"

"For telling me something she was embarrassed to have me know."

I'm sitting in that same spot in the garden room. I still wish Peggy was sitting opposite me but it's nice to chat to David too, now I've decided I trust him.

"Ah," he says. "You mean, how she was being sticky about you?" I wait. "Right, well, yes. I shouldn't have said that. It was me. Not trying to keep you at arm's length! Rather . . . crapping out of telling her any details about you and me. Petty as that sounds. And I didn't want you to know I was such a petty little crapper-outer." He blows out a big breath. "So there it is. Do you still want to come round tonight or do you despise me now?"

"It's a very endearing characteristic," I tell him, "to be a bit shit—"

"Really? Well, I've got a terrible singing voice too, if it helps."

"Don't interrupt me. To be a bit shit and have no trouble admitting it when you get caught. It's almost better than not being shit at all."

"Oh, come off it!"

"No, because that's intimidating, isn't it? Can you imagine going out with someone gorgeous and clever and honest and diligent and organised and energetic?"

"I don't have to."

"Puke," I say. "What time's dinner, when the kids are there?"

"Six," he tells me. "No devices at the table. But there might be a burping competition. Since it's Monday."

◆ ◆ ◆

He's kidding about the burping competition, but not the no-phones rule. My heart bangs in my chest as he calls up the stairs and two huge boys with feet like loaves come thundering down to the kitchen. They stand awkwardly in the doorway, staring at me.

"This is Lindsay," David says. "Edwin. Sean. Sit down and say hello."

They are only a couple of years older than Zak and Nicky and instantly I imagine all four kicking a ball around the back garden at Saint Helen's while David and I and John and Shelley sit on the patio. Although I can't imagine what we would be talking about, the four of us. Maybe we're all admiring the baby I'm feeding, painlessly. But won't these kids be too old for football by then? I bring myself back to the real world and say hello.

They don't look much like David, but they don't look like the whale their mum was at school, allegedly. They're normal, slightly spotty, slightly squeaky-voiced kids, squirming a bit to be sharing dinner with their dad's new girlfriend.

"Lindsay's an audiobook narrator," David says.

The bigger one really tries to think of a follow-up question but fails completely and goes pink, bending over his pasta and shaking his hair over his eyes.

David grimaces at me and I give him a doesn't-matter shake of the head.

Then the two of us adults talk about my new dead room insulation, getting more and more strained, until I want to giggle. I wish Chloe was here. She'd say something outrageous and have both of them wrapped round her little finger in no time.

"Screens off at nine," David says as they scrape their chairs back, having wolfed down their food apparently without chewing it in their desperation to get away.

We sit in silence and listen to their footsteps thump back upstairs, then to the sound of muffled guffaws as a door slams.

"That was excruciating," David says, lying back in his chair and putting his napkin over his face. "I'm knackered."

"At least it's over," I say. "It won't be so bad next time. Poor little loves. God, imagine what it must have been like when they met . . . What's Aileen's wife's name?"

"Christ, I know, right?" says David, taking the napkin off again. "Her name's Medusa."

I snort. "No it is not!"

"In this house, her name is Medusa." He's not quite laughing, so I go round the table and drop a kiss on his head en route to the dishwasher.

"You don't need to do that," he tells me. But I've seen the way he keeps glancing at his briefcase and I shout him down. I ask him how to put the radio on—I'm still loving the schedule coming back to me after all those podcast years—and then I tell him to leave me in peace. He gives me a bear hug that suggests a mountain of work he's been trying not to think about and disappears into the room next door.

In the quiet between tracks, I overhear a whispered conversation, even though he has closed the door. *Mostly* whispered, apart from one "All right!" that's spat with enough vehemence to seem louder than a shout.

I'm instantly convinced it's Aileen on the other end. That one of the boys texted her to report my presence and she's rethought her earlier attitude and demanded I get chucked out.

I'm even more convinced when David sidles round the door a minute later looking . . . *flustered* is the only word for it. His face is red and his hair looks as if he's been running his hands through it.

"I'm really sorry about this," he says. I feel my heart sink. Or rather I feel the pasta in my stomach threaten to rise.

"What's up?" I ask, trying for breezy.

"That was work," he says. It takes me a couple of blinks to catch up with him, not least because it certainly didn't sound like work. Not his kind of work. "I'm going to have to go in. Just for a bit."

"In? To your office?"

"No! God no, not Chambers Street. Just to the Stirling jail. Bloody snafu over an important client who's . . . Well, it's confidential, you know."

"Is Aileen coming?"

"What? No, no. It'll be fine. An hour tops. And I'll keep my phone on while I'm driving."

"David, I can't be left with your children the first night I meet them. Aileen'll do her nut. Rightly."

"Aileen will never know," he says. "I'll tell the boys they can stay online till ten and not to phone Mum. They know the drill. They won't drop me in it."

What drill, I think, wondering how many girlfriends have been left in charge of these kids when David suddenly has to go to some random jail. It also occurs to me that I really don't understand his job. Trotting along to a jail at night sounds pretty junior for all those letters after his name. I still haven't checked what LLM and CC actually stand for.

By the time I decide to agree, he's left the room anyway, telling me to help myself to the whisky and thus proving how he really doesn't know me well enough to have left his kids in my care, because I *loathe* whisky. I hear him upstairs talking in a low voice. I hear the cheer go up about the extra screen time. Then I hear the car start in the drive and I'm left in the kitchen, still holding a tea towel, with two boys I don't know. And—on the bright side—a whole house to snoop around as long as I cock an ear for David returning.

Not that I would actually hear him. Because as soon as he's gone, the boys stop playing whatever games they usually play and start running riot. I can hear them charging about, banging in and out of the rooms up there and laughing their heads off. I stand inside the kitchen door wondering what to do. If I tell them to pipe down, they'll hate me for keeps. And maybe David would be glad they're getting some exercise. Maybe they always do circuits after dinner. I decide to ignore them and go into the room with the leather sofas and the ludicrous telly. I tune out a particularly loud thump as I'm working out how to switch it on. They quieten down after this and I hope they haven't smashed something valuable.

I've just settled on a makeover show and taken one sip of my tea when the bigger one edges round the door.

"Hiya," I say, then I look at him properly. His face is stark although still red from all the high jinks. "What's wrong?"

"Sean fell off the— Sean fell and I think he's hurt himself."

I get up, my stomach turning somersaults, and follow him out into the hall. He hangs back and I brush past him, taking the stairs two at a time. Sean, the little one, is lying on the landing at the foot of a pull-down loft ladder, which he has presumably leapt off.

"You okay?" I ask. I know he isn't. He's flat on his back and he's breathing in whimpering little gasps. "Where does it— Jesus!"

His left wrist, which he's cradling against himself, is puffed up to three times the size it should be and there's a step in it as if his hand has shunted out of line with the rest of his arm. I feel my vision grey out and dig my nails into my palms to get hold of myself. I understand now why Edwin didn't want to rush back and look at his brother again.

"Okay, sweetheart," I say. "You've broken your arm. We need to get you to hospital. Does anything else hurt?"

"It doesn't hurt," Sean says with a waver in his voice. "It just feels really weird."

I've got my phone out but I dither between dialling David and 999.

"Can you sit up, maybe?" I ask. "And could you lift your arm and rest it on top of your head? You need to have it higher than your heart to help with the swelling. Good boy. That's brilliant." I raise my voice. "Edwin? Are you okay? How are you feeling?"

"A bit sick," Edwin calls up the stairs.

"Wee soul," I call back down. I've tried David but he's not answering. First, I flash to angry. How the hell can he not be answering me when he knows I'm alone with his kids? Then my brain catches up. He said he would keep it on while he was driving, but you can't take mobiles into jails, which is where he is. Briefly, I consider Aileen, but I immediately chicken out of that and dial for an ambulance instead.

Ten minutes later, after I've finally understood that a "non-emergency" ambulance will be upwards of four hours, I've got both of them in the car; Edwin in the passenger seat with a sick bowl just in case and poor Sean lying in the back because he can't even contemplate a seat belt.

"Can you help me navigate, Edwin?" I ask. "I've never been to this hospital before. Can you get the map on your phone?"

Of course I've been to Forth Valley Hospital, but I'm hoping giving him a job will take his mind off feeling faint and ill, and guilty, and embarrassed. I wish I knew more about boys. A few weeks with Zak and Nicky haven't trained me for this kind of advanced situation.

"Mmmnnhmm," Sean murmurs from the back seat as we go over a speed bump. I slow until I have to change down into third gear. And thus we make our stately way to the big road.

I try David every few minutes because his "hour tops" is nearly up, but he's still not answering. So, when we're almost there, following the red **H** signs, I finally say it. "Edwin, can you phone your mum, maybe?" This is met with total silence. Sean's breathing quiets too while he waits to hear the response.

"She'll kill both of us," Edwin says. "Maybe all of us. I'll phone Dad."

I swing into the hospital car park and head straight for the big doors to A&E.

"No answer," Edwin says.

"Then your mum it is," I say. Edwin jumps out as I park, going to open the back door for his brother, preferring squeamishness to Aileen, it seems. He has left his phone on the front seat, but I pocket it before I get out to help.

Thank God it's a quiet night in Casualty. From the ambulance wait time I thought it would be pandemonium, but it's mostly muddy men in sports kit and a couple of drunks. Sean gets whisked off into a cubicle as soon as a nurse takes a look at him.

"Looks like he'll be in overnight," she calls back as she disappears. "Have you brought anything for him?"

Edwin follows, disappearing behind the curtain with his brother. He's over the shock and is now being quite sweet. I shift from foot to foot, wondering whether to follow too, until the nurse pokes her head back round and stares at me. "Are you coming?" she says. "Never mind your phone!"

"I'm not their mum," I tell her. "I was babysitting. So—"

"You're a childminder?" she says in a tone that reeks of being about to call social services as soon as she's settled her patient.

"I'm their dad's girlfriend," I say, hoping the boys can't hear me. "I need to let their mum know."

"Ya think?" says the nurse. She rolls her eyes and disappears again.

I try David one last time. His hour is long gone, and I can't believe his phone is still off. I try to get angry at him—what kind of dad would do this?—but what I really think is that something must be wrong. Something else, in this shitshow of an evening.

There's no other way but still I walk up and down the waiting room a couple of times before I start trying to get into Edwin's phone. Thankfully, either David or Aileen has made sure it's not locked and I swipe it open and click his calls app without any trouble.

Mum is saved, of course, and I click on it. It rings three times and a woman answers.

"Ed?" She sounds unlike herself.

"Aileen?"

"Who's this?" she demands. "And why do you have my son's phone?"

"It's Lindsay," I tell her. "Look—"

"Who?" she says.

So this must be "Medusa" and Aileen hasn't told her David's seeing someone. It's sweet that she calls Edwin her son but I wonder what David thinks of it.

"It doesn't matter," I say. "Look, don't worry but I need to tell you that Sean fell over, and he seems to have broken his arm. He's in A&E at Forth Valley and he might be getting admitted."

She starts squawking when I'm only halfway through all of this. "What? What are you telling me? Sean is in the hosp— Jesus Christ! Mike! Michael! Where's Ed?"

I try to break in but I don't think she's got the phone to her ear anymore. I can hear her rushing about, still calling for "Michael" who must be . . . I have no idea. *Her* son?

"Edwin is with Sean," I say as loud as I dare speak in the waiting room. "I can't get hold of David but I'll go in and stay with—"

She *is* listening. She answers this bit. "Look, you," she says. "I don't know who you are or how you came to let my son break his arm, but you stay away from both of them, you hear?"

I hang up without another word. She's being pretty unreasonable, in my opinion, even if it is coming from shock and fear.

I get myself a cup of disgusting tea out of the vending machine and choose a seat where I can see the door to the car park and the corner of the curtain round the cubicle they took Sean to. My ears crackle from straining to hear if he's crying, if Edwin is retching. That same nurse who rolled her eyes comes out but doesn't speak to me as she swishes past, her uniform trousers buzzing as her thighs rub.

I even drink the tea. Taking a sip, then trying David, then taking a sip again. He must be back at the house by now, but he can't be because, coming home and finding it empty, the first thing he would do is phone me. I can't even remember if I locked the front door.

After the last sip of tea, powdery and lukewarm, I finally think of phoning Chloe. I want to be comforted. A babysitter doesn't have to be in the same room as twelve-year-olds. Sean was larking about. A broken arm isn't an aneurism. I know Chloe would tell me all of these things, and I need to hear them, but the fact is I don't want to tell her that David blew out on our date and went to work.

While I'm still going back and forth, I see a woman in business clothes but ballet flats come striding in through the doors and march up to the desk.

"Aileen Prentiss," she says, very clipped. "You've got my son, Sean Prentiss, in here with a broken arm."

So this *is* the wife, I think, gathering courage to go and introduce myself. She's terrifying enough to explain the "Medusa" nickname but she's just lied to the nurse—claiming to be Aileen—and that gives me a bit of a boost. Mind you, if Aileen changed her name when they got married and changed the boys' too, this woman must be as formidable as she sounds. I still make my way towards her, but pretty slowly.

A man barges past me and joins her. "Aileen?" he says. "Is he okay?" He turns to the nurse. "Michael Prentiss, I'm Sean's stepfather. Can we see him?"

What the hell? Who *are* these people? I start forward to tell the nurse that this woman is not Aileen Prentiss and God knows who the man is, but I hear Edwin's voice, wavery and higher than usual.

"Mum?" He comes loping along from the curtained cubicles and throws himself into the woman's arms. "Mum," he says. He either doesn't see me or doesn't care.

"Let's go and see the wounded soldier, shall we?" says Michael and the three of them make their way towards Sean's cubicle as I slip out.

Okay, okay, I say to myself, out in the car park. If this is . . . If this is another . . . whatever those things are, when I know strangers and don't know friends, when I hear what no one's saying and my world flaps and flutters again like when I was a kid . . . then it's the worst one yet and no way I should have been in charge of kids or—God knows—driving them.

I'm in no fit state to drive even myself but I can't face staying here, so I head off out of town, joining the motorway to Glasgow, in exactly the opposite direction from home, from anywhere I need to be, or should be. Exactly the opposite direction from David. Because I can't even begin to straighten out what just happened. I *must* be going mad. Or something is pressing on some bit of my brain. Aileen and Michael Prentiss can't be real. What have I done, leaving the boys there at the mercy of two strangers? Because I *saw* David pick the boys up from Aileen Murdoch that I was at school with, who lost all the weight. I saw it with my own eyes, in the walled bit of the garden centre that day. And I *met* Aileen Murdoch, outside the nursing home.

Something shifts.

But Edwin threw himself at that woman and called her "Mum." And she answered when I dialled *Mum* on—

His phone! It's still in my pocket. I pull over onto the hard shoulder and swipe it open again, not even caring how wrong this thing is that I'm doing. I go to his pictures and scroll through rugby, rugby, rugby, McDonald's, two pretty girls, rugby, rugby and then I find them. Michael and Aileen Prentiss, with Sean and Edwin, muffled up in scarves standing in front of a tall municipal Christmas tree with Stirling Castle just visible in the background.

I am not hallucinating. The world is still and stable and whatever's going on, it's outside of me, not in my mind or my brain.

I rejoin the motorway, come off at the Haggs roundabout, go right round and get back on again, headed for where I've just been. And now my head is completely empty. No, not empty, but still. As if someone has put a nozzle in my ear and filled my skull with expanding foam, muffling every thought, deadening every nerve. I drive at a steady seventy. Fifty on the slip road, forty on the street, fifteen in the hospital grounds, five in the car park, and stop.

I step out, still unthinking, still filled with wadding that's blanketed my brain and left me moving like a zombie. Which is lucky, because that way I miss running into David, who is flinging himself out of his car and running full pelt for the double doors. He doesn't turn his head, doesn't see me. And, given my tortoise plod, he's cleared the desk and gone into the cubicle before I get there.

"Sean Prentiss's brother's phone," I say to the nurse, a new one, when I get to the front of the short queue. It's hotting up in here with the approach of closing time.

"Are you all right?" she says, giving me a sharp look.

"Fine," I tell her. "Nothing wrong with me."

Chapter 20

None of this makes any sense.

None of this tonight makes even a tiny bit of sense.

I try hard to focus, as I roll along through the empty countryside. I haven't had anything to drink since the wine with dinner—that cup of tea doesn't count—and my throat is so dry it sticks shut when I try to swallow. My head is aching too. It feels like a kitchen drawer, jammed shut on its load of batteries and adaptors and ballpoints and bag clips, or a plastic basin full of junk mail. It feels like a dented old biscuit tin, rattling with stale KitKats and Twixes that I'm trying to prise the lid off.

Sort it through.

Aileen Murdoch knew me. *David, this is Lindsay,* she said.

She brought David the boys. *Are the kids in the café?* he asked her. And they were. I saw them minutes later.

Chloe knew Aileen and she knew the story. *So you're the husband. Well, well, well.*

Chloe! I try her number but she's not answering. Probably on a date with "love you too," and she couldn't help me anyway. Because Aileen in the garden centre was a completely different woman from Aileen tonight. The garden centre and the nursing home, I remind myself with a lurch in my chest. The nursing home where Peggy went so I could buy her house. The house that didn't go on the open market and doesn't show up in "recently sold" and was emptied of its owner and all her things so very quickly.

But not by John, I remember. I can still trust *him*. And suddenly, I want to go home. Since home doesn't exist anymore and was thousands of miles away even when it did, though, I'll make do with Lord's Yard.

It's getting dark earlier and earlier, like it always did, I suppose, but I got out of the way of it, all those years in Hawaii. Right now, the clouds over the Ochils are purple and bruised looking and the shadows are deep grey. Here and there, there's a tree whose leaves are starting to turn, not brown, not yet, but the green is fading. The verges and hedgerows are overgrown and getting tangled, long stalks battered by rain and never going to stand up again. They'll die where they are, in souring hanks.

Menstrie is deserted. Two girls in hairnets hang over the counter at the takeaway, looking out for business through the open door. There must be someone drinking at the Phil Inn—I hope so for the landlord's sake—but there's no one smoking outside. Not even a dog walker lingering. And the big gates are shut at the junkyard.

Which seems even stranger when, after I get them open, I see two extra cars parked inside. Shelley comes out onto the step, activating the security light.

"Come in this way," she says. "Poker night."

"I always come in that—"

"He's in a bad mood because they're a man down," Shelley says. "Come and hang out with me."

"Can you *play* poker with three people?" I ask, as I go in through the door she's holding open. She gives my arm a rub on the way past, as if she's comforting me.

"I'm just grateful he didn't ask me to make the numbers up," she says. "What's the matter, Lindsay?"

"Is it that obvious?" I sit down at the kitchen table, still covered with dinner dishes. "Two different things—because life can go wrong in two ways at once, right?"

"At least two," she says.

"Okay, first, I think there's something wrong with me buying that house."

"Bit late now!"

"I don't mean I regret it. I mean I think it's not above board. Thank God John had nothing to do with it. I wish David had had nothing to do with it either. Because I'm trying to believe he's a competent professional and so it must be square but . . ."

"But?" says Shelley.

"But then there's the other thing. He hasn't been straight with me on a personal level."

"Oh?"

"About his ex-wife. He said she was this old school friend from the same class as Chloe and me, and the school friend said she was his ex-wife too. But his ex-wife is a totally different person with a new partner that's nothing like he said his ex's partner was like and I just don't get why he would tell such a weird lie. Or her either. Because she was definitely backing it up."

"How did you find out?" Shelley says. "I mean, yeah that is weird but how did you bust them?"

"I met the real one," I say. I don't have the energy to go into Sean's arm. And my pride is stopping me from telling her David ran out on our date night.

"Yikes," Shelley says. "Do you want a drink?"

I shake my head. "Driving."

"Cuppa then," she says, going to the kettle and reaching for that box of disgusting tea she nevertheless got me hooked on.

"Nothing, thanks," I say, sharply enough that she fires a look at me. "So you agree it's weird then?" I carry on. "It's not just showing off, or hanging back or being a two-timing get or anything normal? It's really off the wall."

Shelley frowns at me. "Of course it's being a two-timing get!" she says. "What else? He's got a side piece and he doesn't want you to know about her, so he says she's his ex-wife to explain her away. Tosser."

"But . . ." I say. I'm so exhausted I'm beginning to feel light-headed. I can't get my thoughts in order, but I know it's not as simple as Shelley's making out. David and I hadn't even met, that day at the walled garden when he pretended Aileen was handing over the kids to him. "Look, I better go," I say instead of trying to explain any of it. "It's late to be landing on you and I'm knackered."

"You're family," Shelley says. "Not a visitor. But you do look pretty wrecked, if I'm honest."

We both stand and she seems like she wants to say more. She's tussling with herself.

"Are *you* okay?" I ask her.

"Me? Oh, can't smile wide enough, me," she says. "I go with the flow. Better than drowning."

Then she seems to realise what a beyond-peculiar thing that is to say and she starts getting bustly, clearing the table and making good night and mind-how-you-go noises. "I recommend it," she says as she walks me to the door. "Go with the flow, Lindsay. By the time you realise you're in the river, it's too late to climb out anyway."

I stop on the top step, gripping the railings and looking out over the parked cars and John's Portakabin. "Don't suppose there's any chance you'll tell me what you're on about?"

"Nothing in particular," she says. "It's general advice. Drive safe, eh?"

But even after she goes back into the house I stand there. I'm right where she's hung that gong from the railings and my fingers trace the cable ties and the holes in the lip of the big brass disc, the rough edges where the drill bit came through.

Why is that bothering me?

I know why it would have bothered Kai. He wasn't a fusspot, not the kind of man who would repack the dishwasher or care how I folded his shirts if I was doing the laundry, but he took a quiet pleasure in a good job well done. He wouldn't have drilled through from the back to the front for a start. And he would have smoothed off those rough edges no matter where they were.

But it's more than that, isn't it? Because why didn't this gong already have a way of hanging up without Shelley having to drill holes through the rim, backwards or otherwise? And why does a gong have a back and a front anyway? They don't usually hang off the railings on a front step. They're usually freestanding. Why has it even got a rim, if it comes to that? I bend right over and look at the thing properly, at the carving of leaves and flowers, and the slight buckling here and there. And it's not the railing cutting into me that makes me feel sick suddenly.

This isn't a gong at all. Shelley repurposed it but it's actually the top of one of those tables, whatever they're called. And suddenly I remember the sound of my mug hitting it when I set it down, so I can see why she got the idea. But this is not a gong. Just like that biscuit tin isn't a replica. I *knew* it wasn't. The daughter of John Lord can tell genuine stuff from faked repro.

I march over to the other door and blat it open, not caring about a stupid poker game.

"You swore on Zak and Nicky's lives you didn't clear Saint Helen's," I say. "Why? How could you?"

John is sitting where he was the last time, a cigar held in his knuckles to keep the lit end away from his cards. I've got a better view of him because the guy with his back to me is missing. The other two are there though. I stall on the doorstep.

It's Farmer George, the estate agent. And Nicotine Ned from the nursing home. I stare at them and they stare back, just as blankly, at me.

"Lindsay, Lindsay, Lindsay," John says. "Didn't Shel tell you to keep out of our way?"

But this is my brother and he can't be for real about that tone. He sounds like a gangster. Not a junkyard owner, husband and father. I can't take his act seriously, but I can't quite dismiss it either. I shift my gaze back to the other two.

"I *knew* I recognised you," I say to Farmer George. "I looked in the window the night I arrived. I *saw* you. And as for *you*?" The nursing home guy cringes under my glare and turns to my brother for help.

I turn back that way too. "John, what's going on?"

"Not very bright, your baby sister, is she?" says Farmer George. His voice is dripping with scorn and I feel the first flicker of actual fear.

"Lindsay, let me introduce my business associates, Robert Walker and Eric McAllan."

"Business—?" I say. "John, you're a scrappie. What business have you got with a nursing home? Overstock?" Nicotine Ned snorts at this. And right enough, why would the sale of overstock make them all act so shifty? And how could overstock involve an estate agent?

"Is it a side hustle?" I ask them, thinking maybe they've all bought shares in a racehorse and their main businesses aren't relevant. *Hoping* their main businesses aren't relevant, more like. Because there's only one way I can connect an estate agent, a nursing home, and a house-clearance specialist. They're all involved, separately mind, at a very particular period in a person's life. And if they're *not* separate, if they're "associated" like John just said, then this shiftiness, this threat I'm feeling, begins to make some kind of sense. I wish I could pretend it doesn't, but I've just been saying it to myself, haven't I? Peggy left too quickly and the house got sold too quietly and the furniture all got shovelled away like a dirty secret. All that hangs together, if the nursing home and the estate agent were working as a team. Only the furniture hardly matters, does it? "You swore on their lives, John," I say. "What are you mixed up in that would make you lie on your children's lives? What are they paying you to cover for them?"

"It doesn't mean anything," he says. "It's just an expression."

"John, please," I say, almost wailing. "What's happened to you? Don't you know how bad it is? Don't you get—?"

"I'm a businessman," John says.

"But what have they got on you?" I say. "Why have you agreed to this? She was an old lady who had every right to stay in her house as long as she wanted to. She had room for a carer to move in. It was no one else's shout what she . . ."

"Really not very bright at all," says Farmer George, leering at me.

"I've got to go," I say to my brother. "I can't even look at you. I don't believe this is happening."

"Sanctimonious bitch," says Nicotine Ned, whatever John said his name is, not cringing now.

I turn to see if my brother is genuinely going to let these two men talk to me like that, right here in his house. He's not even looking my way. His attention has strayed back to his cards and to rolling the end of his cigar around the edge of the ashtray to trim the burning tip. He speaks to me without meeting my eyes. "Keep what you think you know is happening to yourself, Lindsay. Because I'm telling you, you haven't got a clue."

I reel out into the yard and of course, of course, of course, it's happening. There's only ever one answer for when something's too good to be true and John still here, living right here, happy and normal and over it all, was far too good to be true.

Calling it the caravan didn't work for either of us.

Neither of us really got over the reason we needed so many secret ways back into Lord's Yard. All kids sneak *out* sometimes, don't they? Most kids have to make that phone call once in their lives saying, "Mum? Dad? Please come and get me." John and I were different.

We believed what she told us, see? That if we ran away from home again, if we were found out on the road when we shouldn't be, we'd be taken to an orphanage and left there. After that, whenever she put us outside the gate, slammed it shut and locked it up, we had no choice but to break back in again.

We were never punished when we turned up again, hours later, after the danger was past. She hugged us hard enough to break us in two and said nothing. So we told ourselves it was a game. Did we believe ourselves? We had to. John walked me through it until it made sense to me, even at four years old. "We know why she shuts us out, Lindsay," he'd say. I'd nod my head. "But we can't know, can we?" Shake. "So we don't know, do we?" A bigger shake. "Though we do." I'd stare at him and he'd stare at me and then he'd grin and say "Pirates!" Or "Spacemen!" Or, if it had been really bad for me, sometimes "Oz!" Because I was the star of the show in Oz and he was three fools.

And we grew up, John and me. Soon enough he didn't know at all. At least, he took off to the park or a pal's house when we were put out in the cold or the dark and sometimes in the rain. He left me. Because he couldn't know so he didn't. I carried on alone, waiting for that to happen to me too.

I drive back through Menstrie at fifteen miles an hour, no one smoking outside the Phil Inn, no one queueing up for a carry-out.

So, I think, John grew up just like me. I was Chloe's perfect little friend and Kai's perfect little wife and he's the perfect one to clear up the messes of those two men, isn't he?

Chloe!

I try again, but again there's no answer.

I wish I could talk to David but, even if he hadn't lied to me about Aileen, he's at the hospital with his son. I'll need to tell him *sometime* that he helped me buy a house that should never have been for sale, but not tonight.

I wish I could go to Bunny too, both for his wisdom and because he's another elderly person living alone in a house that busybodies would call too big for him, so he's definitely got skin in *this* game. But it's after eleven o'clock.

I'll go home, lock up as tight as I can, read a chapter of *Sleeping Murder*, until I fall asleep with my phone in my hand, and decide what to do in the light of day.

Only when I get back to Saint Helen's, David's car is parked in the drive and he's sitting in it waiting for me.

"How's Sean?" I say when he opens the driver's door and swings his legs round to face me. He looks dog tired, his hands hanging down between his thighs and his shoulders slumped.

"You're a very nice woman," he says. "Do you know that? He's fine. He's in a lump of plaster tonight till they can knock him out and reset it straight tomorrow, then he'll be in a resin cast in any colour he chooses."

"Edwin?"

"Yeah, I heard he took a while to rally. He's upset about that."

"He was great by the time we got to the hospital," I say. "He should be proud. Where is he?"

"At his mum's," he says, rubbing his nose. "All things considered, she's pretty angry with me."

"She needs to get in the queue," I say. "Why the hell was your phone off, for starters?"

He rewards me with the world's smallest laugh. "Yeah," he says. "There goes Dad of the Year." I don't so much as crack a smile. "How are *you* doing?" he asks instead.

"Listening," I say. I go over and sit down on the step to the front door. The stone is warm, and I can smell the grass I cut earlier. We regard each other over seven feet of gravel.

"The boys' mum isn't my ex-wife," he tells me. "But you know that now."

"I hadn't got that far," I say. "And I don't really understand what you mean."

"No wonder," he says. "I'm still fudging. I'm ashamed. And so I should be."

"Go on."

"Right," he says. "Right then. Um, it's been lovely, Lindsay. I like you a lot and that's playing it down. I'm sorry you're probably not going to want to see me again after I tell you this."

"Just spit it out!" I say. "There's more than your shit going on tonight." I hate to hear how much I sound like John when I'm this tired and this pissed off. That same rough Clack accent.

"Of course, the boys' mum *is* my ex-wife," he says. "Just not my most recent one. I divorced Aileen after quite a short marriage, with no children involved."

I sit back and rest my elbows on the top step but it's hard and it hurts them so I crunch forward instead. "I don't believe you," I say, and I notice the startled look he tries to hide. "I mean there must be more to it than that. You pretended before we even met. Aileen handed them over to you that day at the garden centre."

"Oh," he says. "Well, yes, of course there's more to it. It was my weekend and their mum is pretty merciless about things like that, but I was slammed at work, so Aileen took them on the Friday night and spoiled them with movies and pizza. She misses them."

"Jesus Christ," I say. "You palmed your kids off on your other ex-wife because you were busy? Like you asked me to stop 'going out' because you're busy?"

"Yeah," he says. He looks so miserable I want to hug him. He can't possibly know what a massive relief all this is. There's still one bit of it that bothers me though.

"So, you've been married twice and both your wives were called Aileen?" I say.

"What? No," he says. "Their mum's called Eileen. Shit! Did *you* call her Aileen?"

"I don't think she noticed," I said. "Seeing as how the rest of the message was that her kid was in A&E. But yes, I did. So she's *Eileen* Prentiss? And wife number two is Aileen Murdoch?" I am having to work hard not to let a beaming smile spread over my face now. I want to be angry with him but it's so human and messy and normal.

"But I haven't been married twice," he says. He takes a deep breath and holds up three fingers as he lets it creak out again. The sheepish look is definitely half flirty now, though. He's no more managing to pretend to be sorry than I'm managing to pretend to be angry.

"You've been married three times?" I say. "How the hell old *are* you?" I've been wanting to find that out since the start, so this is very unscrupulous. "What order did they happen in? And what was the first one called? Ellen?"

"Elaine," he says. "She *was* first, but it only lasted a year."

"You are shitting me," I say.

"Not about the year," he says. "Fourteen months. But her name was Vesna, not Elaine, and she needed residency."

"Isn't that kind of illegal? For a lawyer?"

"I was a student. And Yugoslavia was collapsing." For a moment he seems lost in memories. Then, as I watch the rest of his life come crashing in on him, I remember mine too. The ugly scheme that got Peggy out of this house. The state my brother must be in to let himself be a part of it. And then there's the selfish bit too.

"Look, do you want to come in?" I say. "Have a nightcap? I need to talk to you."

The hope in his eyes as he lifts them to look at me finishes me off completely. "Of course you do," he says. "Ask me anything. Kick me up the arse for trying to hide my worst bits from you. I deserve it."

"It's not that," I say. "I need to forget about that just now. Although, consider an arse kicking booked in for your future when I've got time to concentrate on it, definitely. No, it's something else."

"The shit going on tonight that's not mine?"

"Well, it's sort of yours," I say. "Some of it. You need to look over the purchase of this house again, because I'm scared I don't own it."

"Eh?"

"I think I've just busted a really sleazy little game that my brother's mixed up in for some reason."

"When was this?" He looks astonished.

"Fifteen minutes ago," I tell him. "I've had quite a night, not even including Sean. Can I tell you about it? And then I really need to go to sleep. If I can order up no nightmares, that'd be great too."

I'm sure I'm dreaming at first, although it's unlike any dream I've had before. This one has the texture of my sheets and the sound of my hair rubbing on the pillow and it moves in real time without the wild swings that telescope and compress dream time usually. And I can smell in this dream. Can you smell in dreams? I smell smoke and sweat and someone else's soap. None of that is too distressing and I'm close to sleep again when suddenly there are hands on my limbs, holding me down, tight around my ankles pressing my heels into the bed, even tighter at my elbows crushing little bones there and sending pain twanging all the way to my fingertips.

I try to cry out but there's something over my mouth, damp and sharply stinking, and just as I come to know for sure that this is real, I feel myself slip and I'm gone. After that, it's a muffled nonsense of half-heard words and a slipping down helter-skelter, sick making and endless, of movement and jostling. I am sure at one point that I'm upside down. There might be a car or perhaps it's a little cart. There was a cart once, low to the ground with enormous wheels, that rattled and juddered as it went. Sometimes I pulled it along and sometimes I was pulled along in it and I remember laughing.

I am sobbing now, sore and scared, and wishing—as I feel myself rise out of the murk into consciousness—that I could stay down in the dark and keep believing that none of it is true.

Chapter 21

When I wake up and turn to look at him on the other pillow, I still can't believe we got from the front step to here. For the first time since Kai died, I really hope he can't see me, isn't watching over me, has moved on to something bigger.

I also tell myself the sex we had last night wasn't the best of my life. Couldn't have been. We were both knackered and upset and we're strangers. It must just be that it's been so long and we'd each just infodumped the other one into the kind of intimacy it usually takes years to build. I know the dead worst about this man: overfocused on work, ready to tell fibs for his image; three times divorced, for God's sake! And he might not know the deepest and darkest secrets of my past, but he knows some pretty squirrelly stuff about my present: horny as hell when I should be grieving, from a murky family that's up to terrible things—I keep hearing Shelley saying "Go with the flow," worried about my house instead of only thinking about poor Peggy March getting shunted off to that nursing home.

It was asking him that, last night, sitting at the kitchen table, that made my mouth go dry. "Are you *sure* there was nothing about the sale that means someone could take it back?" I said. "If Peggy was coerced to sell, if she was hounded into care, if she never agreed even to her stuff getting cleared . . . then could someone pop up and take it back from me?"

David said nothing.

"I mean, obviously, if she was still alive, I wouldn't care about any of that, but since she died, could her son suddenly say he wants the house back? It must be his inheritance."

"But don't you think it was probably the son who did the hounding and coercing?" David said. "That's much more likely than that a troika of—I know one of them's your brother—would target someone who's *got* a son. Don't you think?"

"But don't you know?" I said to him. "I mean, wasn't the son involved in the sale?"

He rubbed his face at that. "I don't know, Lindsay. I can't remember. It was a while back and I was fitting it around a lot of other things. I can dig out the paperwork and go back over it."

"Leave it," I said to him. "You were sure it was okay at the time. That's good enough for me. I'll let the house go anyway, if it comes to that."

"If what comes to what?"

"If dragging the 'troika' out into the open comes to eviction."

"You're definitely going to?" he asked. "Drag them?"

"I've got to! Apart from anything else, if they're not stopped, they might do it again."

So how did we get from there to bed? To furious sex, then languorous sex, then giggly sex, and finally sleep, tangled up together, one of us farting softly as we were dropping off, which only made us both laugh again.

I have no idea. I'm still thinking about it when David opens his eyes. "Wow," he says.

"Wow," I agree, and we stare at each other for a while until he gets taken over by a yawn, which I catch too, and then we both roll over to lie on our backs and face the ceiling.

"I better go," he says after a while, scrabbling on the bedside table for his watch. "Shit!" he says, sitting up. "It's nearly eleven o'clock. I meant to go round and offer to take Sean to the fracture clinic. She'd have refused anyway, and we both knew that, but I need to start building credit to get out of the hole I'm in."

"She's quite . . . Hey, listen, *did* she put up objections to me seeing the boys? Eileen, I mean."

"I don't want to bad-mouth her," he says, which says everything. "Look, I've got a hell of a day. But I could glance at your paperwork again tonight."

"I've had a better idea," I tell him.

"Oh?"

"Don't worry about it. Get going and have first bath. Sorry there's no shower. I'll go and make the coffee. Are you hungry?"

"Am I hungry? How dare you!" he says, grabbing me and shaking me. "After I put in such a hard shift as a demon lover. I'm ravenous!"

So I'm grinning all over my face as I head downstairs and start gathering a restorative breakfast.

He's on his phone in the bathroom when I come back up to ask if he can eat cheese in the morning. An omelette is all I can muster and I haven't got any brunch-style vegetables to go in it, so cheese is the only option. I put my hand on the door but he's locked it.

"Well, you need to do something," I hear him saying. "Today if not yesterday. I don't really care if you're not ready. I'm telling you—scratch that, I'm *warning* you—if this goes tits up because you didn't do something today that you *could* have done today, if you'd just stopped faffing, I will not be standing up saying I'm Spartacus. Got it?"

There's a short silence. The person on the other end must be speaking.

"We'll see," David says. And then I hear his phone hitting a hard surface and a tap turning on.

I creep back downstairs. He doesn't sound like someone who would quail at the idea of eating cheese for brunch. He sounds like . . . My God, he sounds like Kai. Different accent, obviously, and older. But he sounds like Kai when someone pissed him off by not doing their job properly for a crummy reason. I never minded Kai being such a hard nose at work. I got the benefit of it once everyone in the industry knew I was married to him. I never had to do any of the tough stuff for myself.

But, thing is, Kai was the same at home. He flossed and exercised and never ate junk. He always kept his receipts and was the first one to send them to our accountant. Sometimes, he made me feel kind of . . . inadequate? Judged? Below average on some scale I never named.

Name it now, I tell myself, standing whisking eggs for David's omelette. The Goody-Two-Shoes Scale. It comes into my head without invitation. I put the whisk down and hold my hand over my mouth, the cheese smell sickening me. I can't help it though. Kai would never have lied about three ex-wives or palmed his kids off on their stepmother. If I'm honest, Kai would never have laughed at a fart in bed.

I jump back to life as David comes into the kitchen.

"I might have used all your hot water," he says. "So I've left it in for you. I washed my bum at the sink first, though, so it's not too revolting." As if he's on a mission to make my darling American husband, love of my life, look like a prissy little idiot in comparison with him. "And can I just say this, Lindsay? Not to nag but you might not have so many nightmares if you read something a little milder at bedtime."

"Did the plain brown wrapper fall off or something?" I say. "It is a horrible jacket, right enough."

"It was the plain brown wrapper that piqued my interest. I'm serious, though." He gives an ostentatious shudder. "Why would you want to curl up and read about the ghosts of seven dead?"

"What?" I say in a voice so tiny I can hardly hear myself. I don't know if *he* hears me but he says no more.

And I don't ask again.

But once he's gone I go back upstairs and pick up the book, willing it to be what it must be. What I know it is: Dame Agatha toying with her readers, making them wait, and then solving it all, smoothing and soothing and settling. I open up at page one again and, once again, it's George Lee Lutz, of Deer Park, Long Island, and his wife Kathy for the second time and for real, right here by my bed, the Reeds, young and in love, aren't moving to Dillmouth to have an adventure; instead, the Lutzes are moving to Amityville, to start the descent into unending helpless horror. Amityville. Where a family was murdered. Were there seven of them? Could be. And the worst thing of all is that I think I remember hearing that it was true.

I'm not panicking this time. Maybe because of the daylight, or maybe because I'm numb, I feel a sort of calm. "Peggy," I say out loud, sitting on the edge of my bed. "I don't believe in this. I realise there's something wrong with *my* brain, or *my* mind, nothing to do with *you*. I don't actually believe in *you*. I don't even know who I'm talking to."

But I know who I want to talk to next.

Walking down my drive, I take my first proper look at this bit of the garden. From the house, or sweeping past in the car, it's just a lawn with bushes round the edge but, when you get close up, there's about eight feet of dead leaves and bare branches hidden from view. There are ancient crisp bags and dented Coke cans that must have been thrown over the wall year after year by schoolkids on their way past. There's even one of those half bags of cement, now a tatter-covered lump, where a lazy builder hid his leftovers instead of carting them away. And there's the skeleton of a small animal, desiccated and pitiful, with a few scraps of fur left stretched over the ribs and the remnants of a bushy tail.

"Poor Br'er Fox," I say to it. "No one to bury you, eh?" It strikes me, though, that if Peggy March didn't notice the smell of a decomposing fox, maybe it wasn't wrong for her son to . . . Well, the phrase is *put her in a home*, isn't it? I know from the guff of that fox at Lord's Yard that no one in completely robust health could miss it happening in their garden. And what about Bunny, Colonel of the Neighbourhood Watch, for that matter? He obviously didn't notice it either.

As if I've summoned him, I hear the heels of his brogues coming along the road and go to meet him.

"I need to pick your brain," I say.

"It's been many a year since anyone needed my muscle, right enough," Bunny says.

"But what I have to tell you might be upsetting," I add.

"How many times must *I* tell *you*?" says Bunny. "I am not the least concerned. The more the merrier."

"What? Never mind. Bunny, I've been having some strange . . . symptoms, I suppose you'd call them—I just got proof positive that there's something wrong with me—and because of that I've been far too ready to dismiss other things that I should have taken seriously."

He's looking at me polite but bewildered and I can hardly blame him. "Look, I think there's something amiss about Peggy leaving her house. It's been my gain but I want to work out what exactly happened and stop it happening again. Will you help me?"

"I should jolly well think I *will* help you," Bunny says. "I thought it was fishy all along."

"Let's walk into town," I say. "You can get your newspaper and then we can find a comfy seat in a coffee shop and hammer this out between us. How about that, eh?"

Twenty minutes later, we've settled down in comfy seats all right: moulded-plastic Adirondack chairs with footstools outside a chi-chi new café where my order of a latte was almost as old hat as Bunny's Lapsang tea.

"I want to track down Peggy's son," I tell him.

"But you found her," he says. "Where she'd been, I mean."

"Indeed I did," I say. "The Elms, in Kincardine. But now I need Peggy's son for something else."

"Really?" Bunny says. "Another one?"

I have no idea what that means and I'm tempted to leave it alone and stick with the thing I'm actually here to find out: Peggy's son's address or phone number. Even his first name would be a start. Luckily, instead, I decide to let Bunny sidetrack me.

"What are these veiled hints you keep dropping?" I ask him. "Along with the assurances that you're not judging me? The more *what* the merrier? Another one *what*?"

"Oh, ignore me." He flaps his hand. "If I could have had young ladies coming and going the way you have men, I'd have been all for it."

"What men?" I say, feeling my heartbeat begin to quicken.

"Come now, Lindsay. Don't be coy. The first one was the very night you moved in. He strolled up the drive bold as brass at gone midnight and, as far as I could tell, he let himself in through the front door with a key."

"Yes!" I yelp. "He did! But you're supposed to be in the Neighbourhood Watch. Why didn't you do something?" He starts blustering on about the key again but I interrupt him to ask him how slowly a lock picker would have to pick a lock before he called the police.

"You never said anything about it the next day," he points out, sulking.

"I thought I was having a bad dream," I say. "Or a night terror. For half a minute I seriously entertained the idea that the house was haunted." I take a moment. "I don't know if it's better or worse to think there really was someone in there. The very first night!"

"Oh, this was no ghost," Bunny says to me. "Not that I'm ruling out the existence of a spirit dimension, you understand. But this was a great galumphing sort of fellow. Flesh and blood and plenty of it."

"No," I say. "That was the second one. If you're sure it was two different men and not the same one twice." I drop back in my Adirondack chair and let my head rest against the plastic planks. The server inside the window is watching us curiously. Morning coffee with your grandad, as she probably thinks, is usually polite conversation, not gasps and outbursts.

"Have I switched them round?" He puts on a fake-quavery voice. "I'm ninety-six, you know." I can't help laughing. "But the other one was quite a different chap—trust me on that. Oily, I thought. Dreadful posture. And he was smoking a cigarette too. Now, I've nothing against old Lady Nicotine per se, but it's bad form to be puffing away when you let yourself into someone else's house."

"Uh-huh," I say. I'm busy thinking. Or not exactly thinking but trying to keep my mind wide open to let an idea rise from where it's lurking, like a trout at the overhanging bank of a shallow river.

"Next, on an evening when you now say you weren't even *there*, there were three of them! The first two and another. This last one was a very rough-looking type."

"Oh Bunny," I say. "I wish you had told me all this a bit sooner." Because, of course, with the addition of the "very rough-looking" third man, it's easy to work out who these visitors were, even though I cannot begin to account for them rampaging through my place. The ogre was no such thing, for a start. He was—and I knew this even that night—just a big, solid kind of a man, from Perthshire farming stock, like I'd thought when I met him in the daytime. He was, in fact, Farmer George, Mr. Walker of Rattray Walker, whose first name I've forgotten although John introduced him last night. And the oily one who was smoking when Bunny saw him was Nicotine Ned, who permanently reeks of tobacco. Was he Eric Something? And the rough type that made Bunny want to call the police? That was my own dear brother.

And it all seems so very silly. I would almost say they cooked up the midnight visitations, like schoolboys, as a dare.

"Who are they?" Bunny asks.

"They play poker together."

"A card school? Hardly more respectable than my first guess."

"But you only saw the three of them?"

"Wouldn't that be enough!" says Bunny. The server is out wiping tables now, eavesdropping and barely trying to hide it. "I admit I was beginning to wonder how many men friends you had."

"One," I say. "But there are four in the . . . what did you call it? Card school? They were a man down last night, but it's four as a general rule."

"And who the dickens are they?"

Gently and with a watchful eye on him in case he has a heart attack or a fit of apoplexy, I tell him everything. I lay out how a nursing home manager took Peggy in, and Lord's Yard disposed of her stuff, and finally the property centre in BofA handled the sale of her beloved house.

Once I'm finished, I go inside and fetch him a glass of water and a sweet biscuit. The server eyes me closely but says nothing. God knows what she thinks is going on out there but she's definitely on Team Bunny, which I'm very glad to know, considering.

"So," he says when he's had a mouthful and also dipped his handkerchief in the glass and wiped his neck and forehead. "There's a consortium of kidnappers, thieves and fences conspiring to defraud people like me out of their property."

"It looks like it," I say. "Peggy might be the first but she just as easily might not be. And it's all very likely done with the permission of their families, the very people who should be making sure their elderly relatives are looked after."

"Advocating for them," says Bunny, nodding vigorously. "Agitating for pavement dips and grab rails. Quite. Indeed. I agree."

"That sounds personal." He's never mentioned anyone.

"Oh, they're never off the phone," he says. "My daughter would love nothing better than to tidy me away into a little flat somewhere, with a warden, but my grandsons have been marvellous. More or less telling the parents that if they put *me* away then they'd better watch out when it's *their* turn. Don't worry about that for a moment, Lindsay. I'm well looked after."

"Peggy probably thought—" I say, then stop myself. I don't want to make him fret for nothing.

But he's not thinking about himself. "I should have known she couldn't have gone downhill as fast as all that," he says.

"Although she did, didn't she?" I say. "Just in a different order. Not failing health then nursing home. Nursing home then failing health." We stare at one another for a long moment. "I suppose these places are pretty tightly regulated," I say. "I mean, the Elms was suspiciously quiet when I was there but she can't have suffered any actual neglect. Right?"

"No, no, no, none of that," Bunny says. "They will have had an attending physician apart from anything. In fact, it's rather hard to see how the plan could function without one. I'd have said a doctor would be far more use to them than a junk man. The clearing of the house and disposal of the furniture seems rather trivial compared with what the other two do."

"My brother is . . . easily led," I say. "He's had his share of troubles and it's left him . . ."

"The fourth one must be the doctor," Bunny says.

"Not a very good one, going by Peggy. But the other two aren't all that great at their bit either, are they? Like we said, she went downhill fast in the home. And as to the sale of the house, I'm pretty sure they could have got more for it than I paid."

"Perhaps they didn't dare," Bunny says. "What *did* you pay?"

"Seven hundred," I tell him. "But a top lawyer looked at everything and said it was all above board."

"Seven hundred thousand?" says Bunny. "For Saint Helen's? That seems rather scant, my dear, if you don't mind me being blunt with you."

"I'll ask him again," I say. "My lawyer, I mean. I'll double-check. He seemed to think it was unremarkable."

"And where did you find him? This 'top lawyer'?"

I feel a bit sick suddenly. "You're right," I say. "He's not a property specialist. He's a . . ." I've forgotten again but I've still got his card in my wallet and I take it out and show it to Bunny.

"Golly," he says. "Advocate depute. No, I should think it's been a while since this chap did any conveyancing right enough. How did you bend *him* to your will?"

"*He's* my one and only boyfriend," I say. I have no idea what *advocate depute* means. It certainly doesn't say it on David's card. "Have you really never crossed paths with him since I moved in?" I ask. "Some Neighbourhood Watch you are! You clock the uninvited guests and assume I'm on the game and my legitimate gentleman caller is the only one you never see?"

"Not on the game!" Bunny says, quite loud considering the server is out pretending to clear tables again. "Just . . . enjoying life." He rubs his thumb over the engraving on David's name. "Minto," he says. "I might know this chap actually. Minto is a name of great pedigree in Edinburgh circles."

"Yes, he's pretty posh."

"But are you quite sure he's single? I seem to remember a Burns Supper I was dragged to by a pal . . ."

"I've caught him between wives," I say. But I'm not feeling nearly as light-hearted as I sound. I don't know anything about the law but I know there are a lot of professional arenas where truly useless people get kicked upstairs out of harm's way.

"Bunny," I ask. "You knew Peggy better than I got a chance to. Do you think she'd *want* me to have her house? All things being equal? Should I let it go right now? Because the sale is so tainted. Or should I try to hang on to it?"

"Do you love it?" Bunny says.

"I really do."

"And you're not going to ruin it? Put in a gym and a cinema?"

"Not a chance."

"Then I think she'd be delighted." He shivers. "Let's go," he says. "Even in July, it's still Perthshire and my old bones reckon there's rain coming. Anyway, you've got work to do."

"Once I've decided which bloody police station to go to—Fife, Perthshire, Clack, or Stirling," I say, standing and hauling him to his feet too. "If they investigate, they'll be able to track down the doctor, surely. And they'll be able to track down Peggy's son too."

Bunny is standing stock still, staring at me.

"Is your bum numb?" I say. "Those chairs are pretty but brutal."

"I've remembered something," he says. "It was you talking about the coppers tracking down Peggy's son and about a doctor. Oh, my dear girl. Peggy's son *is* a doctor."

"Oh my God, yes," I say. "You told me."

"I can't quite bring his name to mind right now. It'll come back to me."

"Searching for a 'Dr. March, Glasgow' would surely find him," I say. "But . . ."

"But?"

"But no one would do that to their own mother!"

Out of kindness he doesn't mock my naivety and so it's in silence that we make our way home.

I let myself in the back door and sit down with my laptop. "But *which* police station?" I ask myself again. The house is in Perthshire, but the estate agent is in Stirlingshire. Lord's Yard is in Clack, although it still seems like the smallest deal out of everything. The nursing home is definitely the worst angle of the whole scheme, so I decide to go down to Fife, to Kincardine, where there might already be suspicions about the Elms and it won't be such an uphill battle with the cops when I drop my bombshell.

I turn to the keyboard to look up their address and only then notice that I'm still holding David's business card, curled into my fist. Did I really not put it back in my wallet after showing Bunny? I don't know if I'm clutching it to keep him close to me, like a lovesick teenager, or because I'm holding on to the idea that he knew what he was doing about the house sale and I'm not going to lose this place.

Of course I'm not. It doesn't matter what David specialises in now; he did a law degree and conveyancing is ground-level stuff. It's like a pilot could reverse a milk float but a milkman couldn't land a plane. Still, to reassure myself—and I make a promise that it's my last selfish act before I report the whole ugly business and take what's coming—I look him up again, thinking surely one of those 89,000 hits is going to mention that someone in his chambers, or practice, or department, or however Crown counsels organise themselves, will know enough about selling houses that David would have bobbed along the corridor and asked, if he'd seen something fishy.

I let the page fill this time, ignoring the first few entries, which are about some other guy, like they always are: Everyone I've ever stalked online has had the same name as an apartment complex manager in São Paulo or an adjunct professor at Texas A&M.

But I still haven't found David when I've scrolled right down the first page. It's *all* this other guy, bald and sleek and sixty. I read one of his entries, David Minto, LLM, CC, Advocate Depute, Crown Office, 25 Chambers Street, Edinburgh.

That's what Bunny said. And Chambers Street came up too, sometime. Last night, wasn't it? When David went to Stirling jail because an important client snapped their fingers and summoned him.

I'm 99 percent sure what I'm going to find as I type in advocate depute. My mouth is pouring with water like I'm going to vomit and my fingers are trembling, while I wait for the results to load.

I have to blink away tears to read what it says.

Advocates depute are prosecutors. They don't have clients that could suddenly find themselves in jail after dinner one night. One of the tears falls. Either the man I've been calling David Minto doesn't know that, or he thought I wouldn't check.

I walk down the little staircase, letting it all sink in, feeling what I know only too well is advance mourning. I'm an expert at grieving before the actual loss. I fill a glass with water from the tap and stand at the sink looking out over the garden to Shelley's greenhouse she won't get to use, the grass I'll never see four boys having a kickabout on, the trees whose leaves I won't be sweeping up when autumn comes.

It doesn't last long, this glum misery that's almost enjoyable, in a weird way, if you let yourself really wallow in it. It soon departs and leaves room for the anger to come roaring back in. *Why?* That's what I keep asking the absent "David"? How did he get mixed up in all thi—

Then, as quick as a finger snap and as loud as a thunderclap, I know.

Four men round the table that first night I spied on John's poker game: John Lord the scrappie, Farmer George the estate agent, Nicotine Ned from the nursing home and the other one, with the grey hair, who was facing the other way. And then once, when David was facing away from me and I was looking at his back and his grey hair, I felt that same old vertigo.

And, as if I need any more to ram this home, it strikes me that the second poker night—last night—when there were only three, of *course* there were only three! Because the fourth had gone rushing off to Forth Valley Hospital, where his son was in A&E.

Then he'd come back here to give me a load of flannel about himself, all sheepish and "honest."

And then I'd slept with him.

I feel my guts clench at the memory, and I set the glass down in the sink, sure that I'll puke if I try to take another sip.

The phone rings and I grab it without looking. "Chloe?"

"Bunny," comes Bunny's voice. "An easy mistake to make. I remembered Peggy's son's name as I was dropping off, which is better than as I was waking up, because my naps are long. I knew it was something very traditional, such as Robert or William or John or some such."

"Is it David?" I say.

"Oh, splendid. You've found him already. Good work, Lindsay."

I suppose I must say goodbye. Certainly he doesn't notice anything amiss. Maybe I even thank him. After he's rung off, I hit speed dial one. "Chloe," I say to her voicemail. "I've got to talk to you. Code Red, Chlo. Code Red. I need you."

Part Three

Chapter 22

Code Red was born one day at high school when Chloe's period started. I made a pillow of toilet paper for her to stuff in her pants, and then, once she'd got home on the bus without a mishap, started agitating for a machine in the girls' toilets and a supply in the first aid room too. Chloe couldn't see through the mortification to do it for herself.

"It's not first aid," the deputy head told me.

"What is it then?"

"It's a foreseeable requirement," she said.

"So's wiping your bum but you give us bog roll." I was given detention for cheek but we got our vending machine stocked with the cheapest, bulkiest, naffest pads in the chemist's shop. I left it to the girls coming after us to mention tampons.

So today, when I use the code in Chloe's voicemail and she doesn't get back to me immediately, I know for a fact that she's away from her phone. She would never ignore me when I've invoked Code Red. That sets up a worry of its own. I've never seen Chloe without her phone tucked in a pocket or her waistband. Where is she? All last night, she was God knows where too, while I was driving around in a fugue state, bursting in on that horrendous poker game and coming back here to sleep with David "Minto." Where is she now?

My phone rings again and, for the first time since I gave him my number, I hope it's not him.

"What's up, hun?" Finally, it's her.

I let a huge, shaky breath go and don't try to hide that it ends in a sob. "I don't even know where to start," I tell her. "I'm mixed up in something really bad, Chlo, and I didn't know it was happening."

"Eh? Like what?"

"Aileen Murdoch, right? You know how you knew she left her husband for another woman?" I wait for an uh-huh to tell me she's listening, but no sound comes from the other end. "Sorry, I know. It's not as random as it seems. But—you do actually remember her, don't you?"

"What are you babbling about?" says Chloe. "We never misuse the Code, Lindsay. Who cares about bloody Aileen Murdoch?"

"It's the only thing I still don't understand," I say.

"What are the other things?" Chloe says. "The ones you're all over." She's laughing at me and suddenly this pisses me off so much that I let her have the whole lot in a torrent, the words coming out like the vomit that's still threatening.

"This house might not be mine," I say. "I don't know why I got to move in but it might not be legit because my lawyer was a doctor. A bunch of real bastards—one of them is John—tricked poor old Peggy out of here and into care, then sold it to me. And her family is in on it. Lovely David Minto who took me to the ballet and understood about Kai and had an answer for everything and did my legal work for free? He isn't even called David Minto. He's David *March*. He's Peggy's son and he's been lying to me from day one." I take a huge breath. "And so, since I met Aileen on day one, I can't believe that either. Oh Chloe! I slept with him and I feel filthy."

"You slept with him?" Chloe says, her voice a yelp. "When?"

"Last night and I feel sick." Silence. "Chlo?"

"Sorry," she says. "I was thinking. Right, Lindsay, I missed lunch so make me a toastie and I'll be there before it's done. I was going to be coming sometime pretty soon anyway, today or tomorrow."

"What do you mean?"

"There's something I want to show you."

She's always been a bit single-minded, but this is a new level. She wants to *show* me something? Hasn't she been listening to me. "Will you chum me to the police station?" I say. "I'm going to report them. And then can I sleep on your pullout tonight? I don't reckon I'll be allowed back in here and I can't face Shelley if they take John to jail."

"Shoosh," says Chloe. "Shoosh, now. If you still want to go to the police after we talk it over, of course I'll come with you." She's making it sound like this thing she wants to show me is related to what's wrong. Maybe I was being unfair.

"Thanks," I tell her.

"And don't worry about tonight. Everything's going to be okay."

It's not like Chloe to do platitudes. It was one of the best things about her visits towards the end. I'd take her to the farthest bit of the garden, where Kai couldn't overhear me, and rant about the unfairness of it all and the impossibility of me ever coping, all the inarguable reasons I should kill myself as soon as he didn't need me anymore—really bleak stuff—and she only said, "Of course it is. I'm furious too. If God came down, I'd kick him in the nuts for doing this to you. Of course it's impossible, it's unspeakable, no one should have to watch their loved one suffer like this. And of course you want to die with him. How could you feel any other way?"

There wasn't a single "Time will heal" or "Speak to your doctor" or even "One day at a time, Lindsay." So it's kind of astonishing that she would drop an "Everything's going to be okay" on me now when it can't be, not even nearly.

I'm too rattled to make a toastie, but I boil the kettle and put some Penguins and KitKats on a plate. I rub the black biscuit tin as I set it back on the shelf again, polishing it, planning to take it with me wherever I end up when I leave here. I'd like to take the brass tabletop too. I'll probably find the wooden legs if I search the yard hard enough.

As these thoughts wash through me, I can feel something else stirring, a new wave of unease, and I find myself looking upwards as if I can see through the ceiling and the dead room floor even though I don't know what's drawing my attention there. But I hear Chloe arriving before I can chase the thought down and so I shake it off me.

I meet her at the front door after I've heard her screech to a stop on the gravel instead of carrying on round the side. When I get it unlocked and open, she's powering towards the steps through the first of the big, cold raindrops. She barges in, practically knocking me out of her way. This is exactly what I need—Chloe on the warpath—but it's still pretty scary. She's even got her laptop under her arm, as if she's already made a plan that needs spreadsheets.

"Do you want a—?" I say.

"Where's your best Wi-Fi?" she asks, talking over me. "Where's your *alive* room?"

That's not how it works, of course. My dead room is connected to the internet or I couldn't do my job without traipsing around the house, but the phrase has been bothering her ever since she first heard it and I guess she's taking some kind of sideways dig.

"Kitchen should be okay. Why?" I say, following her.

"It's time to move on to the next stage," she says. "No one else agrees with me but I think it's time. Near enough." By the time I reach the kitchen door she's got the laptop open on the table and is tapping away. "Password?"

"Same," I say. She learned it on her first visit to Hilo—Ka1&L1ndsay4evs—but for some reason her lip curls as she types it in.

"Why are you narky at me?" I say. "Or am I getting the benefit of someone else bugging you?"

"Sit down and watch this," she says. "Tell me after you've seen it, if you still want to go to the polis." I slide into the seat and see a stilled video. The counter tells me it's three minutes long. Chloe nods at the screen. "I wasn't *quite* finished, so it's a bit rough."

I hit play and some sort of cheap fade effect clears to reveal a shot of me standing at the dead room window, the day Chloe showed me round the house.

"You filmed me?" I say. "From down in the garden?" My face on the screen is a blank mask. I think this was when I had just found that message scratched in the paint.

That's what it was! The wave of uneasy feeling is getting stronger. It feels like an earthquake's on its way.

The shot changes. It's half of Chloe's face and one of her arms in the kitchen, more or less where I'm sitting right now.

My voice comes out loud and clear from her laptop. *I came to tea here.*

Chloe's voice is even clearer. *And you had the whole idea right then and there?*

"Eh?" I ask her. "I don't remember you saying that. What 'whole idea'?"

I've already got the equipment. My voice again. *I could convert a room this size for about seven hundred quid.*

That's bang on your budget, Lindsay.

"Okay, okay, okay," I say. "I *do* remember you telling me that, but that wasn't when it happened. And why the hell were you recording me? What's going on?"

"Shh," Chloe says.

What are you playing at? comes from the laptop speakers. I said that too, I think. *This isn't one of those stupid shows. This is my stupid life.*

"But that's not *when* I said it," I tell Chloe.

But do you think this place would work for you? Chloe's voice is saying. *You're the boss.*

"What the hell?" I ask her now, twisting away from the screen. "You didn't say that. Not at any point. The sound's a million miles different. Did you even use the same mic?"

"Watch" is all Chloe says.

The film moves on to show us in the bedrooms, our feet knocking loudly on the bare boards. I come to a standstill at a window, facing the other way. Chloe is filming my back. I had no idea. *Gosh, Chloe, I wonder how much this house would cost me?* my voice pipes up, dripping with insincerity.

"Is that when I said that, though?" I ask. "Didn't I say that when you were going on about bathrooms?"

She doesn't answer me here in the kitchen. On the film, her voice says, *I told them you were adamant and—reluctantly, mind—they've agreed.*

"Told who?" I ask her.

"Shut up," she says, leaning in and rewinding the counter. "You've missed a bit."

Well, that's certainly a lovely surprise, my voice says.

"I was outside when I said that!" I yelp. "My God, Chloe, don't give up the day job. You can hear the bloody birds!"

Aw come on, you're getting a deep discount, Chloe says on the film. *They're hardly going to be turning cartwheels for you. I mean, how much of a mark down would you say this is?*

All this house in this location? I can't miss the sneer in my voice. *Nine hundred and fifty thousand pounds. More likely well over a million. But I love it.*

What Lindsay loves, Lindsay gets, Chloe on the film says.

Right, you've had your fun is the last thing my voice says before the film ends.

I close the laptop, unsettled in a way I can't quite account for. "If that's a joke, I don't get it," I say. "Are you . . . trolling me? I'm an audio artist, Chloe, and the way you've plopped in those additions is absolute dog shit. It was like you watching someone wash their kitchen floor with a dishcloth under their shoe."

"I told you I wasn't finished," she says. "I was going to work on it today, so it's still a bit clumsy. I'm the only one besides you—"

"Only one who?"

"—besides you who cares about the quality anyway—I'm a perfectionist; shoot me—and really, what matters is making sure you don't muck this up. So, when you started twatting on about the cops, you know? And to be perfectly honest, like 100 percent open about *all* my motives"—her voice is rising—"when you phoned me up to tell me what you did, I thought, fuck it. This has gone on long enough."

"But . . . what did I do?" I say. "Whatever it is, we can sort it out, but right now we need to talk about—"

"What did you *do*?" Chloe looks me straight in the eye, with a cheerful little smile curling into the corners of her lips. "You slept with Dave."

It takes me a minute and then I repeat it. "Dave."

"You always made out you were so pure and then you go and shag my fella."

Then she watches me as if I'm a trained monkey, that small smile spreading to become a grin as she sees the truth hit me, wash over me, and begin to sink in. The details aren't there, not yet. But the shape of it is clearer and clearer, like a black, bulging thundercloud. Heavier and darker than anything I ever saw coming at Hilo, over the ocean.

"You and David?" I ask her.

"You nearly caught us once," she says. "On the phone. In here. And the night he asked you round to his house? I didn't agree to that."

"I don't und—"

"Fucking you certainly wasn't part of the deal."

I can't help flinching.

"Miss Priss," says Chloe.

I can't bear to look at her, so I put my head in my hands. Maybe it'll help me see what the hell's going on here. "So you knew he was part of this," I say.

"At least you're admitting you know there's a 'this.'"

"You knew this is his mum's house you were determined to show me? And you knew she more than likely didn't want to move to the Elms? I'm sure she didn't want all her stuff to go to Lord's Yard."

"And now . . . ta-da! You know too. But to get back to the subject under discussion." She leans right over the table and hisses into my face. "You had sex with my boyfriend."

"But I didn't know that! He tricked me. *You* tricked me. The pair of you set me up and I don't even know why." My thoughts are racing but I still manage to catch one. "Chloe, this didn't start the day I met David in the garde—" Then everything slips out of my grasp again as a new realisation hits me. "My God, it's been driving me mad how—but Aileen Murdoch probably wasn't even *at* school with us, was she?"

"Probably!" Chloe says, sitting back again and cackling. "Christ, Lindsay, you're not safe to be out on your own. You shouldn't be allowed to cross the road. There *is* no Aileen Murdoch, you plank. That's Sarah McAllan, Eric's wife. They run the Elms together. You nearly made her shit a brick when you met her in the car park."

Another black cloud rolls towards me.

"*You* told him I like the ballet," I say. I don't seem to be in control of what bits hurt most. That shouldn't register, set against him winkling his poor old mother out of her house, but knowing that the night in Glasgow was a con feels as if it's going to shatter me.

"He was bored shitless," Chloe says. "He texted me from the toilet, practically crying."

I'm cracking.

"You told him what I was going to wear and he had on a shirt the same colour."

"And you believed that the universe was smiling on you, because you're soooo special."

And I break.

Now it feels like watching a firework show. Every few seconds, with no warning, a different bit of the darkness splits and blooms, as I remember all the things that haven't made sense. How nothing felt real. How everywhere I went looked like cardboard cutouts, everyone I saw looked like paper dolls. I thought I was cracking up purely because I'd come back to where everything happened to that kid I was. Now I know I was cracking up because of what's happening now to the kid I still am. It's exactly the same.

With one important difference.

The kid I still am isn't alone. It's true that John is nowhere. But she's got me.

"Why did those guys break into the house?" I say, at last, so proud to hear how strong my voice sounds. "In the night, I mean."

"Yeah, that was my fault," Chloe says. "Breakdown of communication. I cleaned it too well after it was emptied, so they both needed to make sure and put their fingerprints back, here and there. Put their fingerprints on all of *your* stuff, in case you tried to claim you weren't in on it."

"In on what, for God's sake? I'm not in on anything! Chloe, I get that you've lost your way. Had your head turned. Look." I sit forward and reach out for her hands. She recoils from me. "Sweetheart, you're obviously not well. And I'm not going to deny that what you're saying right now? How you're behaving? I'm not going to say it doesn't hurt. But I love you. Still. Just."

"Get to the point!"

"But you must understand, I'm going to the police as soon as you leave. You must know that."

"Eh, Lindsay, I know you're not the sharpest pin in the cushion, but did you not see that film I just showed you? It was genius. You put out more solid gold than any of us dreamed—"

"What are you *talking* about?"

"And you should be thanking me because John was ready to kick you till you bled."

"Why?"

Chloe is cackling. "You're as sharp as a spoon, Lindsay. Jesus Christ."

"I know he probably wasn't really worried about me like he pretended but—"

"Oh, he was worried all right. We all were. Worried you were going to sod it up for us. Starting by turning up a day early when we were all set to go. And then you reveal that you met Peggy? That was the fucking tin lid. So overall, we've been worried sick since you came traipsing back, weeping and wailing. You were supposed to be *useful*, Lindsay."

I drive the pain away from me, God knows how, and try to focus yet again on making sense of it. "I don't know what you mean," I say. "Why did you make that film?"

"So that no one could hear your words and think you're not in this up to your neck," she says. "Not that you'd risk it, right? You're not *that* stupid."

"I don't know what you *mean*."

"Oh really? Well, I stand corrected. So let me make it idiot-proof. You bagged one of the houses, Lindsay, at a bargain price too. If you clype to the cops, you'll be going down with the rest of us."

"You make it sound so . . . like a . . ." Then my brain processes what my ears just heard. "*One* of the houses? How many times have you done this?"

"Saint Helen's makes seven," Chloe says.

"Seven?" I can't believe it's so many.

"Yeah, we're only just beginning but already we're getting more efficient."

"And so you make the houses cheap so no one questions it?"

"It is truly exhausting," says Chloe, "talking to someone as dumb as you. Of *course* not. Usually we're screwing the highest price we can get out of the buyer. You're the only one who got a bargain."

"But why?" I say again. "Why? Why did David agree to that?"

"So he hasn't made his move, then?" is all Chloe says. She's being deliberately mysterious. I stare at her blankly, refusing to play her game, refusing to beg for any more information. She gives in first. "John," she says. "*He* wants this house. He reckons he deserves more than his agreed cut. So, he's going to get it off you and make you live at Lord's Yard. Didn't bloody Shelley wade in and half tell you at one point? Thinking she was so clever?"

"But why didn't he just *take* it for himself?" I shake my head, trying to stay focused. "Why involve me?"

"I can't say you're quick, Lindsay, but you're at least asking the right questions."

I stare at her, wishing I knew what she meant, knowing she won't tell me. "And how did John manage to persuade the others?"

"Again," says Chloe, "so close."

I can't stand the way she's teasing me, smug and mocking, but the truth is she's right. I am close. And I know how to get closer. "I'm going to Lord's Yard," I say.

Chloe gives a mirthless laugh. "Closer still. Maybe you're not a complete idiot, after all."

"Because I don't see how John can be calling the shots and giving his sister a cheap house. Offloading the furniture is the least of the wrongdoing here."

"Wrongdoing!" Chloe says. "*Wrongdoing?* Jesus Christ, Lindsay, you really did catch a good dose off of that sanctimonious prick, didn't you?"

They're only words and she's been hurling words at me for ages but this time what she's saying lands like a punch.

"Kai?" I say. "Do you mean Kai? What the fuck, Chloe? What's happened? You sound as if you hated him."

"Oh, don't worry," Chloe says. "I hate you too."

I go up the back stairs to lock my dead room first. God knows where I'm getting this calm resolve from but I know that the equipment in there is my biggest asset. It's what's going to help me rebuild my life once all this is over. The rest of the house doesn't matter. It's not mine and it never will be. I sink into my desk chair, feeling as if someone has removed my bones. *You were supposed to be useful.* So . . . John and Shelley were playing me somehow, using me. Chloe sounds as if she loathes me. *Good dose off of that sanctimonious prick.* Everything I thought I had has gone. Even the thing I thought I'd found—the miracle—was just a sick joke. *We, Lindsay Lord Hale, are trying again.* Everyone pretending to care has been laughing at me. Kai. *Kai.* I wail it inside my head, silent and deafening. There's no answer. Not in the soft, muffled air, not in my head, not even in my heart. "I'm sorry," I say to him, out loud in the warm cocoon of the dead room. But whatever it is that's been here with me, unchanged since the last time he closed his eyes, has gone. I'm speaking to empty space. The worst of it is, I can hardly blame him.

I haul myself to my feet and clump back down.

Chloe is still there, in the kitchen. She doesn't even turn her head.

"Is there any chance you're going to explain why you hate me so much, all of a sudden?" I say.

"All of a sudden!" Chloe jeers, still without facing me.

"Or explain what's going on with John?"

"I thought you were going to see for yourself. Drive recklessly. I wouldn't want you to arrive safe and sound in all this rain."

The door banging shut as I leave is the sound of my oldest friendship ending. Finally, truly, we are absolutely alone, that kid I was and me.

Chapter 23

I stand a minute on the porch, looking out at the steady drilling rain that was the backdrop to most of my childhood. Just like Hawaii, the wind here sweeps in and leaves storm clouds hanging over the hills, then drops to nothing. It's going to be soaking wet for hours now. I sprint to my car and roll down the drive, where the ground beneath the big trees is still dry.

I turn my head as I pass through the gates. It feels like ten years since I paused there and met Bunny. I thought life had been upended then, finding out about the scheme, the scam, the fraud my brother was mixed up in. But I hadn't known a fraction of it.

Now that I've seen it once, I can't help but notice the little fox skeleton as I go by, and I make a promise to myself. I'm going to bury it in the garden before this whole rotten mess collapses and I'm out of Saint Helen's for good. It feels important in a way I can't quite account for, to lay something properly to rest. I missed Peggy completely and even Kai's funeral feels as if it's been sullied. Chloe was there with her arm round me and her soothing voice in my ear. And then, for no reason at all and after Kai was beyond doing anything to harm her, she decided she didn't even like him and despised me for loving him.

So I'll bury the little fox and I'll take what's coming to me from the law. I absolutely trust that Chloe's faked-up videos can't outweigh my sworn testimony. And I absolutely trust that John is the least guilty out of the whole lot because all he did was move furniture and not report the rest of it. I really hope I get the chance to talk to Shelley without him. I need to recruit her, get her to help me persuade him to cut his losses and be the only survivor when this thing falls apart. If the three of us go to the police together today and tell all about the rest of them, maybe John and Shelley can escape the worst of what's coming. I don't care about them exactly—they've been *faking* their concern for me—but I care about Zak and Nicky. I care about *their* little lives.

Except, of course, that I'm lying. I'm so good at lying to myself. I *do* care about John, only . . . admitting that means facing why.

I care about John because he had the same childhood as me. And I'm pretty sure that if I tell people all about it—all about *all* of it—he'll get help, not jail. He'll get treatment. He needs it. He went white that first time I mentioned the caravan after I got back here. And he had no clue why I said "Dad." He needs a kindly, clever doctor to dig down under the caravan on the top, and the so-called game underneath that, and help him face the full truth about the life we lived here. No one with a heart will question why he got manipulated by the other three. We turned into such good little soldiers, John and me, both of us so easily led, so desperate to please.

I wish, though, that these thoughts didn't feel so much as if I was trying to convince myself. I wish what I'm telling myself didn't seem so rickety and there wasn't that gnawing dread that something far worse is just out of view. I can still hear Chloe's voice saying *so close* and *see for yourself.*

The climb up to BofA is nerve racking—I'm out of practice driving in weather like this—the windscreen wipers struggling and the tyres skiting over sheets of water as the gutters fill. The main street is a nightmare of scurrying shoppers with their hoods up, peripheral vision abandoned, crisscrossing the road to get into shelter while the peering drivers hunch over their steering wheels, cursing. The rain has emptied the park as I skirt round the top of Stirling too, battering the beds of flowers flat, bowing the shade umbrellas outside the hotel until every segment is a hammock full of water and the spokes are buckling.

The Hillfoots Road is flooding. I slow down to thirty-five and put my full-beam headlights on, flashing the oncomers that I'm straddling the line to keep from aquaplaning.

I give them plenty of warning that I'm turning off at Lord's Yard, but I still see the car behind skid too close for comfort before it swerves around me and keeps going. The gates are shut. Maybe John doesn't want the ground churned, or maybe he reckons no one will be out in this and he's taken the chance for a break. Or maybe they're out.

"God, I hope they're out," I mutter to myself. Then I catch my lip in my teeth. Why did I say that? My mind is reeling and I pray that my brain hasn't chosen this moment to start sending my speech off the rails as well as my hearing and my vision. Only . . . *was* my hearing off the rails? No, of course it wasn't. *Nice save* makes perfect sense for Sarah McAllan to tell her husband when I turned up at the nursing home. And I can work out what I overheard John saying now too, when I thought I heard *North Wind and the Sun*. It's not difficult once you know what they were discussing: how to get away with it, how to make sure David bears the brunt, how the best plan of all is to make sure that there's *more pinned on the son*.

Only . . . what aspect of John's bit could be pinned on the doctor instead? I wish I could be sure I'd never work *that* out, but I've got a deep-down—bone-deep—feeling that something is more wrong than I've admitted yet and that some bit of me knows what it is, even though the rest of me can't bear to. Poor little fox, I think. I look at myself in the driving mirror and from nowhere, my voice says, "Seven dead."

I step out of the car. Coatless, my hair and shoulders soaked through before I even reach it, I go for the little pedestrian gate cut into the big one but, try as I might, I can't get it to open. The latch looks the same as it always did but, from the way the lock bows and clanks, I think it's bolted on the inside.

I stand there a moment, so wet I can't get any wetter, letting the rain stream down my face and feeling the water saturate my clothes. In the front of my mind, I'm still coming to tell Shelley and John to confess and get themselves some benefit, so what I should be doing is getting into my car, into the dry, and phoning them.

In the back of my mind, though—not even that, in the pit of my belly—there's a truth growing too big to be denied. And so maybe it's for the best that this gate is locked. Maybe, just maybe, I can get in under my own steam and face what I already know to be true.

But is there any chance one of our secret routes is still there? He's definitely been working on the side fence. It's now as sturdy as any wall and six feet high from the level ground, rising to eight because of the drainage ditch at the field edge. So it's not going to be easy, but I can use the depth of the ditch and the fence shadow as cover while I make my way to the end, where the land starts to rise, the hills looking down like a judge from his bench, like God from his throne.

The ditch is filling and my Converse are sodden and squelching on my feet, blisters already rising on my heels as my wet socks start to work their way down. But not for one minute do I consider giving up.

I get to the back corner and the fence is as stout as ever. My heart starts to sink. How likely is it that any of the old tricks are still there to be played? I'm drenched to the skin now, glad I've left my phone in the car and that I don't wear a watch. My eyes are smarting as my day cream streams into them and I can smell the conditioner in my hair as it washes out and pours down my neck. I'm shivering. Still, I stand a moment with my eyes squeezed shut, remembering and hoping. I even cross my fingers and try, inside my cold socks, to cross my toes.

I knew the tree with the overhanging branch was still there—I could see it from Zak's bedroom—but when I splash and clamber my way over to it, it's as I thought: The nails are gone, nothing left but scars in the bark to show where they were.

On to the next one. I thought I remembered where the leaning sheet of corrugated iron was, but after I've squelched and skidded back and forth for what feels like half an hour, I'm forced to admit that either I've forgotten or—more likely—it's gone too.

The third route was always my best shot anyway, because no one else knew about it. Chloe didn't know because we never told anyone anything, John and me. And John didn't know because, by then, he had turned crude and tough and scornful, forgetting where the library was and what time *Blue Peter* was on, and only caring about the price of Strongbow and whose big sister might buy it for him because she thought he was a ride. That's why I kept *this* secret entrance—the best one, the Narnia wardrobe—to myself.

I turn to scan along the length of the back boundary, but it's so dark—in the shadow of the hill, the clouds as black as a new bruise, the rain a veil of grey—that I accept I'll have to go by memory. That and hope. Maybe a stroke of luck too.

I get to the spot, hauling myself up a steep bank by digging my fingernails round the tree roots and jabbing my feet into the mud to make toeholds. I'm almost sure that this fence panel I'm touching right now is no such thing. It's too narrow and too tall, and I'm sure my fingers can feel swirls of walnut wood, rough now without a shred of varnish left, raised into a topography by the seasons of rain and sunshine. I'm sure of it. This is my Welsh dresser, here as it's always been.

The rusted filing cabinets to one side are still there too and so is the shipping container, its mustard paint peeling. When I stretch out to touch it, I feel the flakes come away.

I gasp and pull my hand into my chest. Flakes, I think. It's only flakes, not splinters. Why is my heart hammering? I can feel the answer starting to rise, and so I force my thoughts away. I drive my whole mind to remembering how it's done, to hoping it still works. Then I drop down into a crouch.

I need to clear twenty years' worth of weeds and leaf litter from where it's banked up before I can even try to slide the bottom panel. My hands are numb with wet and cold and my nails bend and break with the first few handfuls, but I stick at it, scraping and gouging, shoving clods of mud and dead grass back between my bent legs until I feel like a mole making a burrow. It's endless, or it seems so until I hit an enormous dandelion—I know what it is from the sudden sharp stink; it's grown sappy nestled down in mud and mulch this way.

I pull it out by its roots and fall on my backside as it comes clear. When I roll forward again, there's a different smell. This isn't decaying vegetation. This is a dry smell. It's dust and paper and carpet and fabric and old clothes and stale air. It's the smell of Lord's Yard. I'm as good as in.

I wipe my muddy hands on the sides of my jumper, under my arms where it's still almost dry, then I feel for the grooves on the baseboard, where my fingers fit same as they always did, or even better now that I'm bigger. I give one tug and, with a screech of wood on wood, the board starts to slide towards me. I wriggle backwards on my bum, scrabbling for purchase with the sides of my trainers, slipping and sliding, but inching back steadily, until—just like it used to and like I should have been ready for—the board comes free and flips, sending me sprawling down the bank and knocking me hard in the neck with one corner.

I clamber clear of it and crawl back up again. I need to do this next bit without letting myself think about it too much, so I fall onto my front, full length, and wriggle forward until I can squeeze my head and shoulders in, pausing to work one arm through then the other, next my chest, then I pause half in and half out of the cave of dresser base that I've opened up.

I'm so much bigger. When I was wee, it was a thrill to crouch in here, but now my elbows are bruising through my wet sleeves and I can feel pins and needles starting to tingle in my calves. I've never been claustrophobic but this dark box is making me shudder. Or maybe it's the cold now that I've finally stopped moving.

Either way, I stretch forward and shove the nearest door, the click of the latch releasing such a familiar sound that I find myself gasping. There before me is the place John called the Barrens, same as it always was. It's neither inside nor out, like so much of the yard, where skyscraper piles make canyons and, if boards get laid on top of the canyons, turn into caves. Here, it was rusted scaffold poles stored along the tops of buckling old wardrobes, and then at some point my dad shoved a load of corrugated plastic up there too, not deliberately trying to make a roof—more trying to clear space below—but it turned into a roof just the same, turned what was under it into a room. A room with no walls as such, except that the press of junk all around makes them.

I haul my torso out of the dresser base and wriggle my legs up through the hole behind me, walking forward on my hands in a way I haven't done since wheelbarrow races at school. When my knees hit the hard ground in front of the dresser, sending needles of pain down my shins, I ball myself up and sit huddled against the other dresser door, feeling the knobs of those carved flowers digging into my spine.

The Barrens. John named it and so it was his. It still is. He has protected it. He has found a use for it. Huddled there chilled and shivering, I cannot deny for one more second what I came to find, even though I couldn't admit I was searching. I'm looking at them right now, here in the no longer forgotten, no longer abandoned, no longer neglected, no longer cluttered, far end of the junkyard, with its straight path from the Portakabin and its—oh God—its vegetable patch where Shelley grows such healthy crops to give away so very generously to the poor. Here in the Barrens, in the dirt, in the dark, some almost gone and starting to blend with the earth around them, others not even begun to settle, here are the graves that John protects with cameras and a new path, with a better fence and different lighting.

I start to count them but feel my gorge rise. I squeeze my eyes shut, swallow hard and manage not to throw up. There's nothing inside me to come out anyway.

I realise I'm rubbing my fingertips against each other, cold mud and rain making them slide numbly over and back, over and back. But I'm thinking of them warm and dry, touching the rough edges of the new holes Shelley drilled into the brass table to turn it into a gong. And when I did *that*, I was remembering flakes of paint that I brushed off my fingers, looking down at Chloe in the garden, still reeling from reading those words scratched into the wall.

Help, they're going to kill m—

Only those flakes of paint should have been long gone. If that message, scraped out under the windowsill of my dead room, was an old game played by children at an earlier stage in the house's life, or parlourmaids unhappy or dramatic, then the flakes would have been swept up decades ago. But there they were the day I toured the house and there they probably still are, behind the soundproof boards, stuck in the grooves of the old skirtings where even Chloe's cleaning didn't find them because she hadn't seen the message and didn't know they were there.

I should have realised right then, I tell myself. And, even if I didn't, I should have known better than what I believed about the poor dead fox back here. I should have had the wit to know that that terrible smell, the grim rage on John's face, the blank look on Shelley's, were all wrong. And I should have known for sure, beyond all doubt and wishful thinking, when the gods sent me the long-dead fox right there in my own front garden—sent me the gift of knowledge yet again, saying, "Look, Lindsay. Look how mild a poor little fox is as it dies and goes back to the earth. No one even noticed this one."

I *did* know. I've been feeling knowledge starting to bulge at me from the inside all day until I could burst. I should have stopped resisting it. Then I would have been spared what I'm seeing now.

Or, if the plain sight of a fox's bones and its poor scraps of fur didn't shout loud enough, then what about the sound good sense I started dishing out to myself when I found out what those four poker players had done?

I said it over and over again: The junkyard owner is not the same as the rest of them. A doctor, the care home guy and someone to sell the houses shouldn't be bossed around by the scrappie. No way should *he* get a house for himself, via his sister or not, just to say thanks for clearing out furniture and taking it away.

Now, sitting here, covered in mud and soaking wet, I'm looking at the reason John Lord is the kingpin.

He's got the most to lose.

He did the thing no one else would do.

And did it seven times.

"Seven dead," I whisper to myself, but I still can't count them, because I can't tear my burning eyes away from the newest—*Peggy*—where the turned dirt is still dark and mounded high, the shadows black and the peaty earth the colour of dried blood where a glimmer of faded light hits it.

Nothing *here* is flat. Nothing's paper. Nothing flutters. This is dry dirt crumbling and wet dirt clumping. And down below there will be the suck of mud, close and cloying around hair and skin and eyes and teeth. This is bones and nails and rotting clothes. That's Peggy I'm staring at. It's my brother and his wife and my friend who are propped-up cardboard that my own brain tried to tell me weren't there, weren't real. My own brain, that I thought was sick like Kai's or broken by losing him, was telling me the truth all along: This life I've come home to live is nothing. God knows why John wanted me back here. I don't know who he is, this brother of mine. I don't know anything.

I crawl away on my hands and knees, no idea where I'm going, no idea what I'm going to do, and only realise where I am when I see the chipped and battered paint on four crooked legs, the hooves up off the ground, just the pole supporting it.

I'm at the fairground horse. Of course I am. I'm right where I was that day when I smelled the smell John said was a fox, a poor harmless, lonely little fox. I stand up and look around in the gloom, searching for that plastic washing-up basin full of paper recycling. If only I had glanced at the address labels on all those flyers and catalogues that day. Or if only I had wondered why exactly that handy little letterbox cage was such a perfect fit for my new front door, I could have put this all together as soon as I moved into the house.

I tell myself that was still too late to help Peggy, but I start to go through the leaflets and flyers all the same, searching for something with her name on it. Am I hoping for a piece of evidence to show the police, to make them come here and start digging? Or am I simply desperate for something of Peggy's to hold in my hand? I have no idea but what I find makes my blood sink until it's pooled in my legs. I know my heart can't really have stopped but it feels that way. I drop to the ground, strings cut.

I still can't read the writing but I feel the smooth, expensive slipperiness of my business card, that Kai told me was worth the money. The business card I dropped through her door that first day. And I know at once what it means. I was a day early and they were aghast to see me. I slept right round the clock, only surfacing briefly because my window was open. I heard screams and *that* wasn't a fox either. That was Peggy, dying. And I didn't save her.

I crawl back to her, to all of them, but I'm too ashamed to tell them I'm sorry. I'm too ashamed of how stupid I've been to even try.

I don't know how long I sit huddled and frozen, willing time to turn back, willing myself into staying in Hilo, making new friends there, blocking Chloe's number, forgetting I've got nephews, making this unhappen, making myself unknow. Making it so I wasn't *so* close to saving Peggy, didn't hear her screaming, didn't stay there in my bed blaming jet lag and nightmares and grief. I curl myself as small as I can go and wait for it to not happen, because it can't.

I don't know how much time passes, but the light has changed and I'm so cold and stiff that I don't jump when I hear the voice. I make no noise.

"Aye, but her car's there." It's John and he's near me. As quietly as I can, I ease open the dresser door and pack myself inside. There's a faint imprint from my wet bum and legs, but it's dark in this corner and I swish some dust around to hide the outline, then I pull the door shut on myself, as silently as I can, and I pray.

Chapter 24

He's right beside the dresser, about two feet from where I'm crouched, trying not to breathe.

"Nah," he says to whoever's on the phone. "I told you. I'm standing in the dead room right now and there's nae sign of her."

Oh, Chloe, I think. And, Why didn't I ever ask myself why that bothered you so much?

"I told you," John says. "The whole of the front is covered and we've been watching. She couldn't have got here." He listens. "There's no way in the back." So *he* thinks. "Robert, Eric, and me have been right round," he says next. "Calm down. She'll be hiding somewhere out on the road waiting for the gate to open and nip in."

Then a silence. Who is he talking to?

"I've got her phone."

He waits.

"Nah, she took the car key with her. But—"

He's interrupted.

"Yeah, but you don't know her like me," he says when he gets the chance to talk again. "She'll not be able to stand being shut out like this. My old dear used to kick us out when we'd been wee shits—I did it too, till Shelley put her foot down! Thing is, it never did me any harm but it wrecked *her* head. She'll be scratching at the gate like a lost pup, I tell you."

Never did him any harm. He did it to Zak and Nicky until Shelley put her foot down. I can't—But he's talking again.

"Well, if she does," John says next, "which she won't, I'm telling you, but if she does, Robert's watching the front and we'll hear the car start. Pick her up back at Saint Helen's and take it from there."

Another silence.

"It won't," he says. "Sort of thing happens every day." What the hell is he talking about now? "Grieving and lonely, eh no? Getting to lodge in a pal's big posh house isn't enough to lift her spirits and all that. Take it from me."

Yesterday, I would have tried to believe his meaning wasn't clear, but I'm done with that. Look where refusing to meet the worst head-on has got me.

"Aye, but you're forgetting that her brother and her best friend'll confirm the state she was in. Aye, aye—'reluctantly.' Good call. But who else has she seen since she got back? Shelley and me, Chloe and you."

So he's talking to David. Together they are all calmly planning to kill me and make it look like suicide.

"No, stay at home," he's saying now. "We're covered. Eric's in the office watching the screens, Sarah's in the house with Shelley. But she'll not get in the gate. And, if she thinks she can hide all night in this, she'll get hypothermia and do the job for us." He cuts this off quickly as if he's been interrupted. "You're too soft," he says. "Get a grip, man."

Then his footsteps move away and, unbelievably, he's whistling.

For some reason, I feel perfectly calm. Maybe it's because at last I understand. I have no idea—and I don't care either—what happened to the other three to get them here. But I know what happened to John. He didn't recover from our childhood. And he didn't do what I did either. *He* didn't bury it too deep to find until reading a self-help book out loud unearthed it. And he didn't stay broken and hurting either. Now I understand why he couldn't talk about "Dad." Why he pretended I'd made a silly mistake, saying that when I meant "Mum." It's because he moved into the space our dad left. You hurt old people with big houses different from how you hurt little kids who trust you, but it takes the same kind of man to do both. Our dad did what he did to John and to me. I ran away from him. John became him.

The journey back under the dresser base, along the edge of the field and out onto the road is a hell that feels a week long although it can't even be fifteen minutes. I fall twice, now that my feet are so cold I can't tell where I'm putting them. The second time, I graze my cheekbone on a rock and twist my ankle trying to get back up again. But eventually, in the failing light and sheets of rain, I'm standing on the verge, a good bit along from the yard gates, waiting for a car to come so I can flag it down.

When I do see lights at last, I don't just stick out my thumb; I step right out into the path of a lorry, waving my arms and saying "Please, please, please," hoping the driver can see me, then hoping the driver can stop in time. I want to jump out of the way but I want even more to show him how desperate I am, so I stand there wailing, mouth wide open like a baby.

He stops, air brakes hissing and engine shifting down and down until it's just a grumble under the sound of the lashing rain. I get myself moving somehow, and totter forward to thank him.

Thank *her*. She waits for me up in the cab and gives me a long look up and down as I scramble in and sit back with my head resting on a fluffy cushion Velcroed to the passenger seat.

She twists the control on her heater until hot air blasts out. Immediately, I start steaming up the side window and my bit of the windscreen.

"Who did that, then?" she says, gesturing to her own cheekbone, as she starts up again.

I pull down the sun visor, taking two goes to make my arm swing that high and my fingers grasp the edge of it. "I fell," I say. Then as she makes a scoffing noise halfway to a spit I add, "You can check if you like. There's grit in it."

Then we're passing Lord's Yard and I bend over in my seat out of view until I judge we're beyond it.

"Is that where you live?" she says.

"I used to," I tell her. "But—"

"Fucking bastard," the lorry driver says. I don't care that she's got the wrong end of a very long stick. She has no idea how right she is, essentially.

"So where are we going?" she says, another few miles along. "Police?"

"Police," I agree.

"Good girl," she says, still not understanding. "I was headed to Stirling. Do you know where the Stirling police station is or will I get it on the satnav?"

I don't answer her. I'm thinking. But my thoughts aren't swirling the way they've been. These thoughts are orderly and they're taking me somewhere. If I heard Peggy at the junkyard that night, the day she was taken from her house, then when did she scratch that message into the paint? And if I heard Peggy at the junkyard that night, if those screams were because they were killing her, then what's the nursing home for?

I get that far then let my head fall back. The police will sort it out for me.

Except . . . John told David to stay at home. And he said Eric was watching the screens and Sarah was in the house with Shelley. Chloe is at Saint Helen's. So maybe, just maybe, no one is at the Elms.

I wish I hadn't stopped counting the graves, because a notion is taking shape in me, and I can't stop it growing. I close my eyes and try to bring the sight of the Barrens—John's *dead room*—back into my mind. One grave was slightly rounded and one was dark and steep. Were there four flat places where older bones had settled? There were more than three. But were there really as many as five?

"Actually," I say, "if it's not too much bother, could you do a drive-by of a house in Kincardine? I need to check something."

"Always a treat to take my rig over that bridge," the driver says, but she's smirking and I can tell she's going to do it for me.

"Thanks."

"But then you'll go to the police." It's not a question.

"Oh, I'll go to the police," I assure her. "Keep your eye on the news. You'll see."

"Good girl," she says again.

"I'll go to the police," I repeat, half to her and half to myself. I'll go to the police. I won't excuse, or explain, or try to find a workaround. I won't be Shelley. I won't be my mum. Because the thing is I know she put us out on the road so he wouldn't find us, when he was looking. I know she did it to protect us, time after time. I know she meant something with those fierce hugs she gave us afterwards. But the first time we got away from him all by ourselves? When we made ourselves a hidey-hole in the caravan? She was angry. She was livid when she found out how come we'd managed it. And it was her who told us it wasn't safe to run away, that we'd get put in a home. I try to think about what he might have put her through when he was looking for us and couldn't find us. I try to care what punishment she had to bear when he wanted his children and they weren't there for him. I fail. She could have broken her life into bits, lost her home and her husband and her pride. She could have saved her kids.

"It's not right that women get blamed for not stopping men from doing what they do," I say to the lorry driver.

"Depends what they're doing," she says grimly. "Usually there's enough blame to go round, if you ask me."

Twenty minutes later, the lorry lumbers along the quiet street towards the Elms like a monster come to ravage the city. I see curtains move and lamps snap on. But not at the nursing home; it's in darkness.

"This the spot?" she says, braking and then idling.

"I'll take it from here," I tell her, opening the door and slithering down.

I wait until her compression brakes have disengaged, like the breath of a snorting dragon, and her "rig" has rumbled away, leaving utter silence and total blackness in its enormous wake. I slip inside the gates, still shivering and squelching, and walk up the drive.

It was six graves, I tell myself. And Chloe said Peggy's was their seventh house. And this nursing home must be part of the plan for *something*.

But dare I break in? I try all the doors, of course, and of course they're locked up tight. And I've got no phone. But Eric and Sarah McAllan are at Lord's Yard and there won't be anyone else here. Surely. There wasn't anyone else here either day I was here before. Besides, if you're letting old ladies die and hoping no one notices, you don't employ witnesses.

By this time, I've found the window I'd break if I could summon the nerve to break a window. It's a half basement, hidden from view by a bin store and a straggly hedge. What if there's an alarm, though?

Again, I need to consider what's going on here at the Elms. The last thing they'd want is an alarm going off and someone calling the cops or the fire brigade.

Before I can talk myself out of it, I jab my elbow hard into a pane of glass, then crouch, waiting. Nothing happens, so I kick the shards away from around the break and, hoping I don't cut myself on bits I've missed, I edge forward, hauling myself inside and then jumping down from the deep windowsill onto a concrete floor, wincing as my ankle flares again.

There's still no alarm and I make for the door into a dimly lit passageway. It's damp and musty smelling, almost as bad as Lord's, and I make sure to take shallow breaths until I find the door hiding the old servants' stairs up to the front hall, where I stand in the middle of the floor, halfway between that covered office window and the grand staircase to the bedroom level, straining to hear any signs of stirring, any sound at all.

The smell of cigarettes is sickening and I want to kick myself for not realising no way Eric was smoking like a train in a house full of paying residents. At least the smell fades as I make my way up the creaking steps, one hand on the polished banister and the other clenched into a fist, wishing I had tried to find a weapon.

On the landing, I start to try doors but find room after room empty, nothing but stripped single beds, their plastic-covered mattresses gleaming in the scant light from the nearest streetlamp. When I've been round them all once, I retrace my steps and check inside the cheap wardrobes but find nothing but coat hangers and stale air.

There must be an attic floor, but I can't find the door to the staircase anywhere on this landing. I take a deep breath and go back round the main rooms again, wondering if there's a hatch. Wondering too what's bothering me, beyond everything I know is bothering me. There's definitely something else wrong too.

In the second big bedroom, I spot what was troubling my subconscious: There's a door in the middle of a blank wall and, trying to picture the layout of the other rooms, I can't think what lies behind it. So, crossing my fingers for an attic stairway, I try the handle.

Then I leap backwards, with my heart hammering. The door is locked and on the other side of it, in response to the handle moving, someone lets out a weak cry.

I back up and take a run, lifting my leg on my last step and aiming the flat of my foot at the lock plate. If the door opened towards me, I might have broken my good ankle but instead I fall through, after the crash and splintering, and find myself careering towards another of those single beds, cartwheeling my arms to try to stop but tripping, coming down hard on one knee and finishing with my panting face less than a foot from the stark-eyed, shaking, whimpering sight of Peggy March, huddled under a blanket in the dark, staring back at me and babbling.

"Help me," she says. "Who are you? You have to help me. Help me."

"Peggy, don't you remember me?" I say. "Lindsay Hale, from Hawaii."

"Help me," she says again. "Help me."

I get her to her feet, steadying her with both my hands, horrified by how thin she is and how bad she smells. "Can you walk? I haven't got a phone, Peggy, and I really want to get you out of here in case they come back."

"I can walk if you help me," she says, but I end up half dragging and half carrying her down the stairs to the front hall. It seems lighter than it did before and I'm suddenly convinced that there's a car on the drive shining its headlamps in through the fanlight. I turn to Peggy to ask her if she could try to crawl back out through that window, but I gasp when I see her face.

"What happened? You're covered in bruises!"

"My idiot son forgot that he wouldn't be able to sign my death certificate," she says. "I'd have to be signed off by a doctor I'm not related to. So I hit myself—and not just my face, all over—and they've had to keep me alive!"

"Oh my God," I say. "You're amazing." Then I say, "Oh my *God*!" Because from outside we have just heard the blaring, blessed, unmistakable sound of an articulated lorry's horn, leaned on hard.

I leap forward and start unfastening bolts and flipping locks and, when I open the door, there she is, just swinging down from her cab to come and pound on the door.

"It didn't feel right," she says to me. Then she catches sight of Peggy. "Jesus fucking Christ."

"A good point well made," Peggy says. "Lindsay? Can I have an arm? I think I'm going to pass out."

"Police or hospital?" the lorry driver says after we've got Peggy into the cab and wrapped her in the duvet from the little bunk tucked in behind.

But something new has occurred to me. If we take her to hospital, where she most definitely belongs, and she starts telling the staff her tale, they're going to think she's got dementia. Then, even if she doesn't name her next of kin, someone on the staff's bound to know that nice Dr. March from Glasgow, and they'll call him, and no one's going to stop him visiting his poor old mixed-up mum. And if we go to the police, me soaked and muddy and apparently raving, we'll *both* end up in hospital and David March might pop in to see me too. I have no idea how I'm going to convince someone to believe me but I need to keep Peggy safe until I've done it.

It's then that Peggy says, "I know I probably *need* a hospital, but I want to go home. If I've finished myself off, I want to die in my own bed."

"Would you settle for the home of a friendly neighbour?" I ask.

"Bunny?" she says and, despite her exhaustion and frailty, the sudden sparkle in her eyes is all the answer I need.

"Can I use your phone?" I ask the driver, after I've told her the address and she's said it must be her night for taking the scenic route.

"Knock yourself out," she says.

"Police," I tell the operator. "My name is Lindsay Hale," I say when I'm put through. "Saint Helen's, Dunblane. I need to report a crime. There are seven—no, six bodies buried—"

"Hello again, Lindsay," the dispatcher says. "You having another tough night?"

"What?" I say, then it hits me. "Oh! It's you again from when that guy was in my house? Well, he was. And I know why now."

"You sound as if you're driving, Lindsay. Are you driving?"

"I'm being driven," I say.

"Because if you're not at home, we can't send anyone out to check on you, you know. Why don't you go home and have a nice cup of tea, maybe a hot bath, and then phone us again if you need to? How about that, eh?"

"You don't und—" I begin. Then I catch myself. "Thanks," I say. "I'll do that. Thank you."

"You take care now, you hear?" the woman says. She's being more patient with me than I would be, even if it's making me want to scream. "Maybe have a word with your doctor about all this. Would you do that for me?"

I say nothing more for the rest of the journey, plotting furiously, until the lorry driver pulls right into Bunny's turning circle and deposits us practically out on the doorstep. "And I'm to keep an eye on the news, eh?" she says before she pulls away. I'm so shattered and so scared, so unsure whether I'm doing the right thing, so unable to decide what to do next, I don't even ask her name. I just watch her go.

We don't have to ring the bell, of course, after the racket the lorry made.

"Who's there?" Bunny shouts through the door, sounding fierce and brave but with a tremor underneath it.

"It's me, Bunny," I say. "Lindsay. I'm sorry it's so late. Can I come in?"

He takes a good old while to unlock and unbolt the door and even longer to haul it open and peer round it at us. "Lindsay, what the dev—?" he says, then his eyes land on Peggy.

"There's no time to explain," I say, barging past him into a cluttered wood-panelled hallway and guiding Peggy into a chair. "Hot sweet tea and a little bland food," I say. "Don't tell anyone she's here—*anyone!*—and don't let *anyone* in unless I'm with them, okay? I'll try to be as quick as I can."

Bunny has sunk down onto his knees in front of the hall chair, his bare feet half out of his leather slippers and his old knees surely screaming in protest. He wriggles out of his dressing gown and sweeps it round Peggy's shoulders. He looks at her with brimming eyes. "How? Where?"

"They abducted me," she says. "They took me to show me my own grave. They tried to keep me locked up in my own house. Finally, they moved me to a nursing home to rot there."

"Who?" says Bunny. "Why?" He turns to see if I can help him and gets another shock. "Lindsay, what happened to you? You need dry clothes."

I don't stay to argue. I let myself out, shout, "Lock up behind me" through the letterbox and scurry down the drive.

Chapter 25

Saint Helen's is in darkness. I slip in the back door, lock it behind me for what it's worth—who the hell knows who's got keys to this place—and go straight up the small stairs to the dead room. I shut this door too and lock it, then I put the light on, squinting against the brightness. It feels as if I've been in the dark—of rain, tree shadow, tunnels of junk, the lorry cab, the nursing home and Bunny's gloomy hallway—for hours now.

But the bright light is soothing, once my eyes have adjusted. It's warm and sane and all around this room are familiar objects. Even the smell of the new panels reminds me of home, although here in the cool of a Scottish summer, it's fainter than it was when Kai and I put it up last time, the plastic reeking until our heads ached. I pull my laptop down from the desk onto the floor beside me and log in. It takes me less than a minute to download a VoIP softphone and dial, praying it'll be that same dispatcher when I get through.

"I'm home now," I tell her. "Saint Helen's, Dunblane."

"I remember."

"I've discovered six dead bodies buried at Lord's Yard in Menstrie," I say, trying to stay as calm and measured as humanly possible. She doesn't answer. "I can give you the names of some of the people involved. Not all, because I've forgotten them, but John Lord, Shelley Lord, Chloe Crozier, David March, Aileen—no that's a lie. There are three more and I know where they work."

"I think I *will* request that safe-and-well check on you, Lindsay," she says.

"I hoped you would."

"Don't you worry anymore. You stay on the phone till the officers get there and we'll take care of everything."

I keep the line open but I can't just sit there, so I grab the small polka dot hammer with the screwdriver hidden in the false handle that I brought in here to bang picture hooks. It was always mine, along with a pink measuring tape and flowery pliers; feminine tools that wouldn't migrate to the workshop along with the sharpest scissors and handiest little knives.

Aching with memories, I crawl towards where the window was and, not pausing to think, I lift the hammer and bring its claws down hard on the soundproofing board, making an instant ragged hole that I pull outward, once again sobbing. Not because of hacking at my precious dead room, more basic than that, more animal. It's the simple act of violence upsetting and dismaying me. It's the first hint of how badly I'm coming apart and how long it's going to take me ever to put myself back together again, after this. If there is an after this. Right now, it doesn't matter. I want to see that message that's hiding behind the boards, fresh and sharp and so obviously not left over from someone's childhood years ago. I hate myself for how quick I was to crawl back into stories again. It might have saved me when I was a kid, but I'm a woman now and I'm ashamed. I want to torture myself with how I should have faced facts. I could have saved Peggy months of horror.

I steel myself, raise the hammer again and drive another hole in beside the first one. Underneath I can already see the old wallpaper. I peer at the top of the skirting board and the edge of the linoleum. There it is. I was right. There are the little chips and flecks of white, even some splinters of yellow wood, lying where they fell, where they lodged, when Peggy scratched that desperate message into the paint. I contort myself to see the words but they're lost in the shadow of the windowsill, in the dark of the soundproofing. I lift the hammer again.

I've made one more decent hole when I hear what my hammering and sobbing have disguised until now.

It's Chloe. "You won't tunnel out, Lindsay," she shouts, muffled by the panels on the door but audible. She must be yelling at the top of her lungs. "You're trapped."

"Can you hear that?" I say into the laptop mic.

"I hear you doing something," the dispatcher says. "It sounds like you're breaking things."

I say nothing, just keep gouging at the boards and ripping away bigger and bigger chunks until I've uncovered part of the window.

Chloe must hear me scrabbling at the glass because she shouts again. "Look out, by all means, if you're planning to climb down a drainpipe."

I cup my hands around my eyes and rest my head on the glass to peer out into the dark garden. David March is standing there, arms folded, staring up at me. How could I ever have thought he had a kind face, a warm face? He's wearing a sneer and his eyes look half shut, as if he's bored with what he's caused, as if it's tiring him.

"Can you hear that voice?" I ask the dispatcher.

"Are *you* hearing a voice, Lindsay?" she asks me.

"The door's locked on my side, Chloe," I shout. "How am I *trapped*, exactly?" I'm trying to sound strong and angry, although my voice is reedy even to me.

"Not long now, sweetheart," the dispatcher says. "They're on their way and they'll be there soon. Don't shout. And don't go breaking things, eh? Case you hurt yourself."

Chloe is trying to tell me something else at the same time though, and I can't listen to both of them. So I kill the call.

"—trapped because you won't get past me," Chloe is bellowing at me, so loud that the bass of it is distorting the vowels: "WANT GAT PAHST MY." She sounds like an ogre from the fairy tales we read when we were kids together. A real ogre this time. "I'll stay here as long as I have to," she shouts. "We'll take shifts. You'll starve in there, Lindsay. Poor Lindsay. Poor grieving stupid Lindsay, boo-hoo-hoo."

"Why do you hate me?" I shout at her.

"I don't hate you," she bellows back at me, but her voice is thrumming with rage. "You're in the WAY. You're SPOILING it. And you're too STUPID to LIVE. You've run away from your PHONE and locked yourself in a DEAD room, Lindsay. You've trapped yourself in a DEAD room. You're hiding, cut off from the WORLD. You might as well be in a CAVE, Lindsay. You might as well be in a TOMB."

She really has never listened to me. She wasn't interested and so she never gave a moment's thought to my job or how I might do it. She thinks I'm air-gapped from everyone who could help me.

So it's half because I want to see her face when the police come that I open the door. The other half is because I still don't understand and I need so much to understand something. She is standing four-square at the top of the stairs, her head hanging down, her mouth hanging open. There is drool darkening her T-shirt and sweat showing under her arms too.

"Chloe," I say, more gently than I feel. "Why was I useful? Why did you need me to take this house from David and then give it to John?"

But even just the way I've put the question together begins to give me a glimmer of the answer. Only it can't be that, can it? It can't be something so grubby, so *small*.

"We didn't need *you*, Lindsay," she says. "Nobody needs *you*. We needed your lovely clean American insurance money. How the hell could a junkman afford Saint Helen's? A widowed sister from Hawaii is another thing completely."

So it really is that tawdry and that shameful. And why am I surprised? These are people who care more about the price of a house than the life being lived in a home.

"So . . . you cooked this up after I decided to come back?" I say. "Since spring?"

"And the funny thing is you're not even kidding," Chloe says. "No, Lindsay, I cooked this up starting two years ago, when I knew the handy widow was on her way."

"On my way?" I repeat. "But I didn't decide to come home till—" Then it hits me, and I can feel all the blood draining out of my face. She sees it too and raises an eyebrow. "The widow was on her way . . . because . . ."

"Brain tumours, Linds," she says. "We were getting worried about all the cash stacking up, knowing if we really got into the swing we were hoping to, then we'd need an accomplice who wasn't right here in the nanny state. Of course, recently, John got greedy and decided he *did* want you here, so he could get this house as a bonus. But back at the start, when John told me his little sister, my old friend, was ripe for a bit of sympathy, and I remembered what a complete pushover you always were, I decided I could probably stomach being your rock for a few months to get you onside."

"You're a monster," I say.

"If I'd known it would be nine*teen* months!" says Chloe.

"You really are a complete monster."

"Yeah well, it takes one to know one," she says. "You're so self-absorbed you never even questioned whether someone who'd scraped you off her shoe eight years before would be up for wiping your tears and listening to your endless whining. Of course you didn't. Like you never questioned why I couldn't stand being near you and Mr. Incredible in your heyday. 'Oh come to Hawaii, Chloe, you poor little failure. Come and marvel at my wonderful life, Chloe, you hometown joke.'"

"You-You were jealous of me?"

"I was sickened by you." But she's raising her voice again. She's lying.

"Jealous of *me*? Of me getting to be happy? After the childhood I had?"

"Oh, don't forget the *childhood*, boo-hoo-hoo. How could anyone forget your childhood, Lindsay? You never stopped bloody living it! Storybooks and nicey-nice and someone to take care of you. Poor guy.

At least I got away from you." She smirks. "Or maybe *he* was happy to get his escape too."

But I can't bear any more and I slam the door on her cackling, evil face then go to sit on the floor and sob my life out of my chest before I break in two.

I don't know what the sound is that makes me raise my head at last. Something is scraping and scratching, sounds like it's in the walls, and then there's a soft thump and out of the corner of my eye I see a small movement. Something is lying on the thick carpet by the door. I wipe my eyes and squint at it.

It's a key. It's *the* key. It's the key I boasted out loud to Chloe was in the door on my side. I let out one more sob and scrabble over there on hands and knees, fumbling it back into the keyhole, weeping and shaking, jabbing and poking, trying to force it back where it belongs.

But she has—they have—done something, plugged the keyhole up with something. It sticks to the end of the key and comes through in long strings that scorch my nostrils with the stench and make my fingertips stick to the key and then to the floor.

I can hear Chloe laugh and thump on the door, and I know she shouts more jeering words at me, but I can't hear her over my own weeping.

I'm still trying to get the key into the glued-up hole, jabbing and twisting, ripping my skin and beginning to despair when I hear Chloe's footsteps race away. She must be thundering down the stairs but it comes to me through the soundproofed door like the patter of little mice feet.

And I'm sure I know what's happened to make her go. She didn't know I'd called the police, did she? I scurry back over to the window and press myself hard up against the hole I made. David is gone, and I can see—I'm sure I can see, almost convinced I'm not imagining—a faint blue cast coming and going rhythmically on the dark trees at the end of the back garden.

I don't hesitate. I take my stupid little floral hammer and break the biggest pane of glass, tapping out all the shards at the edges just like I did at the nursing home, then I back through the hole, gripping onto the windowsill under my arms, feeling my legs dangle into terrifying emptiness until I find the tiniest toehold in the mortar between two blocks of stone.

For what feels like ten minutes but must be mere seconds, I crouch there, hugging the windowsill, pressed against the wall like a limpet. John flashes in my mind, standing under the tree, jeering at me, and I start to whimper. I am finished. I can't do this. I've got no courage left.

My plan might have worked if I'd got the chance to carry it out. But I can't. I'm done. I've come this far, survived this long, hiding my body and my mind from what they couldn't bear, living in my stories, willing my brain not to break, brave enough to recognise love when it came, strong enough to keep going when I lost it. But I'm finished.

"Sorry, Peggy," I whisper.

Then I gasp. Peggy! I take a deep breath and tell myself that if Peggy could do what she did, I can do this. This window isn't so very high; maids don't get soaring ceilings. The worst that will happen is a broken ankle. I have to try.

I shift first one hand and then the other, chickening out when I feel the weight of my dangling body. If I was a weightlifter maybe I could do this slowly, in complete control, but I know, as soon as I stop gripping with the whole length of my arms, I'm going to slither down the wall and hit the ground. I just need to do it, and maybe pray.

"Peggy," I say, and let go.

It takes me a good couple of seconds of sprawling on the wet grass before I can believe that I haven't smashed any bit of myself. I roll onto my side, clamber to my feet, and totter towards the back door.

I burst into the kitchen to find the four of them sitting cosily round the table, Chloe and David, wearing worried faces, side-by-side like the couple they are and two police—a man and a woman—calm and steady, like they've seen it all before. "Lindsay, sweetheart!" Chloe says, jumping up and coming towards me. I put my arm straight out with my hand up to stop her from touching me. She turns to the police and gives a helpless gesture, as if to say that this is what she's been telling them: I'm crazy.

"Where did you spring from then?" says David, smiling at me. "I thought you were holed up for the night."

"I got out the window," I said.

"You jumped out of an upstairs—?" Chloe tries to say, all fake concern.

I turn to address the coppers as if she doesn't exist. "Has someone gone to Lord's Yard?" I say. "There are six bodies buried there."

"Lindsay, darling," says Chloe. "You're soaking wet. How long have you been out in the garden? We thought you were in your little safe room."

The male copper stands up. "All right, hen," he says to Chloe. "All right. We're going to take care of all that for you. Lindsay, is it? Well, don't you worry about a thing, Lindsay. Everything's going to be okay."

"I don't know what they've told you," I say, "but you need to check every word of it. This is my house, and I don't want them in it. Please get rid of them and then I'd really appreciate it if you put someone on the gate overnight till I can find somewhere else to go."

"We've found you somewhere, Lindsay love," says the woman copper. She's younger than her colleague and less world weary. She looks embarrassed, but not for herself. For me. It's pity I can see in her eyes. "You'll be safe and comfortable there till we can get you the help you need."

"It's my house!" I say, louder and not quite so in control of my voice suddenly.

"Now, now," says the man, "you must know that's not true. It's Dr. March's house, isn't it? He was born here. And maybe you can come back when you're feeling better but we'll have to see."

"There are six bodies buried in the back of Lord's Yard in Menstrie," I say. "Six elderly people, murdered by these two who've fooled you here tonight. And John Lord, and Farmer George and Nicotine Ned—that's not their names—but you need to believe me."

"We do believe you," says the woman. She's been on a course, I think. She's learned not to argue with deluded people. "And we want to hear all about it. So why don't you come with us?"

"Where?" I ask. If it's a hospital, they'll phone John. But, it only right now occurs to me, if I'm headed to a jail cell, it'll be a lawyer.

Chloe turns sharply to look at David and he gives his head a tiny warning shake.

"There!" I say. "Did you see that?"

"We can help you not see whatever it is you can see that's upsetting you," the woman says. "Come with us."

"And don't worry," the sergeant says. "You're not under arrest, Lindsay."

No, I think. But I will be.

Because it's just occurred to me exactly who I need to speak to and how I'm going to make it happen too.

I go quietly, keeping up just enough resistance and distress to stop Chloe and David from getting suspicious. I let the two coppers lead me squelching through the hall and out the front door. I let them help me into the back of the panda, the woman even laying a gentle hand on my head, although I've not got cuffs on and I could do it without assistance. David and Chloe stand together on the step, all concerned and united.

I sit quietly on the back seat, soaking it, breathing in the stink of booze and puke from their usual customers and the fug of fried food and old coffee from the coppers themselves, until they get me to the emergency parking space at Forth Valley.

Then, when I step out, before I've even finished moving, I punch the sergeant in the throat as hard as I can. He must be trained in self-defence, surely, but maybe because it's so unexpected he doesn't get a hand up to stop the blow. He swears and bends over, coughing. His colleague hasn't a clue what to do. She moves a hand towards her belt as if to get her handcuffs, but she's still dithering when the sergeant straightens up again. There's fury in his eyes, a rage born of wounded pride as much as physical pain. It doesn't help that a couple of drunks standing smoking at the A&E doorway give me a cheer and a shout of encouragement.

Well, it doesn't help *him* and his ego, but I'm hoping it helps me. I'm hoping I've read him right. I certainly don't want to hit the girl.

Apart from anything else, now that they're on their guard, she'd no doubt hit me back a lot harder.

But all's well. I've got the sergeant taped. "Aye right, have it your own way," he says in a hard voice, spiriting a set of handcuffs into being and clicking them smoothly onto my wrists before I can move. "A night in the tank it is. Lindsay Lord, I am arresting you for unlawful entry of private property, verbal assault, physical assault, assaulting a police officer . . ."

"Lindsay Hale," I say. "And now I get my phone call. Thank you."

He smirks at me, which I don't understand, but he says nothing.

First I get an overnight stay in jail. The sergeant I hit and the guy who books me in seem to think, quite sincerely, that I must be upset about this development, but as far as I'm concerned I'm safer here in this concrete box than anywhere else I can think of. John and Shelley could probably have talked me out of a psychiatric ward and then God knows what would have become of me.

I'm safe, but not comfortable. There's a stink worse than the squad car—of cheap bleach and disinfectant over a base note of drains and damp—and the paint on the concrete is shiny and comfortless. It's blinding white too, and the light is kept on all night, bouncing off the floor, walls, bunk shelf, desk shelf, stool shelf, and ceiling, until my head aches from it. The only relief is to pull the thin blanket over my face, breathing in the soap powder until my nostrils start to sting, and think about Peggy drinking Bunny's tea (I hope he doesn't make her Lapsang), standing in Bunny's shower (I hope she doesn't feel faint again), or lying in Bunny's bath (I hope they're not too prudish to do the sensible thing and let him help her). I'm pretty sure they're not. They're made of stern stuff, both of them.

Then I turn my thoughts away and try to come up with a detailed plan. There's not a hope of sleeping, between my wet clothes, the concrete, the light, the smells, and the endless shouts and bangs from elsewhere in the lock-ups, but I don't care. I'm glad. I need all night to work out how I'm going to swing this in the morning. My brilliant idea. My long shot.

Once again, I am lying in the dark, after an extraordinary journey.

But I'm not alone. I reach out a hand and find Bunny's, lacing my old fingers in with his.

"I've always wanted to go for a drive in one of those huge lorries," he says.

"I thought you were asleep."

"I'm awake again. Keep talking,"

"I knew I was in Kincardine, at the . . . nursing home, Lindsay said it was . . . because I felt us going over the bridge. And I knew where I was when they had me in the maid's room next door. But the other place? I had no idea. It was terrifying. It was like a nightmare."

Bunny squeezes my hand.

"Of course, it was supposed to terrify me. That was the point. It was supposed to cow me and break me. Make me biddable."

"You?" says Bunny. "Never!"

He is trying to be kind but the truth is not so rousing. "Almost," I tell him. "If Lindsay hadn't come when she did."

"Splendid girl," Bunny says. "I hope—"

Now it's my turn to squeeze his hand. I hope too. I can't imagine where Lindsay is or what she's doing but I hope too.

Chapter 26

When the door opens, I jolt awake so suddenly that I bang my elbow bone—right where it hums—and feel tears in my eyes.

"There you go," says a woman in a plastic apron, shoving a tray down on the desk shelf. "A bit of toast and a kind word for you."

"Don't eat the toast?" I say, remembering the old joke.

"Don't, whatever you do, eat the toast," she says, chuckling. "The tea's no bad if you're quick." She's gone again before I can ask her for any clue about what's going to happen, but she wasn't in uniform anyway, so I doubt she'd know.

The tea is so terrible that I take a bite of toast out of fascination and curiosity. It tastes as if it's been rubbed with lard. It won't even flush down the stainless steel toilet. It just sits there in the water, swelling and making me feel sick. Only the thought of having to retch onto it keeps my stomach from turning completely.

Then the sergeant I punched comes along the corridor. I know it's him before I see him. I recognise the arrogant ring of his feet as he strolls towards me.

"Right then, Lindsay *Hale*," he says when he's opened my door and is lounging against the jamb. "What have you got to say for yourself this morning?"

"I need to speak to my lawyer," I say. "When can I phone him?"

"I'll hand you over to the desk for all that," says the sergeant, smirking again as he steps to one side and makes a flourishing gesture to invite me out into the corridor. He takes me back to where I answered their questions and signed God knows what forms last night. I was so tired by then that I didn't read a word of it. I'm hoping he's too grand to hang around; certainly he left me to the desk guy when he brought me in and, right enough, after he's said, "This one wants 'to phone her lawyer'" to the older man who's there today, he strolls away. The scare quotes unnerve me but I shake it off.

"So you want me to get you a lawyer," the desk guy says, not unkindly. I think he's a sergeant too. He's got the same stripes on his jumper.

"I want to *speak* to *my* lawyer," I tell him.

He heaves a huge sigh and shakes his head. "You should have watched more *Shetland* and less *Vera*."

"What?"

"You're in Scotland, hen. You've no right to a nice wee phone chat here. You should have broken into a house in Carlisle."

"Shit, really?" I say. I'm thinking furiously. Will it work if this guy calls? On the one hand, he's got his rank to help him but on the other, he won't say the things I think might make the difference.

"Do you know the number, hen?" He's still being quite kind. He's taken no pleasure in setting me straight.

"It was on a business card I had in my pocket," I say. "But they took it off me. Can I get it back?" I don't know what I'll do if he says yes.

"Ehhhhh," the man says, thank God. "Awkward, but I'll look it up for you instead." He jiggles a mouse and waits with an expectant expression on his face.

"David Minto," I say. "He's from Edinburgh."

"Minto," the sergeant repeats. Then he frowns.

"Ehhhhhh," he says again. "Mr. Minto's no a solicitor, hen."

"I know," I say. "He's a Crown counsel, but he's my lawyer. I had his business card until they took it off me."

"He's a writer—"

"To the signet, yes," I say, trying to sound clipped and confident, the way someone would who actually knew the real David Minto and knew what a writer to the signet was, and a Crown counsel, and an advocate depute. I want to be back in Hawaii where lawyers are called lawyers. But I mustn't start crying. If I'm going to get this plan to work, I need to act as if I'm anyone but me.

"Look, hen," the sergeant says. His endearments are beginning to grate on me. "Will I just call the duty solicitor, eh?"

"I am asking you to contact *my* lawyer. David Minto, LLM, CC. His number is on the business card I had taken away from me last night. I can't really see the problem, and I don't suppose David will be able to see what the problem was either, when this is sorted out and I tell him what happened to me."

The sergeant sucks his teeth for a moment. He's caught between resenting the way I'm talking to him and realising that he doesn't want to get into bother with a big boss Edinburgh lawyer if he can help it. He clicks to another screen. "Watch, earrings, earring posts, wallet, thirty-seven pounds, driving licence, debit card, credit card, Tesco Clubcard, Nectar card, ah! Business card. Doesn't say here whose name was on it."

"You can check," I say. This is taking far too long and I'm beginning to sweat. If the other sergeant comes back, he'll shut me down in a heartbeat, and if this sergeant actually gets that business card out of my bag of belongings, it'll have David *March*'s phone number on it, which won't be any use at all. I feel tears threaten. Getting this close after everything I've been through and then not being able to take that one last step . . . "Please help me," I say.

"Don't upset yourself," he says. "I'm just not keen to make a tit of myself with Chambers Street."

"Well, let me then," I say. "I know you told me it's not a protected right, but it's not banned, is it? Believe me, I'd have stolen a car and driven over the border to punch a Carlisle policeman, if I'd known."

He opens his eyes very wide and looks down at my paperwork. When he lifts his head again, he's beaming at me. "You *punched* that puffed-up twat?"

"In the neck, yes."

"I'll just get Mr. Minto's number, madam," he says. "Then pass the phone to you."

But he's still not speedy as he keys in a name and waits for results to load.

"David Minto," he mutters under his breath at last, then he picks up the external landline that sits on the desk between us, painstakingly copies the number from his search result into the keypad and hands the phone to me.

I have no expectation that the real David Minto himself will answer and, right enough, it's an assistant of some kind that I get through to. I try to speak very clearly and plainly, knowing I might only have one chance to make this stick.

"My name is Lindsay Hale," I say. "I'm trying to report a string of serious crimes that have taken place across Stirlingshire, Perthshire, Fife, and Clackmannanshire over the last few months or perhaps longer. I've uncovered the fact that someone by the name of David March has been impersonating Mr. Minto, to the extent of handing out fake business cards bearing his name and I would like to make sure that Mr. Minto is aware of the fact."

"Eh?" says the desk sergeant.

"Em," says the assistant, over the line, "you need to report to the police, Miss . . . Hale." At least she's written my name down. "They will contact Mr.—"

"I'm actually calling from Stirling Police Station right now," I say, "but I'm not getting anywhere with them. I've told them about a series of six murders in great detail, including where the bodies are buried, but for some reason that completely escapes me—"

"Now look," says the desk sergeant. "I'm no fan of Sergeant—"

"—they're hell bent on making sure nothing is done."

"But this is—"

"I'm not entirely clear whether the police are aware of the identity fraud concerning Mr. Minto—"

"What the fuck—?" The desk sergeant is grabbing for me and I have to dance backwards.

"I also know the current whereabouts of the victim of a seventh attempted murder who needs urgent medical attention—"

Then the phone is wrenched out of my hand and the call is killed. The desk sergeant is looking at me as if he's just stepped in something, wearing new white shoes. "It's aye the ones that look normal," he says. "Fucking nutter. Brian!"

The sergeant who arrested me appears as if he's been waiting behind a door. "All done?" he says.

"Not even close," says his colleague. "This one's just called the CCs in Edinburgh and told them some daft fairy tale. Duty solicitor it is and I'll tell them there's no need to hurry, okay? Absolute mental case."

"Back you go," says the one I punched. "Your shout. You'll learn that it's on you whether this goes rough or smooth, Lindsay. It's up to you."

I am halfway to the door when the phone rings. I stop moving.

"Wait," I say.

The guy on the desk is listening to whoever's on the other end and, as he does so, he straightens up until he's standing to attention. "Yes, that's right," he says in the end. Then he looks over. "Bri," he says, flashing his eyes. "Minto, Chambers Street, asking for this one."

As I walk back to the desk, I try to copy the swagger of the man I'm leaving behind, gawping at me. I don't have the metalled heels but I make a pretty decent job of it anyway.

Part Four

September

Epilogue

I'm in the garden room, at Saint Helen's, on a late summer day as the light starts to fade, sitting more or less where that armchair was when Peggy lived here all alone with her treasured possessions. Some of them are back, anything that could be scrubbed clean of the taint of Lord's Yard, but no one could face the upholstered furniture, or any of the curtains and cushions. They looked fine as long as they stayed in situ but even Bunny agreed, when we surveyed them in the cold light of day, that they "didn't owe us anything." And then the new curtains made the walls look dingy, and the new paint made the floors look scruffy so, step by step, Saint Helen's has been spruced up from the ground to the chimney pots. I even got my en-suite bathroom.

And I got my daydream of four boys having a kickabout on the back lawn too. They're out there now, the game moving ever closer to the greenhouse without them noticing. I don't really care if they smash the glass. It only reminds me of Shelley now and I'd be happy if it was gone. I'd get more upset if they snapped Nelly Moser.

I didn't think the four of them would have anything in common and I sure as hell didn't think Eileen Prentiss would let her two anywhere near my nephews. But I hadn't thought it through. Sean and Edwin have a murderer for a father, same as Zak and Nicky. So it's only when the four of them are together that they can stop bracing themselves for questions and piss taking. Besides, Eileen's a snob and, now that Zak and Nicky live in this gorgeous house, they've got a lot more to recommend them than when they lived in the chalet bungalow behind the gates of the scrapyard.

But I'm not being fair. She and I talk a lot about how to support them, about school and the future and the fact that Sean and Zak want to go on family access visits and Ed and Nicky have refused to consider it.

It had to be that the boys came here. I couldn't join them in their home because it's not there anymore. None of Lord's is there anymore: not the containers, not the Portakabin, not the sheds, the trailers, the horseboxes, the carports, the piles of tyres, the rusting bikes . . . all of it is gone. In its place is a garden to commemorate and honour the people who had their homes stolen by Robert Walker, were kept at the Elms by Eric and Sarah McAllan, were killed by David March, were buried by John Lord.

Shelley might be out before they're both eighteen, I suppose, but it's touch and go if she'd get custody. Until then, and maybe forever, I've got two boys to feed and love and help and scold and watch get bad skin and broken hearts and all the rest of it. Seeing them messing up my grass with sliding tackles is the easy bit. Someone in a shop assumed I was their mum yesterday. She must have wondered what the hell was wrong, the way our three faces fell.

And if the thought of their mum is impossible . . .

John's never getting out of the state hospital, I wouldn't think. Nicky's got plenty time to come round to the idea of visiting.

Ed too. Because David March will be very lucky if he sees a far view before he's an old man.

The prosecutor—not Mr. Minto, because of the conflict of interest, but he kept a close eye on the case—wasn't moved, and neither was the jury, by the argument David kept on advancing about the difference between killing and letting die. He sometimes even strayed into claiming that the first six deaths were gentler than the natural ones that were coming, sooner or later. He had nothing to say about how Peggy scuppered the seventh, about his own stupidity in realising he couldn't sign off on the death of his mother. I'll never stop marvelling at her courage, to keep her body too bruised to let another doctor see it.

And I didn't believe a word of David's excuse anyway. I saw Chloe's hand in it. Chloe's planning. Chloe's cunning. Speaking of Chloe, I can't say anything about prison visits to Ed and Nicky really. I've no intention of dropping by to see my oldest friend, no matter how long she's in there. Apart from anything else, it would creep me out too much if she started going on about how clever they'd all been, like she did during her trial. She sounded proud of it, didn't do herself any favours.

"We moved the victim out of the house, see, with the family's consent and encouragement, and kept them at the Elms until the sale was through and the dust was settled." She seemed to think she had the jury in the palm of her hand. "Until any long-lost relative or persistent friend who might be troubled by a tale of sudden decline had given up and gone away." There was a sneer in her voice and on her face. "If someone insisted on making a fuss," she explained, "the old person could be produced, frail and fading." She actually opened her hands and held them out, displaying her cleverness, she thought. Displaying her brokenness.

I had to turn away. Half the jury did the same, men and women—they couldn't stand the sight of her. I try so hard not to join in with it, the way the jury and then the press hated Chloe with a different hatred from how they felt about David, Robert, Eric, and John. They judged Sarah and Shelley more harshly than the men too. But am I any better, finding it so easy to call my dad a monster and move on, so impossible to accept my mum choosing peace and comfort with the monster and letting John and me pay the price?

Sometimes I think I understand. If I could make myself read that wise and brutal book again, maybe I would get it. It's something to do with how my dad only caught us once more, John and me, after we hid in the caravan. But my mum knowing, and choosing, was over and over again for years. It's not fair. I know that. Everyone knows that. But everyone in that courtroom was a child once and you can't tell little children what they can survive and what's going to destroy them. Hating

Chloe while she explained the final bit of the plan that they carried out six times came from deep inside every lawyer, cop, juror, reporter, and even the judge herself.

Six times.

Until Peggy. You could feel the wave of fierce joy and sheer relief all over the court whenever we got to turn our thoughts back to Peggy. As well as keeping herself visibly injured, she would not learn her lesson. She refused to settle, whether in the locked room in her house, on that short visit to the junkyard, or at the Elms. She kept raging on about escape, and revenge, and reporting them to . . . well, someone or other.

That was half the problem.

There were four local authorities, each with jurisdiction over just one quarter of the scheme—so a planning department might get involved in a new owner's vision for their house, and a social care department might wonder about the Elms' accreditation, but the two women doing the filing would never have lunch in the same canteen and get to wondering. And John would fill in all the forms to dispose of old fridges with God knows what leaking out of them, while family doctors might be sorry their patients left without saying goodbye, but why would waste services speak to community health across the miles and begin to spin tales for themselves?

Slowly, steadily, and separately, officialdom ground its way to the end of all the forms and fees. Only when every official body, with any skin in any game, was satisfied, then the victim was "let die" and taken to what turned out *not* to be their final resting place, but only a short interlude before they were given the honour they deserved.

That nearly derailed the entire plan, we learned, day after day as the details came out in the press. They almost blew it over the question of the bodies. They never considered for one second the scrupulous probity and bone-deep goodness of the funeral homes.

Sarah McAllan waltzed into a place in yet another county—Grangemouth, down in Falkirk—away back in the planning stage, telling a sad tale of a never-married, childless, long-time friend. She was "just double-checking," she told the funeral director, to see if she could bring in the death certificate and arrange a private cremation, with no announcement and no attendance. When the funeral director's eyes narrowed and his hand twitched towards his phone, she had to fake a forgotten appointment to get out of there quick. And that was when John became an essential cog in the wheel.

Along with the other three. They did it six times all the way through and nearly made it seven. Different methods every time, all seven pretty easy. When someone's up there in their late eighties and beyond, a bit of work with their meds is all it takes, usually. I feel sick when I think about how slight and frail Peggy was the night I found her, how reedy her whimpering behind that locked door. There wasn't much raging left by then and it took months until she began to rally.

She's almost back to her old self again now. She's out in the garden watching the boys playing football, her grandsons and her . . . sons, I suppose. I feel myself start to laugh again.

David March was absolutely bloody livid when we visited him yesterday. For the last time, Peggy tells me. It takes far too much out of her to expose herself to his vitriol, to his poison, at her age and after everything she's been through, but she wanted to tell him to his face. She wanted to show him.

Because he had been insisting to her, both on visits and over the phone, that he was going to stop her doing what she meant to do, which was leave her house, her beloved house, to me, her friend.

"Apart from anything else," she told him, "after we got Lindsay's money back, she sank quite half of it into doing the place up. So many bathrooms!"

David said he would find a way to stop her if it took the last breath in his body. That's how much he hates me. He hates me almost as much as Chloe does now. And the only person Chloe hates more than she hates me is David.

It was during the trial it changed. "*What?*" he'd said, in answer to a question. "My dear man, she's a *cleaner*." If I was going to feel a single flicker of pity for her, it would have been then. I fought the urge.

All in all, both of them look set to serve their long sentences distilling more and more bile and loathing until they corrode themselves from the skin to the marrow. It couldn't happen to a nicer pair.

While we're on the subject of pity, I almost felt sorry for David yesterday when Peggy and I visited.

"I have outflanked you," Peggy said, over the table in the visitors' room. David sat back with his arms crossed over his grey sweatshirt, one foot drumming on the floor and a muscle flickering at the hinge of his jaw. "I've outwitted you," she went on. "I've scuppered you. I've wiped the floor with you. Poor floor."

"What are you talking about?" he said. "I've barely started planning how to get that bloody house off you. Who's going to argue your case once you're gone? Eileen? She *wants* it to stay in the family. For the boys. Who else is there?"

"Oh, it's going to stay in the family," Peggy told him, calm and slightly amused. God, she's magnificent. I'm planning to be exactly like her when I'm that age. "It's all very straightforward. I'll make a will, of course, to leave some little gifts to friends and to make a bequest to the memorial garden, but my home and the rest of my estate, as is very normal, will go to my spouse."

"Your what?" David said. It came out like a bark.

"My wife," Peggy said. She waggled her left hand with the brand-new, bright wedding ring on the fourth finger.

I waggled mine too. It matches. White gold with a thin band of pink tourmaline running through. We reckoned pink wedding rings were just right for—as Peggy insists on calling us—two girls. Usually I wear Kai's ring on my wedding finger and Peggy wears Richard's but we swapped them that morning to show David. For effect, basically.

"Thank you for giving us the idea," I said to him. "With your Aileen story. I never thought I'd get two step-grandsons before I was forty and, let me assure you, I'm going to be a wonderful granny to Edwin and Sean. But I'm going to be a fucking nightmare of a stepmother to you."

"I've made her promise as much," Peggy added. "For later, when I'm gone."

It was mostly bravado. She wept bitterly as we drove back from the prison. I don't know if she'll ever get over what he did. What he is. But I'm going to help as much as I can.

I smile and lay my book down as she comes in at the French window. "They've got ten times more energy than David had at that age," she says. That's what she does. She mentions him in a normal way as if it stops some of the pain. "How are you liking Poirot?" she asks, dropping into a chair.

"I prefer the divine Miss M," I say.

Peggy makes the tsk-tsk sound she always makes when she remembers that amongst Chloe's other crimes there was this: She took a book and didn't return it. We've replaced it since, but there's no forgiveness.

Peggy lays her head back and closes her eyes. "Or perhaps I've got ten times *less* energy than I had back then." She does that too: mentions her age, how little time she's got left, how I must prepare myself for another widowhood. I can't bear to think of the day when I lose Peggy again, for real this time.

But I'll have the children, my two and shares in the other two, and I'll love all four of them. All five of them. I rub my hand over my pumpkin stomach, my belly button sticking out like its stalk, and I look ruefully at my ankles. I was terrified, after that night with David, that I'd find myself pregnant with his child. Then, when my period came, I cried for three days.

The letter from the fertility clinic in Honolulu arrived just before Christmas. I have no idea why Kai didn't tell me. But I'm glad of it. I couldn't have coped with the knowledge when I was preparing to lose him. He did it all on his own, as soon as he found out he was ill. He banked sperm and paid for four years' storage.

It was madness to think about paying for another four, halfway round the world. I went over and had the insemination purely because the thought of them there, frozen in the dark, gave me worse nightmares than the ones I had about the six graves in Lord's Yard. Job done, I thought when I got home again. The last of Kai.

When I started being sick in the morning, I convinced myself it was psychosomatic. The day I did the test, I sat in my new en-suite bathroom and howled. Poor little baby, little embryo, little zygote it was then. Welcome to your new existence. Have some cortisol. Peggy heated me some soup and made me sip it sitting up in bed.

That's when I listened to Kai's last recording, for what I thought would be the final time. To feel close while I told him about the baby.

> *If you're there, Lindsay, that means I managed to shift this file to somewhere you're going to find it. I didn't want to leave it too long. I wanted to sound like me and I can feel my range narrowing every day. Anyway. So I died, huh? What a downer. You okay, babe? I want you to be okay. I want you to be happy. I want you to meet a nice guy—not too nice, but solid, you know? He'll cope with living in my shadow if he gets you thrown in. And then you and him can get started on those babies we were going to have if it had turned out that way. Deal? We got a deal? Try not to mind them being basic issue and not the angels we would have made. Love them anyway. And even if he doesn't show up, just go ahead and have the babies.*
>
> *Seriously, Lin. I'm not going to tell you not to mourn. I would be ready to burn the earth to embers if it was me losing you. So, mourn. Grieve. Don't forget me. But be happy. You're living for two now, sweetheart. You're living for me as well as yourself. No slacking.*

I try to laugh this time. I'm beyond being angry.

"On it," I tell him. "All over it."

I sit watching the counter, feeling stupid for thinking maybe he was going to answer me.

I'm swiping at tears when his voice comes back, making me jump because there's no buzz, no background noise. Of course not. Kai was too good a technician for that.

> *I don't know if I want you to hear this part or not, Lin. You're in the kitchen right now, washing towels I threw up in. You're trying to cry quietly and I'm so tired, babe. I'm so sc—*

I jabbed at the pause button then and put my hands over my face. In all the time he was ill, Kai never once said he was scared and only said he was tired in the usual way, after a hospital visit or some other kind of hard day. This message at the end of the file was the only time I'd heard him tell me he was tired and known he meant tired of life, tired of trying.

But if he could say it—if he could live it—then I had to find the strength to hear it. I jumped it back five seconds and hit play.

> *—so tired, babe. I'm so scared. But my heart is bursting with love for you. I am as deeply in love with you today as I was the night we met, the day I proposed, the day I married you. Remember that day we ate lobster in bed in that stupid little B&B and they charged us for extra cleaning? I love you today like I loved you then. I'll love you forever.*

"Why didn't you open with that?" I asked him. "I would have listened to it every day."

I could hear his voice in my memory saying "Yeah, I think I'll play the brain tumour card on that one," and I found myself laughing.

"I can see her!" Peggy says to me, startling me back into the present. She peers over her reading glasses and points. "That was a foot, clear as anything. I must say, I still find it odd to know she's a she but I approve of these unapologetic maternity clothes. A crop top! I went about like a cross between a nun and a toddler, which makes no sense at all whichever way you slice it."

"The boys don't know where to look," I say, running both hands over my belly now, trying to settle her. Both feet and both elbows going at once can still make me feel queasy. "Even Bunny's a bit hot under the collar sometimes."

"Wait till the breastfeeding starts!" Peggy says. Then she catches herself. "If you want to. I was scolded out of it by Richard's mother and it was a great sadness. But of course, it's up to you."

"We'll see," I say. It's what I say to the boys, my two boys, about some of their wilder plans. About *all* of their suggested baby names: Dua, Billie, Kesha, Wing. Myself, I like Kaila. It breaks open warm and round and it ends light and gentle. Kaila Hale. Although Billie March is the happiest pair of words ever joined together.

But the boys will not get to name my daughter. I try to strike a balance between giving them some leeway and keeping them grounded. The latest is they want the old maid's room, my dead room, as a gaming centre, because of the soundproofing and the Wi-Fi. Peggy says she'll never set foot in it again as long as she lives. "Which, of course, might not be that long," she adds, as if it's an obligation. I pretend I can't hear her.

"And you're not going to be doing much audio work with a screaming baby strapped to your chest for the next two years, are you Linds?" Nicky says.

"Babies don't scream for two years," I tell him.

"Can we get that in writing?" says Zak. "And can we have the room?"

"We'll see," I say again. It's the most important lesson I can teach them, I reckon—that none of us will ever know what the future holds and that's okay. "We'll see," I keep telling them. "We'll see."

Facts and Fictions

The towns and counties in *The Dead Room* are real places and I've tried to show the topography of the Ochils and southern Cairngorms as best I can. Lord's Yard, though, is not real. Nor are any of the nursing homes, property centres, or other businesses referenced in the book. None of the characters is based on a real person, but Chloe is especially not based on *my* best-friend-from-babyhood, Catherine Lepreux, and neither Kai nor David is anything like my husband, Neil. Plus I've only got sisters—good ones too.

When I started writing "the new story," I described it to my agent as "*Gaslight* meets *Sleeping Murder*" and that's stayed true through the rewriting and editing, which isn't always the case. But *Gaslight* didn't get any more relevant as I went on. *Sleeping Murder*, on the other hand, my cofavourite Agatha Christie (along with *The Moving Finger*) has popped up in numerous little unplanned Easter eggs.

Saint Helen's—speaking of Easter eggs—owes a lot to a real house I found on a property website once, but please don't go looking for it in Dunblane because it's many miles away in another bit of Scotland entirely. Andy Murray's gold pillar box, on the other hand, is right where I put it and perfect for a selfie.

Finally, I'm saying "I did this" and "I didn't do that" and I mean it. That is, no generative AI was used to create this story. It was all me.

Acknowledgements

I would like to thank Lisa Moylett, Zoë Apostolides, Elena Langtry, and Jamie Maclean at the agency; Jessica Tribble Wells, Juliet Stevenson, Charlotte Herscher, Katherine Kirk, Alicia Lea, Damon Freeman, Allyson Cullinan, Bella Roberts, Andrew George, Brittany Morris and Nicole Burns-Ascue at Thomas and Mercer; Raquel Reyes, Rob Osler, Linda Joffe Hull, Tracy Clark, Mysti and Dale Berry, Leslie Karst, Leslie Budewitz, Susan Shea, Ellen Byron, Lisa Weddle, Megan Peto, Edith Maxwell, S. J. Rozan, Lucinda Surber, Stan Ulrich, Laura Hayden (and the rest of the team at Author, Author!), Laurie Sheehan and Gigi Pandian (*they* know); so many other friends and family that I can't begin to—well okay, I can begin, but I certainly can't complete. Here goes: Eileen Rendahl, Tamsen Schultz, Lisa Nalbone, and Spring Warren—the Wednesday writers; Sarah and Dave Rizzo; Laura and Michael Walker; Andy Wallace, Sally Madden and Matt Holland—the Vincibles; Kristopher Zgorski, Dru Ann Love and Kathy Reel—who've read more crime fiction than I could in a hundred lifetimes; Shannon Baker, Jess Lourey and Erica Ruth Neubauer—pop-up pep squad; Catherine Lepreux—the original and best; Louise Kelly—every step of the way; Stuart and May McCormack and Kathryn and Tommy Morrison—who have no idea how much; Wendy Bellars; Olivier Lepreux; Nancy Balfour; Megan McPherson—an unexpected silver lining to the blackest cloud; Jean McPherson, Audrey Ford and

Wendy Keegan—the women at the heart of the sprawling clan I was lucky enough to be born into; Nan McRoberts, Suzanne Thomson, Gillian Paterson and Bogusia McRoberts—the women at the heart of the sprawling clan I stumbled into. And Neil McRoberts, the one who tripped me.

Book club questions

1. What part do you think grief plays in Lindsay's response to her fears and suspicions?
2. What do you think of Lindsay's decision to go home again, after the childhood she had there?
3. Could the scheme dreamed up by the poker players work where you live? Why (not)?
4. What do you think about Lindsay's shifting opinions of Kai in the course of the book?
5. Do John and Lindsay's very different reactions to their shared childhood chime with anything you've come across?
6. I often wonder what a story would look like from one of the minor characters' points of view. Whose story, running in parallel with Lindsay's, would you most enjoy making up?
7. Care of elderly people is at the heart of the book. What do you think of the British system as it's depicted here? How about the system nearest you, if you live somewhere else?
8. Have you ever revisited places you thought magical when you were a child, as Lindsay did Lord's Yard? How did it go?
9. Do you read horror novels or watch adaptations of them on television? Could you, if you were alone in a house? Why do you think they have the power to affect us so much?
10. Does *The Dead Room* have a happy ending? If you rewrite endings for yourself (I do) what would you change?

Reading List

I recommend most of these in their entirety, without hesitation. A couple of exceptions: Aesop's complete fables take a lot of reading; and Herman's terrific book about PTSD and C-PTSD is fascinating but be careful with yourself if it's directly relevant to your life.

- *Aesop's Fables*
- *The Amityville Horror*, Jay Anson
- *The Handmaid's Tale*, Margaret Atwood
- *Jaws*, Peter Benchley
- *Sleeping Murder*, Agatha Christie
- The Little School by the Sea series (*Class, Rules, Lessons, Studies*), Jenny Colgan
- *Trauma and Recovery: The Aftermath of Violence—From Domestic Abuse to Political Terror*, Judith Lewis Herman, MD
- *It*, Stephen King
- *The Monarch of the Glen*, Compton Mackenzie
- *Peter Pan and Wendy*, J. M. Barrie